# DARKNESS
## BEFORE DAWN

Darkness #2

CLAIRE CONTRERAS

Copyright © 2013 Claire Contreras

Cover design by Sarah Hansen of www.OkayCreations.net

Photo credit: Mathilde Skrzyniarz

Edited by Lori Sabin

Interior Design by Angela McLaurin, Fictional Formats

Without limiting the rights under copyright reserved above, no part of this publication may be reproduced, stored in or introduced into a retrieval system, or transmitted, in any form, or by any means (electronic, mechanical, photocopying, recording, or otherwise) without the prior written permission of the above author of this book.

This is a work of fiction. Names, characters, places, brands, media, and incidents are either the product of the author's imagination or have been used fictitiously. Any resemblance to actual persons, living or dead, events, or locales is entirely coincidental.

The author acknowledges the trademarked status and trademark owners of various products referenced in this work of fiction, which have been used without permission. The publication/use of these trademarks is not authorized, associated with, or sponsored by the trademark owners.

# Table of Contents

Darkness                    1

Chapter One                 3

Chapter Two                17

Chapter Three              22

Chapter Four               28

Chapter Five               32

Chapter Six                45

Chapter Seven              56

Chapter Eight              63

Chapter Nine               76

Dusk                       85

Chapter Ten                87

Chapter Eleven             95

Chapter Twelve            104

Chapter Thirteen               109

Chapter Fourteen               118

Chapter Fifteen                126

Chapter Sixteen                135

Chapter Seventeen              143

Chapter Eighteen               152

Chapter Nineteen               160

Dawn                           175

Chapter Twenty                 177

Chapter Twenty-One             184

Chapter Twenty-Two             191

Chapter Twenty-Three           204

Chapter Twenty-Four            212

Chapter Twenty-Five            219

Chapter Twenty-Six             229

Chapter Twenty-Seven           235

Chapter Twenty-Eight           239

Chapter Twenty-Nine          245

Chapter Thirty               256

Chapter Thirty-One           261

Sunlight                     269

Chapter Thirty-Two           271

Chapter Thirty-Three         280

Chapter Thirty-Four          291

Chapter Thirty-Five          298

Chapter Thirty-Six           306

Epilogue                     311

Acknowledgements             333

# Dedication

*A & M,*

*Don't let anybody tell you that you can't do something.*
*Not even me.*
*You want it, you go after it.*
*No excuses.*

*Christian,*

*For not giving up on me,*
*even when I want to give up on myself.*

"Lend me your hand and we'll conquer them all

But lend me your heart and I'll just let you fall

Lend me your eyes I can change what you see

But your soul you must keep, totally free"


—Awake My Soul, *Mumford & Sons*

WARNING:

IF YOU HAVE NOT READ
*THERE IS NO LIGHT IN DARKNESS*,
YOU MUST DO SO
BEFORE READING THIS BOOK.

darkness

/'därknis/

Noun

1. The partial or total absence of light.

2. Night

Synonyms:

dark; obscurity; gloom; murk; mirk; night

# Chapter One
## ~Blake~

Squeezing my eyes shut, I hug my shivering body and try to picture myself somewhere far, far away. Other than the dirty mattress I lay on, there is nothing here—nothing but the darkness that surrounds me. At the sound of footsteps approaching, my breathing pounds in anticipation. As he draws closer, it begins to shallow. When I hear the doorknob turn, I stop breathing altogether. The steps get closer...closer...until they reach me.

The sound of shifting denim fills the empty room as he crouches down in front of me, and I try to hold in my breath as the smell of cigarettes and bourbon that seeps from him tickles my nostrils.

A small whimper escapes me when his calloused hands caress my face and I stifle a frightened quiver that threatens to break out over my body. I never know if I'm going to get nice Alex or not, but if I had a choice I'd go with the latter. Not that I like him either way. I figured I would place him on my shelf of villains. Alex is kind of like Dr. Jekyll and Mr. Hyde. That's what he reminds me of. He grabs both sides of my face in one of his hands and squeezes it, my own yelp dragging me out of my thoughts.

"Look at me," he demands gruffly.

My eyes peel open slowly to meet his blue eye greets me, soft and warm. His glass eye reflecting the sadness in my own.

"Are you feeling well?" he asks after a beat.

I grind my jaw and glare at him in response. I like it better when he's mean to me, when he's sober. When I don't respond, he sighs deeply, letting go of my face, and sits down in front of me. I loosen the grip I have around myself and sit up, mimicking him.

"Did you eat today?" he asks.

"Yes," I whisper, flinching when he pushes himself up to his knees suddenly and buries his face in his hands. I stare wide-eyed at the back of his blond head before I look around the now dimly lit room. If I had something heavy I could knock him out right now, but of course there's nothing here except that damn broken television and I can't lift that. He takes a long, deep breath before he looks up again, his face glistening.

"It wasn't supposed to be you," he whispers hoarsely, extending his arm to touch my face, brushing my left cheek.

I don't understand what he means by this. If it wasn't supposed to be me, why did he take me? Instead of asking, I close my eyes and think of my rock during these hours, days, months, years. His bright green eyes, crooked smile, dimple, and messy hair. His protective arms and everything they offer me when I need it most. My eyes begin to burn with unshed tears, and for a moment I find my zen because in that moment I'm with Cole.

"I'm sorry," Alex says brokenly. "I'm so sorry," he cries, bringing his face to his knees and clutching the mattress below me with the palms of his hands. My body shakes along with the mattress as he continues to sob in front of me. I don't know what to do, so I just sit wallowing in my own sadness and examining his wide, scraped knuckles.

"Are you going to let me go?" I ask quietly.

Suddenly, he lifts up and sits back on his heels very slowly. His eye darkens as it narrows on mine and the disapproval in them makes my stomach plummet.

"What?" he asks through gritted teeth. "What do you mean, let you go?"

"You...you said you were sorry," I stammer.

"I'm never letting you go again, Cory," he huffs, his face hardening as he gets up and walks to the door.

"I'm not Cory," I whisper, more to myself than to him, but my voice bounces off the walls of the small empty room and I know he hears me.

"What did you say?" he growls, pivoting around swiftly.

"I'm not Cory," I whimper.

He stomps over to me and before I can move back, the back of his hand makes contact with my face, causing my entire head to jerk sideways. My painful cry is cut short when he yanks me by the hair and drags me off the mattress, making me scramble awkwardly on my hands and feet in an attempt to lessen the pain on my scalp.

"I KNOW YOU'RE NOT CORY," he bellows as he continues to drag me around the room while I hold on to my head to stop the burn. "If it weren't for you, maybe she'd still be here! With me!" He lets me go suddenly, bumping me against the side of the dresser, before he walks over and crouches down in front of me, his breathing harsh in my ear. I force myself to look up and when our eyes lock, his entire demeanor changes. His eyes widen and he stumbles back, grumbling an apology under his breath before walking out and slamming the door behind him. I wait until I hear the lock click on the other side of the door, then I lurch over to gasp for air, letting myself crumble.

I lie on the cold floor willing my heart to calm. I try to recall everything that's happened while I've been here, hoping to figure out how long I've been gone. I unsuccessfully do this every day—I just know it has been too long. I can barely hear Cole's voice in my head anymore; the one there fades with each passing day and I can't allow myself to forget what he sounds like. If I do, I'll lose hope.

I've already lost too much though. And for him, for us, I can't afford that. I make the painful crawl back to the mattress and sob into the pillow until it's covered in blood and salty tears. I close my eyes and picture Cole's green eyes looking back at me, pleading with me to stay strong, as I drift into sleep.

The click of the lock jerks me awake, but I keep my eyes closed even when the door is shoved open and bangs onto the wall beside it. I bury my face deeper into the pillow and bite down on it, refusing to make a sound as pain shoots through my body.

"Wake up, girl!" His booming voice echoes in the room as he switches on the light. "Wake UP!"

I shift and sit up, carefully squinting my eyes and whimpering from the pain in my back. My eyes blink a couple of times until they adjust to my surroundings and widen when I see Alex standing in the threshold with his arms crossed. He's dressed in dark jeans, and a button down shirt, not his usual business clothing. His tall physique blocks most of the entryway, and it takes everything in me to look at his face. The circles under his eyes are more prominent every time I see him. The blond shadow on his jaw filling a little more. As I examine him, the fleeting thought crosses my mind that he must have been a handsome man once upon a time, before life took his eye. Although it's hard to conceive, I like to believe that light may have once resided in them. Sometimes his eyes look so gentle, and I wonder if he has children of his own or anybody to love. I like to believe that about everybody though. Tearing my gaze away from his, I see another figure behind him and swallow a gasp as I clutch the sheets beneath me.

"Look familiar?" Alex asks gruffly when the young man stands beside him. A man that can't be much older than me dressed in jeans, a white T-shirt and black leather jacket. He has the kind of face that I would normally consider a baby face if it weren't for the clear mischief in his eyes and light hair that aligns his jaw. I nod in reply to Alex's question because I can't afford to make him angry again. "This is Dean, he'll be watching over you for a couple of days. He's good at that. Do as he says and don't try and get smart with him. If you try anything stupid-"

"I won't," I interrupt in a low voice, flinching when he takes a step forward.

"Good," he says. "You have work to do today."

They walk out without another word and I get up carefully, dragging my feet to the bathroom. I brush my teeth, careful not to hit the inner wall of my bruised right cheek. Once I'm done rinsing, I stare at the woman in the mirror, a ghost of my former self. With the exception of the bruises, my skin looks pale, almost translucent; a far cry from the golden skin I had before I got here. I don't know her anymore, and I'm not sure if I'll become her again. I don't even know that I want to. That woman, that scared woman, the one that locked all of her doors because she thought it kept her safe, is now locked in a room with no way out. How fitting.

I shower as quickly as I can without causing my body more pain, dress in gray sweat pants and a white baggy T-shirt, and carefully bend back down to sit on the uncomfortable mattress again. I'm lost in thoughts of Cole when I hear a single knock on the door. It opens slightly and Dean tucks his head in. After seeing me dressed and ready, he steps in and places a tray of food in front of me, which I devour in two seconds. When I look up from the empty plate, he's eyeing me curiously.

"Have they been feeding you?" he asks, his voice low.

"Yes."

"Hmm. And you've been doing the laundry for them?"

I nod slowly as I look into his confused hazel eyes.

"Well, let's go," he says, getting up and taking the tray with him before extending a hand to help me up, which I refuse. I place both hands on the mattress and awkwardly push myself up so that I don't flinch in pain.

I take a step forward, and my knees buckle before I straighten both legs and push my shoulders back. Dean puts the tray on top of the TV and takes two strides until he's directly in front of me. I stumble two steps back, blinking rapidly while looking at his narrowed eyes.

"Where else did he hit you?" he asks, grinding his teeth. Bewildered by the hostile tone in his voice, I just stare at him, my breathing becoming ragged. I'm unsure of what to expect. Alex had never really hit me before last night, and even though I'm afraid of him, he's still the lesser of two evils.

"He...why does it matter?" I ask as my eyebrows knit together.

Dean exhales and ruffles his brown hair before extending his hand and touching my bottom lip with his thumb. I take in a breath; my feet cemented not letting me move away. "Let's just say I have an issue with women being hit." He shrugs, dropping his hand from my face.

I nod once and finally let out the breath I'm holding. I contemplate not replying to him, it's not like he can or will help me anyway. He helped get me here, after all. He's just as bad as they are. I brush past him and walk out of the room as he trails behind me.

"He's not the one I worry about," I mutter, looking around at the three men that are already here and breathing a sigh of relief when I see that the one I'm referring to isn't one of them. Dean grabs my elbow and pulls me back harshly.

"What does that mean?" he asks with narrowed eyes.

8

I squint back. "What are you my savior? Where the hell have you been for the past...whatever amount of days?" I ask angrily before yanking my arm away from him.

He lets out a short laugh behind me before mumbling, "Savior...that's new."

I continue down the path that leads to the laundry room and begin my daily task, which unfortunately doesn't take long enough. I throw the white coats that the men in the other room use into the washing machine, and throw their stained gloves into the trash can, before sitting on the floor. Dean sits down on the wall opposite of me and we both stare at the floor.

"Look, chick, I don't want you to get the wrong idea, I'm not here to save you or anything." He starts running his hand through his hair and exhaling. "Gimme some time to figure shit out. Maybe I can help you out," he says quietly. I can feel his gaze on my face, but I refuse to turn and confirm that he's staring at me.

"Why would you help me?" I ask, my voice dripping in disbelief.

"Because I know who you are. Because helping you might help me," he states simply.

I turn my face and glare at him. "Yeah, you made that perfectly clear the last time we had a run-in, remember?"

"Of course I remember. But I didn't know what I know now and I changed my mind about helping him," he replies with a slight shrug as if a life, MY life, is a freaking game.

"Oh, you changed your mind?" I scoff.

He gives me a menacing stare. "Yes. You don't have to believe me. Like I said, I'm not here to be your fucking prince charming, you already have one of those, remember?" he says with a raised eyebrow. My jaw unhinges and my heart begins to thump rapidly against my chest, but before I can reply to him, the door beside me suddenly kicks open full force. I shriek, crawling backwards when I look up and see dark eyes narrowing in on me, until my back collides with the tips of Dean's boots.

"What are you doing here?" Benny snarls looking over my head.

My stomach clenches when I notice the absence of Dean's shoes on my back. I bring my legs up to me, clasping my knees together and wrap my arms around my legs, my eyes glued to Benny's cold black eyes. I want to avert my eyes from his, I wish I could so bad, but he holds me there; holds me prisoner. Chaining my insides slowly together and tugging, waiting for me to crumble. But I won't. He tears his glare from me to look at Dean in disdain, waiting for an answer.

"Alex told me to watch her, the fuck do you care?" Dean snaps back, making my eyes widen. I've never seen anybody talk back to Benny, other than Alex. Benny is not really a big guy, but he has the most menacing face, with a scar that trails from his right eyebrow to the top of his lip. His jaw is always hardened and his lips remain set in a grim line, but it's his eyes—his soulless eyes make him menacing.

"Why would you have to watch her?" Benny asks, even his question sounding like a demand.

Dean shifts his feet and stands in front of me, blocking me from Benny. They're now standing face to face, testing each other. They both have an athletic figure, but Dean is actually fit, whereas Benny looks like he drank an entire Corona delivery truck.

"You've been beating her?" Dean asks in a low voice, stepping closer and causing Benny to back up a step. I scoot back a little more, just in case this turns into a full-out brawl.

"What's it to you?" Benny spits back. "You can't fuck 'er, ya know? Alex will cut off your balls and feed 'em to ya."

"Fuck you. You touch her again and I'll cut yours," Dean grinds out.

Benny shakes his head in amusement as he laughs. "So fucking touchy when it comes to women. What ever happened to Sarah, anyway?"

Dean's nostrils flare and he lets out a growl before his fist collides with Benny's jaw, making him fall back. I gasp and scoot my back flush against the wall before clasping both hands over my mouth to keep myself from screaming. Benny attacks back by punching Dean in the stomach, making him hurl over. He recovers quickly and lurches his body forward, slamming Benny's back against the wall.

"That's enough!" a man shouts loudly. My hands start quivering over my mouth and tears form in my eyes. "Benny, I told you not to come down here unless I was here!" he screams.

"You're too easy on her! She ruined your life! MY LIFE!" Benny screams loudly. I press my back further into the wall and bite down on the inside of my hands when a sob threatens to escape. I shut my eyes, praying for a way out of the scene before me.

"Get out! Get the fuck out!" Alex yells. "This is business! This isn't for your personal fucking pleasure! We got her here and now we wait! She stays unharmed, and you don't get near her until it's time to turn her over. YOU GOT ME?"

Benny mumbles something I can't hear and I hear his stomps begin to fade away. My body goes rigid when I hear footsteps approach, and I snap my eyes open in a panic.

"Sorry about that, chick," Dean says, crouching down in front of me. His face and T-shirt are full of blood as his hazel eyes search my face.

"What the fuck was that about?" Alex asks gruffly, standing by the door with his arms crossed over his chest.

"He beat her," Dean explains casually and I feel my eyes go as wide as saucers. Benny has hit me, but he wasn't the one who did this to me. I swallow loudly and avert my eyes from Dean, hoping I can cover up my discomfort before looking back at them.

Alex gives me a long thoughtful look before he shakes his head slowly and looks at his feet. He doesn't apologize, but he makes me feel it. The washer timer goes off and I force myself to get up and tend to it.

"I'm leaving. Watch her 'round the clock. I don't care what you gotta do outside of here, cancel. Tell Jamie you got something else to do and let someone else handle it for you," Alex says before walking away.

"Got it," Dean replies with a nod.

The next morning, I'm awakened by the sound of clattering dishes nearby. I sit up, startled, when I see Dean standing in my room holding a tray. I'm surprised that he changed into a pair of jeans and a black leather jacket. I don't know where I figured he would be staying, but since he's supposed to watch me around the clock, I didn't think he would go home. For some reason the thought of him going home in the middle of the night bothers me.

"Sorry, chick. I knocked and called out for you, but you never answered. Brought you food," he says as he puts the tray down on the floor beside me. I nod in appreciation and am once again thankful, when I watch his eyes trail down my body, that they provide me with clothes that fully cover me.

He clears his throat. "Not much to do here, huh?" he asks, averting his eyes to survey the empty room. The only thing here is the mattress and a tiny television that sits on the floor across from me. It gets three channels and I stopped watching it when the news came on, showing a picture of me and Cole last Christmas. The reporter said the authorities were losing hope in the search for my body, as if they assumed I was dead. After that, I decided that I'd rather not know when they were calling off the search. It's not like they would ever find me here anyway. Not that I know where I am, but I know it's not easy to find. That much is obvious from all of the illegal drug activity going on right outside this door.

I shrug before placing the tray on my lap. "Guess not."

I can feel Dean watching me as I eat and my chewing begins to slow. I put my fork town and wipe my clammy hand over my sweats, my eyes searching the eggs and eyeing the orange juice.

"What's wrong?" he asks, his face scrunched in confusion when I look at him.

"Why are you looking at me?" I ask, irritated.

His eyes widen, registering my insinuation. "You think I put something in your food?" he asks incredulously.

"You say that like it's impossible," I scoff with an eye roll.

His scowl deepens and he shakes his head slowly. "I can't believe you still don't trust me."

My jaw unhinges. "I can't believe you expect me to!"

He draws an O with his lips as he lets out a slow breath. "I guess I can't, but I would never put something in your food."

"So why are you staring at me?" I ask, picking up my fork to play with the eggs that I so badly want to finish eating.

The side of his mouth turns upward. "Just trying to figure something out."

I inhale and exhale a breath before I continue eating. I groan when I find that he's still staring at me.

"Well, figure it out and stop looking at me!" I snap.

He laughs a little and I glower at him, refusing to share his amusement over my annoyance.

"Oh, chick. You're actually pretty cute when you're upset."

I roll my eyes and take a sip of juice. "Why are you even here? With these people?" I ask in a whisper and watch his eyes widen in surprise.

Dean doesn't seem like he belongs with Benny or Alex or even any of the men that work outside my door every day. He just seems like a regular guy. He's oddly mysterious, but he still seems like a regular guy that I would see around school. I just don't get it.

"I..." He clears his throat. "They're family," he replies with a casual shrug.

My lips twist in disgust. "My condolences."

His answering grin makes his face light up and I catch myself staring at it before I remind myself who he is and snap the hell out of it. He may be nice to me, but I don't know what he's capable of. I know he's capable of stalking me, and I know he was okay with Alex and Benny taking me before he found out "who I was"—whatever that means.

"They're not all bad," he says after a couple of seconds of us looking at each other. "Benny and Alex are just more fucked up than the rest of them."

"Well, you kidnapped me," I retort with a raised eyebrow.

"No, I didn't. I watched you, I didn't actually take you," he replies slowly.

My mind drifts back to that day. I was in the park enjoying the spring breeze while reading Cole's letter. Text messaging Cole and getting his response before getting up and walking away without a care in the world, then hearing gunshots at a distance and people screaming.

"Did you kill my bodyguard?" I ask quietly. Every time I replay what happened in my head, I wonder what the hell happened to him. Those shots I heard must have been aimed at him.

Dean exhales and shakes his head. "Bruce? Contrary to what you probably think of me, I don't kill for anybody."

I avert my eyes from his and let his words saunter in my head for a while before I look at him again.

"How do you know his name?" I ask quietly.

"I know everybody in your life, Blake," he replies slowly.

I'm not really surprised by that. He did follow me around, after all. He was bound to see me with everyone I was around, but I wonder just how much he knows about me that he's not letting out. He may know more about me than I do. In fact, I know he does, and although that scares me, I think I'm more terrified of finding out more information about myself. That's what got me here in the first place, my constant need to solve this puzzle. I decide to steer this subject in his direction instead.

"Are you like...a mobster?" I ask, my eyebrows knitting together.

His laugh answers my question. "I...oh shit, I don't even know how to...you don't want me to answer that," he says in between laughs.

His carefree laugh makes my blood boil and the fact that I keep staring at his mouth while he does it makes me even angrier.

"Who's Sarah?" I ask, cutting his laughter short. He narrows his eyes at me and leans forward. I instinctively clutch on to the sheets under me and rock my body back. He looks from my hands to my face and shakes his head, his eyes full of remorse.

"I would never hit you, chick. I swear I won't. Sarah's...she's just an ex-girlfriend of mine. Long story," he says quietly before leaning back.

"Forget I asked," I mumble. It's not like I want to make small talk with this criminal.

"It's cool. Like I said...you really shouldn't be here, but I don't know how to get you out. Shit is really fucking complicated around here, in case you haven't figured that out yet."

"Why can't you...can't you sneak me out while he's away?" I ask, trying not to sound as hopeful as I feel.

"Hell no. I wanna help you, not get myself killed!" he scoffs.

I blink at him. "They'd kill you? But you just said they're your family!"

A bitter laugh escapes him before he says, "Yeah...family. Family means everything and nothing to people like Benny. These people have your back until you fuck up, chick. It's an eye for an eye out there. You cross them—you die."

I get lost in a trance, pondering his words. I wonder who has the vendetta against my supposed family. Is it Alex or is it Benny? And who's ultimately in charge of my fate in all of this? I know that if Benny is the one in charge, I am royally screwed because he clearly hates me beyond anything I've ever seen before. He acts as though I killed his dog or something. Alex doesn't like me either, he'd rather not look at me at all. It just doesn't seem fair that I would have to pay for something that people I don't even know did to them over twenty years ago. Not only that, they seem convinced that my father, who is supposedly alive, and his people, are going to want me back. But why would he? Why would any of them want me back? If they did, wouldn't they have looked for me years ago? I mull over these thoughts as I drift to sleep, hoping I'm wrong and that they do want me and do believe I'm alive. Because the only thing I know without a doubt is that whoever they are, they're the only ones keeping me alive. Just like Cole is the only one keeping me sane.

# Chapter Two

## ~Blake~

I rub my eyes and stretch with a yawn, rolling over to look for Cole until I feel the cold of the sheets beside me. When I open my eyes I realize I'm not home but still trapped in this hell. The voices coming from outside the door confirm it. The light that seeps in from under the door is the only thing brightening the room a little. Sitting up, I try to listen closely, hoping to make out who's here before heading to the bathroom. I step into the bathroom and close the door, locking the dread behind me before leaning against it and sliding down to the floor. My eyes jump from one tiny white tile to the other and I look around at the bathroom that has become my sanctuary. I examine my arms and notice that the bruises are slowly disappearing. Thanks to Dean's daily visits, Benny hasn't been able to lay a hand on me. I finally gather the strength to pick up my lethargic body and head straight to the shower, peeling off my clothes on the way. I stand below the water before it gets too cold, not that it's warm to begin with. As I lather my hair, my mind drifts to my loved ones, as it always does. I wonder what Cole is doing today, how he's coping. How Aubry's doing and whether Becky and Greg have gone to visit them. So many questions that I don't have the answers to, and the longer I'm here, the less likely that I will.

Sitting under the shower head, I bring my knees up to my chest and let the water prickle my back as I watch it drain away the soap and tears. I close my eyes and think of Maggie and Aunt Shelley, the women I leaned on during the most important years of my life. I haven't let myself think of either one of them in a long time, not wanting to experience the pain of losing them again, but I can't help it as I wonder what they would do in this situation, what kind of advice they would provide me with. They were so caring, so patient, so resilient. Even in her last days, Aunt Shelley never let me see her break down, not once.

Loud pounding on the bathroom door breaks me from my daydream, and I get up quickly to turn off the water and get out of the shower. The pounding on the door continues until I yell out that I'm almost done. Once I'm dressed, I take a deep breath and decide that I will not let them break me; I won't let my family down. I open the door and see Dean on the other side, wearing a plaid blue button down shirt with the sleeves rolled up, jeans, and black boots. His dark hair is perfectly styled, and even the shadow of a beard looks pretty good on him. My eyes trail down his slim body and stay glued to the tattoos I see on his left forearm, until his chuckle brings me to meet his twinkling hazel eyes.

"Well, this is a change," he says, the side of his mouth forming in a slight smile.

"What is?" I ask, crinkling my eyebrows.

"You. Checking me out instead of glaring at me," he says as a slow smile spreads on his face.

My mouth pops open for a moment before I recover my thoughts. "I was not checking you out! I was trying to figure out what your tattoo is. There's a difference. Besides, you're not in your uniform today. It's weird to see you wearing grown up clothes." He doesn't really wear a uniform, but most of the time he's dressed in jeans, a white T-shirt and a leather jacket.

He shakes his head. "If you say so." I can hear the disbelief in his voice and it makes me want to throw something at him.

I roll my eyes. "Do you have another magazine for me?"

He's been bringing me magazines to help my boredom. I have to hide them whenever Alex comes to check up on me just in case, but that's a small price to pay for entertainment. I may not know what's going on in the world, but I know which celebrity couples are together and what the latest trend fashion is. So far, Drew Barrymore got married and Jessica Simpson had a baby. Maybe if I had kept up with gossip before, this would be exciting for me to know, but frankly, I don't give a damn. I sigh dreamily at my own thoughts as I daze off thinking of Gerald O'Hara. God, I need to get the fuck out of here! You know it's bad when you're daydreaming of an old dead guy.

"You're such a pain in the ass," Dean says with a laugh, and then suddenly stops when he sees me wipe my tears. "Shit. I was kidding, chick, you didn't have to go and cry about it." I bury my face in my hands before more sobs can escape. How pathetic am I that I can't be called a pain in the ass without crying? Once I calm down, I wipe my face again and bring the tray onto my lap, avoiding his gaze.

"So, you don't like being called a pain in the ass?" he asks quietly. I know he's trying to keep the conversation light, but I'm not in the mood for any of it.

"No," I grumble before taking a bite of toast. "I don't like being called anything."

He sits in front of me and watches me eat in silence. When I finish, I get up and head to the bathroom, leaving him sitting on the floor by my bed.

I sit up on the counter and begin to draw circles over the green bruises on my calf. That's all I am these days, cuts and bruises—inside and out. I snap back to reality and hop off the counter, picking up my hair in a messy ponytail as I open the door, hoping to walk into an empty room, but Dean is still there flipping through my magazine.

"You gonna sit here and read old gossip all day or you gonna try to help me out?"

He raises an eyebrow. "This is new gossip and I *am* trying to help you out."

As he walks over to me, I notice our difference in height. For some reason I've never noticed the way he towers over me. Probably because I'm always looking at the ground, unless I'm sitting on it. He's definitely not as tall as Cole, nothing about his physical appearance is like Cole's. Cole is tall and muscular, Dean is tall and lean. Cole has more of a playboy face, whereas Dean is more of a rugged pretty boy. The only thing they have in common is that swagger, or spark that some guys have. The one that draws you to them, even though you know in the back of your mind that you will get burned once you get too close. When he leans close to me, I take in his scent of nicotine and cinnamon before he hands me the magazine, making me flinch a little.

He holds my stare as we both grip either side of the magazine. "Chill out, I'm not gonna hurt you, chick."

"You are hurting me," I whisper as I sit down on the bed and look down at the magazine. It looks blurry through my eyes, so I can't make out who's on the cover of this one. He cups his hand under my chin and lifts my face to look at him, but I turn out of his hold. "Don't touch me, please."

He exhales heavily. "I'm sorry about your sucky situation, and I'm sorry you're the one that has to deal with the mess others have made."

"I just wish I knew why this was happening to me," I say quietly as I stare at my chipped red nail polish.

"I dunno the whole story, but from what I've heard your dad screwed Benny over. Alex's beef with your dad is personal though," he says quietly.

I take a deep shaky breath. "How did my 'dad' screw them over?" I ask, emphasizing the word that's so unfamiliar to me, just like the man himself.

"Well, from what I've heard-"

"Dean! I've been calling you, where's your goddamn phone?" Alex shouts as he stomps over to my room. I hide the magazines under my pillow and bring my knees up to my chest, wrapping my arms around myself. Dean gives me a grateful look before picking up the tray and standing.

"I came down to bring her food," he replies to Alex, who is now standing in the threshold looking at me. I try my best not to squirm or look away from his stare.

"Good. You can go," Alex says in a gruff voice. I close my eyes, grab a handful of the sheets beside me, and pray Dean stays a little while longer.

"I'll see you, chick," Dean says, looking at me with regret in his eyes. I nod in response and watch him walk out, leaving me alone with Alex.

Alex looks at me for a long time, his eyes drifting all over my face until they settle on my eyes.

# Chapter Three

## ~ COLE ~

I take a fourth gulp of whiskey and welcome the burn in the back of my throat, praying that numbness engulfs my pain soon. The camera flashes that bolt through the windows remind me that four drinks isn't going to be enough to hold me off tonight. I can't believe I agreed to come to this shit; the last thing I wanted to do was fly out of Chicago, but attending a social event takes the freaking cake. People would've understood if I would've skipped out on the event, but Greg was acting like a little bitch, begging me to come with him because Becky couldn't make it. After two years of trying and failing, she got some in-vitro treatment done and finally got pregnant. Unfortunately, she's been having a rough first trimester, and Blake's kidnapping hasn't helped her stress level.

I put down the glass and run my hands over my buzz cut and rough beard, before picking it back up and drinking what's left. To say that I'm going fucking crazy without her would be the understatement of the century. I went back to work two weeks after she disappeared thinking that I could use the distraction, but I couldn't. I had to take a leave of absence and I don't know if I ever want to go back. I don't know if I can.

"Yo, what's up?" Greg asks, stirring me out of my angry daze. He's holding a beer bottle, pointing at my hand with his pinky.

I look down and growl when I realize that I shattered the glass in my hand. I clean up, tossing the broken glass into the tiny ass garbage can next to me, before getting napkins and wiping the blood from my hands.

"Shit. Does it hurt?" Greg asks as he examines my hand.

I shrug. "Not enough." He exhales and shakes his head. "You ready?" I ask before he says anything else.

He nods once and takes a deep breath, stretching his neck the way he does before he goes on the field. I know he's mentally preparing himself to deal with my wrath in public. I heard him on the phone with Becky last night and from what I gathered, she was coaching him on how to handle me. As if I'm some kind of wild animal or something.

As soon as we step out of the limo, the camera lights start flashing. Greg turns to me. "You know you don't have to talk about anything, right? If they ask you questions, just ignore them, or let me handle it."

I shake my head. "Let them ask. Maybe it'll help." The authorities are calling Blake's kidnapping a disappearance, as in she left without leaving a trace. They're saying there were no eyewitnesses around that saw her being taken. They even had the audacity to ask me if maybe she was involved with somebody else and doesn't want to be found. At least the news reporters are still talking about it and speculating that it was a kidnapping, which I'm getting tired of confirming. It doesn't help that Bruce has no recollection of anything that happened that day, so at this point, I'll take any help I can get. Maybe keeping my face in the news is the right step.

We walk down the red carpet, and Greg and I stop to pose for a couple of photos. Reporters are yelling from all directions, asking me questions. "Mr. Murphy, how are you holding up? Have you learned any information about Miss. Brennan's disappearance?"

I take a deep breath and turn to the reporter. "We're still searching. I'm not losing hope. I know I'll get her back.

If anybody sees or hears anything, please contact the police immediately!"

Everything is going fine, until some idiot yells, "Have they found her body?" and I feel the blood drain from my face. I close my eyes and clench my jaw as Greg puts a hand on my shoulder and squeezes. I'm silently hoping my anger will pass, but the fucker repeats the question, louder this time.

"Who the fuck asked that question?" I growl.

The flashes continue. You'd think they would stop because they know I'm pissed. Instead these dumb mother fuckers are eating this up. I know this, and I don't want to give them a fucking show, but damn if I can stop myself. I feel Greg place his other hand on my shoulder and start ushering me out. I hear his voice, but I don't know what the fuck he's telling me. When we reach the next batch of photographers I bump into a woman in a gold dress. I'm about to apologize and walk away, but she turns around and my eyes get caught in Erin's pale blue eyes. She smiles sympathetically and before I know it, she pulls me into a hug.

"I'm so, so sorry, Cole. So sorry. I tried calling you, but it always goes straight to voicemail. How are you doing?" she asks sweetly.

Erin's a class act and by far the sweetest girl I've dated. I ran into her after we broke up. She'd heard I started dating Blake, and instead of being angry, she congratulated me and smiled. She said she always had a feeling we were meant to be together.

"Thanks, Erin. Where's Tom?" I ask as I lean out of her embrace. She's been dating Tom Buck, the quarterback for Chicago, for a while now.

She smiles brightly. "He's around. He's nominated, so he went to do a couple of interviews with his agent. He should be back soon. I'm handing out the awards, I'm sure you noticed," she replies gesturing her dress.

I look down at her golden dress and nod, realizing she'll be one of those girls that stands on stage all night. For a fleeting second I picture that dress on Blake and think about how good it would look on her. Blake. Thinking of her brings back the tightness in my chest and the ball in my throat. I clear it, hoping to rid myself of emotion for now.

"That's great, Erin. I'll catch you later, Greg's waiting for me."

"Sure. Cole?" she says before I turn away. "She'll come back to you. I know she will."

I nod, because if I say anything right now, I would sob it out. I walk over to Greg, who's talking to his teammate, Trevor, the fucking asshole that was all over Blake when she went to New York last year. Trevor's not really an asshole, though, and I can see the sympathy written all over his face.

"Sup, Cole?" Trevor says, extending his hand. I take it and nod once in reply.

"I'm sure you're sick of hearing this shit, but I'm sorry about Blake, bro. If you need anything, I'm there," Trevor says.

"Thanks, man," I reply.

I greet the petite woman wearing a black dress standing next to him and she smiles at me sympathetically before putting her hand in Trevor's. I rub my forehead in frustration. Does everybody here have a fucking date? I guess I need to get over that, at least, but every time I see couples being affectionate it gets under my skin. Blake and I aren't even the type to hold hands. Now I wish I had held her fucking hand every chance I got. I wish I could go back to that fucking day and not have taken that damn flight to New York.

The rest of the evening went well enough. I got more "I'm sorrys" and shit, but other than that, I was able to present the award, and get the fuck out of there with no issues. Greg left when I did and opted to skip out on the after parties; I'm not sure if he wanted to spend time with me, or not piss Becky off.

I lay in the queen size bed of the hotel room staring at the ceiling, listening to Greg snore his ass off. How the fuck does Becky sleep with this every night? Fuuuck, this shit is annoying. I glance over at the time, three fucking thirty. *Fuck me. Of course it is.* This time, the sobs win. I hear the bed creaking from my shaking body. This shit happens to me every night. I want to say that this is when I miss her the most, but the truth is, I always miss her. Even in my sleep, I miss her warmth beside me. Why the fuck did they have to take her from me? Why? Why her?

"Damn, man," Greg rasps. "I'm so sorry, dude." I hear him sit up, but he leaves the lights off. Thank God. If he turned them on and exposed me, I'd fucking kill him. I feel vulnerable enough already. I hear him sniffling, and I know he's crying too. I know he misses her too. He loves Blake. Everyone does. I can't get her image out of my head. Her long, wavy dirty-blond hair, her big, stormy gray eyes, her plump lips, her pink cheeks, her perfect tits, her perfect ass, her perfect fucking legs. My princess. She flips the fuck out whenever I call her that. Even as kids, I thought of her as my princess. Now I only call her that when she's being a bitch, which is often. Damn, I miss her smart mouth, her fuck off attitude, our banter, our sex, our laughs. I miss everything about my life with her.

"You talk to Mark lately?" Greg asks hoarsely.

"Yeah, every fucking day. Fucker won't tell me shit. I'm gonna have to kick it out of him if he keeps playing games with me. Godfather or not, I don't give a fuck. I already warned him. He keeps saying he's handling it, but I don't see shit being handled. He won't tell me shit. Fucking Bruce didn't see anyone coming for her, which says a lot, since, well, you know Bruce. He's a fucking ex-Marine for Christ sake. What the fuck, man. What the fuck?" I sob.

"I know, dude. I fucking know. Becky can't fucking think, she's not eating right and that shit's unhealthy for the baby. She keeps talking crazy, saying she doesn't wanna be pregnant if Blake's not here. Doesn't wanna fucking have a kid if Blake's not gonna be around for it. I miss Cowboy to death, yo, but fuck, that's my fucking kid she's talking 'bout. I don't think she'd do anything stupid, but I'm fucking scared to leave her crazy ass for too long. With Mags gone, and now Blake missing, I'm about to fucking take Aubry's ass to live with us for a while."

I let out a shaky laugh thinking about that. "I doubt he'd go. Aubry loves Becks, I'm sure he wants to be there for her, but he's out of his mind without Cowboy." I hear Greg snicker. "Fuck you. I know I'm out of my damn mind without her, but he's hurting too, they fucking lived together their whole lives. They were attached at the hip. I swear if I didn't know for a fact that Aubry is scared shitless of me, I would have a problem with that."

Greg laughs loudly, making the bed creak. "Aubry wouldn't try to get with Blake because he knows she'd kick his ass."

I smile at the thought. "As long as he never touched my girl, we're good."

"Yeah," Greg yawned, "good night, man. Try to get some rest, tomorrow's gonna be a long day."

He's right. Tomorrow I go back to hell. Back home. Without her...again.

# Chapter Four

## ~Blake~

I turn my tender body in the mattress that has become an extension of my body. Sensitive to my surroundings, I pick up the sounds and smells around me. The voices outside the door and opening and closing of the fridge clue me in to the time of day. The schedule rarely changes, which is one reason I can't differentiate weekdays from weekends. Not that a Monday is different from a Friday to me, though it would make it easier for me to figure out how long I've actually been here. I could ask, but I doubt I'd get an answer. I only care because I like to torture myself wondering whether or not anybody is still looking for me. I know Cole's still looking for me though. He has to be.

When Dean comes to bring my food, he tells me that I'll be helping out in the kitchen upstairs, which surprises me since I'm rarely allowed up there.

"Why? What about Benny? Is he here?" I ask as my heart hammers in my chest. I don't want to think about seeing Benny or the possibility of him cornering me. I've only seen him once up there, and thankfully Dean was nearby, but even with the distance between us, he scares the shit out of me.

"I dunno where Benny's at, but you know he won't get near you. The maid's not here today and they have company tonight, so the kitchen needs to be cleaned," Dean says as he hands me my silverware.

As soon as I take a bite of the bagel with cream cheese I get grossed out and toss it back on the plate. I get up and let him escort me, passing the men sorting out pills and powder on the table in the middle of the room. I walk up the stairs behind Dean and finally into the house, and a shudder runs through me when my bare feet meet the cold marble floor of the mansion. I look around, taking in the details of my luxurious surroundings, a far cry from the murky basement below. When we walk into the open kitchen, I eye the clock that reads 11:00 as I roll up my sweat pants to just above my ankle and my sleeves to my elbows before filling the bucket Dean hands me with water and Pine Sol. The intense smell of the product makes me gag, but I take a deep breath and block everything out of my mind as I begin to clean, scrubbing and wiping down the surfaces while Dean calls some restaurants and finds out about food delivery.

By two o'clock, my hands feel sore, but I'm done and the place looks spotless. Dean looks impressed when I tell him that I think I'm finished. He walks over to the fridge, pulling out two beers and handing me one. I give him a wide-eyed stare, not sure if he's really offering it to me or just testing me to see if I'd take it.

"What? You don't drink Bud?" he asks with a raised eyebrow.

"Umm...not usually, and I'm not sure if I should. What if they get here and get mad that I'm in the kitchen drinking?" I really can't afford to make anybody angrier than they already are. My bruises are gone, but my body is sorer than ever. I don't even want to think about getting hit right now—and for a Bud Light? Definitely not worth it.

"Chick, just drink the damn beer. We'll take them downstairs."

I shrug and take it from him, letting the cold bottle sooth the pain in my hands before taking a sip of it and making my way back downstairs.

"Are you going to be upstairs the whole night then?" I ask him, sitting down cross-legged on the mattress.

"I dunno," he replies with a shrug. "I got some shit to do tonight, so I'll probably do that and then come back."

Panic must be written all over my face at hearing he'll be gone tonight, while who knows what sort of people are here for some twisted dinner party, because he chuckles.

"What kind of party are they having?" I ask.

"It's not really a party, it's just men getting together for dinner and drinks. No big deal, but you don't gotta worry about it. They'll be busy upstairs. Benny won't come down here in the middle of all that."

I humph my response because I highly doubt that. The only reason Benny's been absent to begin with is Dean. Once he gets wind that he won't be here, he'll definitely come down here to bother me. I don't voice my concern about it because it's clear that Dean believes what he believes and isn't going to sway from that. Who knows, maybe he's right.

"I heard from a trustworthy source that your dad did that shit on his face, you know?"

My lips pause on the brim of the beer bottle and I lower it from my mouth. "What...that scar?" I ask, horrified.

"Yeah. I heard he did it after he found out Benny supposedly killed you and that other kid."

"Cole," I say quietly.

"Cole your boyfriend?" Dean asks surprised.

"No, Cole your *uncle*. Obviously my boyfriend!" I deadpan with an eye roll.

He laughs, finding my outburst amusing, which makes me want to chuck the beer bottle in my hand at him. Instead, I take a couple of deep breaths and focus on the brown grout in between the tiles.

"Shit. I kinda feel bad for the guy now. Going through that as a kid and now losing his girlfriend. No wonder he's going out of his damn mind."

A loud gasp involuntarily escapes me and the bottle slips from my hand, clinking on the floor. Luckily I'm low enough that it doesn't cause it to break, and it's empty enough that it rolls a little but doesn't spill.

"You've seen him?" I ask, trying and failing to steady my breath.

"Yeah, I've seen him. He's been acting a fool everywhere he goes, kinda hard to miss."

My already broken heart cracks a little more as my imagination wanders to Cole getting drunk and doing God knows what. I know I should have more faith than to doubt him, but damn if these unwanted thoughts don't cross my mind anyway. It's not like it's the first time I've thought about it. I know Cole's coping methods are pretty slim. He gets drunk and gets laid, that pretty much sums it up. I close my eyes and will the tears from spilling. I can't think like that; he wouldn't do that to me.

"Look, chick, I told you I'd help you get out, and I will. Hanging out with a kidnapped girl isn't my idea of a fun time. Not that you're not fun, but I have a bad feeling about this. I don't see a good ending to it either. Gimme a couple more days."

I blink before looking at his serious face and nodding. When he leaves me alone with my thoughts, I finally let my sobs break free. I miss my family so much that I get actual chest pains when I think about them. I need to keep my head up and stay positive, come up with a plan to get myself out of here. I need to break free, and even though Dean says he's going to help me get out, I keep plotting ways to do it on my own.

# Chapter Five

## ~ COLE ~

Fucking hell. That's what this place feels like without her. There's not enough oxygen to fill my lungs as I look around the lifeless apartment. *Our* apartment. Every day in this place brings memories of what we had. All the laughs, the fights, the sex. Those memories haunt my waking hours. I walk over to the guest room, where I've been sleeping since that night. That dreadful night, when I landed in the fucking Twilight Zone.

I replay that day at least a hundred times in my head every day. I got out of my meeting early and went straight to the airport after making a pit stop. I got on the first flight available and called her when I landed. I called Bruce after not reaching Blake's phone. When his phone kept going to voicemail, I started panicking and called Aubry, Aimee, Becky, Greg, and Mark. I was even desperate enough to call fucking Russell. A few minutes after I got home, Mark called to tell me that Bruce was in the hospital. That's when my chest started to ache worse than it ever had before. I put my hand in the breast pocket of my jacket, right over my heart, and felt the velvet box that I'd brought back from New York.

According to Mark, Bruce had gotten knocked out with a hit in the back of the head, and shot in the leg. He said he didn't see anybody, didn't see it coming. He had been watching some guy across the street that he'd seen Blake speak to a couple of weeks before, and was blindsided when he got hit. He said he knew it had something to do with that guy.

I shake my head from the awful memories and pull out my phone to call Aimee. I've been avoiding her and Aubry and anybody that reminds me of Blake, really, which has pretty much made me a fucking hermit. An hour later, when I open the door for them, I'm greeted with two shocked faces.

"Hey," Aimee greets, giving me a half-assed smile.

"Hey, sorry I've been...out of touch," I reply as I hug her.

"I haven't wanted to see you either," Aubry mutters quietly. "You look like shit, by the way."

I raise my eyebrows. "Uh...thanks?"

I offer them something to drink before we settle down in the living room. After small talking about nothing of importance, I figure I might as well bring up the reason I called. Might as well get this shit over with.

"Aimee, I've been thinking that maybe your parents...our parents, whatever...can help me look for Blake. They have a lot of pull, so maybe...I don't know, maybe I can meet them and we'll go from there?"

Aimee's eyebrows hike up. "Sure, I mean, I guess it wouldn't hurt to try. Are you ready to meet them? Do you want me to tell them?"

I let out a breath and scratch my beard. "I guess. It's not that I don't wanna meet them, it's just...I don't know, Maggie was my mom," I say in a shaky voice before clearing my throat. "I remember some things from when I was with you guys, but it almost feels like that was in a different life."

"I know, but they'll be happy to see you. I'm just glad I haven't seen much of them, because I don't know how I would have kept this whole thing to myself."

"Yeah, well, the only way I wanted to meet them was with Blake by my side, but seeing my fucking father on TV giving news conference after news conference with *my* girlfriend's face on the screen is wearing me down."

She sighs. "I know, trust me, I know. I'll see when their schedule looks clear so we can go over there. I'll have to figure out when Dad can see me so I can break the news to him first anyway."

It sounds so businesslike. I know he's the mayor, but damn. Whatever. I don't really give a shit. I need him on my side. He has the power to help me find Blake; and that's all I care about right now.

I wake up in the middle of the night drenched in sweat and my chest heaving. I just had the worst dream to date, just thinking about it makes me shudder. I get up and take a shower, hoping to rid myself of the sweat and my nasty dream, but it replays in my head every time I close my eyes. Blake is sitting on a dirty floor, tied up, with a man caressing a knife lightly over her body. I close my eyes tight and try to erase the images from my head. It was only a nightmare. A fucking nightmare, but every day I wake up wondering if they're feeding her, hurting her, touching her. My stomach turns at the thought and I double over in the shower, coughing up some of the bourbon I drank earlier. They better not fucking touch her. I know she's alive, I can feel it with every fiber in my being.

When I walk into the lobby of Mark's office the next day, I'm greeted by the blond that's always here. I remember Blake telling me that she couldn't stand them. Them. I guess there are two of them. Whatever, they look and act the same to me. This one is practically salivating as she eye fucks me. I try not to roll my eyes, because I don't have an appointment to see Mark, and I really don't want to barge into his office, though I will if I have to.

"Mr. Murphy," she coos as she leans forward, blatantly trying to entice me with her fake tits. "It's great to see you again. Do you have an appointment with Mr. Lewis?"

I grin at her, noticing her eyelids flutter before I feed her my bullshit. "I don't, actually. I was wondering if you could squeeze me in." I drop my voice as I say the last words, and I swear this girl is about to come in her tight ass pencil skirt.

She clears her throat as she smooths the front of her skirt. "Well, Mr. Lewis is a very busy man, Mr. Murphy. His morning is booked. His next client should be here in ten minutes. He won't be happy with me if I squeezed you in," she replies breathlessly.

I walk toward her and lean on the desk and ask, "Are you sure about that?"

With great effort, I don't cringe at her shiver or the strong perfume that consumes the airways as I stand so close to her. Blake rarely wears perfume and when she shivers, my cock instantly starts twitching. This bleach blond Barbie look alike is just not Blake...and the perfume she wears makes her smell like an old lady.

"I'll...umm...see what I can do, Mr. Murphy," she replies, flustered.

I grin again, wondering if it looks genuine or more like a grimace before turning back to the waiting area when she picks up her phone and makes the call.

"Mr. Murphy, you may go inside," she says right before I sit down.

"Thank you, Miss—"

"Tanner," she replies huskily.

"Miss Tanner, you have a good day, now."

When I get to Mark's door, I don't knock. I just push it open and walk straight toward him.

"Mark. What the fuck?" I bite out.

He rolls his eyes dramatically, and I swear I'm going to punch the motherfucker today.

"Cole," he says flatly. "What a surprise."

I slam my fists on his desk. "Do you think this is a fucking game? My fucking girlfriend has been missing for almost a month. The cops won't even look for her anymore. I have no help, I'm about to meet my long-lost fucking parents because I'm that damn desperate. So I'll ask you again, what the fuck do you know?" I growl.

He takes a deep breath. "You're going to meet your parents? Cole..."

"Don't even think about giving me your advice," I grind out.

He closes his eyes and rubs his forehead. "Cole, the people that are involved in this are big time. I can't have this conversation," he says as he looks around making a face at me.

I crinkle my eyebrows. "What the fuck does that mean?"

Mark stands up quickly, making his chair fly behind him and hit the glass wall.

"Listen, Cole, I know you're pissed, sad, and scared. Trust me, I am too, but it doesn't give you the right to disrespect your fucking godfather. I suggest you shut the fuck up, and go take a fucking walk. I'm going to lunch in five minutes. We'll talk about this when you've calmed down."

As he says this, he's stalking toward me. He grabs my arm and pulls me toward the door. He's fucking kicking me out. This asshole thinks he's going to kick me out? Is he fucking crazy? I snap my arm from his and push him off me. I can tell it's taking a lot for him not to push me back. I decide that I'm going to wait for him to leave on his little lunch break for his meeting, and I'm going to follow him around until he tells me what he knows. Fuck. This.

I push past him and walk out. I hear his footsteps behind me, but I refuse to look back. I walk toward the elevators and hear Miss Blondie say my name, but I don't turn around. When the doors open, I step in, and Mark steps in behind me. The doors close.

"Dickhead, did it ever occur to you, that *maybe,* I'm being fucking recorded and I can't talk about certain things in my office?" Mark asks angrily.

I narrow my eyes at him. "Does that mean you're gonna answer my fucking questions?"

"Yes, asshole. I'll take you to lunch, but I swear, you disrespect me again, and I'm going to teach you some fucking manners."

I rub my face with my hands. My beard is itchy and hot and I fucking hate it. I know Blake would hate it, but I'm not shaving until I find her. Even if I start to look like Santa Claus, or Jesus. I'm not fucking shaving.

"I would apologize, but you're past pushing my fucking limits, Lewis."

We take a cab to a little Irish pub. From the outside, it looks shitty. I'd never noticed it before, and I drive by here often enough.

"How long has this shit hole been here? Is it even open?" I ask, confused.

Mark shakes his head. "I wouldn't bring you for lunch if it was closed. And it's not a shit hole."

Inside, the place is nice. The booths are kept up, there's a huge bar in the center of the place, a stage across from it, a dance floor in front of that. Foo Fighters are blaring through the speakers.

"Shit, this place is actually nice," I say as we scoot in a booth.

"I know," he replies with a smirk.

"So, do you know who took her?"

"Yes," he sighs.

My eyes shoot out of my face. "You've known this whole time?"

"Yes," he says in a grave voice. "It's complicated, Cole."

"Fuck complicated!" I shout. "Stop fucking telling me things are complicated. I fucking know complicated. I've lived complicated. My fucking girlfriend...oh my God, Mark. Oh my God. Mother of fucking fuck. Is...please tell me it's not the same people," I whisper.

Mark looks me in the eyes, and the pain I see in them answers my question. Fuck.

"Who are they, Mark? What do they want? Why her?"

The waitress comes and gets our drink orders, and we order our food so she won't bother us again until it's ready.

"Cole," he says sternly. "If I tell you-" I make a face. "*When* I tell you, you have to promise me that you'll let me handle it. Please let me do this."

I pound my fist on the table, making our waters spill over a little. I practice on my breathing so I won't lose my temper again.

"Mark, just tell me," I demand through gritted teeth.

"Blake's father's last name is Brennan. Her mother's was Benson. As in Brian Benson."

He says it with such assurance, as if I'm supposed to know who the hell that is. As if he's saying...oh shit, Brian Benson? My eyes shoot up to his. Son of a...no way. I shake my head vehemently as I look into his expectant wide blue eyes.

"Brian Benson?" I whisper hoarsely. When he nods his head, I want to die.

He nods his head. "—is Blake's grandfather."

My head feels like it's inside a hamster ball, spinning and hitting everything in sight. Brian Benson is like the fucking Godfather. No, not like, he *is* the fucking godfather. He's *the* mob boss of mob bosses. Brian fucking Benson. Oh my God. It's all starting to come back to me. Blake's grandfather's farm. My farm now. What the fuck?

"Why the hell do I own Brian Benson's farm?" I whisper.

Mark's eyebrows shoot up. "His farm?"

I shoot him a look. "Don't be stupid. I know that you know."

Mark looks confused. "No, I really don't. What the hell are you talking about?"

I let out a breath and rub my forehead, trying to rein in my impending headache.

"Forget it. How do I find Brian?"

He chokes on the sip of water he's taking. "What?" he coughs out.

"Brian. How do I find him?" I ask, exasperated.

"You don't, Cole. Are you out of your fucking mind?"

"Yes, I fucking am," I shout. "I've *been* out of my fucking mind. I'm dying over here. I can't breathe, I can't sleep, I can't think! My mind is running marathons half the time. You know what? Forget it! I'll figure it out my own damn self!"

He exhales sharply. "Calm down!" he bellows. "I'll take you to him. I'll fucking take you to him!"

My eyes bug out of my face. "What? How?"

He tells me to let him handle that and that he'll take me to meet Brian soon. I just need to give him more time, but he's running out of time with me. Meanwhile, I can't even begin to process how the hell Mr. Fucking Big Time Attorney knows Brian motherfucking Benson. Well, he is a criminal attorney, maybe he's pulling in a favor. I don't care what he's doing, I need to find my girl.

A couple of days later, I'm standing outside my building waiting for Mark to pick me up and take me to see Brian. I hear Mark's Aston Martin before he pulls up to me and unlocks the doors. Before my ass even hits the seat, he's handing me a flask. I take it, giving him a confused look as I bring it up to my lips.

"Trust me, you'll need it," he says as he speeds off.

We're silent during the ride, no sounds other than the cool breeze powering out of the air vents. Comfortable silence is just about the only thing I can handle right now because I sure as shit don't want to talk, and I don't care much to hear what he has to say. Instead, I focus my attention on the LED lights that glow against the darkness before us, the only thing illuminating our journey. As my mind drifts to Blake, I stop paying attention to the roads and signs around me. Again I wonder why they have her, what they're feeding her, and where they're keeping her.

I put my face in my hands and feel the steel of the flask hit my forehead. The pain in my chest is becoming unbearable. Why couldn't they fucking take me? I'd gladly take her place. God, please let her be okay. She has to be okay. I don't realize I'm breathing heavily until Mark places his hand on my shoulder and looks at me with concern. I take a couple of deep breaths to calm down before staring back out into the night.

We pull up to a mansion with a massive iron gate that has the initial *B* in the middle. Mark opens his window and punches in a code to open the gates. He has the damn code?

"How do you know Brian?" I ask cautiously.

He turns to me with a smirk. "Oh...he's my father."

My jaw drops and all I can do is gape at him while he laughs at the shock on my face.

"Are you fucking kidding me?" I growl when I finally come to my senses.

Before he can even make a coherent reply without laughing at me, I'm standing in front of the large oval dungeon door in the front of the house. Mark rings the doorbell as I nervously wipe my sweaty hands on my pant legs. Moments later, we're greeted by an elderly woman dressed in a French maid outfit. No joke. I try not to laugh but surely that is just about as weird as it gets. I nod my head and smile politely, as Mark greets her with a hug. He turns and introduces me to Ethel and I shake her hand before we walk past her.

We approach what I'm assuming is a smoking room, because it smells like straight wood and cigar smoke. When we walk in, a gray-haired old man is sitting on one side of a poker table reading a newspaper.

"Pops," Mark greets, making the old man look up over his paper.

My stomach drops when I meet his big, piercing gray eyes. Brian fucking Benson. Any doubt I may have had about him being related to Blake vanishes along with my dignity, because I'm pretty sure I'm going to sell my soul to this guy so I can get my girl back. The longer I stand staring into his stormy eyes, the bigger the hole in my chest gets. Those eyes have haunted and saved me for the past twenty-six years. I clear my throat so I don't start crying like a little bitch in front of one of the most notorious men I've heard of.

"Nathan," the old man says as he searches my face.

I clear my throat again, trying to get rid of the fucking golf ball stuck in it. "Cole...but yes, sir," I say as I extend a hand out to him.

He shakes it. He's a tall man, almost as tall as I am and he's wearing khaki shorts and a polo. I don't know what the fuck I was expecting him to be wearing, but it sure as shit wasn't this.

"You've grown up, son," he says with a smile. I must have made a face because he starts laughing. "Were you expecting me to scream or be a pissed off old man?" he asks, amused.

"I didn't really think about it, sir, but I didn't expect you to be wearing regular clothes, that's for sure," I reply honestly.

His laughter fills the room, and Mark joins in shortly after. My mind is still reeling as I watch him hug Mark tightly and kiss him on both cheeks before turning back to me.

"Don't *sir* me, call me Brian. You used to call me Grandpa as a kid, but I don't expect you to remember that. Sit," he says, pointing at the chair across from the one he was sitting in. "Mark filled me in on everything. I gotta say, I was shocked as shit when I found out about Blake. I thought they were trying to play me, until Mark here came to me about it. Anyway, I'm expecting company tonight, so we need to air this shit about before they get here. There will be no mention of Blake around anybody else in this house. Understand?"

His eyes go cold when he says the last part to me, and suddenly the stories about how ruthless he is are a little more real to me. I know I can take this man down in a fight, but the intensity in his voice makes me shake in my fucking boots.

"Yes, sir," I reply. "I just need to know who took her and I need to get her back."

He picks up the set of dice in front of him and starts shaking them in his right hand, his eyes never leaving mine.

"I know who has her, they won't hurt her, son," he says firmly.

"Is it the same people that took us when we were kids?" I ask, working my jaw.

He nods and sadness pools his thunderous eyes before he fixes his stare on the die in his hand. Their gray is so much like Blake's, that I feel my throat tighten again and have to avert my own to the door just in time to catch Mark, who had seemingly left the room, stepping back inside.

"You tell him?" Mark asks Brian with a nod to me.

Brian takes a breath and looks at me. "I'm sure you are now aware of who I am. You've probably heard things; some true, some not. The men that took you were like family to us until we started having some issues over twenty years ago over some land...and other things that you don't need to know about. But I beat them out on something and that was the last straw for them. You dad was in charge of approving proposals in the city at the time, each of us turned our own things in. Everybody knew that because of the relationship I had built with your dad, I would get the approval. One of the guys thought it would make a difference to kidnap you and Blake. One thing we had in common is that we never involved children in our business. That night things just..." his voice trails off. "Anyway, Blake's father went nuts after that and did some things he can't take back. And there's just been bad blood between us and the O'Brien's since then. We've managed to keep them buried," he pauses and throws the dice down onto the green table. "Until now. They got something we want. I already told them I'd give them what they want. But he's not after that anymore, it's become some sort of obsession of his. Blake's pops don't know about it, don't know about you either, and I wanna keep it that way as long as I can. If anything happens to her and he finds out she was alive all this time, when he thought she was dead, he'll...fuck, I don't even know what else he can do," he says as he eyes Mark, who raises and drops his shoulders in response.

"So Jamie O'Brien is the one that has her?" I ask, ignoring the rest of the story.

Brian shakes his head slowly. "No. Him and I go way back and despite this shit, we have the same ideals. One of his guys does. It's complicated, kid. We'll handle it though," he replies, looking at Mark again.

"You talk to Benny?" Mark asks.

He scoffs. "Fucking kid wouldn't know his head from his ass. I talked to Alex, though," he replies with a sigh. "Alex ain't gonna hurt the girl, Marky, you've seen her."

*What the hell does that mean?* I'm ready to ask questions, but Ethel interrupts us to let Brian know his guests have arrived. We say our goodbyes and leave through the back door.

On the way home, we're quiet again, even though I have so many questions to ask, but for some reason I keep getting stuck on the stupidest one.

"Mark." My voice slices through the silence as I pivot my body as much as I can in the tiny seat. "Why the fuck is your last name Lewis?"

He gives a carefree laugh. "I changed it after they took you. I refused to hide, so I changed it and continued law school instead. They know who I am, of course, but the rest of the world doesn't need to know that a criminal attorney is the son of...well..."

The fact that he can't even say it makes it funnier than it is. The mix of confusion, anger, and anxiety drives me into a hysteric laugh and tears start rolling down my face as I clutch my stomach. Mark slaps my shoulder, which makes me laugh harder, and finally joins me laughing.

What a strange, fucked up world we live in.

"So Brian is Blake's grandfather, and...you're her uncle...from the farm?"

"Nope, that must've been my brother. I rarely visited the farm," he replies with an exhale.

# Chapter Six
## ~Blake~

My clattering teeth echo in the dark empty room, as I lay in the fetal position, holding myself together, trying to keep myself warm. When the door bursts open, I hold myself tighter and squeeze my eyes shut as I try to control my breathing. *Please think I'm asleep. Please think I'm asleep.* Sometimes Alex comes in here and sits on the floor staring at me when he thinks I'm asleep. Most of the time I hear him weeping as I lie here with my eyes shut, waiting for him to leave. Sometimes he mutters apologies under his breath as he touches my face lightly, and I try my best not to flinch or cry. Then he leaves quietly after bidding me goodnight. I don't feel well enough to pretend right now, though.

"Blake," he whispers roughly.

My heart begins to slow down, and I open my eyes as I stir my body.

"What?" I ask groggily, sitting up on the uncomfortable mattress. My back is killing me from this damn mattress. And the smell. I just can't take it anymore! The smell of chlorine overpowers any other lingering scent and just thinking about it makes me gag. I can even smell it through my stuffy nose from the terrible cold I have, which is pretty telling.

"How do you feel?" he asks, leaning over me and touching my forehead softly, making my stomach churn from the cigarette smell on his clothing.

"Like shit. How do you think I feel?" I reply weakly.

"I'm going to take you to the doctor in the morning," he says in a concerned tone.

I cough out a laugh. "You really think Alex or Benny are going to let you take me out of this place?

"Don't worry about them. You're going to die if you stay in here without a doctor. You've had a fever for four days now."

"They'd be happy to let me die," I reply tiredly.

"They need you alive, Blake. Trust me."

"Trust you," I whisper, mostly to myself.

"Yes, trust me. I haven't done you wrong, have I?" he asks, his hazel eyes narrowing at me angrily.

I shake my head slowly.

"Besides, you know better than to say anything or try to run. He's already warned you before. If you say anything to anybody, Cole's dead. If you try to run, we'll add Aubry to that," he says flatly.

A whimper escapes me. "You're a heartless son of a bitch," I say hoarsely.

"You have no idea," he replies. "So don't fuck with me. I like you and I don't agree with what they're doing, but if I have to pick between my life and one of theirs, it sure as fuck isn't going to be mine. Understood?"

I nod yes with tears in my eyes and remind myself that even the nicest people can't be trusted.

He groans. "Damn it, chick. Just be good and nothing will happen. I brought you something for your fever, drink it and go back to sleep. I'll come get you in the morning."

I do as I'm told and watch him leave the room. Leaving me in the darkness, nursing my ailments with my tears—again.

I go to sleep thinking of Cole. Wishing it was his arms around me, instead of my own.

I wake up sometime after Dean left, my stuffy nose not letting me go back to sleep. After a while of just staying in bed, I get up and dress before lying back down to wait for Dean. I look up when I hear the door unlock and find Benny staring at me angrily. My instinct is to push myself back, toward the wall. He's pushed me around, and I still have a couple of bruises on my arms from the last time he was here.

"Dean's taking you to the doctor today, girl. Don't you for a second think this is your chance to escape. Try something, your famous boyfriend gets hit first. Got it?" he says in his icy voice, gruff from his smoke-filled lungs.

"Got it," I whisper.

"I can't hear you. Speak up, girl," he spits.

"Got it," I say loudly. I stiffen when he stalks over to me. He grabs me by the throat and squeezes, cutting my breathing as he pushes my head roughly into the wall.

"Don't fucking talk to me like that," he spits.

"BENNY!" Dean screams as he rushes toward us and tears him away from me.

Benny looks over to Dean and hacks out a maniacal laugh. "You keep playing knight in fucking shining armor for her, don't you?"

Dean's eyes narrow. "I'd rather keep her safe while you figure out what the fuck you're going to tell Jamie when he finds out."

"I call the shots 'round here. Fuck Jamie! He didn't do shit when her pops did this to me, did he?" Benny screams as he points to his face.

I clasp my mouth with both hands. It's not that I care that my father did that to this monster, sad excuse for a man. My father is a stranger to me anyway, but the thought of him being anything like these people doesn't sit well with me. I clutch on to my stomach and try not to lose my breakfast.

"She had nothing to do with that," Dean responds as Benny walks away.

"She had everything to do with that!" Benny shouts over his shoulder not turning back around.

Dean looks at me with guilt in his eyes, and for the hundredth time since I've been here, I can't figure out why he's chosen this life for himself. He crouches down directly in front of me.

"You okay?" he asks, searching my face. I nod rapidly, my heart still drumming loudly in my chest as he helps me up.

I follow Dean out of the room in the basement and up the stairs. When we make it to the top step, I squint at the brightly lit house. We round the corner and end up in a living room where the walls are white and the decor is opulent. Not what I expected. I hear loud male voices and instinctively plaster myself to Dean's back, clutching on to his shirt. I feel his body stiffen under my hold, and he turns around, placing me by his side. His hazel eyes are looking at me, wildly confused.

"I'm scared," I whisper, because I am. I'm scared out of my mind.

His eyes soften. "Don't be scared. I got you."

I nod, but his words don't soothe me. Nothing about this place makes me feel safe, not even him.

He leads me toward the back door, the opposite direction of the voices, and outside. He holds my hand tight in his, and I know it's not to make me feel safe, but to make sure I don't run.

"Blake, remember what I told you. You run, Cole's dead. You wouldn't want that, now would you?" Dean asks in a soft voice that contradicts the severity of his threat. He says he wouldn't kill for anybody, and I wonder how much truth is in that. It doesn't matter, the threat is there and I have no desire to find out whether or not they'd do it. I can't afford to mess around, for all I know these are the people who killed Maggie. That thought alone churns my stomach.

"No, I wouldn't," I whisper. "I won't run, I promise."

"Good."

I take a deep breath and let the fresh air fill my lungs. I've smelled the nasty smell in the room for so long, I'd forgotten what breathing clean air is like. When the sun hits my face, I begin to weep quietly. When Dean opens the door of the pick up truck we're riding in, I wipe the tears from my eyes. He gives me a sad look and slumps his shoulders.

"I'm sorry, chick. Really. This is just the way it has to be," he says as I climb in.

I don't believe that he's sorry. If he had the chance, I think he'd do it all the same. He followed me around for who knows how long. He told me I had a price on my head. He knew about my fucked up past, saw my lovely life, and he still tore me from all of it. I try to huff in response, but instead I fall into a full-out cough attack. As he pulls out of the immense driveway and into the neighborhood, I look for anything that may look familiar. Most of the houses are huge and far apart from each other. It's very much a white picket fence community. *I'm being held hostage in the middle of a safe, high class neighborhood. The irony.*

We drive about twenty minutes, listening to Nickelback, of all things. *Might as well kill me now.* We pull up to a cottage-looking house and he tells me to wait so he can open the door for me. I let out a frustrated breath, which makes him laugh. I don't understand why we stopped here to begin with. He drags me to the front of the house and knocks on the door three times. An older gentleman with a white beard in a doctor's coat greets us. *This can't be the doctor he brought me to.* I'm sweating a fever that I've had for almost a week, I've been coughing up a lung, vomiting, and he brings me to see this old man *at his house?*

I narrow my eyes at Dean and stomp inside. The old man looks at me over his glasses and extends his hand out to greet me.

"I'm Dr. Kellogg. Dean tells me you've had a fever for a couple of days and haven't been feeling well?" he asks patiently.

"That's right," I reply with a cough. I extend my hand. "I'm Blake." I look around, quickly averting my eyes from his curious look. The house is cozy; I can tell he has a wife to look after him.

"Blake," he repeats with a smile as he shakes my hand, "let's go to my clinic."

I follow him to the back of his house. Dean is behind me and has his hand on the small of my back. I turn around and glare at him before I slap his hand off. He chuckles softly and shakes his head.

When we get to the room, Dr. Kellogg opens the door and ushers me in. "Now Blake," he says, handing me a robe, "I need you to undress and put this on."

I reach out and clutch the robe to my chest. "Thank you." I raise an eyebrow at Dean. "I'm not undressing in front of you two," I say flatly.

"Of course not. We'll step outside and give you privacy," Dr. Kellogg says.

"She's not staying here alone," Dean counters.

"Dean, I'm not going anywhere. This room doesn't even have windows," I snap.

"What if you try to kill yourself with one of his tools?" he asks as he waves his hand at some scalpels and other things on a table.

"Are you serious?" I say, gritting my teeth. "You think what you guys are doing to me is worth me killing myself over?"

Dean's eyes are blazing and his jaw is clenched. He takes a deep breath and runs his hands through his unruly brown hair. I know he's trying to rein in his temper while Dr. Kellogg is silent, just watching us.

"Dean, step outside with me," the doctor says again, and this time, he goes.

When I'm done putting on the robe, I sit on the exam table and wrap my arms in front of my chest in an attempt to warm up.

Doctor Kellogg walks back in by himself and begins asking me questions as he listens to my chest.

"When was your last period?" he asks as he presses down on my lower abdomen.

"Umm..." I don't know how to answer that because I don't know how long I've been gone. I contemplate asking him what date it is, telling him what my situation is, but the sinking feeling in my stomach reminds me that Dean brought me here for a reason. I wonder how many women he's had to bring here. Dr. Kellogg stops examining me and looks at me expectedly.

"I'm not pregnant, if that's why you're asking. I'm on birth control, or at least I was on birth control before..." I answer quietly. I was supposed to refill my prescription, but never got around to it, obviously.

Cole and I were always careful, wearing condoms, pulling out, even though, a couple of times he didn't pull out, which pissed me off. Cole seemed to think it would be okay if I got pregnant, but told me it wouldn't happen anyway and alas, he was right.

"Well, let's have you take a test anyway, just in case."

"Sure," I say with a shrug as I take the little see-through cup from his hands and head to the bathroom.

When I come back, I place it on the table and go back to the exam table.

"Sore throat?" he asks and jots something down when I nod in agreement. Every time I try to swallow, it hurts.

"Nausea?"

"Hmmm...not really. Well, lately yes, but my throat hurts so much and anytime I try to eat anything it's just...yuck."

He nods. "That's understandable, stick to soups and liquids until you start to feel better." He gets up and takes the urine sample and puts a stick in it, then takes it out and places it on the table.

"You can get dressed while this gives us a result. I'll step out and give you some privacy," he says with a smile.

I get dressed and sit back down until I hear him knock lightly again. He comes in, sits down beside me, and we continue to small talk about his wife, where I went to school, what I studied. He's telling me about a nephew of his who had gone to law school and dropped out as he gets up to look at the test. I breathe a sigh of relief at the look on his face, even though I knew I had nothing to worry about.

He jots something down and looks up at me smiling. "The test is positive," he says softly, still smiling.

My stomach drops. "What? Like positive I'm not pregnant? Or positive..." I ask numbly, expecting him to tell me this is some kind of sick joke.

His smile falters and he gives me a confused look. "You're pregnant."

I gape at him as my hands fly over my mouth. "I can't be pregnant," I say in a muffled voice. I'm stunned silent, watching him, waiting for him to tell me it's some type of sick joke they're playing on me. When I see his unchanging expression, I think of Cole and how happy he'd be if he were here with me. I start to sob quietly into my hands. Doctor Kellogg puts a hand on my shoulder and gives me a sympathetic look.

"I'll have to do an ultrasound. My machine is in the basement. Do you think you'll be okay to walk down there?" he asks softly.

I nod my head as unwanted tears spill down my face. *Oh my God. I'm really pregnant?* I wipe my tears and walk out of the room clutching my robe closed. Dean is sitting right outside the door, but stands up quickly when he sees me.

"Are you okay?"

"No," I answer hoarsely. "I'm not okay, at all."

"What's wrong with her?" he demands as he looks at the doctor.

"I can't say, kid," Doctor Kellogg replies with a shake of his head.

"Blake, what's wrong with you?" Dean asks as he holds my shoulders firmly.

A sob escapes me as I look into his worried eyes, and I start to cry again. Dean pulls me in and holds me while I sob.

"Oh my God. I can't. I can't," I say through my sobs. When I calm down, I take a deep breath and inhale his cigarette and cinnamon smell. "I'm pregnant," I whisper brokenly against his chest.

I feel him stiffen. "What?" Shocked, he lifts my chin to look at him. "How can you be pregnant?"

I push off his chest and give him a "how the fuck do you think?" look.

"Is it Cole's?" he asks, his expression hardening.

I refuse to comment and continue to walk toward Kellogg and follow him downstairs to his basement, leaving a shocked Dean behind. Kellogg explains to me that it has to be a vaginal ultrasound, and shows me a dildo with a condom over it.

"You're kidding, right?" I ask, horrified as I look at the instrument.

He laughs. "No, it'll be painless, trust me."

I hear stomping footsteps coming downstairs and tense.

"Dean! I don't want you here, this is uncomfortable enough," I yell.

"I don't give a fuck. I wanna be here. You don't got nothing I haven't seen before, trust me," he yells back as he walks toward us.

I let my head hit the cushion under me and exhale. Dean takes a seat next to me, and looks at me with an expression on his face that I don't understand. More guilt, I guess. *Good.*

I gasp and bite down on my lip when I feel the dildo thing sliding inside me slowly.

"Relax," the doctor tells me.

I take a deep breath and try to do as I'm told. Dean grabs on to the hand closest to his and holds it in both of his. I can only stare at him as he stares back and suddenly this feels way too intimate. All my thoughts vanish when I hear ruffling on the monitor beside me and see a little peanut pop on the screen me.

"There's your baby," the doctor says, pointing at it.

"It's so...tiny," I muse, in awe despite myself, as tears well in my eyes again.

Dr. Kellogg laughs. "You're still early in the pregnancy."

When Dean squeezes my hand, I start to cry again.

"I can't do this," I whimper as Dean soothes me by caressing my hair. I want to tell him to stop. Demand him to stop. But I can't. Instead, I lean into him and let him comfort me as I close my eyes and pretend it's Cole. But it's not, and it won't be, and I hate it. I hate that they've not only taken me from him, but also robbed us of this moment together. He should be the one sitting beside me watching our baby with me.

On the ride back home, I'm still sniffling back tears and distantly staring at the houses we're driving by. The last thing I expected to hear today was that I was pregnant. What am I supposed to do now?

"Alex used to go out with your mom," Dean says suddenly, snapping me out of my daydream.

"What?" I ask, turning my head slowly to look at him.

"That's what I heard. That's what I know. He hadn't seen her in a while before he went to your house that night...when you were little," he says, giving me a sad smile. "She wouldn't return his phone calls, and he showed up there. But I don't know what happened after that. Nobody will talk about it. I just know things went horribly wrong that night."

"That's an understatement," I scoff.

"Sorry, chick. You've been through a lot."

I nod, contradicting my thoughts. A lot doesn't even begin to cover it.

# Chapter Seven

## ~Blake~

*Cole and I went to get an ultrasound done today. We were able to see our baby boy moving around on the screen. I've never seen Cole so happy before, he keeps smiling and kissing my bump as he talks to the baby about baseball games he's going to take him to. The sparkle in his green eyes is so beautiful—it almost makes me forget all of the heartache we've been through. This moment makes it all worth it. My heart melts when he runs his hand lightly down my arm and smiles at me, showing me that dimple that I love. Yes, this moment definitely makes it all worth it.*

"Blake, I brought you food," he says slowly, at a distance, breaking my gaze away from the beautiful smile before me. "Blake! Wake up."

"No! No! No!" I shout as tears trickle down my face. It was just a dream? Just a dream.

"Hey, it's okay, you're okay," Dean says quietly.

I sit up quickly and glare at him. "I am not okay! I am not okay!" I shriek before taking deep breaths and wiping my face. "Don't tell me that. Ever. I'm not fucking okay. I need to get out of here!"

"Blake," he says with a sigh as he looks at me sadly, "let's go upstairs so you can eat."

"Right now?" I ask as I wipe the tears from my face.

"Yes, right now." He takes a deep breath and runs his fingers through his unruly hair. "I just don't know what the fuck Alex is thinking. He's fucking crazy. And Benny..." Dean says his name as if it leaves a bad taste in his mouth, which is precisely the way I feel about Benny.

I get up and follow him upstairs. They've been letting me come upstairs every day now. I guess they figured out that I really wouldn't run. Not with the threats they hold over my head about Cole and Aubry. When we round the corner, I'm surprised to see a guy with short blond hair sitting on a stool around the kitchen island. His back is facing us and he turns in his seat when he hears us approach. Both of our eyes widen when we look at each other, and I force myself to look away quickly, biting the inside of my lip before my jaw hits the floor.

"The fuck are you doing here, Con?" Dean asks from behind me.

"Grace asked me to wait for her while she showers," he replies with a shrug, not taking his eyes off me.

"Huh. When did you start dating?" Dean asks curiously, as I look between the two of them, wondering who the hell Grace is.

"Not long ago," the guy replies vaguely before returning his attention to me. His eyes travel my body, but something about the way he does it doesn't make me feel uncomfortable. When he looks back into my eyes his forehead wrinkles together, and he shakes his head in disbelief.

"How long?" he asks, turning around to face Dean.

"Soon. Fucking Fort Knox, you know."

"Yeah, dude, but...shit's gonna hit the fan soon. Rumors are going around and—fuck. You hear Jamie talked to my grandpa?" he asks.

Dean formally introduces me to Connor, who shakes my hand firmly and holds it in his grasp for a little too long.

For the next fifteen or twenty minutes I just sit there, quietly eating the pasta that Dean plated for me, while he and Connor speak in code. It's worse than listening to a conversation between Cole, Aubry, and Greg. I can tell these two have known each other for a long time. I don't know what shocks me more—the fact that they're such good friends, or the fact that Connor Benson, Mark's former client, that looks like he could be his own son, is sitting inches away from me and I can't say anything to him.

When I'm done eating, Dean takes my plate and waits for me to get up. The Grace girl never came down, so I guess I won't get to see her. Dean and Connor say goodbye to each other with a handshake and shoulder pat. I wave to Connor, but he strides over to me and wraps his arms around me, making me stiffen. His embrace reminds me of Cole's, and even though the thought of that makes me sad, something about it soothes me.

"I'm going to get you out of here," he whispers against my head before letting me go. He winks at me and turns around, leaving me gaping at his retreating figure.

Confusion clouds my head as I walk down the stairs, through the commercial kitchen of illegal shit, and into my room. I continue my dazed walk to the bathroom and think about Connor and his familiar face. Flashbacks of seeing him on the news with Mark at some point earlier this year invade my thoughts. He obviously knows who I am and the possibilities of what he could've been discussing with Dean make my heart flutter. When I walk back in the room, I see Dean sitting in the corner, playing with his phone. The phone I've dreamed of snatching away from him countless times so that I could use it to call somebody for help. The logical thing to do would be to call the police if I ever get a phone in my hands, but I'm too scared of what the consequences may be if I did that. I push my phone jacking thoughts aside and lay in bed quietly as I listen to him ramble about Alex and Jamie. I drift off into sleep and am awakened by the vibrating of his phone. I blink my eyes open, shifting in the bed to face Dean in the dark room, the only light coming from the phone held at his ear.

"Hey," he murmurs quietly. The softness in his voice sparks my interest; he never picks up the phone around me. "Nah, I'm still at Alex's. Yeah. You need anything? Call me if you do. And if he comes back you call the cops and call me next."

"Who was that? And why didn't you turn the light on?" I rasp as I sit up on the mattress. It is now pitch black in here and I can't see anything at all.

"My sister and I didn't wanna wake you up after I bored you to sleep giving you information about your kidnappers," he replies sarcastically.

I exhale harshly. "Sorry, I'm just so sleepy." I've never been this tired before in my life, so I chalk it up to the pregnancy. Dean has been giving me prenatal vitamins every day; he won't leave them here because he says it's not safe for anybody to know my *situation*. Because that's what it is, growing a child inside of one's body when you're being held hostage—a situation.

"I didn't know you had a sister."

He chuckles. "There's a lot you don't know about me, chick."

His words clink around in my head until they wedge themselves into my curiosity folder, and I'm thankful that he can't see my gaping face in the darkness.

I clear my throat. "You're right, so tell me. How old is your sister?"

I hear him exhale and shift off of the floor and I think he's leaving, until the edge of the mattress dips. My heart begins to beat rapidly, even though he's not close enough to touch me...yet. I squirm, moving myself back a little closer to the wall behind me and away from where I feel he is.

"Relax, chick. My ass was hurting from sitting on the floor. I'm not gonna hurt you." He takes a deep breath before muttering, "What the hell do I need to do to get you to understand I don't want to hurt you?"

"Why don't you? Everyone else here seems to not care whether or not I'm hurt."

"Hmm, why not hurt a pretty and innocent pregnant girl locked up? Eh...not my style," he says and I can hear the smile in his voice.

"You're an idiot," I mutter.

"Yeah, you've said," he replies, still smiling.

"So tell me," I push.

He groans. "My sister's twenty-four, has a three-year-old son. Cutest little boy in the world, really." My heart skips a beat, hearing the pride in his voice as he talks about his nephew.

"Do you have pictures?" I ask, already knowing the answer to that.

"Of course I do, what kind of uncle do you think I am?"

His phone lights up and he begins to scroll through his photo album. I try not to look too interested in seeing his pictures, I mean, I don't know if there are any naked people on there, but I'm too curious to care. I end up scooting right beside him and watching as he scrolls through photos of him by himself, with friends, Alex, and other people I don't recognize. There are a couple of him with a pretty brunette, he hovers on one of them before clicking on one of him with the most adorable little boy. In the picture, Dean is wearing a navy blue Cubs T-shirt and carrying the little boy, who is wearing the same outfit, on his shoulders. They're both smiling happily at the camera. I put my hand over his slowly, taking the phone from him, and he lets me. I can feel his eyes on me the entire time as I sit there, staring at the picture of him and the little boy. Tears fill my eyes as I look at their bright smiles and the bright sun and green grass around them. They're so happy. So free. And I'm so jealous.

"He really is the cutest kid ever," I say with a sniffle. "Can I look through the rest?"

"Sure," he whispers.

I scroll through the photos, stopping at the one he hovered on before. It's him and a beautiful girl with shoulder length dark brown hair and caramel colored eyes. She has a button nose and a dazzling smile, and Dean is standing beside her with an arm draped over her shoulder as he kisses the side of her face. The strangest sensation moves through me as I stare at them together.

"Who is she?" I ask in a clipped tone.

He laughs softly and scoots closer and he cups my chin to look at his face, which I can make out with the phone's light. "That's my sister Sandra," he replies, his eyes boring into mine. We look at each other for a long moment, drowning in silence, before he brushes his thumb over my cheek. I lick my dry lips, watching as his eyes drift down to them and his own lips part. "Do you want me to kiss you, chick?" he asks in a whisper that I can barely hear through the loud pounding in my ears.

My breath falters for a moment as I stare at him, wide-eyed, pondering his question, even though there's nothing to ponder. He can't. We can't.

"I'm pregnant," I whisper back, as if that places a chastity belt over my lips.

"I know," he says back just as quietly, moving his face closer to mine until I can feel his breath over my lips, though they're still not touching. "Fuck," he mutters before barely brushing my lips with his. The smell of cinnamon and cigarettes makes me snap out of the moment and I gulp down loudly while backing away from him. He follows suit, scooting his body so that our knees are no longer touching.

"Sorry," he says quietly.

I shake my head even though he can't see me without the light of the phone. "No. I just-"

"I know," he responds before I finish my sentence.

He takes the phone from my hands and gets up, muttering his good night as he steps out of the room, leaving me staring into the dark.

What the hell just happened?

# Chapter Eight
## ~ COLE ~

Aimee and I pull up in front of her parents' house, our parents...I guess. I look up at the house I haven't seen in twenty-two years and feel absolutely nothing. According to Aimee, when she told her mom, Colleen, about me a couple of weeks ago, she fainted. Her dad, Camden, still doesn't believe it, and I don't blame him. I don't think I would believe it either. I step out of the car and look around, and that's when I see the house across the street and my chest starts to ache. The Home Alone house. *Blake.* I can't go anywhere without seeing her in everything I do. She's rooted so deep into me that no matter what happens, Blake has ruined me forever. She fixed me and broke me all at once.

Aimee stands next to me, wraps her arms around my waist and lays her head on my chest. "Don't worry. She'll come back to us, I know she will," she whispers.

I want nothing more than to believe that, but it's been so long. I do believe it, but I think she needs to be found, and I'm going to look for her.

"I know, Aimee. I know," I reply and steer her toward the front door.

She takes a step back and looks at me, holding my hands between us. "You know Blake would be horrified if she saw you right now, right? We're all hurting and worried about her, but you need to stay strong. Take care of yourself so that when you get her back you can take care of her too. You look like a mess. A ghost of yourself," she says, her voice breaking as her eyes fill with tears.

I take a breath, wishing I could offer positive words, but come up short. "That's all I am, Aim. A ghost of myself. I don't even know who I am without her."

A soft sob escapes her and she hugs me one last time, comforting me and herself at once. When she backs away again she wipes her tears and sniffles before leading the way again.

As we make it up the steps, the door swings open and a man and a woman appear in front of us. I've been seeing them on television for a while now, so I'm not surprised by how they look. Still, seeing them makes the color drain from my face as I stand on the steps of their colonial style house. The house I was taken from. The house I slept in, played in, potty trained in. The woman is looking at me with eyes that only a mother could have for her son, lost or not.

"Oh my god," she gasps as she clasps her hands over her mouth and tears stream out of her big green eyes. "It's really you."

Camden is staring at me as if he's trying to figure out whether or not I'm real.

I surprise myself, by stepping forward and extending my arms out to them before they both rush toward me. The woman clings to my neck as the man sandwiches her between us, holding us tightly. Aimee grabs on to my left arm and squeezes it. For a couple of minutes, we're as united as our family could be. Yet the more I think about family, the more I think of Blake. And even though these people, my blood, are holding me up, I feel myself shattering beneath them.

They eagerly lead me inside and we settle down in their living room.

"Wow," Camden says, his eyebrows pinched together. "I just can't believe it!"

I nod and give him a shrug and a slight smile, as Colleen looks at me, and touches my face and my arms continuously. I let her, because that's probably what I'll do when I finally have Blake in my arms again. Though it is a little strange coming from a woman that hasn't seen me in over twenty years, but a mother is a mother and her touch doesn't make me uncomfortable.

"Aimee tells us that you were involved with Blake Brennan before she went missing?" Camden asks, and I know I shouldn't feel the rage I feel at the question. He makes it sound so insignificant. No, I was not *involved* with Blake. You are not just *involved* with the person that causes your world to make sense. You live for that person. You breathe for that person. So no, *involved*, is not the word I would use to describe my relationship with Blake.

"Blake is everything to me. She's not somebody I'm *involved* with, she is my reason, my everything," I say calmly.

His eyebrows shoot up and I see the surprise in Colleen's eyes. I wonder if they think that because I've been lost all these years without them as my family, that I'm incapable of love. I look over at Aimee, who now has tears in her eyes, and I think again of how funny life is. Here she is, in the house she grew up in, with the people who raised her, and she goes through life isolating herself from most people. She's the opposite of what you would expect somebody in this upbringing to be.

I, on the other hand, am whole. My friends are whole, and if you look through my family photos growing up, you won't find absent souls in our eyes. You'll see laughing, amused, caring, loving eyes. As I look at the photos on their end tables, all I see are ghosts. In that moment, I understand. I am not the orphan--they are. I am not the broken child, Aimee is. I didn't grow up going to private school or surrounded by socialites, but I grew up with love.

"I thought you were dating that model, Erin Andrews?" Colleen asks quietly.

"That was a long time ago," I reply.

"I just saw your pictures together at an event. I even bought the magazine because I loved the dress she was wearing," my mother says.

"And because you're a gossip queen," Aimee chimes in rolling her eyes.

"You can't believe anything you see or read in those things. They probably took pictures of us talking and decided to make it into a story about us getting back together. Erin is happily dating somebody," I answer, and am annoyed that I have to explain this to a politician's wife. Of all people, she must know that the media is always full of shit.

"So, Blake Brennan, huh...Aimee says you met her in foster care. I'm so sorry that you had to live there, son. If I had known..." Camden's voice breaks and he looks pained.

"Don't feel bad about something that you couldn't have fixed. Even if you would have known, I'm glad I was there. I met the best people in my life there. We're a family, and yes, Blake is one of them," I answer.

I can tell it's a lot for him to process, so I give him time before I continue.

"I met with Blake's grandfather yesterday, Brian Benson—I'm sure you've heard of him," I say, raising an eyebrow, because everybody knows that name.

"Brian?" Camden gasps. "Blake?" He has a horrified look on his face, and I know it's because he's judging Brian's reputation.

"Yes, Brian, that Brian. I need help finding Blake. I don't have time for you to sit here and judge whose granddaughter she is," I bite out.

Camden looks as if I've slapped him. "Judge? You're confusing shock with judging, son. I'm not judging anybody. I could never judge Brian. Hell, Mark is your damn godfather, for crying out loud," he exclaims. My eyes widen at that because I know not many people, if any, know that Mark and Brian are related.

"How do you know Brian?" I ask suspiciously.

He smiles. "He's an old friend." His smile falters and he crinkles his eyebrows. "So you're saying that Blake is Liam's little girl?"

I run my hands down my face. "I don't know who Liam is," I sigh, "I don't know who Blake's father is, I just know that Brian is her grandfather. I do know that Brian doesn't want her father to know that she's alive yet."

Colleen gasps and she cups her mouth closed. "Oh my god, that poor man," she says as tears fill her eyes.

"Honey, can you get us a drink, please? Aimee, go help your mother," Camden demands quietly. They don't question him, they just go toward the kitchen and leave me sitting there with my shocked father.

He turns to me and closes his eyes. When he opens them I see pain. "Liam doesn't know his little girl is alive?" he asks in a whisper.

"I guess not. Do you think he'd help me find her?" I ask desperately.

He looks at me like I have two heads. "That's his daughter, of course he'll help...but it won't be pretty. Does Brian know who has her?"

"He said it was the O'Brien's," I mutter under my breath.

His sharp intake of breath makes my stomach drop.

"Then it's best that Liam doesn't find out," he states gravely.

"Why? You were just looking all heartbroken that this Liam guy doesn't know his daughter is alive and now you say it's best he doesn't find out?"

Camden's eyes widen. "Your tantrums were definitely cuter when you were a little boy," he says with a huff.

A growl escapes me as I stand up. "I'm not throwing a tantrum! This is not a goddamn game to me! I need to find my girlfriend and I would appreciate a little cooperation. I'm going crazy over here, can't you see that?" I shout, throwing my hands up.

Aimee and Colleen run back into the room and straight toward me, putting their arms around me. I'm too fucking pissed to calm down and the only person that has the power to calm me down has been fucking kidnapped by some fucking Irish mob boss.

"Take a deep breath, Cole. Please," Aimee pleads as she lets me go.

I do as I'm told and begin to pace the room with my hands on my head. Once I feel like I can speak again, I sit in a chair on the opposite side.

"Who is Liam in all this? Why do they keep taking his daughter?" I ask quietly.

"He's Brian's right hand."

I close my eyes and try to process this. "Why isn't Brian out there trying to get his granddaughter back?"

"He is, Cole. Brian's a smart man. He thinks things through. He's lost a lot, too. Trust that he's doing his best to get her back."

None of this shit makes sense and none of it makes me want to trust a fucking mobster. They're the ones that have some kind of fucking pissing contest going on and my girlfriend is stuck in the middle of it.

"Camden, I need your help. I need you to help me look for Blake. I can't live like this anymore," I plead as I look into his eyes, hoping he can see how serious I am about this shit. If it takes me joining the damn mafia to find her, I'll fucking do it.

"Cole, the police have searched everywhere for her. If you say that Brian knows where she is, just let him do what he needs to do. I can't step on his toes," my father pleads back.

"Why? Doesn't the government pay you for justice?" I spit angrily.

Now it's his turn to rein in his temper. "Brian is a good friend, those people are like family to me. Brian's kids and I have been best friends since we were kids. I don't need you to tell me where my priorities lay. If you're trying to make me feel guilty for not being a good fucking mayor, you might as well save your bullshit. I am a damn good mayor, but I am also loyal to the people that have always been there for me," he says, rubbing his face roughly.

"What do you know about that old farm we used to go to when I was little?" I ask suddenly.

I watch his face ashen in surprise. "I...sold it. Why?"

"Who did you sell it to?"

"Cole," Camden says dragging a hand over his face. "Why are you asking me about that place?"

I clench my jaw. "Blake thought it was her grandfather's farm..."

"It was originally," he replies tiredly. "He gave it to me when I was a kid because I loved it so much. Don't you remember all of us spending our summers there? I couldn't keep it after you were taken. That was your favorite place in the world. I couldn't bear to look at it without you."

I nod my head, but don't reply. That was my favorite place, but I don't remember ever going there as a family.

"The only reason I loved going there so much was because of Blake," I mutter under my breath.

He chuckles. "You were a kid. I'm not going to say you didn't enjoy playing with her, but you always liked going, with or without her."

"Trust me, I only liked going because I thought she was going to be there."

He shakes his head. "Okay, if you say so. Just let Brian do what he can, okay?"

"Sure."

After we leave their house, I drop off Aimee feeling no better than I did on the way there. My heart still aches, my muscles feel exhausted, my eyes still burn, and my mind is burnt out. The only thing I can think about is Blake and wonder where they took her. Wonder if they're feeding her and what they're doing to her. I look in the rearview mirror when I come to a stop light and all I see is a life-less soul staring back at me. The pain in my eyes no longer a visitor, but a full time resident. He and his buddy rage have taken over every ounce of me and I'm not sure if they'll ever get out; not sure if I want them to until I get my girl.

A honking car behind me makes me tear my eyes away from myself and look at the streets before me. I call Mark and practically beg him to get somebody in his family to help me get Blake. He finally caves and tells me to go to his house for drinks with him and his nephew. I don't question him before speeding over to his condo before he changes his mind or makes up some bullshit excuse.

I hand my keys over to the valet and jog to the elevator. As soon as I get in, I hear someone call out for me to hold the door open for them. Fucking A, of course somebody needs to get into the damn elevator at the same time I do. I push down to hold it and slide an arm between the closing doors as I wait for an old lady with an oversized purse and grocery bag to catch up and come inside. I smile politely and step aside, pressing down the button to the forty-fifth floor again.

I'm still replaying the incident at Camden and Colleen's house when I reach his door and snap out of my thoughts when it swings open before I knock. Standing on the other side, holding it open for me is a younger version of Mark.

"Who are you?" I ask, confused.

He has a scar on his top lip that spreads slightly when he smiles. He's a big guy too, I notice as I size him up. I'm thinking he probably weighs about 220, and he's a little taller than me, so probably 6'3.

"I'm Connor. I would ask who the fuck you are, but Uncle Mark doesn't have people over too much. I'm guessing you're Cole?" he asks, his voice full of amusement.

"Yeah," I reply as we shake hands. "Uncle Mark, huh?"

"Yep."

I turn around and look at Connor again. He looks so familiar, but I can't really place him.

"You still not done checking me out, bro?" he asks with a smirk.

I take a step back. "I'm not checking you out. You just look familiar."

He snickers. "Yeah, I get that a lot after the arrest. They made a big fucking deal and accused me of attacking a city employee outside of city hall."

"Ohhhh yeah," I draw out after realization dawns on me. "Well, did you?"

He laughs and puts his hands up defensively. "I cannot confirm nor deny that. My attorney is in the shower. He must be present to make any statement about my whereabouts that day."

"Impressive."

Mark steps out of his room wearing sweats and a T-shirt. "What's up, Cole? You met Connor. Connor, Cole is the missing kid."

"That's right. The kid Benny took?" Connor asks, obviously familiar with the story. The way he says their names surprises me, it sounds like he knows them, but I'm not about to ask him any personal questions. Mark was there that night, I know that much, but I never considered that he could have been friendly with the other men that took us.

Connor sighs and runs his hand over his buzz cut hair. "Well, I met Blake yesterday," he says over a mouthful of chips.

That stops me dead in my tracks. "What?" I ask, feeling my heart rate quicken. "MY Blake? What the fuck do you mean you met her *yesterday?*" My stomach drops when I run through everything I was doing yesterday when this dude was meeting my lost girlfriend.

"And that's why I haven't handed you your beer yet," Mark mutters under his breath.

I glare at Mark before looking back to Connor. "What the fuck do you mean you met Blake?" I ask through gritted teeth.

Connor puts down his beer and rubs his forehead. "I met her-" he says quietly before looking at Mark for reassurance. Mark nods and shrugs his shoulders.

I take a deep breath and grab on to the back of the couch before I take the fucker down on Mark's glass coffee table. "Can you just cut to the chase?"

"Well, I went to my girlfriend's house yesterday to pick her up, and Dean brought Blake into the kitchen to eat while I was in there. She freaked out when she saw me...I guess I kind of did too. I mean—I knew she would look like her mom, but damn. Not that I ever saw her mom, obviously, but pictures. I talked to Dean a little but she just sat there playing with her food before they went back to the basement. Dean said he's gonna help me get her out. She's fine, though. She looks...I mean...she looks good, considering." His shoulders slump and he sits down.

"Considering what? That she's been fucking kidnapped?" I shout desperately.

He crinkles his eyebrows and I see the uncertainty in his blue eyes before he clears his throat. "Yeah. Anyway, I'm getting her out of there."

"Connor," Mark starts in a warning tone before I interrupt him.

"Mark, shut up and let the kid talk!" I say, exasperated.

"Dean and I talked about it. They're having a huge party in a couple of days and won't notice if she slips out. It'll be quick." Connor shrugs before Mark's laughter cuts his words short.

"It'll be quick?" Mark asks in disbelief. "You know how Benny and Alex work. Hell, you know how Jamie works. You've been around their shit long enough to know nothing is ever that simple."

Connor gets up from the couch and crosses over to stand in front of Mark. "What the fuck do you think is gonna happen when Uncle Liam finds out about this shit? You think he's gonna call Jamie and be all fine and dandy about it?"

"Jamie doesn't even know about it!" Mark shouts, making Connor's brows rise to his hairline as I sit there watching on.

"Ha! You think Jamie doesn't know? Damn, Uncle Mark, you're a dumb sonofabitch sometimes. No disrespect," Connor replies, raising his hands in defense.

Mark scowls at him. "He would've called Pops by now if he knew!"

Connor sucks his teeth. "You think Dad and Grandpa always give you the inside scoop or something? You're a lawyer, dude!"

"First of all, WHO THE FUCK IS DEAN? And can someone get a pen and paper and start drawing out the family trees and everyone's connection to everyone else?" I demand. And I mean it, this shit gets exhausting and keeping up is impossible. I should've brought Aubry so he could give me the cliff notes on these people and their complicated issues.

Connor laughs and walks over to me, sitting on the couch in front of me, as Mark follows him and takes a seat on the other side of the couch I'm on.

"Dean's a good guy, don't worry about him, he's family. Anyway, Alex and Benny are the guys that took Blake. They work for Jamie. Blake's parents and them go way back. Like waaaay back. They were all best friends, grew up together, ran with the same crowds. They were all friends until Benny started fucking shit up," Connor explains before taking a swig of beer.

Talk about information overload. I think my brain just exploded. I sit here dumbly staring at Connor for a bit with my mouth hanging open, still processing everything and trying to figure out why, but still come up blank. I just keep mulling over the *Dean is family* part.

"What do you mean Dean's family? Whose family is he?" I ask.

Connor exhales. "Look, like I said, our families used to be close. Even after that whole thing went down, some of us stayed close. You have nothing to worry about with Dean. Benny's the scariest motherfucker in the equation."

I shake my head. "You guys use the term *family* really fucking loosely. So why did they take me and Blake? Why the hell did they take you?" I ask Mark, turning my body to face him.

Mark shrugs. "Wrong place, wrong time. Benny started complicating things when your dad was working in the city and Jamie O'Brien and Brian Benson couldn't come to an agreement over some stuff. There was *a lot* of money involved, Benny took it a step further and kidnapped you and Blake. I still don't know why the fuck they took me, to be entirely honest with you. I've learned to let it go though. I got sick of trying to figure it all out, and I was fine with knowing that you and Blake were safe. At least I did something right."

I nod in agreement and appreciation because he's right, if it wasn't for him, who knows where we'd be right now. I just can't believe all of these people were friends before all of this and lost their ties because of one guy.

"Why did that Benny guy start so much shit? What's his deal?" I ask curiously.

"He's a psycho, that's his deal," Connor says, as Mark nods his head in agreement.

"He's never been right in the head, but I think greed is the root of his problem," Mark adds.

"We're all greedy," Connor mutters below his breath.

"Yeah, and we're all fucked up," Mark replies with a shrug before taking another swig of beer.

# Chapter Nine

*~Blake~*

I've been staring at the door, waiting for Dean to come in any minute, but the minute never seems to come. I've already been to the bathroom ten times since I woke up, and each time I feel like somebody is drilling my lower back—that's how much it hurts. I run my hands over my neck for what seems like the millionth time since I've been here. I was wearing the necklace Cole gave me the day they took me, and I miss having it around my neck. Not that I need it to remember him, but I hate that they took it from me. When will they stop taking? I don't even want the answer to that question.

My ears perk up when I hear the door unlock quietly, followed by the quickening heart when I see Dean appear in the threshold wearing a pair of dark jeans and a black hooded sweater that's fitted to his body. His hair is damp and messy, not his usual style. We haven't spoken about the moment we shared the other day. In fact, we haven't spoken much at all. He's been here every day since, but our conversations are always short and to the point. He asks how I'm feeling, gives me my food, and leaves. Sometimes I could swear he's standing right outside the door and the thought that he'd rather leave me alone here bothers me endlessly. It was nothing, dammit!

My eyes travel down his body and I notice the brown paper bag in his hand as he strides over to me and sits down beside me.

"Hungry?" he asks casually.

I nod and he hands me the bag. When I open it I find a sandwich, chips and a can of pop.

"Are you going to talk to me or run away like a little girl?" I ask when I finish chewing my first bite. His chuckle makes my eyes roam over his lips before I look into his eyes.

"I haven't been running away like a little girl, chick. I just...it's not right for me to have almost done that and then come back in here wanting to do more. It's just not right. Even I know that."

The side of my lip twitches. "Since when do you care about what's right or wrong?"

"Are you testing me? If you start testing me, I'll cave," he says with a half smile, walking closer to me.

I shake my head vigorously and put my hands up. "Nah, I think we should just be friends."

He stops walking and laughs loudly, throwing his head back. "It's not you, it's me?"

I crinkle my nose. "Something like that," I reply with a laugh.

And just like that, we're back to being us.

"Tonight's the big party here," he whispers as I take a sip of Coke. "I'm going to leave the door unlocked for you and this under the bed." He pulls out a small flip phone from his back pocket and slides it under the mattress. "Listen to me very fucking carefully, Blake, because I don't want this to get fucked up. You don't use that phone—period. I call you, it vibrates, you get it and do not pick it up. You'll see Unknown Caller on the screen, and you get up, turn the bathroom light on, lock the door and close it. Then you leave this room and go the back way to the right of the kitchen, everyone will be in the yard. You open the front door and fucking run— not walk, not jog—you fucking run, do you understand?" he whispers harshly.

I nod, my eyes wide, mouth slack just staring at him. "And then what?" I whisper back softly.

"You run out of the gates and make a right, my truck will be there. If you're not there twelve minutes after I call you, I'm coming for you."

"Okay."

"Okay? This is important shit, Blake. We can't fuck up," he says, his eyes growing serious. "Run it by me. Tell me everything you're going to do."

So I do.

Three times.

I tell him step by step exactly what I'll do when the phone under my mattress vibrates. By the time I repeat it a third time, my words are strained and I have tears in my eyes because it's real and I can't believe I'm finally getting the hell out of here. As he stands up, he eyes me sadly and cups the back of my head, gently tugging the hair in my ponytail and tilting my head to place a soft kiss on the top of my head.

"Everything will be fine, chick. I'll see you later," he whispers before walking out and closing the door. I hold my breath and lean forward on the mattress, sitting on pins and needles, waiting to hear whether or not the door will lock. When I can no longer hold my breath, I exhale, my heart beating erratically at the realization that he left it unlocked. This is real. I'm that much closer to my escape. After looking at the back of the door for what feels like an eternity, I stand and pace back and forth a couple of times while rubbing my lower back with both hands. I plop down on the mattress and look around the empty, dark room. The only light shining is coming from the squiggly lines on the messed up TV on the old brown dresser. I am so not going to miss this place. When the pain in my lower back begins to worsen again, I close my eyes and lie on the bed, placing an arm over my eyes even though I'm trying to fight my exhaustion in efforts to stay awake. I can't miss the call.

Eventually, I gasp awake at muffled vibrations and sit up quickly, sliding my hand under the mattress to get the flip phone. My heart hammers against my chest when I read Unknown Caller on the screen. I clutch it in my hands and get up swiftly, moaning from the pain in my back that I no longer have time to worry about. I speed to the bathroom and flip the light on, look around and blink away the tears that threaten to surface as I recall the dreadful memories I've had in here. I turn around and step back into the room, locking and closing the bathroom door behind me. I leave the television on and put on the pair of tattered flip flops they gave me before heading to the door. I roll up my too-long-to-walk sweats up to my knees and place one hand on the knob, taking a deep breath.

Butterflies swarm my core as I turn the doorknob and open the door slowly, sticking my head out to make sure nobody is around. I tiptoe out and close it quietly behind me before placing the lock on it. I allow myself to dwell on it for a couple of seconds before shaking my head and continuing to tiptoe toward the stairs. A shiver runs through me as I ascend to the main story of the house, standing for a count of two and rocking on my heels as I clutch on to the doorknob with a shaky hand. I slip off my sandals after I turn the knob and open it slightly, listening acutely to the muted conversations. I tuck my head in, tilting it to the right, then left before stepping out and shutting the door behind me. I stride to the right, walking as quickly as I can on the palms of my feet, passing the kitchen entrance, a formal living room, a dual staircase and lavish entryway before I reach the front door. The house is well lit but quiet on this side, just as Dean said it would be since the party is going on out back. I open the door and breathe a sigh of relief when the fresh air greets me. I bend down to slip my feet back into the sandals and look at the phone in my hand, but it's still blank. I contemplate opening it and calling the police, Cole, anybody, but Dean's words ring louder than my gut feeling, so I opt against it. I continue my walk across the vast lawn, listening to Frank's Sinatra's melodic voice and the mix of men's loud chatter and women's laughter. I am thoroughly disgusted that they are having a full on party, all while thinking that I'm locked up in their basement. A part of me wants to run out there, scream my head off and let everybody know that they kidnapped me, but the smarter part of me just wants to get out of here as soon as possible. My breathing is ragged as I continue shuffling my feet to the gate, which I'm supposed to walk out of and meet Dean on the other side. I pick up the pace a little when I reach it and hold one of the cool iron bars between my hands, pulling it a little. When it doesn't budge, I put my strength into it, pulling it with both hands. I let out a breath and wipe my sweaty hands over my sweats before trying again. A sudden sharp pain stabs my abdomen, making me gasp and let go of the bars to place my hands on my midriff. I look down at myself and squeeze my eyes shut. "We're going to be okay. We're going to be okay. I'm going to get us out of here," I whisper, channeling this baby and praying for our safety.

The sound of rustling behind me jars me out of my thoughts and makes my head snap in that direction. My stomach drops when I see a large figure approaching me in the darkness. I don't need light or sound to tell me who it is, I'd know that body, that walk, anywhere. The fact that it's coming my way causes my heart to kick into overdrive. I whimper, turning my body slightly to hold on to the bars and begin to pull again with all my might, making the gate finally creek in motion.

He runs up behind me and closes a rough hand over the top of my arm, making me shriek in surprise as he jerks me to him. He turns me around to face him and lets go of my arm, taking a step back to narrow his eyes at me.

"The FUCK do you think you're going?" Benny snarls. "You thought you could be slick and get the fuck out?"

I clamp my mouth shut and shake my head vigorously, refusing to answer him with words. How did he find me so fast? Was he on to Dean and me the entire time? Did he hear our conversations? Where in the world is Dean? Was it all a set up?

"ANSWER ME!" he booms, jarring me from my thoughts. "Did you think you could get away from me? I'M NOT DONE WITH YOU!"

With the dim streetlight, I can make out the wildness in his dark eyes before he charges toward me.

I don't have much time to react, my only instinct is to curl up and protect my barely visible pregnant stomach before he reaches me. He grabs me by the hair and jerks me forward, dragging me along with him. Tears well up in my eyes and a scream escapes me when I realize he's heading back toward the house. I can't go back there. I can't. Shivered sobs rake through my body as I lurch forward and carve my fingers into the wet grass below me, but he's stronger than I am and in one hard pull has me tumbling over myself.

"GET UP! GET UP, BITCH!" he shouts loudly. So loudly that I can just silently hope that somebody in the party hears him and comes out front.

I shake my head, still sobbing and look around at the neighboring homes that are too far to detect any noise. The chatter from the party hasn't died down so I know they haven't heard his shouts or my sobs. I place the palms of my hands flat on the ground relying on them and my scraped knees to keep myself up as I try to steady my breath. My eyes find his black pointy dress shoes and I notice he's wearing dress pants. I make the effort to crane my head, taking in his formal attire before I see the grim look on his scarred face. When his eyes meet mine, he hawks a spit at me that grazes the tip of my nose before landing on my chin. I close my eyes, sobbing louder at the pain, the thought that I don't know how I'll get out of this if I can't even let go of the ground long enough to wipe my face. I try to take a breath to calm the waves of fear that are radiating through my body.

He shifts his feet so that his body is beside me, and suddenly kicks my stomach with such bluntness, that I instantly fall over and gasp for air. I roll onto my side, placing my hands over my lower abdomen to keep it safe, mentally praying, BEGGING the God I was taught but have never really known to believe in, to help me and my baby get through this. After finding out I was pregnant, not once did I touch my stomach, not once did I speak to it, not once did I feel excited about it, but now that it's in danger I feel like it's the only thing I have. It's the only part of me that I want to keep safe. *Need* to keep safe.

He crouches down and grabs me by the hair, making me squeeze my eyes shut at the pain before placing his lips over my ear. "You never answered me, bitch. You thought you were gonna leave here? You thought I was done with you?" he rages.

"No," I whimper.

"NO WHAT?" he shouts, causing an instant ache in my eardrum.

"Didn't think-" I begin.

"NO! YOU DIDN'T THINK!" he shouts again before grabbing a handful of my hair and pounding my head to the floor.

He gets up, scooping my body with him before slamming me back down on the ground, making my head tilt back and forth like a rag doll. He gives me no time to collect myself before kicking sharply on my right side.

"Ah!" I shriek. "Please!"

"Shut up, bitch! Shut the fuck up!" he yells.

"Please stop!" I say, my voice low and guttural, before he slams his fist against my face. I hear more than I feel the crack and instantly taste the iron in my mouth.

He kicks me again, closer to my stomach, right over my left hand making me scream in agony. "Please!" I beg in a whisper, feeling the strength in my fight fade with each blow. "Please...baby..."

"What? You don't like to be hit? You think I didn't scream when they did this to my fucking face? THIS," he shouts, and I know he's pointing at his face, but my heavy eyes won't open to let me see. "OPEN YOUR EYES, GODDAMMIT! THIS IS YOUR FAULT!"

I pry my eyes open as far as they go, tears spilling down my face and sobs sputtering out of me. "Baby," I plead, my voice barely a whisper. My eyes shut again before I can stop them.

The next time I flutter my eyes open a little, I see him put his arm behind his back and bring something to the front of his body. My eyes open as wide as my face allows and I bring my hands up to shield my face. I hear Dean screaming loudly and rushing toward us. The last thing I see are Benny's dark hateful eyes before he slams the bottle of liquor over my head and pushes me into blackness.

dusk

/dəsk/

Noun

1. Early evening

Synonyms

gloaming. nightfall. sundown

# Chapter Ten

## ~ COLE ~

The sound of my ringing phone makes my heart and stomach simultaneously clench. Anytime it rings, a surge of hope streams through me only to be quickly covered in dread because every time it rings it's a let down. I stare at it for a second longer before answering.

"Hello?" I ask and hold my breath.

"This Cole?" asks a male voice I don't recognize.

"Who's this?" I ask quietly.

"Blake's at St. Joseph's Hospital. You should probably go as soon as you can. Critical."

The air swishes in and out of my body so quickly, I barely have time to recover my breath before answering. "What? Who...who is this?" I stammer.

"Blake. St. Joseph's. Critical. Don't got time." Then the line goes dead. I look at my phone for a minute and shut my mouth before my brain kicks in again, adrenaline already a resident in my heart. I grab my keys and run out of the apartment dialing Aubry's number on the way to the car. When it goes to his voicemail, I try Connor's number instead to see if he heard anything. Today was supposed to be the day he picked me up to get Blake wherever she is and my stomach is in knots thinking about something going wrong.

"Yo, bad news," he says as a greeting.

"What?" I ask, anxiety overtaking my body.

"It's not happening today," he replies, sounding exhausted.

It occurs to me that this wasn't a prank call—this wasn't a way for them to get me there so they could take me too.

This is real. Blake's really at the hospital, and the thought of the words Blake, hospital, and critical being in the same sentence hit me like a ton of bricks.

"Fuck. Fuck. Fuck. I just got a call," I mutter, letting go of a sharp breath.

"No shit? What's going on?" he asks and sounds genuinely confused, but then, he always does.

"Some guy said Blake is at St. Joseph's and critical."

"Fuck. Meet you there," he says and hangs up.

I contemplate calling Mark or Aubry but I can't process anything more. My mind is a jumbled mess, yet blank at the same time, so I just repeat the mantra: *Please let her be okay*, all the way there.

I arrive at the hospital and run full speed to the ER. I tell the front nurse that I'm looking for Blake Brennan.

"Are you family?" she asks.

"Yes."

"What's your relation?"

"Husband."

She crinkles her salt and pepper eyebrows together and eyes my ring finger before her eyes trail over my wrinkled shirt.

"Uncomfortable," I explain as I wiggle my fingers. "I don't wear it."

"So you're Mr. Brennan?" she asks with a raised brow.

I let out a breath. "Yes," I reply through gritted teeth. I swear to God, I'm going to marry that fucking girl and change her last name as soon as she gets out of this damn hospital.

"Hmm."

"Hmm? What does that mean? Where is my wife?" I growl, no longer able to keep my feelings pacified.

"With her husband," she replies with a raised eyebrow. "I'm assuming the two of you should probably have a little chat? Unless of course there is such a thing as brother husbands?"

I grind my teeth together a couple of times. "Look..."

"Ginger," she replies quickly, still looking at me with naked amusement.

"Ginger, if there's another man playing the role of her husband, I'm going to advise that you start calling security right now. I am her husband. I'm the only husband she's ever had and ever will have, and I'll be damned if there's another man holding her hand in there right now instead of me."

Ginger smiles. "She just got out of surgery, she didn't have her insurance card or any information when they brought her in. I'm assuming you would have that since you're her real husband?" The way she emphasizes the word real as if she doesn't believe me, makes me want to choke her. Thankfully, I have all of Blake's shit in my wallet, so I just give her a tight smile and hand over the stuff.

"Where is she?" I ask again, more impatiently.

"She's upstairs in room 4020, she's stable," she announces as she clicks through the computer.

Apprehension hits my stomach. Hard. "Stable?" I ask quietly.

"The doctor will speak to you about that, you can go up to see her after you fill out her paperwork," she says as she hands me a clipboard. I look at her with my mouth hanging open. She cannot be serious.

"Can I take these with me and give them to the nurse in there? I need to see my wife!" I shout out.

She rolls her eyes. "Fine."

I run to the elevators and take them up to the fourth floor. When I get there, I have to check in with the security guard and go over who I am—again. When I round the corner and finally reach the hallway to her room, I see a doctor talking to a guy I don't know. The guy's clothes are covered in blood, he has a black eye that's closed shut and stitches above his eyebrow. He's a little shorter than me, less built than me and has a worried look on his face. For a minute I feel like we're feeling the same thing. That is, until his body turns toward room 4020 and any sympathy I might've felt is slapped away from me.

"Who the fuck are you?" I demand, shoving his shoulder away from her door. His eyes snap to mine and he just stares, saying nothing. "Who. The. Fuck. Are. You?" I ask again.

"Dean," he responds after clearing his throat.

"Dean," I repeat, the name tastes like straight shit in my mouth. I turn my back to him and take a couple of deep breaths while I count to ten. I feel unshed, angry tears sting my eyes thinking about this asshole being with my girl every day for the past three and a half weeks. I decide not to waste energy thinking about that and turn back around to face him and the doctor.

"How is she?" I ask the doctor, who looks at me with a confused expression on his face. "Get out of my way," I grit, pushing past them to find out for myself. Seeing her in the dim light of the room, surrounded by white walls, draped in teal hospital blankets makes it real. My girl, my beautiful girl came back to me. My chest heaves in suppressed sobs as I toss the clipboard full of papers by the sink. The closer I get to her, the clearer she becomes. I take in her messy hair, the bruises on her pale face, the gash on her temple, and the slow rise and fall of her chest. I take one more uneasy step toward her before the enormity of this moment crashes down on me and my legs give out. I fall to my knees, my chest rising and falling in heavy pants and my sobs begin to break free.

"She's okay," Dean says quietly behind me, his voice barely registering over the pounding in my ears. "She's going to be okay. She's out now because of the meds, but she's fine."

I shake my head because I don't want to hear his voice, I don't want to hear his words, I just...

"I'm sorry," he says before I can respond. "I tried to get to her, I tried to-" his words fade into my strangled sobs and I can no longer hear them. When I'm able to compose myself again, taking a series of deep breaths, he clears his throat before continuing, "I got there too late, I failed her."

I nod slowly and wipe my face not able to answer him or confirm that he did fail her. Even though I have a million questions and accusations to make toward him, I have no words right now. I pick myself up using the edge of the bed as a crutch, lift up her sheets and crawl in beside her.

I adjust my body toward her and wrap my arms around her, burying my face in her neck before I lose it again. The bed creaks from my shaking body, and I have to remind myself to loosen my hold around her so that I won't crush her tender body.

I hear the door open but don't look up, I'm assuming Dean is leaving and I don't care to watch him walk out.

"I'm Dyann. I'm taking over for Ronda," a woman's voice says, making me lift my head and wipe my face quickly.

I blink a couple of times trying to focus on the blonde nurse in the green scrubs.

"Which one of you is the husband?" she asks, looking between Dean and I.

I clear my throat. "Me," I reply while glaring at Dean, daring him to say anything.

He shakes his head and puts up his palms defensively.

"What's your name?" Dyann asks me.

"Cole. Cole Brennan," I respond, not missing a beat and not caring how ridiculous Blake's last name may sound as mine.

Dyann nods and gives me a small smile while jotting something down on her chart. "Mr. Brennan, I'm sorry for your loss. I'm just going to adjust Mrs. Brennan's morphine, and I'll be out of your hair in a bit."

Despite my confusion at her choice of words, my heart constricts in my chest. What loss? Is Blake not okay? Please tell me she's okay. "What loss?" I ask hoarsely.

Her eyebrows pinch together as her green eyes look from mine down to her chart and back to mine. "Oh...the um...the baby," she responds quietly. "I assumed you knew?" she continues with a worried look on her face as she adjusts Blake's morphine and pillow.

I clamp my mouth shut with a sharp nod when she apologizes one more time before walking out of the room.

I'm frozen in place, my heart hammering against my chest as I continue to stare at the door she closed behind her. Her words echo in my head: The baby. The baby. The baby.

I shift my body to face Blake again, ignoring Dean who still hasn't moved an inch from his spot by the bathroom. I lift up one of Blake's hands in mine and kiss the palm.

"Baby," I whisper as I caress her bruised cheek. "It's me." She doesn't respond, doesn't move. The only sound in the room is coming from our breathing and the beeping machines she's hooked up to.

Dean clears his throat, making my eyes snap in his direction. "I'm going to go out into the hall."

I glare at him. "Who did this to her? Connor said you were trustworthy, so how the fuck did this happen?" I spit.

"I told you, I tried to get there as soon as I could. She didn't come outside to meet me where we agreed and-" his voice cracks and he shakes his head, unwilling to finish his story.

"The baby?" I ask in a hoarse whisper.

"Was yours," Dean replies firmly. "I'm sorry." His hazel eyes are laced with regret, which makes me believe him, but not hate him any less.

"You can leave now," I quietly inform him, and he nods in agreement.

"I'll be back later," he replies.

I get up, careful not to hurt Blake, and stomp over to Dean until I'm right in front of his face.

"Listen to me, you little shit," I say quietly, hoping to scare him, but one look at him and I know I don't scare him at all. "If you EVER refer to yourself as Blake's husband again, I'll fucking kill you."

His lips curl up in response. "Well, I don't think of myself as her brother and I had to be family," he explains with a smirk and a shrug that I don't care for.

"Get out! You've done enough. If I never see you again, it'll be too soon. In case I'm not being clear enough, don't come back!"

Dean takes a step back and looks at me, at Blake, and back at me again before he turns and leaves, closing the door behind him. I lie back down and turn my body to Blake's again, braiding our fingers together and burying my face in her hair. I inhale her, the hospital smell on her overpowering her natural scent, but I don't mind.

"I'm so sorry," I whisper into her hair. "I'm sorry I wasn't there for you."

I stroke her face lightly before running my hand to finger comb her hair some. She looks so pale, so small beside me. It cracks my heart to even fathom what they've done to my girl. And a baby. She was pregnant with my baby this entire time? I shake the thought away from my head, not wanting the pain of that loss to overshadow my happiness of having her back in my arms. My phone vibrates in my pocket and I take it out to see Aubry calling me back from earlier.

"Hey," I croak, picking it up on the first ring.

"What's up man? Rough day?" he asks.

"Blake. I'm with Blake," I stammer and I start sobbing hard when it hits me—really hits me—that I am really with her, that she's really lying beside me and that this nightmare is finally over.

"What?" he whispers. "Where are you? Is she? Oh my God. Is she-"

"She's okay, we're at St. Joseph's."

"On my way," he says and hangs up.

I can't bring myself to call anybody else so I send Connor a text message saying where I am and one to Mark asking him to get us security. The paparazzi has been security enough for me since Blake's been gone. They're annoying as shit, but nobody would think of coming near me when they're around, and they're always around trying to snoop for a new story.

I lie back down and for the first time in three and a half weeks, I drift off to sleep without the help of alcohol.

# Chapter Eleven
## ~Blake~

*BANG! BANG! BANG! are the sounds I hear before running down the stairs and into the kitchen. I let my eyes roam over the princess decorations and the cupcakes with the number four on top of the counter before I look at my daddy holding a knife in his hand. An angry dark-eyed man is standing before him with a gun in his hand, and my mother is lying in a pool of blood. My chest heaves, my eyes filling with tears before I let out a scream, "Mommy!" The man narrows his black eyes, and tears roll down my daddy's face as they both look at me. My daddy starts to cry loud and scream at the man with the black eyes before the man hits him in the stomach and carries him over his shoulder out of my sight. I run up to Mommy and drop next to her on the floor, shaking her roughly, begging her to wake up before a young man comes into the kitchen.*

*"Let's go, baby girl," he says to me.*

*"Mark! She won't wake up! Wake her up!" I shriek.*

*"No, baby, she's not going to wake up," he replies sadly, as he, too, begins to cry while holding on to me.*

*"Get her out of here!!" another man screams as he walks in, taking in the scene. His chest heaves rapidly as he looks between Mommy and me. "GET OUT!" he says louder.*

*Mark carries me in his arms, my blood-soaked pajamas hanging heavily from my body and sticking to his, as he takes me to the black van.*

*"Why my mommy?" I wail.*

*I look up at Mark, his face suddenly becoming Benny's. "That wasn't your mommy," he says with a harsh laugh before pinning me with his crazed eyes. "That was you."*

I gasp, trying and failing to sit up. I cringe from the pain that runs from the tip of my head all the way down my body. I blink at the bright lights around me and blink some more until I can focus and see that I'm in a hospital. The last thing I remember is Dean holding my hand and telling me everything was going to be fine. A sudden shift in the bed fills my stomach with apprehension.

"Oh, thank God," he says hoarsely and pulls my face into his hard chest. I squeeze my eyes shut and will my heart to slow because I know that my sick imagination is playing tricks on me again. I miss that voice so much it hurts. When I sniffle my tears, I'm consumed with his unmistakable fresh scent, and I know this has to be real...unless I'm dead.

"Blake, look at me," he says quietly as he touches the side of my face and backs away from me a little. My breath starts coming out quickly, in gasps as I tilt my head and open my eyes slowly to meet the most brilliant green eyes I've ever seen. We stare at each other for a long moment with tears in our eyes, before his arms swallow my body in his, shielding me from everything—the light, the dark, and everything in between. For the first time in a very long time, I feel safe. Truly safe. My body begins to shake from my muffled sobs and I cling on to him tighter, not daring to let him go. I pour all of my angst out, trying to let go of the bad and really just grateful that I have something good. Finally.

"Please don't leave me," I whisper against his chest once our sobbing calms. "Please, please don't let them take me away from you again."

"Oh God, baby, I'm so sorry. I'm so sorry I wasn't there. I'm so sorry they took you and I wasn't there to protect you. I'm sorry you had to go through that by yourself," he whispers hoarsely. I nod against him, inhaling his scent, that scent I missed so damn much and was beginning to forget.

We separate and wipe our faces as we study each other. He lightly caresses my face with his thumb. "You have some bruising...and stitches on your head," he says with furrowed eyebrows.

As I move away, I feel a heavy, gooey pool in between my legs. My eyes widen and I look at Cole, completely horrified. "What about-" I stop myself before I can continue because I already know the answer, but for some reason I need to hear somebody say it. I'm not even sure if he would have heard about it though.

"What about what?" he asks, his hand stilling on my cheek when he registers the scared look in my eyes.

"The baby," I whisper, dropping my gaze from his and holding my stomach with my hands.

"I'm sorry," he replies huskily. I bury my face in my hands and let out a strangled, tearless sob before I take a couple of breaths, struggling for air. When I'm able to look at him again, I place my hand on top of his and we give each other a squeeze.

"Me too," I reply quietly. "I should've tried harder."

"No, Blake. You had nothing to do with losing the baby, please don't think that," he says, looking at me with loving eyes as he strokes my cheek softly.

I nod, blinking away the tears pooling in my eyes again. He carefully adjusts my body to face his and we lay there for a long time cataloging every inch of each other's faces.

He presses a kiss on my lips and for a moment I forget everything. I grab both sides of his face and plunge my tongue into his mouth. He groans deeply and grabs me by the back of the neck, pulling us as close together as we can be. I hear one of the monitors behind me start beeping uncontrollably, but I don't care to check it. Somebody clearing their throat causes us to break apart, but we don't look away from each other's eyes. In this moment I realize that I'm not sure how long I was kidnapped, but nothing, nobody, can hold me hostage like Cole's eyes can. "Welcome back, Blake. I'm glad to see you're feeling better. We got notified about the increase in heart rate so I came to check up on you. Now I know why it happened, though," she says with a smile and a raised eyebrow. "You should rest."

I smile back at her, and just as I'm about to thank her, the door opens behind her and our heads turn to watch Aubry step in. He looks at me for what seems like an eternity before he buries his face in his hands and starts to cry. Cole shifts off the bed and walks over to him and hugs him, telling him that I'm okay before they walk over to me.

"Cowboy," Aubry says, his voice wavering. "I can't..." he pauses to swallow, but doesn't say anything else, just sits where Cole was previously laying and pulls me into a hug.

"I'm fine, Aub. You can't get rid of me or my laundry," I say, muffled into his chest.

He laughs and pulls away from me as tears roll down his cheeks. "I missed you so fucking much, Cowboy. You don't even know."

"Is she okay to walk?" Cole asks Dyann as she fixes my IV.

"Sure, if she's up for it," she replies, looking at me with a smile before she leaves the room.

"I missed you too, Aub," I mutter leaning the side of my head into his chest. He rests his chin on top of my head, and Cole moves to the other side of the bed to sit by my feet.

For the next hour, we alternate between just staring at each other and verbalizing how much we missed each other. I ask them about Aimee, Greg and Becky and they ask me about where I was being kept and what was going on there.

"You want me to get you some real food?" Aubry asks suddenly.

"I would kill for a pizza right now," I respond, making them both chuckle.

"Becky has been calling me non-stop since she heard, has she called you?" Aubry asks, looking at Cole.

"My reception sucks in here. I wanted to let Blake rest anyway, and you know Becky-"

"It's fine, I'll call her," I say.

"I'm going to get you your pizza. Want something, Cole?" Aubry asks as he heads out.

"Nah, thanks. I have everything I need right here," Cole replies, looking at me as he grabs my feet. When Aubry leaves, Cole moves back to his original spot beside me.

"I was pregnant and now I'm not," I say quietly as I touch my flat stomach.

"Shh, it's okay," he says as he strokes my hair softly. "Right now, the important thing is that you're here and you're okay."

"But I lost our baby, Cole," I say before I start to sob again. "I lost your baby. I'm so sorry."

"No, baby, no," he coos. "You didn't lose our baby. It just wasn't his time to come into our lives. He'll come back to us, you'll see."

I wipe my tears away to look at him. I can tell it's taking a lot for him to say those words. "Do you really believe that?" I ask hopefully.

"I do. I think everybody comes into our lives at the perfect time, and it just wasn't his time," he replies quietly before kissing the tip of my nose.

"Thank you." I lean back on his chest.

"I met my parents," he says suddenly, making me shift my body as much as it lets me.

"What?" I gasp. "How? What happened?"

"I went to their house with Aimee," he says with a shrug as if it's no big deal.

"Cole! What happened? What made you finally do it?"

"The same thing that makes me do all the crazy shit I do," he replies, shaking his head. "You."

"Me?" I ask in confusion.

"Baby, you'd been missing for over two weeks, I was desperate to find you. The cops had stopped searching, Mark was being an asshole. God, I have so much to tell you, but I want to make sure you're up for it, so I'll wait until we get out of here, okay?"

I groan and throw my head back. "Just tell me about your parents."

"So I went to their house...I saw the Home Alone house, by the way."

"Cole! Focus!" I interrupt impatiently.

He leans in and grabs me by the nape of my neck before he pulls me in and ravishes my mouth, making the heart monitor beep wildly again. "God, I fucking missed you."

"Cole," I plead.

He groans. "I went to their house-" he pauses and puts up his hands to air quote, "my *mom* fainted, my *dad* couldn't believe it, we got into an argument, and we talked about how to keep your story in the public eye. Yada yada yada, big fucking welcoming. I've been in touch with them since. I'm sure they'll be around when Aimee tells them you're here. Only if you're up for it, though."

I look at him and sigh. "I guess." I know I can't escape the press for too long, but if the mayor comes to visit me, it's going to be all over the papers and news and then they'll know where I am.

"Not today. Nobody comes in here today. Today, you're mine and mine alone," he says as he presses his lips to my forehead. We wrap our arms around each other, exhaling tranquil breaths, until Aubry comes back into the room with the pizza. "And Aubry," Cole grumbles. "Of course, I have to share you with fucking Aubry."

I laugh but stop when I get a pain in my side as I sit up slowly. Thankfully, my soreness is getting better, which I'm sure has to do with the last dose of morphine Dyann gave me.

"There are a shit load of news trucks outside," Aubry announces as he puts the pizza box down.

"Yeah, I figured," Cole replies. They both look at me for a while. I know they're dying to ask questions but are trying to give me time, and I appreciate it because I'm not ready to talk about everything I've been through.

A loud knock on the door makes us pause mid-chew and put our slices of pie down. Cole calls out for them to come in, and when the door opens, we're greeted by police officers. My body instantly goes rigid. I haven't had time to think of what I'm going to tell the authorities. I didn't even have time to discuss it with Cole! As if he senses my discomfort, Cole places his hands over my fidgety fingers and holds them firmly.

"How can we help you?" Cole asks, getting up from the bed to greet them.

They introduce themselves as Detective Ginsburg and Officer Emmanuel, and ask to speak with me privately. Aubry steps out of the room, and after going back and forth with Cole, he sits down beside me and tells the officers to carry on with their visit because he's not leaving. They start off by asking me how I'm feeling and making small talk before drilling me with the more difficult questions, the ones I cannot answer.

"Do you remember what happened the day they took you? What were you doing? Who had you spoken to? Where did they take you? Who took you? Did you catch any names? Did you see their faces?"

They're all completely valid questions, but I cannot answer them truthfully, so I do the only thing I can do. I lie. A lot.

"I was getting ready to leave the park and head home, they knocked me unconscious so I couldn't see my kidnapper. I was kept in a dark room by myself and only saw them when they brought me food. They had their faces covered the entire time we interacted. I didn't catch any names. I'm sorry I can't help any more than that."

The older gentleman, Detective Ginsburg, looks at me with disbelieving eyes and continues to ask more questions. At this point, his questions are in the form of demands, not leaving me much room to answer anything. He says I know who took me, I know where they kept me, and I did interact with them more than I say I did. His accusations make me angrier than they should. He's right, after all—I do know the answer to those questions. Still, the fact that he's trying to push me for answers bothers me.

"Miss Brennan, we can provide you with security and put you in our protective plans so that you may live your life under the radar. Just help us find the people who did this to you. Don't you want to put this past you?" the detective asks in a softer voice than he's been using. Put it past me, that's one thing I wish I had learned to do years ago.

"Baby," Cole says softly as he squeezes my hand so I will look at him. When I do, his eyes are pleading with me to tell them what they ask, but I can't. I convey that back to him with my own eyes, speaking our own silent language, and he stops squeezing my hand.

"I'm sorry, detective, but I really don't remember anything. I was drugged the entire time I was there."

As they excuse themselves, they hand me a card with their information on it and let me know they'll be in touch. I look at the card until it's blurry through my eyes and snap out of it when Cole caresses my back and brings me back to reality.

"I don't trust them," I whisper.

"I don't blame you," he whispers back while placing a kiss on my head.

# Chapter Twelve
## ~ COLE ~

"What's up with your beard?" she asks, tugging the short hair on my face.

"You like?" I ask, smiling and wagging my eyebrows for effect.

"I hate," she replies, twisting her lips in disgust, making me laugh.

"Why don't you go home to shower...and shave?" Blake crinkles her nose as she plucks my beard with her fingers. I smile in response. I was already thinking of doing that, but I'm waiting for Aubry and Aimee to get here. There's no way in hell I'm leaving her alone. Connor has been in the waiting room every day, and Mark comes around to check on her after work, but I need someone she feels completely safe with and that means Aubry. Bruce is back and watching her, along with a new guy, Spencer, but I only trust Aubry to watch her right now.

"I will, baby, just relax," I respond, holding her close. The door opens and Dyann comes in wheeling in the blood pressure machine. She's the only nurse I can stand in this place, the other ones are nice enough, but they give me shit for sleeping next to Blake on the bed.

"Hey, Blake, Cole, I'll be out of your hair in a minute," Dyann says as she stops next to Blake.

"No worries, you know you're our favorite nurse," I reply with a smile, making her blush slightly.

"Well, you're my favorite non-patient, Cole," Dyann says with a small smile. "Are you ready to go home, Blake?

The doctor should be in here soon. I think you'll be getting discharged today."

Blake shrugs slightly. "I guess," she says, her voice barely a whisper. I know she's scared of facing the real world again, even though she won't admit it to me. I give her hand a squeeze and she turns her face to give me a slightly reassuring smile. I frown at her and her smile gets a little bigger. I know it's going to take a little while for her to come to terms with the loss of our baby; it's going to take me some time too, but I have to be strong for her—for us.

As Dyann is leaving, Aubry and Aimee are walking in with balloons and flowers. I shoot them a confused look as I get up to stretch.

"Hey, guys," Blake says in her fake happy voice. Aubry and I look at each other, relaying the same message through our eyes, even though I know it's going to take a while to get our normal Blake back. It's only been three days, and although most of her bruises are fading, that's only in the exterior.

"Hey, Cowboy," Aubry says as Aimee walks over and sits at the foot of her bed. "Cole, you going home then?"

"Yeah, I'll be back soon. Don't leave this room. If you have to pee, grab the bedpan from under her bed and pee in that. And Dean isn't allowed in this room—period," I say, looking at Aubry and Aimee for emphasis. Dean has been here every day, but I refuse to let him see Blake. She knows he's been around and asked to see him once, but I put a stop to that shit real quick. I don't want him anywhere near her, and I'm pretty sure she won't fight me on this for now.

"Eww, Cole, what the hell?" Blake says, sitting up and cringing as she raises her knees. "He can go to the bathroom when he wants."

"Dude, I got it. I'm not an idiot," Aubry says before I reply to Blake. I walk over to her and lean down to give her a long kiss before leaving.

When I walk by the waiting area, I see Connor talking to Dean, looking like they're plotting something. As I walk over to them, they stop talking and look at me expectantly. I look around and see Bruce sitting on one side glaring at Dean, and Spencer standing near the elevators. At least some people are taking this seriously.

"You heading out?" Connor asks as he stands.

"Going to take a shower and get Blake some stuff, I'll be right back," I reply, taking my eyes off his and narrowing them at Dean, who I can tell is trying to not smile at the news that I'm leaving. Between the smirk, the leather jacket that he doesn't need in this weather, and his perfect hair...I can't fucking stand his ass. The only thing I can stand seeing on him is the black eye on his face.

"All right, well, I'll be here," Connor replies as he eyes his watch. "Fuck, five o'clock already."

"Like I said, I'll be right back," I call out over my shoulder as I walk away.

On my way home I call Greg and Becky to see if their flight landed. I can't make it to the airport to pick them up, but I want to leave them a key to my place so they can be there when Blake gets home. As happy as I am for Becky to be here, I'm also nervous about Blake seeing her pregnant so soon after she just lost our baby. They've been speaking every day, so Blake knows and says she's really happy about it. I guess we'll see.

When I get to our place, I go straight to the fridge and make sure we have everything we need, but, of course, we don't. I take my phone out and dial Becky's number.

"Didn't you just speak to Greg?" she greets.

"Hello to you too, Becky. I did, but I need a favor. Can you guys go to the grocery store for me? I don't wanna leave Blake for too long and that shit takes me forever."

She laughs. "Yeah, we'll go. Are you taking the key to the hotel?"

"Yeah, I'll leave it at the front desk, though. I'm sorry I don't have time to wait for you, but you know."

"Yeah, I know. Don't worry about it, we got you."

Once that's settled, I shower and shave. I splash water on my face once I'm done and smile at my hairless face, a reminder that I finally got my girl back I start sorting through Blake's drawers, trying to pick something out for her, which is a bitch to do. I'm a good dresser; I know what looks good with what, but she has so many clothes. I end up choosing some loose, ripped jeans and a gray Foo Fighters T-shirt. I figure she'll want to be comfortable. Becky better not say shit about it, either.

Dean and Connor are noticeably absent when I walk by the waiting area, which I'm glad for. I continue down the hall, checking in with the security guard, when I see Bruce walking up to me with a worried look on his face.

"What happened?" I ask before he says anything.

"Blake asked to see Dean," he replies with a shake of his head. I look around and notice Spencer is nowhere to be found.

"And you let her? Are you out of your damn mind?" I growl. "What the fuck is she thinking?" I say as I storm over to her room.

I swing the door open and look around the crowded room. Aubry, who is standing beside Blake, puts his hands up in defeat. My feet stay frozen on the spot when I see Blake standing in front of Dean, staring at him with tears running down her face. Both Connor and Aubry have their hands on her shoulders.

"So they've been using me as some sort of pawn?" Blake asks Dean, snapping me out of my trance, making me step toward them.

"What the fuck are you doing in here?" I ask Dean as I walk up to Blake and bury her face in my chest. She lets out a muffled sob against me before turning her head and placing her cheek against me.

"I asked you a question," I say loudly.

Dean shakes his head and shrugs his shoulder. "Not my place to say."

I feel my body burning from the inside as I continue to stare at him. He has an attitude that mirrors my own, and normally that would be a good thing, but between the way he looks at my girl and the fact that he helped take her—I will never like him. To add insult to injury, Blake acts like the motherfucker is welcome around her, and it pisses me off to no end.

"Cole, just drop it, please. We'll talk about it later," Blake whispers against my chest, making me get even angrier, but when I look down and see her pleading eyes, I let out a deep breath and nod.

"Has the doctor come by?" I ask as I caress her face lightly. Her eyes gleam at me and she gives me a small smile before nodding. "Are you ready to go home?" She nods enthusiastically which makes me smile and duck my head to kiss her.

# Chapter Thirteen
~Blake~

I look up, still reeling from the information Dean gave me earlier, and catch him watching me intently from across the stuffy hospital room. I'm not sure how he can be so casual in such an uncomfortable situation. Cole has been shooting daggers at him since he got here, yet there he is leaning against the wall with his legs crossed out in front of him—not a care in the world. I know he's used to dealing with much scarier people than Cole, but still. I don't think I've ever met a man that's not afraid of Cole ripping their head off. Maybe he just doesn't get it, poor bastard. I shake my head and drag my eyes away from his to Cole, who's standing on the other side of the room watching me as well.

"I'm ready," I announce once I have my shoes on. Both Cole and Dean lean forward and walk toward me, Dean stopping short and smirking when Cole shoots him a warning glare. Cole reaches me and holds me at arms' length, his eyes traveling up and down my body a couple of times before he pulls me into his side. I take a deep breath looking around once more and make a silent wish that I never have to visit this place again.

I hug all of the nurses and thank them for putting up with us and our dysfunctional friends before one of them wheels me out of the hospital. A mix of emotions washes over me as we take the elevator to the bottom floor, knowing that in a couple of seconds I'll be heading out into the world again. I think of the last time I stepped outside and glance at Dean, who has a clenched jaw and is fidgeting with the sleeves of his jacket. He looks over at me and our eyes lock for a couple of seconds before he gives me a small smile and looks at the floor in front of him. When the elevator reaches the bottom, I get up from the wheel chair and hold onto Cole's hand as we walk out. The wind hits me and I take a moment to breathe in the cool air and look up at the dark sky before I turn to say goodbye to everybody. I hug Connor first and he promises to visit me tomorrow to check up on me. I then turn to Dean, stepping forward to speak to him and am thankful when Cole moves back and lets me have this moment.

I see a myriad of emotions in Dean's eyes before they settle into a passive stare. "Thanks for telling me and for helping me," I say quietly.

"No big deal," he replies with a shrug. I gape at him in response, which makes him start laughing. "Really, chick. I'm sorry."

Cole places his hand on my shoulder and squeezes gently, letting out a harsh sigh when I tell Dean it's okay. I let Cole escort me away, Bruce and Spencer on either side of us as we walk toward the car in the back of the hospital. When we drive off, I see the news trucks on either side of us and the photographers flock to the car to take photos of us. Aubry's been warning me about them being out here, but seeing them makes it all real. Even though the windows of our truck are tinted, I hide my face behind Cole's back to keep them from getting a clear picture of my face. I don't want Benny to get a chance to see me at all, though I know it's inevitable.

I take a deep breath, letting Cole's familiar scent of Christmas and Jean Paul Gaultier wash away my ambiguity.

"You okay?" he asks softly as he leans back and nestles me under his arm.

I tilt my head to look into the night, watching cars drive by and admiring the city lights. I think back to how only a few minutes ago I was still in a hospital bed, and how I begged Aimee to go get Dean so that I could speak to him. When she agreed and Dean made his way over to me, I asked him to tell me everything he knew about me because I couldn't go back to living the way I had before. I couldn't go back to living a shadow of a life, without knowing with certainty who my family was and who they were involved with. I already figured it was mafia related, but I didn't know the extent of it. According to Dean, my grandfather is Brian Benson, THE Brian Benson. After hearing that, I figured everything else would be less daunting, but hearing that the Bensons and O'Briens had a falling out, and in turn, made Benny turn against everybody, didn't make things easier on me. Dean seems to think Benny's vendetta is against my father, who is indeed alive and remarried.

"Blake?" Cole says, snapping me out of my reverie.

"Yeah?"

"Are you okay?" he repeats.

I turn my face to him, loving the way his big green eyes twinkle in the dim lighting. Loving the way I feel here in his arms, safe. I give him the best smile I can muster as I blink away tears of gratitude. "I think I will be," I whisper honestly.

He nods and pulls me tighter into his side, kissing the top of my head softly as we pull into the parking garage of our apartment.

My hands feel clammy as I walk into the building, and suddenly I'm not so sure I want to be back here. What if Benny is watching us right now? I look skeptically at Bruce and Spencer as they walk on either side of us. I've spoken to Bruce about what happened that day a couple of times and although I know that none of it is his fault, I can't help not trusting him anymore. I cling on to Cole's arm a little tighter and he stops walking, looking down at me with questioning eyes.

He snaps his head up. "Go ahead," he says to our security guards as we reach the elevators.

"Sir, Spencer will go up first and check things out while I wait here with you," Bruce says as Cole waves his response off.

"No, go ahead. I'll take her up by myself in the next one."

Both men look at us with dumbfounded expressions before shrugging and muttering an "as you wish" and getting on.

Cole turns his body to me. "Look at me," he says quietly, and I comply. "Everything is going to be fine."

"I don't trust them," I whisper. "I don't want them watching me anymore."

He frowns before shaking his head on an exhale. "Baby, we need the security," he says as he combs my hair away from my face. "If you want we can get new people, but you can't just parade around by yourself."

I shake my head. "I'm not planning on it."

His eyes soften as he regards me. "Good, because I don't think I can handle another blow to my heart."

I sigh. "I guess we'll keep them for now, but I don't know, it just feels weird. Will Connor be around too?" I ask quietly.

His face grows serious as he searches my eyes and takes both sides of my face in his hands. "Yeah, unless you don't want him to be? I trust him though, and I know you'll like him. He's really excited to have a cousin, you know? And if you don't feel safe with Bruce and Spencer, we'll get rid of them." I give him a small smile and he leans in to kiss me softly.

"I want Connor around," I whisper quietly. Truth is, I get a good vibe from him, and he gives me an ounce of hope that maybe my family isn't all that bad.

"Good," he replies with a nod as he tilts his head to search my face. "Now, let's go home, yeah?"

"Yeah," I reply quietly, feeling a little less breathless, despite the lack of air in my lungs.

The walk to our apartment is long, as I take my time, savoring each step of freedom that I take. Every step brings me closer to our home together, our life together, the life I've been missing for the past month. When we open the door, I see a fury of red hair bouncing toward me, making me gasp and take a step back.

"Blakey!" she shrieks as she wraps her arms around me, her large, obviously pregnant midriff crashing against me. My breaths start coming in gasps as I wrap my own arms around her and begin to weep. I see a large figure from the corner of my eye before feeling Greg's big brown arms wrap around both Becky and me.

"I missed you so fucking much," Becky says in between sobs.

"We're so glad you're safe," Greg says above us.

"Let the girl breathe!" Aubry shouts from behind us, making us step away from each other and chuckle as we wipe our tears.

I fully take in Becky's short navy wrap around dress that hugs her body perfectly, and I can't stop my tears from running. Despite my broken heart, I step forward and place my hands on her pregnant belly. A soft sob escapes her as she places her own hands above mine.

"I heard. I'm so sorry, babe," she whispers.

Once I'm sure the knot in my throat will let me speak, I clear my throat. "I'm so happy for you," I say quietly. And despite the sadness I feel about my own lost pregnancy, I am happy for them. They tried to get pregnant for so long, and I know it's unfair for me to feel the pang that I feel in my chest. I turn to Greg and smile at him. "Congratulations, Gregory."

His mouth turns up slightly before he steps forward and wraps his arms around me and kisses the top of my head. "I love you, Cowboy. I'm sorry for your loss. I missed you so much." I feel new tears sting my eyes before I rapidly blink them away. I will not cry anymore, dammit!

Cole walks over and hugs Becky and Greg before putting an arm over my shoulder and pulling me into him. "You hungry, baby? Becky stocked our fridge."

"I wanna shower first, is that okay?" I ask, looking from face to face.

"Of course, we're not going anywhere!" Becky responds, sitting down on the couch and perching her feet on our coffee table, which makes me smile.

I excuse myself and walk to my room in long strides, soaking in every detail of our apartment. Everything looks the same. My jean jacket is still thrown over the back of a stool in the kitchen. My slippers are by the sliding glass door that leads to the balcony. The memories of that day make me shudder slightly as I open my bedroom door. Stepping in, I frown at the disheveled gray sheets on our bed, the same ones on it when I left that day. I feel Cole's warmth behind me before his arms wrap over my shoulders from behind.

"You okay?" he murmurs against my hair. I nod in response before turning my body around to face his.

"You didn't make the bed," I say quietly. Cole is anal about making the bed in the morning. So much so, that if he leaves the bed unmade and comes home throughout the day, he makes it before he leaves again, whereas I just always leave it unmade.

A flash of pain clouds his eyes and he gives me a sad smile, tucking my hair behind my ears with both hands. "It's been that way since you left. I couldn't bring myself to sleep here without you."

"But that drives you crazy," I reply, looking at the bed and back at him with furrowed eyebrows. He pulls my face against his chest and holds me there, his deep chuckle making my body hum.

"I know, but I wanted to make you make the bed when you got here."

I laugh and shake my head a little at his ridiculousness, because he always does things like that just to "teach me a lesson".

"I forgot what a pain in the ass you are," I mumble into his shirt.

He drops his arms and takes a step back, ducking his head to look me square in the eyes. "Don't worry, I'll never let you forget again." He kisses me slowly, his tongue leisurely stroking against mine before pulling away. "Let's get you showered."

He's helped me shower every day at the hospital, even though after the second day, I was fully capable of doing it myself. I go into my walk-in closet and get my most comfortable sweat pants and my favorite red Murphy shirt before making my way to the bathroom.

"I can wash myself, you know?" I say with a raised eyebrow as I peel off my shirt, noticing the way his eyes travel slowly down my body. The up side to being in the hospital for a week is that other than the bruises, I feel fine. My face isn't swollen anymore and for the most part, the soreness is gone from my body.

"I know," he replies quietly, his eyes darkening when I shimmy out of the black yoga pants I'm wearing.

By the time I lean into the shower to switch it on, he's staring at me with hungry eyes. I smirk at him before taking off my bra slowly and tossing it in his face, and then fall into a fit of laughter when he wraps his arms around me and follows me into the shower.

"Cole! You're dressed!" I screech as I try to wiggle out of his hold.

"I don't care," he replies before biting my neck. "You're teasing me. You know I can't handle that."

He runs the tips of his fingers from my waist up my sides slowly before stopping below my breasts. My legs pool in anticipation and my eyes flutter closed as I toss my head back on to his chest, arching my back, begging for him to touch me.

"Are you sure you're ready for this, baby?" he asks, his voice hoarse with need. I whimper and rock my body against him in response. He finally fans his fingers over my breasts before plucking at them slightly, making a tremor run through me. Suddenly, he drops his hands and places them on my hips. I focus on the sound of the water mixed with our heavy breathing, and when I notice that Cole isn't moving, I turn around to face him. His eyes are ablaze with desire, but I can also see the concern there that makes him second-guess this. I look down look and let the water hit my back. I focus on his wet shirt that's clinging to the cuts on his stomach and snap out of my daydream at the sound of Becky's loud laughter coming from our living room. *Becky, my beautiful best friend who's pregnant*, I think, my eyes trailing over my flat stomach as water pools my eyes. I blink them back, hoping they get mixed in with the rest of the water, unnoticed by Cole.

"Hey, what's wrong?" he asks, cupping my chin to look into my eyes.

I try to restrain my head from moving just for a second so that I can train my eyes into a blank stare, but he's too quick for me...and he knows me.

"We'll wait. You're not ready and that's okay. I'm not going anywhere," he whispers.

I nod slowly in response, my eyes filling with tears I can no longer hide, my shoulders beginning to quake from sobs I can no longer hold back. He pulls me into his chest, kissing the top of my head and holds me there letting me cry, letting me pour out the conflicted feelings that flow through my veins. Feelings that make me feel disgusted at myself for having toward my own best friend.

"I'm a horrible person," I whisper into his chest.

He grabs me by the shoulders and holds me at arm's length as he searches my face. "Why would you say that?" he asks, confusion and alarm clear in his voice.

"Because I am." I shake my head sadly. "I saw Becky and all I can think about is that I'm supposed to be pregnant too. After all she's been through...after all the years she's been trying to conceive and that's the first thought that crossed my mind. I'm a terrible person," I finish, my voice breaking and turning into a loud sob as I lean back into his chest.

"Oh, baby," he says quietly, wrapping his arms tightly around me, letting me cry for the two of us.

# Chapter Fourteen

## ~Blake~

I feel like I'm having an out of body experience sitting in my living room surrounded by the people I love. I can't stop the tears from running down my face. But this time they're not sad tears, or scared tears, they're thankful tears. I am so thankful to be sitting on Cole's lap as Becky runs her fingers through my hair, Aubry holds my hand, and Greg catches me up on what has been going on in their lives. The discomfort in my chest stabs at me with each mention of their baby, but I smile nonetheless. I'm sure it'll get easier to deal with and despite my own sadness, I find myself placing my hand on Becky's growing belly and smiling at the knowledge that she's carrying a life inside of her.

"I'm sorry," Becky whispers as she places her hand over mine. I sniffle back new tears and look into her wet blue eyes with a nod. Cole shifts me so that I'm sitting sideways in his arms and cradles me into his chest, covering most of my body with his arms and kissing the top of my head. I bury my face into him before deciding that I really need to stop crying. I wipe my face, take a deep breath and sit back up.

"I'm sorry. I'm fine, I swear I'm happy for you guys," I say softly, looking at Becky first and then Greg.

"Cowboy, this is all new for you, you've been through hell, we understand if you're sad. We're sad about your loss too, and it's okay to be sad," Greg says before he leans forward and wipes a stray tear from my face with his thumb. Becky hugs me and kisses my cheek before she excuses herself to go to the bathroom.

"Where's Aimee?" I ask, looking at Aubry.

"She'll be here later, she had to go do some stuff with her mom," he replies, looking at Cole for a beat before grabbing my hand and kissing the back of it. Cole pulls my hand away from Aubry's and shoots him a look that makes us laugh. He scowls at Aubry and Greg before winking at me and pulls me closer against him.

"What do you feel like eating?" he asks before pressing his lips to my neck.

"I don't know," I mumble, tilting my head to welcome the trail of kisses he's showering me with.

"Oh nooo," Becky groans as she makes her way back to us. Cole stops kissing me and we all turn our heads toward her. "You guys are not going to start acting like horny teenagers already, are you?"

The guys shake their heads while muttering their agreement with her.

I crinkle my nose, looking from one face to the other. "We do not act like horny teenagers!"

Aubry, Greg and Becky start to laugh before Cole joins in, as I look at them with wide eyes and my mouth hanging open.

"Babe, I'm pretty sure we do." Cole taps my nose while giving me his dazzling smile. My gaze shifts from his smile, to his sole dimple and back to his twinkling eyes before I feel myself beam back at him.

"No, we don't," I say unconvincingly, trying to think of examples that will help me plead my case. Cole shifts under, me making me gasp and feel automatically turned on when I feel how hard he is.

"You see why we act like horny teenagers?" he murmurs behind my ear before nipping it with his teeth. When I face him he gives me a crooked smile before biting and sucking my bottom lip into his mouth. Greg's chuckle and Becky clearing her throat reminds us of our audience, and we pull apart slowly.

"Ugh," Aubry groans exaggeratedly. "Thank God I don't live with you guys anymore."

"You can say that again," Cole says as he flashes him with his middle finger.

As promised, Greg and Becky stay for the rest of the week and even though they got a hotel room, they end up sleeping at our place every night. Aubry and Aimee take the couch in the living room and Greg and Becky take the bed. It almost feels like the sleepover parties we used to have when we were kids. Connor has kept me informed in regards to Dean, telling me that Dean has called every day to check up on me. I've kept conversations about Dean to a minimum because Cole hates him and sometimes I think that I should too, despite the ways he helped me. Connor also says that nobody has heard from Benny, and that is enough to keep me on edge.

I clutch on to the sandals in my hands when the thought that maybe he's keeping tabs on me runs through my mind. Thoughts of his mean snarl, his scarred face, his hateful eyes as he charges toward me while I try to open the iron gate of Alex' house making me cringe.

"Hey," Cole says in a low voice snapping me out of my horrible daydream. I blink away the images running through my mind and I look at him from the floor of my closet.

"Hey," I respond, smiling when I see he's wearing a sleeveless black work out shirt and a pair of Chicago Bulls basketball shorts I'd gotten him last year.

He tilts his head and furrows his eyebrows. "You okay?" he asks quietly.

I take a deep breath. "Yeah, I'm fine. Just sorting through clothes I need to get rid of," I offer.

He nods, seemingly not believing me entirely, but doesn't push me. "Are you going to go pick up those papers from Mark tomorrow?"

"I guess so. Might as well do that since you're going back to work," I respond with a slight shrug.

He strides into the closet and crouches down so that we're at eye level. I focus on the way his basketball shorts ride up his defined golden thighs and raise my eyes back to his when the palm of his hand caresses my cheek softly.

"Talk to me," he whispers, his thumb dropping from my cheek to my bottom lip. "Do you not want me to go back to work?" he asks, his voice still low. My head spinning between the longing in his eyes, the sound of his voice, and the way the pad of his thumb run over my lip.

"You need it," I reply breathlessly, my breathing ragged.

He shakes his head slowly, his gaze dropping to my lips. "I need you," he husks inching his face closer to mine.

"I need you too," I reply, my voice barely a whisper as my heart begins to spike in my chest.

"You sure?" he murmurs with his lips against mine.

I inhale a deep breath, the smell of Christmas and Jean Paul cologne invading my senses. "Yes," I rasp.

My eyes flutter closed when his tongue darts out and he licks his lips. I part my lips slightly, letting my tongue meet his in a sensual dance, his deep groan sending a warm hum through me.

"I want you so bad right now," he says hoarsely against my lips, his fingers trailing softly over my shoulders and down my arms making me quiver.

"Nobody's stopping you," I murmur.

He groans dropping his forehead against mine and letting out a breath. "Are you sure you're ready for that?" he asks, his voice strained with need.

"Yes. So ready," I reply, my chest rising and falling rapidly.

"I'm so glad you said that," he growls against my lips before scooping me up in his arms and walking me to our bed.

He puts me down slowly, his eyes searching mine before running down my body once as he sits beside me and turns his body toward mine. I sit up slowly and peel my shirt off over my head and hear him suck in his breath when he sees my exposed breasts.

Cole squeezes his eyes shut and I wish I didn't still have a bruise over my ribs. And that the stitches on my temple were fully healed and that my skin wasn't as pale as it is.

"Please look at me," I whisper fidgeting with my cotton shorts.

He takes a deep breath and re-opens his eyes, they train on my breasts for a second before he looks back into mine.

The corner of his mouth tilts. "I can't believe you weren't wearing a bra."

I smile back, thankful that he can see past the broken girl that I am. He dips his head and leans into me, taking my mouth in his, igniting the yearning I have for him deep within my core. I shift my body so that he can hover on top of me and grab on to the hem of his shirt, inching it above his stomach. Cole finishes pulling it over his head before taking my shorts off in one swift motion. I splay my hands over his chest and run them down his body, reveling in the way his stomach clenches in the places I touch, until I reach the band of his shorts.

He places his hands over mine and pauses them there, looking at me through heavily hooded eyes. "Baby, if we do this...we have to take it slow, okay?" he says huskily.

I nod my head vigorously, panting when he lowers his head to suck the spot below my ear.

"Slow," he whispers against my neck and I'm not sure if he's saying it as a reminder to himself or me.

"Slow," I repeat breathlessly when his fingers trail over my body stopping to trace my nipple and continue their way south stopping at my pelvis.

He kisses my temple softly, where my stitches are before continuing to rain soft kisses over my face. When he reaches my lips, he brushes them with his a couple of times. "I love you so much," he whispers before kissing me, his tongue slowly delving into my mouth and dancing against mine. "I missed you so much," he continues. "I was going crazy without you," he says as he kisses my jaw and down my neck. "I couldn't think without you." He places an open mouthed kiss between my breasts. "I couldn't sleep without you." He places a kiss in the middle of my abdomen. "I couldn't eat without you." He scoots lower, hovering over the apex of my thigh and places a kiss on either one. "I couldn't breathe without you." He tongue flicks against me, making me throb in want for him. "I didn't want to livet without you." He swipes his tongue again, making me moan and writhe against his mouth as my chest panting heavily. I close my eyes as his tongue continues it's sensual dance along my folds and he inches his hands up my body until they reach my breasts. My breathing is heavy, rapid, and I lose myself in pleasure, my core tightening and body bowing off the bed in abandonment when he sucks against me one last time and lets go with a pop. Opening my eyes slowly, I find Cole hovering over me with one arm on either side of me. He's just watching me, his lips parted and his eyes glistening as if in a trance. My gaze traces his body and I realize that he's naked and ready for me as he settles in between my legs. He dips his head, his lips sealing mine as he pushes himself into me slowly. I gasp at the feel of his tip entering me before he continues to stretch me, his sharp intake of breath matching my own. I bite down on my lip to keep from screaming out.

"Are you okay?" he croaks, backing away from my face to look at me.

I nod, still biting down on my lip. "Don't stop. Please," I beg in a whisper.

He shakes his head, his green eyes lidded and chest expanding as it rises. "I don't think I can," he whispers back.

My eyes are wide and on his as I nod, giving him permission to move inside of me. He lets out a breath and leans his body over mine, resting his elbows beside my face and ducks his head to kiss me. "I didn't want to live without you," he murmurs against me as he pivots his hips into me. "I couldn't bear to live without this again," he says, his eyes glistening as mine fill with tears. I put my arms around his neck and wrap my legs around his hips, pulling him into me.

"I didn't want to live without you either," I whisper back, tilting my hips to meet him.

"I can't lose you again," he replies, his hips moving enticingly slowly.

"You won't," I breathe.

"Promise me I won't," Cole husks picking up the pace.

"I promise," I gasp, arching my back and throwing my head back onto the pillow.

"I'm nothing." He thrusts deeply making me moan loudly. "Without you." He thrusts again, sucking a breath between his teeth. "I can't." He moans. "Live without you." He continues to press inside me and wash kisses over my jaw, my neck, before looking at me. Blood pumps through my veins and I moan once more as pleasure ripples through me from head to toe. Beads of sweat form above Cole's eyebrows, his eyes half closed and coated with a lustful glaze as he stills inside me, pouring himself into me and moaning out my name loudly.

"I love you. So much. So much," he growls as he fills me, never taking his eyes off of me, his pulsing pushing me over the edge again and making me clench around him.

"I love you too," I murmur against his lips when he lowers them to mine again.

He places his forehead on mine as we catch our breath, our bodies slick with exhaustion. We both let out a long breath and look at each other for a long silent moment, basking in the aftermath of our pleasure.

He caresses my cheek with his thumb as he shakes his head looking into my eyes. "I was empty without you, baby," he whispers.

I think about him going to work tomorrow and suddenly my chest begins to ache. The seriousness in his eyes makes me wish I never had to live without him, not even for a day, not even for an hour. And the more I think about it, the less I know if I can handle it. He pulls out of me slowly, slower when he sees me cringe, and lays beside me.

He shifts my body to face him and tilts my face to him, looking at me with concerned eyes. "What's wrong?" he coos.

"I don't think I can do it," I cry. "I don't think I can stay here without you."

"Shhh," he soothes, pulling my face to his chest. "We're going to be okay, baby. Everything's going to be okay."

# Chapter Fifteen

~Blake~

The next morning, feather soft kisses all over my face wake me up. I stretch out my body and open my eyes and my smile falters when I see that Cole is already wearing a sharp charcoal business suit and tie. My stomach drops at the sight of him ready to go, despite my being the reason he's going back to work. I do want him to go, I just feel uneasy about being without him again so soon. I just got him back.

"You're leaving?" I groan.

He chuckles, shaking his head. "Yes, sleepyhead...and you're coming with me."

"I am?" I ask wide-eyed.

"You are," he replies with a crooked grin.

"Are you sure?" I ask, fidgeting my fingers, which he stills with his hand so that I look at him.

"I'm positive. Get up."

I do as I'm told and get ready as fast as I can before hopping to the kitchen on one foot as I put on my other shoe. I smile at Cole's broad back and watch him as he washes the dishes and hums along to whatever tune is playing in his head.

"Ready?" he asks, his back still facing me.

"Yes, sir," I reply sweetly while fluttering my eyes even though he can't see me.

He turns around with heated eyes that roam my body slowly. "I like that," he says before winking at me and walking toward me, handing me a brown paper bag and a cup of coffee. "Let's go, school girl," he adds with a laugh.

"School girl?" I ask, smiling as I look into the bag. "Oh this smells so good. Thank you."

"Bacon and egg wrap. I didn't have time to make you pancakes this morning."

I smile at his thoughtfulness. It's cute that he would apologize for not making me my favorite breakfast, even though he made me something anyway. He kisses the top of my head and grabs his jacket from the couch before escorting me out. Bruce and Spencer meet us outside the door and Cole informs them that we're going to a building downtown. We sit in the backseat of my car and let Bruce drive us since Cole is already running late to catch his flight.

"Did you get my ticket?" I ask, suddenly panicking.

He looks at his watch and exhales. "Yup. Got it while you showered. I hope we make the damn flight. I hate running late-" His voice fades off as he continues to ramble about being late and I stop paying attention.

"Who are you interviewing?" I ask as I wipe his eyebrow with my thumb. He gives me a crooked smile and I stop mid-wipe and scrunch my eyebrows in expectation.

"A pitcher from the Mets," he replies, his eyes sparkling in amusement. "Number twenty-three." My hand and mouth drop simultaneously and I can only stare at him as he bites down on his lip to stifle a laugh.

"No way! You're interviewing Jack Carter?" I squeal, fully turning in my seat to face him. "Like THE Jack Carter? Like Jack Effin' Carter?"

He laughs, pulling me close to him in the seat, but I back away with my hand on his chest and look at him expectantly.

"Yes, 'the' Jack Carter," he says, air quoting as he rolls his eyes. "Are you going to go all groupie on him and shit? You know, now that I think about it, the only sports item you have in your closet is his jersey. Maybe I'll make you wait outside while I interview him."

I gasp, widening my eyes in disbelief. "You wouldn't! He's my favorite player ever! Besides, I have Gregory's jersey too!"

"Babe, you have Greg's jersey because it's him and he sent it to you as a gift! You're sitting here fucking drooling over Carter and we're not even in New York yet."

He shakes lint off the sleeve of his suit jacket and turns his head to face his window, looking away from me.

"Aww you're jealous! How cute," I say playfully as I laugh and take my seat belt off to sit on his lap, gaining his full attention again. "But you know you're the only guy I would ever drool over, right?" I kiss him on both cheeks and then on the lips.

"I better be," he growls as he bites down on my lip. When I shimmy out of his lap and back to my side of the seat, I smile widely at him.

"He does have a nice ass, though," I reply, trying to hold in my laughter.

He looks at me with a serious face for a couple of seconds before his lips break out in a grin. "Nice ass?" he asks, pursing his lips and nodding his head slowly. "All right, I'll remember where your eyes are the next time we're at a game and the cheerleaders stand in front of us to do their little routine."

"Not funny, jerk," I say, flashing him my middle finger, which makes him laugh loudly and lean in for a kiss before he wraps his arm around my shoulder and tucks me into his side. I sigh happily as I lean into the comfort of his hold, but my heart drops when we drive by the park and awful memories flood my mind. I feel him stiffen beside me and hug me a little tighter.

"I read your letter," I whisper. He backs away a little and lifts my chin to look at him.

"Which one?" he asks softly.

"The one you wrote after I broke up with you. How many were there?" I ask with a small laugh, hoping to lighten the mood a little.

"There were many letters," he says with a sad smile before kissing the top of my head.

"Well, I read that one. Aubry brought it-"

"We're here," Bruce interrupts as the car comes to a stop in front of the airport.

Cole searches my face before exhaling. "I meant every word that letter said, but it doesn't matter anymore. I have you now and neither of us is going anywhere. I loved you then, I love you now, and I'll love you always. You've always been it for me, Blake." He kisses my smiling lips before opening the door and pulling me out of the car with him. Photographers and journalists are waiting for us as soon as we step out of the car. They're all shouting questions about my disappearance and my kidnapper as Spencer shields us from them and Cole rushes me into the airport.

I leaf through a magazine while Cole gets our trip sorted out in the business lounge of the airline. When he comes back, he hands me our tickets, and I put down the magazine to make sure our seats are together.

"I think I got the window seat," I say with a smile, making him frown. Cole hates not sitting by the window.

"Nope, I doubt it," he replies as he scrolls through his phone and types.

"Umm...I'm pretty sure A is the window seat, just saying," I say still smiling.

"It doesn't really matter, Blake, you know I'm sitting there anyway," he quips.

"I wouldn't bet on it," I respond, picking the magazine back up to continue idly looking at pictures. I don't care where I sit, I just love that he gets defensive about his window seats. I've had to listen to enough of his stories to know that he hates arguing with passengers about sitting there.

He lets out a breath and puts his phone away in the breast pocket of his jacket. "Are we seriously having this conversation right now?"

I bite down on my lip to keep from laughing at his serious face. "Are you really going to pout about it?" I razz.

"I'm not pouting! You know I hate sitting in the aisle and middle seat! My legs are too long for people to cross and go to the bathroom! And why the hell do people go to the bathroom during a two-hour flight anyway? I don't get it! Did they not know they had to pee before boarding the airplane?" he exclaims, throwing his hands up as his eyebrows draw together and his jaw grinds.

I sputter in laughter, tears forming in my eyes at his outburst. "You're so cute," I say with a smile, grabbing both sides of his face and giving him a smack on the lips.

"You're such a pain in the ass," he says with a light laugh as he flicks my hair away from my eyes.

Our trip to New York ends up being the best idea ever. Cole fills me in on why the interview is so important. Apparently, it's a pilot they're filming for a new show. It isn't news to me, as he's been talking about the plans for this show for what seems like three years now, but the fact that they gave him the opportunity and he almost passed it up is a lot to take in. His interview with Jack is the first for the show called *Inside the Locker Room With Cole Murphy*.

Everything is a success and the views are amazing, which means he gets to film four more interviews in hopes that the show will continue to air. It bothers me that Cole even worries about things like his show flopping, when he knows it won't. He's too charismatic for anybody not to want to watch, and every time he mentions being worried about it, I find myself trying not to roll my eyes at him.

We spend most of Saturday morning packing up his house, which he was finally able to sell. I'm sure he didn't profit from the sale because he hasn't mentioned it to me, but I don't have the heart to ask, even if he says it doesn't matter.

"Let's go to the city for lunch," he says after taking the last box of things downstairs. The only thing left is the clothes in our closets. The mention of food makes my stomach rumble in anticipation.

"Sure," I reply, giving myself a once over in the full-length mirror beside me, and shrugging when I decide that denim capris and a T-shirt should be fine.

"Nope, you have to change," Cole says, interrupting my thoughts. I purse my lips and raise an eyebrow as I wait for him to elaborate on that. "We're going somewhere after lunch and I know you would kill me if I let you leave dressed that way. Just put on whatever cute little dress you have in the closet."

I gape at him. "Are you serious? Whatever cute little dress I have in the closet? I only have a handful of things here and half of them are cocktail dresses!"

"So wear a cocktail dress," he replies with a shrug.

"It's three o'clock in the afternoon!"

"So wear what you're wearing. Let's go," he says with an eye roll.

I return his eye roll and place a hand on my hip. "Umm...no. I'll change, thank you very much." I disappear into the closet and angrily sort through my wardrobe, dismissing everything. Everything either makes me look fat, is for cold weather, or isn't cute enough. I wish I hadn't decided to join him on his trip so last minute.

"Cole," I shout from the closet. "Can we go to a store and buy something that I can wear?"

His laugh resonates through the almost bare room and I hear his footsteps approaching.

"Blake, it's not that big a deal, I shouldn't have said anything. Just wear what you want," he says with a comforting smile.

"Except you did say something and now that's it, the seed is in my head and whatever I wear isn't going to be good enough," I reply, throwing my hands up in frustration. He strides up to me, backing me against the wall, making the wire hangers clink and the clothes scatter to the floor. He cups my chin and looks straight into my eyes, his green eyes warm and serious.

"Anything you wear is good enough. Anything. You make everything look good. Just wear what you're wearing," he says before dipping his head to kiss my lips softly. When he pulls back, he brushes the hair out of my face and taps my nose, walking back out.

"Yeah, but you're wearing a sports jacket," I mutter at his back. He shakes his head and shrugs off the jacket. "You're still wearing a nice Polo," I say, looking down at myself again. I'm wearing an old Kiss shirt, capris and a pair of flip flops. I look like a bum compared to him. He pulls his shirt over his head and I am momentarily frozen, torn between running up to him and jumping on his muscular back so I can bite his shoulder blade or letting it go because I'm starving, for food. The way his wide back looks and his jeans hang off his hips makes thirty different scenarios of us naked and sweaty cross my mind. He twists his body around, the movement causing my eyes to trail down his rippling abs and back up to his face slowly.

"One track mind," he teases with a smirk on his face, before turning back around and continuing his walk out. I drop the dress I have in my hand and break into a sprint, jumping on his back and circling my legs and arms around him before biting his shoulder, his neck and placing a wet kiss on his cheek as his body shakes in laughter. I bury my face in his neck and squeeze him as hard as I can.

"I love you," I murmur against his neck before sliding off slowly.

He turns around and smiles softly at me. "I know, baby. Now let me go dress like a bum." My mouth pops open as he laughs and gives me a hard smack on the ass before turning back around.

Once we're both dressed casually in jeans and T-shirts, we leave the house and take a train to the city. Despite his original plans, I convince him to take me to Serendipity because I am dying for a deep fried Oreo ice cream. We eat and he humors me by pretending to be John Cusack while I pretend to be Kate Beckinsale, because I mean, isn't that what the cool kids do at Serendipity?

"You suck at remembering lines," I say with a smile and an eye roll.

"That movie is way ahead of my time," he says with a deep chuckle.

"Oh please, how many times have you watched it?" I snort, knowing that he's seen it at least five times with me. Nineties movies are our thing, granted, Home Alone always takes the cake, but I still love them all.

"It's always playing on AMC, dammit," he mumbles below his breath, making me laugh loudly before I turn to see Spencer watching us, equally amused.

"We have no privacy," I whisper. "At all. Am I the only one that gets annoyed with that?"

Cole groans. "Blake, we need them, please don't start this again. They're good people and they are going to make sure nothing happens again. And we have Connor and them."

"Don't remind me," I reply, swirling my spoon around the melted ice cream. If it weren't for Mark and Connor confirming who my grandfather is, I would think they were trying to play a bad joke on me. It's just too much to deal with, which is why I haven't even considered meeting him yet. As much as I want to see my father because I'm morbidly curious, I'm not sure I can go through with it. Connor says he doesn't even know I'm alive, which makes it easier to stay in hiding. It also makes me wonder how he doesn't know I'm alive if Connor, Mark and my grandfather all know that I am.

"Are you sure you don't want to meet them?" Cole asks, disrupting my thoughts.

"I don't know, Cole. I don't know anything anymore," I whisper, looking up from the ice cream for a second before returning my gaze to it. He puts down his spoon and places his hand over mine, completely covering it before squeezing it once.

"You know me," he says in a low voice that makes me snap my eyes back to his.

"And that's all I need to know," I reply just as quietly.

# Chapter Sixteen
~Blake~

As we stroll hand in hand around the city, which proves to be sticky, as summers in New York usually are, we fall into comfortable conversation about the buildings and how much nicer the people are in Chicago.

"Don't say I didn't warn you about your clothes," he says, giving me a pointed look.

"You keep saying that!" I say, exasperated. "Let's just go buy some damn clothes."

He grins widely. "Okay, let's do that."

I'd forgotten how much I absolutely hate shopping with Cole. I've been standing around playing hanger rack for him and following him around the entire department store as he looks at all the sports jackets.

"I've never met anybody that needed this many freaking sports jackets!" I exclaim when he places the fifth one on my aching forearm.

"I'm not getting all of them, don't worry," he says with a wink.

I let out a huff and take a seat on a couch while he continues to walk around and I see a pretty sales girl walk up to him and take out her measuring tape. Cole shakes his head and smiles at her, politely declining, but she continues to follow him around while I just watch as an amused spectator. Cole keeps looking over his shoulder and smiling stiffly at her, but she's clearly not getting the picture. She just keeps following him and checking out his ass while I laugh from my seat. Cole snaps his head to me and pleads for me to help him but I decline, still laughing. He narrows his eyes at me and laughs a little, shaking his head in disbelief before making his way over to me. The girl, who is still following him, looks at me with wide eyes when she spots me and realizes that he's not alone. I smile at her for a moment before Cole covers me with his body, making me squeal as I lay back completely on the flat surface of the couch. He bites my bottom lip lightly before sucking it into his mouth.

"You like that? Watching other girls flirt with me knowing I only have eyes for you?" he murmurs against my lips. I gasp in surprise as his body leaves mine with a push up. His green eyes sparkle with mischief as he runs his tongue between his teeth ever so slowly, calling my attention to his mouth. The clearing of somebody's throat causes us both to snap our heads in that direction. Watching us with dropped jaws are two blond curly haired kids, no older than ten and their pissed off mother. I look at Cole, who is smiling sheepishly as stands, pulling me up with him. We stand awkwardly in front of the family, apologizing with our eyes and facial expressions as the mother continues to scold us with hers.

"That was pretty hot." Our heads turn in unison to a teenager standing by with a pair of jeans in his hand and a Slurpie in the other. He sips on his drink and shrugs at the woman who is glaring at him.

"Jonathan, you do not make comments of approval about those things in front of your brother and sister!" she says before turning to us. "And you two should be ashamed of yourselves! This is a public store!"

"Honey, what's going on?" A deep male voice chimes in from behind, making us turn around. "Oh hey, Murphy! Are you back on the night show?" the man asks cheerfully when he sees Cole.

Cole recovers his composure and chuckles, extending his hand to the stranger. "I'm actually filming a new segment for the channel. It'll air on Sunday nights. It's called "Inside the Locker Room." Check it out, I just did an interview with Jack Carter." The man's eyebrows raise in approval as he nods his head.

"Nice. I'll be sure to tune in! I miss hearing your take on games—you and I have similar views on things. Well, it was great to meet you, sorry I can't stick around to talk longer but we're back to school shopping, you know," he says with a bored expression before signaling toward his family. "Oh, I'm so glad you're safe! Martha, this is the girl that was kidnapped by those people." Martha's glare eases on me before she says that she's glad I'm safe. We awkwardly wave goodbye to the teenager and little kids before turning to pay.

"That. Was so freaking weird," I mutter under my breath. Once we pay, we both go to separate dressing rooms and change into our new clothes, at Cole's insistence. I think it's strange that he wants us to wear something nicer so much that he's not willing to go back home, but it's Cole, his appearance is everything. He was probably embarrassed to be spotted looking like "a bum" to begin with. *No wonder he dated so many models.*

As soon as we get in the cab my phone starts to ring. I pick it up while Cole informs the driver where to take us, but the line is silent. For the first time since we got to New York, I start to feel panicky. Cole questions the call and I tell him it was nobody. When the cab starts to slow down and asks us to pay, I get a text message from the same number.

**We need to talk. Call me when he's not around. D.**

My eyes widen at his message. Why would Dean call me and not talk?

"We're here," Cole says as he hands the cabbie the money. I shake the thoughts out of my head and slide out of the cab, careful not to flash anyone.

"What about our bags?" I ask.

"Spencer can carry them," Cole says with a shrug that I have to laugh at.

"He's our bodyguard, not our butler."

"Yeah, well, where we're going, we don't need security. He can wait outside with our bag. It's only one, I'd do him the favor if he needed to pee," he replies with another shrug.

I look around Fifth Avenue and wonder where we're going next. I look down at the short coral peplum dress and nude heels I'm wearing and look at Cole who looks edible in his dark jeans, dress shoes, shirt and jacket. His short hair is getting long enough for me to run my hands through it and grab it. I realize I'm biting down on my lips at where my thoughts are taking me when I see him look at them and smirk.

"I'd rather do that to you for real...at home, now let's go," he says with a laugh as he grabs my hand and pulls me to him.

"Do what?" I ask, confused, as I try to figure out what to do with my oversized handbag.

"Fuck you," he replies nonchalantly.

I gape at the sidewalk, which I'm concentrating on as I walk in my new shoes, before looking around to make sure nobody heard him.

"Cole," I warn in a hush whisper.

"What? You're looking at me like you want to fuck me and I'd rather not do that in public," he adds with a shrug.

I laugh loudly, throwing my head back, causing myself to stumble before I take a breath and go back to paying attention to my walk.

"You suck at walking in heels."

"And you suck at trying not to fuck me in public," I retort.

He groans and stops walking before he tugs my arm and dips his head to suck my lip into his mouth. He loves doing that. Hell, I love him doing that. I moan when his tongue slides into my mouth. He pulls back quickly and takes a deep breath. "You drive me crazy. You need to stop talking about fucking you in public unless you're okay with me walking around with a hard on."

I laugh lightly and we step back into walking. "Nah, although I don't think the cameras will mind if they zone in on it," I say with a sly smile.

I'm so lost in our conversation that I completely forget trying to figure out where we're going. When we stop in front of very familiar large iron doors, I'm completely frozen in shock. My mouth is still hanging open when Cole opens the door for me so I can walk inside of Tiffany & Co. We greet the sales people, and realization dawns on me as to why Cole needed us to be dressed up. I almost laugh, but am offered a glass of champagne, which I gladly accept, before I can comment on anything.

My mind is running a mile a minute because from the second we walked in the door I already knew we were here to look at engagement rings. I mean, why else would he bring me here? I don't even want to look at prices in here. I kind of want to call Becky and scream into the phone as I jump up and down and she tells me that I should have worn a black dress and pearls. I groan loudly and shake my head. I so should have worn a black dress and pearls. Damn it.

"See anything you like?" Cole murmurs against my ear, making me shiver. I turn around and face him with a smile.

"Umm...everything?" I reply with a quiet laugh.

"I brought you here so you can pick one of these out," he explains, grabbing my hand and walking me to the other side of the store. My heart is pounding so wildly, my chest is beginning to cramp. He stops in front of a glass case and gives me a knowing smile, which I return until I look at the case. There are about fifty skeleton keys looking back at me. *Not* what I was expecting. Bubbled laughter escapes my lips before I can stop it and I look up to meet Cole's laughing eyes as he purses his lips.

"What's so funny?" he asks.

"Nothing," I reply between laughter as I shake my head slowly. "Nothing at all."

He furrows his eyebrows, but I know him enough to know he's anything but confused. "The key to my heart," he says by way of explanation. "You lost it, so I figured I would get you a new and improved version. Even though, you are my heart." The sales lady behind the counter sighs dreamily along with me.

"Mr. Murphy," she says in a chirpy voice. "Nice to see you again. Is there anything you'd like to see from here?" I frown at the way she says his name, as if she's seen him here dozens of times. She's probably a little older than us, but not by much, maybe thirty. She's tall and has dark auburn hair and pretty hazel colored eyes. She's dressed impeccably and has blinding diamond earrings on. He did live in New York for a long time, so it is a possibility that he bought something for his past girlfriends here. The thought doesn't even bother me. We've been through enough together and apart for something that petty to get to me, but still, I am curious. Cole turns to me expectantly and I realize they're waiting for me to pick out a pendant.

"Oh...well, can I see that one right there," I ask, pointing at an oval key pendant. It looks the most like a normal skeleton key does.

"You sure?" Cole asks with a raised eyebrow. "You don't like that one better?" he asks pointing at a different one.

"Oh, that's our Blossom key pendant, that one is marvelous," the sales lady, Sarah chimes in. I take a deep breath and look up at Cole.

"Why don't you decide?" I say to him. "You bought it for me in the first place."

He gives me a thoughtful look before a grin spreads over his face. "Okay, go look around while I pick something out." My mouth drops, but I nod dumbly before walking away and looking around.

By the time Cole finishes picking the pendant, I've made my way over to the engagement and wedding bands. Walt, who has told me exactly how many diamonds and how expensive everything in the store is, is now pointing out a beautiful three carat oval engagement ring. I feel my cell phone vibrate in my purse, but am too worried about looking weird fishing it out, so I decide to let it ring.

"See anything you like?" Cole asks with a smirk.

"You got eighteen-thousand dollars to waste?" I ask with a raised eyebrow.

He chuckles lightly as he threads our fingers together and kisses the palm of my hand. "For you, nothing is a waste, baby," he whispers against it before placing my hand at his side. The butterflies in my stomach swirl and I give him a small smile before thanking and waving at my new friend Walt.

When we step outside I notice that Cole has no bag in his hand.

"You didn't end up liking anything?" I ask.

"Huh?" he asks distractedly as he scrolls through his phone.

"The skeleton keys. You didn't like any of them?"

"Oh, yeah, I liked one but they didn't have it here so I ordered it. They'll FedEx it to us."

"Hmmm," I reply thoughtfully before I remember to get my phone out to check it. Four missed calls. Three text messages. The calls are from Aubry, Aimee, Becky, and two from Connor. Odd. I scroll to open the text messages.

**Connor: You wanna come over for dinner on Friday with my pops and stuff?**

**Unknown Number: Chick, call me. We need to talk.**

**Unknown Number: Just making sure you're all right, chick. Just hit me back.**

I reply to Connor's text message saying that I'll think about it. I'm not sure I have the courage or will to meet those people yet. I make a quick reply to Dean while Cole is still typing away on his own phone.

**Me: I'm fine. I'll call you this week. Out of town.**

**Unknown Number: Thanks for the reply. Let me know when you get back.**

I have to figure out how to tell Cole that I'm in touch with Dean, but I'm not going to ruin our trip over that. I'll tell him when we get home.

# Chapter Seventeen

~Blake~

"Are you coming over for dinner tonight?" Connor asks as he sorts through everything inside my fridge.

"I don't know, Con. This whole thing still has me kind of on edge."

"Still?" he asks incredulously.

Connor has been pretty much a fixture in our home ever since I got home from the hospital, but since we got back from New York a few weeks ago, he seems to have practically moved in here. He leaves at night because that's when he works, not that he has a legitimate job, but that's neither here nor there since we don't discuss it. At first I was hesitant to have him around, knowing what I know about him and the people in his family—our family, I guess. But he's a good guy, that much is obvious. And Cole trusts him.

After the New York assignment, Cole has been called on five different ones. I accompanied him to two of them before deciding that I couldn't just trail him every time he went away to work. His absence is starting to bother me, even though I know it shouldn't. It never bothered me before and I understand that work is work. I just wish his job didn't demand him getting on an airplane every other day! It seems like we haven't had time to be together and work on our relationship now that we're together again.

I know that's entirely my fault because I act like everything is fine when he's around, even when I don't feel like it is. We haven't spoken about the time we were apart other than his questions on whether or not they fed me, if they touched me, where they kept me. I'm half scared to ask what he was up to, even though he's made it pretty clear that he was going through hell. Connor has been hanging around our apartment every day, and Aubry usually comes over later on after work. Aimee comes over sometimes when she takes a break from studying for the Bar, but even when she does that she brings her book along and studies here. I still have no clue what I'm going to do with myself or whether or not I want to take the test or do something else. The more time that passes, the less I want to practice law, though. I started on that path because I thought I could help people. I thought I could keep monsters behind bars, but after what happened to me, I'm not so sure anybody can.

"I don't know, I just don't think I'd feel comfortable in your grandfather's house, you know?"

He turns around, his blond brows crinkling in confusion. "Your grandfather too, you know. And I think you'd feel safe around them."

"Safe around *them*?" I ask in disbelief. "Safe around a bunch of men that go around killing people?"

"They don't go around killing people." He laughs before his face grows serious and he purses his lips as if to contemplate it. "I mean, I guess...whatever, it doesn't matter. Nobody's gonna die in front of you. It's not like we walk around the house flashing our guns around."

"Yeah, I'm sure you don't," I say with an eye roll before nodding pointedly to his hip where I know he has his gun.

"I carry it on my back," he replies casually as he turns around and lifts up his loose T-shirt revealing his toned back and the tip of the cross tattoo he has splayed on it. The handgun is tucked into his jeans. "But not when we're at home. Ma would kill me if she saw one on me."

"Hmm. Tell me about her," I say, making my way to the couch so he can follow me. Connor has practically become my free personal therapist, but better because he doesn't ask me stupid questions like "how did that make you feel?" He just sits there and laughs or comments once in a while. It feels good being able to rant to someone. Normally that someone would be Becky, but I still have some healing to do before I can get back to normal with her. I let her ramble on about how much her back hurts, but I'd rather not say too much because I don't want to say the wrong thing and make her feel bad that I'm not pregnant and she is. She doesn't deserve to not enjoy this time in her life.

"She's cool, you'd like her. Real quiet, cooks a mean meal, over protective. I don't know, just a regular mom, I guess," he replies with a shrug.

"What's her name?"

"Cindy," he replies as he dips his nacho in the cheese sauce he heated up.

"And your dad is Michael...my Uncle Michael." I state half-heartedly.

He laughs as he crunches on the nacho. "Yeah, hopefully you'll see him again soon. He's always out of town though, spends more time in Boston than he does here these days. Anyway, you know my mom's Cindy, my dad's Michael and my son is Elijah, are gonna go over this again?"

I smile at him, he talks more about his three-year-old son than he does anything else. It's cute, and makes me laugh when he says the things he does. It's hard to believe he rarely sees him since he lives a couple of hours away.

"Didn't you say he's staying with you this weekend?" I ask.

"He is, my ex is bringing him over on Friday. Should be fun," he says, the scar on his top lip expanding as he smiles widely.

"So she brings him over and goes back home? How does that work?" I ask curiously.

"Sometimes she stays, sometimes she goes back. Depends, I guess," he says with a small shrug as he flips through channels.

"How come you've never shown me any pictures of him?"

A smile plays on his face as he turns his attention to me. "You've never asked."

He shifts on the couch and takes his cell phone out of his pocket and starts to sort through it, his blond brows furrowed in concentration until he reaches the photo he wants and smiles at the screen.

"This is him last month at Navy Pier." He extends the phone to me and I take it in my hand, fumbling when I see the photograph.

A loud gasp escapes me as my jaw unhinges on its own accord. "Oh my God. What the hell?" I ask looking at him wide-eyed.

Connor chuckles and shakes his head. "Dean showed you a picture before, huh? I swear he shows him off any chance he gets"

I uncurl my legs from under me and stand up waving the phone dramatically in front of him. "How could you not tell me?"

His eyes widen before he begins to laugh. "Was I supposed to? What difference does it make?"

I narrow my eyes at him, pursing my lips before realizing that it doesn't make a difference to me that my cousin is an ex brother-in-law with Dean. It's still a little weird though, and I can't help but to play out different family function scenarios in my head. Will he be there? Will his sister be there? How awkward will it be with Cole and Dean in the same room all the time? Is Dean even allowed to step foot in a Benson house?

"What does your grandfather think of all that?" I ask curiously.

"What's he supposed to think? Nothing," Connor says with a shrug. "He loves his great grand-kid, what's there to think about?"

"Why aren't you with your ex then?"

Connor lets out a breath. "How much time you got?" he asks with a laugh.

"Loads," I reply with a raised eyebrow.

"Sit your ass back down then!"

I sit in the couch across from his and curl my feet beneath me before I click the button on his phone to turn it back on and continue staring at the picture of the smiley blond boy with brown eyes.

"So?" I ask expectantly.

"You can scroll through them, by the way. I don't have any naked pictures on there or anything," he says and laughs when he sees my horrified face.

"You're such a clown. Continue—I believe you were about to tell me why it is that you're not with the beautiful woman in the pictures."

Connor rolls his eyes. "There's not much to it, I guess. Sandra and I were high school sweethearts, got married right after graduation, had a kid two years later and separated a year and a half after that." He adds a shrug for good measure to try to bore me or keep his story as nonchalant as possible, but I'm not going to let it go.

"Huh. So why the separation part? You're not legally divorced?"

"Nah, divorces cost money."

"Your uncle is an attorney, ass-wipe. Save the bullshit for someone who buys it. What happened?" I press.

"Damn, you're nosey! Nothing really happened!" he exclaims. "What happened with you and Cole? From what I hear you guys weren't together for what? Like seven years?"

I roll my eyes at him. "Yeah, that was different, Cole's an idiot."

"And you're not?" he asks with a sarcastic laugh.

"Stop trying to change the subject," I mutter, trying to fight a smile.

The side of his mouth turns up a little more and his eyes grow sad. "You know when you love someone so much that you make them miserable? You push them away any chance you get because you know they can do better than you. It kills you, but you do it anyway...because you know, you just know that they can't possibly be happy with you. That they'll figure out at some point that you're a piece of shit and they're so much better and they'll leave you anyway?" I nod slowly, blinking back tears.

"Well, that's what happened. And now I can't get her back."

The tears I was trying to blink back begin to run down my face and I wipe them quickly as Connor looks at me, his own eyes clouding. He clears his throat loudly.

"I told her I didn't love her anymore...like that," he continues. "Fucking ripped my heart open, but I had to."

"Wow," I say, my voice barely audible. "That's messed up. You're worse than I am."

He nods. "I'm worse than a lot of people are, Blake."

"You're not. The big guys never are," I say, shaking my head and offering a smile, making him smile back. "So are you still in love with her?"

"Always have been, always will be. She knows that too. She let me walk away because she was hurt and hurt more with what I told her...but she's not stupid. She knows she has my heart forever."

"Do you think love conquers all?" I ask quietly.

"I hope so. If it doesn't, we're all doomed," he replies seriously.

My phone chirps while I'm washing the dishes and I lean over to look at the screen.

**Cole: I miss you.**

I smile at the screen and wipe my hands to respond.

**Me: I miss you more. Thinking of going to Mark's.**

**Cole: Be careful.**

**Me: Taking Connor.**

**Cole: Be careful.**

**Me: I got that part.**

**Cole: K I love you. See you later.**

**Me: Love you too.**

I smile at the screen for a couple of seconds before I shuffle off to my room.

"Con, I'm going to Mark's. Wanna come?" I ask once I'm dressed in presentable clothes.

"I guess. He know we're going?" he asks with scrunched eyebrows.

"Nope. Figured we can show up and sneak in there in between his meetings. I have to get some papers he owes me from a while back anyway," I say with a shrug. He agrees and helps me finish cleaning up before we head out.

We have Bruce and Spencer meet us downstairs and make the drive to Mark's office, but when we get there, Connor says that he can't go inside. I give him a confused look and he explains that nobody can know that he's Mark's nephew because "shit will get ugly", his words. I contemplate heading back home, but Connor assures me that he doesn't mind waiting in the car with Bruce while Spencer goes inside with me. I shrug off my worry and head up to Mark's office with Spencer on my tail. Everything about this place is so familiar; it's oddly comforting, all things considered. Once we reach the firm's lobby on the eighteenth floor, I see one of the Barbies behind the desk. She sees me and her smile goes from brilliant to snarl before it fixes on fake.

"Hmm. Miss. Brennan, do you have an appointment?" she asks, clearly annoyed. I'm taken aback by her attitude, she's never been nice to me but this is just...weird.

"No, I don't. Do you think you can squeeze me in between appointments?" I ask, watching her expression sour suddenly. Before she can answer me, the door that leads to the offices opens and Mark and a couple of men in business suits walk into the lobby. They're all so lost in conversation that they don't look around or notice me. One of them is an older man with salt and pepper hair that looks familiar, but I can't place him. As I study his face, my phone vibrates with a message in my purse.

**Connor: Abort mission. I have to get home ASAP.**

I look at the message for a couple of seconds before I reply.

**Me: Abort mission? Lol I'll be quick. He's already out here.**

**Connor: Alone?**

**Me: No. Saying bye to clients.**

I stay staring at the phone, but his reply never comes, so I put it away and look up. The men are still talking and I decide to walk a little closer to make my presence known to Mark. Both of his clients are wearing black suits and have serious yet easygoing expressions on their faces as they speak. The other man is probably in his fifties and has brown hair and light brown eyes, he has a laid back smile that I find myself entranced with. I don't realize how close I've walked to them until the three of them turn their heads to face me.

When they see me, it's as if time stops. Suddenly the chatter, the ringing phone, the elevator ding, the closing and opening of doors—everything is muted except for my harsh breathing. I stare wide-eyed, first at the older man that has eyes so similar to mine, I feel like I'm looking at myself. Then at the younger man, who now looks so familiar, but I cannot figure out where I know him. I search my mind through all of the catalogs of faces that I have stored and come up short, yet I know him. Last, I look at Mark, whose face has gone completely pale. The loud ding of the elevator and a large male form running toward me makes me take a defensive step back and look at Connor, who is running at me full speed.

"Fuck," he says, breathing heavily and holding onto his knees. "Fuck."

I stare at him willing myself to speak, to ask, to demand, but produce nothing.

Nothing.

I feel my body temperature drop and the walls start to close in on me as I place my hand over my chest and begin to loudly gasp for air. I blink away the tiny white dots that my vision produces before I feel Connor or Mark or one of the men, somebody begins to move me. They walk with me before I completely black out.

# Chapter Eighteen

## ~Blake~

"How could you not fucking tell me?" a man shouts angrily. "I can't fucking believe-" his voice trails off before he begins to wail loudly.

When my eyes flutter open, I see Connor's concerned baby blues as he squeezes my hand.

"Sorry, B," he whispers, not giving him a chance to explain why before the brown haired man launches himself at us, falling to his knees beside me and Connor. He awkwardly pulls me into his arms and presses my face to his chest as he cries openly, loudly. I stare at Connor, with saucer wide eyes, not quite understanding his emotion.

"Liam, let the girl go, you're scaring her," says the old man in a gruff, smoky voice.

The man loosens his hold on me and holds me at arms' distance as he examines my face. His face and eyes are wet with tears and they continue to flow freely before he lets out a sob. He drops his hands from my arms and wipes his face with the backs of them.

"Sorry," he says with a sniffle. "I didn't mean to scare you, it's just-" his voice breaks before he begins to cry again. For a moment I hear no sound except for the pitter-patter of my heartbeat. And then I see, feel, *hear* the pain that the man before me is bearing. And even though I don't know him, even though I haven't seen him in an eternity, locked memories flood my mind. Memories of that smile, those eyes, that voice, that smell. Especially that smell. He smells like a rainy day, he smells of home, or what I considered home many moons ago.

Sorrow bubbles deep in my stomach as I stare at the man who was once my father. And even though I've always imagined what it would be like if I ever saw him again, this doesn't add up. In my lifetime, I've pictured millions of scenarios in which I'd run into his arms laughing and crying of happiness. Where he would go to Maggie's house and find me sitting in my room listening to music or show up after school and announce that he'd searched high and low until he found me. It's not that I wanted our reunion to be deemed good enough to be featured on an episode of Oprah, but I expected to feel...something. Something happy. Something hopeful. All I feel is blank. And sadness. Bleak sadness. What a fucking thing to feel when you're looking in the eyes of the person who helped create you.

Somebody clears their throat and I tear my eyes away from Liam's to look up at Mark who is watching me carefully, with sadness in his own eyes. The old man standing beside him has unshed tears in his own eyes and from how much he looks like Mark, there's not much of a question that they're related. Then again, I know who he is, and I know he's my grandfather. I stand up on wobbly legs, and am thankful when Connor helps steady me by holding my arm.

"I...I have to go," I say in a hushed, hoarse voice. "I can't-" I don't even finish the sentence before I dash out of the room, holding my empty sobs inside. When I make it to the elevator I press down on the button furiously and cross my arms while I wait. I see Spencer from the corner of my eye, but refuse to look around me. I don't want anything to trigger my impending tears.

"Tell Cole I say hi, Miss Brennan," says a chirpy, annoying voice behind me. I instinctively turn around with my eyes narrowed and look at Skipper the bitch.

"What?" I seethe as my heart starts skipping beats and my ears start steaming.

She smirks. "Tell him I had a blast with him at the bar a couple of weeks ago. Wouldn't mind a repeat of us sneaking off alone together," she says with a wink as the elevator chimes and its doors open behind me. I feel my jaw working as I glare at her with her fake nose and her short blond perfect bob, and her low-cut blouse and too tight pencil gray skirt. I nod once sharply before turning around and stomping into the elevator. I don't have the energy or time to reply to her and I don't have to. Connor runs into the elevator and steps inside next to me, holding the door open as he too glares at Skipper. Her smile falters when she sees the angry look on his face.

"Nobody wants to fuck you, gold digging slut!" Connor states angrily before dropping his hand and letting the doors close in front of us, leaving her with a shocked expression on her face.

"I hate stupid bitches," he mutters under his breath.

In spite of everything, a soft giggle escapes me right before I start to ugly cry. Connor wraps his arm around me and pulls me into the side of his chest and lets me without saying a word.

When we make it back to my apartment, I text message Aubry asking him to come over. I'm still shocked and reeling over seeing my father, my long lost father for the first time that way. And as petty as fake Barbie's accusation is, my chest physically aches from the idea she insinuated. In spite of everything I experienced today, her words are the ones I keep on replaying. Unwanted flashbacks of Sasha, Cole's mistake in high school and then college, seep into my mind every time I picture fake Barbie's proud face. I close my eyes and am transported back to the college party and hear Sasha's moans of desire behind that door, making my stomach weaken. Aubry's responding text message snaps me out of the reverie.

**Aubry: @ work. U OK?**

**Me: No. Need you.**

Seconds after I hit reply, my phone rings and I see Aubry's curly blond hair and smiling blue eyes as his incoming call flashes my screen.

"Hello?"

"What's wrong, Cowboy?" he asks anxiously.

A broken sob escapes me before I can reply. "Can you leave work? I'm sorry."

"Oh my god. What happened? Are you okay? Are you hurt?"

"I'm fine. I just...I need someone..."

"Is Connor there?" he asks desperately.

"Yeah, but I need someone I know," I whisper brokenly.

He exhales into the line. "I'll be right there."

"I'm sorry," I repeat, hating that I'm having a weak moment.

Connor makes a few calls and announces that he doesn't have to work tonight, whatever work means to him. I excuse myself, letting him know he's welcome to stay as long as he wants, but that I need to lie down for a while. I contemplate calling Becky, but I don't want to get her worked up, and I don't want to call Aimee because she's too close to Cole in all of this and it'll just make me angrier at him. I start scrolling through my phone and hover over a familiar name before hitting send.

"Hello?" he answers in a confused tone.

"Hey."

"Hey back. What's up, chick?" he asks, and I can tell he's smiling.

"Not much, yet everything. How does that happen?"

He laughs. "I don't know, you tell me."

"I don't know either," I reply as a small smile touches my lips.

"You had a shit day, huh?"

"Yep, pretty much."

"Wanna talk about it?"

"Not really."

He laughs again. "Nice conversation."

"It's perfect."

We continue our mindless banter back and forth for a while before he tells me he needs to go. By the time Aubry knocks on my door, I don't feel the urge to cry anymore. Instead, I sit up on the bed with my legs crossed and smile sadly at him. He eyes me curiously and walks over to me, unfastening his purple tie in the process. Once he sits down in front of me, I replay my entire day for him and am surprised to find that I don't shed a tear.

"Shit, Cowboy. What a fucking day," Aubry says, shaking his head slowly in disbelief. "Wanna get fucked up?"

"Hell yes."

Drinking with Aubry is always fun, and drinking with Aubry while we listen to hip hop is hilarious. He always gets in a zone and pulls out all the cards, singing everything that blares through the speakers. Connor and I watch on, doubling in laughter, as Aubry untucks his shirt and starts walking around like a G, his words. Around seven o'clock Aimee joins us, thankfully bringing us pizza as we continue to drink. We're in tears as Aubry does his best Nelly impersonation with Greg on speakerphone.

"You're the blackest white guy I know, dude, that's for damn sure," Greg says, laughing into the phone.

The five of us fall into a fit of laughter, theirs dying out before Aubry and mine. Greg hangs up the phone and Aimee announces that she has to get home soon.

"But you just got here," I whine annoyingly, immediately cringing at how needy my voice sounds.

"I know, Blakey, but I have to study," she replies softly.

"Ugh. The Bar," I groan. "I don't even know what I'm going to do anymore."

"You could always take it," she chimes.

"No, I don't even wanna be a lawyer anymore," I slur as I sway to get more whiskey.

"What!" she shrieks. "You went through three years of law school and now you don't know if you want to be a lawyer? Are you fucking crazy?"

"Babe, just leave her alone. Talk about this tomorrow," Aubry says before he kisses Aimee's lips shut. She shakes her head in disbelief as she tells us to be careful and says goodbye.

Connor heads out shortly after she leaves, and as I lock the door behind him I realize that Cole hasn't called me all day. I groan loudly as I flop back on the couch across from Aubry and sip on my drink. Maybe I should go out tonight. I mull over reasons why going out wouldn't be a good idea and come up short. Then again, I am justifying everything with "Cole screwed that Barbie bitch while I was kidnapped." My stomach turns at the thought. What an asshole. I was kidnapped, living in a fucking basement and he was screwing around with other women. The more I think about him being away so much in the past weeks, the angrier I get at everything. The rational person in me knows that he wouldn't cheat on me, but I wasn't gone long enough for him to have to...whatever.

"Aubry, we're going out!" I announce as I walk to my room, tipping my cup a little too much and spilling some whiskey on my feet. "Fuck," I grumble as I wipe the top of my barefoot clean with the bottom of the other. Aubry says something behind me and when I walk out of my room I find him on the verge of falling asleep on the couch. I wake him up with a couple of light slaps on the face and lead him out of the apartment.

"Where are we going anyway?" he asks sleepily.

"Out. Anywhere that has a bar."

He shrugs his answer and we ask Spencer to drive us to a small place nearby. Cole is supposed to get in later tonight and I do not plan on being home at that time, I'm afraid of what I'll do when I see him.

We sit around the bar, and to my dismay, there's a Cubs game on TV, which means my drinking partner is solely focused on that. I roll my eyes and take my phone out of my purse. I find two missed calls from Cole and a text message that says he'll be home at nine o'clock. I ignore him and call the last person on my call log instead.

"Two calls in one day? I feel honored," Dean says in an amused tone.

"Shut up. I had no one else to call," I reply. "Besides, we haven't really gotten to talk."

"Not my fault," he quips.

"I forgot how annoying you were." He laughs loudly into the receiver, making me back it away from my ear. "I met my dad today."

He lets out a low whistle on the other side of the line. "So you know."

My eyebrow lifts and I remember he can't see me. "Know what?"

"About your dad and Alex."

My heart drops. "What about them?"

He exhales sharply. "Where are you? I'm assuming lover boy isn't with you since you're calling."

"No. I hate him. I'm at a bar."

"Hate him, huh?" Dean says in a playful tone.

"Don't start. I'm at Jimmy Green's. You coming or not?" I ask shortly.

"Be right there, Princess."

An unwanted shiver runs through me. "Don't call me that. Ever."

He hangs up the phone on me so I turn my attention to Aubry, who, of course, was listening to my entire conversation.

"You told him to come here?" Aubry asks angrily.

"Maybe?" I whimper.

"I can't fucking believe you, Blake. I can't fucking believe you." I cringe at his tone. He never calls me by my name unless he's beyond pissed off.

I try to appease him by finishing the story and making him feel guilty for not wanting Dean to tell me what he knows. I really need to know, now more than ever.

# Chapter Nineteen

## ~ COLE ~

I rub my forehead trying to contain the impending headache that I feel coming my way as I pace our empty apartment.

"Call again," I growl at Bruce who has been trying to reach Spencer for the past half hour.

As usual, when my flight landed I called Blake, and to my pure horror, she didn't answer the phone. She hasn't been answering her phone all day and the one time she did call me, I couldn't answer mine. Everything is exactly as it was that day. That horrible day. I don't think I can deal with any more heart palpitations.

"Let's go," I demand. "We're going to Mark's. That's where she was going when I spoke to her."

I call Connor's cell phone again and this time he picks up. He tells me that he left Blake with Aubry in the apartment earlier tonight and hadn't checked in since he'd been busy.

"I'm going to Mark's."

"Don't bother, he left the office after we did. Dude, you don't even know what happened..." Connor says before he proceeds to explain.

Needless to say, I feel like absolute shit that once again I wasn't here when she needed me the most. I know there's nothing I can do about it, my only options are to quit my job or take her with me everywhere I go. Since she's not going to let me do either one of those, I need to figure out another solution to this. The worst part is, I wasn't even working today. Not that I was any less busy, but on top of not being here for her, the fact that I was a car ride away and ignoring her calls because I was under pressure to finish shit...it doesn't sit well with me.

"So she met her dad?" I ask to be absolutely sure.

"Yeah, man. It wasn't pretty. She walked out of there...it was bad, Cole. She was pretty fucking upset."

"Fuck," I mutter. "Thanks. I have to keep looking."

"Hold on," Connor says as he switches over to the other line.

I put the phone on speaker and place it on the seat next to me as I crack my knuckles and try to figure out who else to call. Aimee! I haven't called her yet. I'm about to hang up the phone, but Connor comes back to the line and apologizes.

"I know where she is," he breathes.

"Where?" I ask on edge.

"Green's with Aubry."

"Did she just fucking call you?" I growl, not able to hide my annoyance about it.

"Nope. Dean did."

My mouth pops open in disbelief. I close my eyes and take deep breaths to control the rage I feel rippling through my body. "I need to get to Jimmy Green's, Bruce," I say through gritted teeth, trying to figure out why the hell neither she nor Aubry decided to let me know they were going to a sports bar.

"She called him, Cole. Remember that when you get there."

I let out a harsh laugh. "Oh yeah, that makes me feel so much fucking better, asshole. Fuck. Why would she call him?" I mumble to myself.

"I don't know, but...just be careful. Dean's nice, but don't try him, dude."

"Don't try him? Are you fucking kidding me?" I shout.

"Just be smart and rein in that temper of yours before you find yourself in some shit you don't wanna deal with. Get Blake and get out of there. I wish I could go, but I still have some shit to take care of."

I hang up with Connor and place my elbows on my knees while I will myself to calm down. I know I need to be open-minded about this. Blake wants her answers and he's one of the only people willing to answer her, but fuck. And what the fuck is Aubry thinking? I'm going to kill him when I see him. I can't wrap my head around why she would contact him and have him meet her at a bar. I decide to call Aimee, which ends up being a bad idea because she tells me that when she left our place Blake and Aubry were already pretty drunk. So Blake drunk dialed Dean, lovely. This just gets better and better. I'm working my ass off trying to build something for us, and she's calling a guy that helped kidnap her behind my back. I shake my head in amazement and turn my attention to the city lights around me. At least she's okay, that's all that matters.

When we pull up to the bar, I take one more minute to calm down before wiping my clammy hands over my dress pants and getting out. I look inside and see Aubry sitting in the bar watching highlights of the game and I anxiously look around for Blake. When I spot her looking beautiful yet sad, so fucking sad, in a dark booth with a guy sitting across from her, I close my eyes and count to ten. I see that Spencer isn't far away from her and is watching them intently, and that calms my nerves some. I walk in and go straight up to Aubry and smack him in the back of the head.

"Shit. What the fuck?" Aubry says, ducking his head and glaring at me. "Oh. Cole."

"Oh. Cole?" I growl. "Oh, *Cole*? Where the fuck is your phone?"

"Out of battery," he slurs, his blue eyes glazed over.

"You're so drunk."

He laughs humorously. "So is Cowboy!" His eyes widen when he realizes his own words. "Shit. She's with Dean."

I narrow my eyes at him, but make no comment before I walk up to the booth they're in and stand with my arms crossed at my chest glaring at both of them. Their hushed conversation ceases and their heads turn to me. When they see me, their eyes go wide. Dean recovers quickly and raises an eyebrow at me. Blake recovers just as quickly and glares at me. She's pissed at me. SHE is pissed at me? Hell no.

"What is that face for?" I ask, feeling my jaw work as I place my hands on the edge of the table, clutching it to try to keep from making a spectacle by chocking Dean and pulling her out of here.

"I don't want to talk to you. You can go home," she says flatly, her eyes blazing, before returning her attention to Dean, which pisses me off even more. I feel my body shake and I grip the table harder.

"You don't want to talk to me?" I ask in disbelief, gaping at her. "You don't want to talk to me? DO YOU KNOW WHAT THE FUCK I'VE BEEN THROUGH IN THE PAST HOUR?"

"You need to chill out," Dean says.

I push the table, picturing it hitting his face but it doesn't budge. "Stay the fuck out of this!" I growl, anger taking over my veins. I let go of the table and watch his eyes flash when I lean over to grab him. My ragged breathing and blazing thoughts interrupted by the sound of Blake pounding her small fists on the table, which makes the cups of ice clatter. I blink away the cloud of rage that masks my eyes before looking at her.

Her gray eyes thunder before they become cat-like slits. "You?" she asks, sliding out of the booth to stand in front of me. I take a step back so I can see her face better. "You?" she repeats pounding one fist on my chest. "Fuck. You!" she screams loudly before turning around and storming away. I grab her forearm and pull her back to me, which makes her turn around and glare at me. She then jerks her arm away and proceeds to walk to the front of the bar. By the time I reach her I'm fully aware that every head in this place is turned to us, as Blake sways drunkenly away from me, and I shake in rage behind her.

"Blake, you better turn around and talk to me. NOW," I shout when I get outside.

"Go home, Cole," she shouts back as she continues to walk down the street. Both Spencer and Bruce are scrambling to get on either side of us, and I just want to tell them to leave us alone for a goddamn minute.

"I am going home. We're going home right now, dammit!" I yell back.

She stops walking suddenly, making me crash into her back and put my arm around her waist to keep her from falling. I lean forward just for a second, just long enough to fill my airways with her scent. That flowery scent that makes me think of Spring and sunshine and drives me wild. She turns slowly and shimmies in my hold, pushing me away from her and I step back enough so that I can see her face.

"We," she slurs while sloppily signaling her hand between us, "are not going anywhere. You can go home. I'll talk to you tomorrow." The mixture of the tone of her voice and her troubled eyes makes my heart beat ten times more rapidly than normal. I feel the air constricting in my lungs, as her eyes continue to suck the life out of me.

My stomach drops. "What do you mean?" I ask quietly, ignoring the pain I feel wedging in my chest. The pain that I've felt so many times before, you'd think I would no longer be phased by it. But it hurts. It hurts when she pushes me away.

"I mean that I'm not going home with you tonight. You can go home by your damn self," she says, stomping her foot for good measure. I know she's drunk and acting irrational, but something about the way she's looking at me while she throws her fit doesn't sit well with me.

"Blake, just talk to me. What's wrong? What did I do?" I plead.

She shakes her head somberly, tears pooling her eyes. "What did you not do?" she whispers hoarsely. "You know what? It doesn't matter. I'll talk to you tomorrow. I can't even think straight right now."

I watch her walk away from me again as I mull over what just happened.

"You just gonna let your girl go like that?" Dean's voice asks behind me, snapping me out of my trance.

I turn around to see him leaning against the wall, smoking a cigarette, with his legs crossed out in front of him. I blink a couple of times, processing his words and what just happened.

"Stay out of our lives!" I demand, narrowing my eyes at him before taking off in a sprint toward Blake. I run up behind her, lifting her off the ground on my way to the car.

"Put me down, Cole," she demands, which makes me tuck her face into my chest and hold her tighter. When we make it to the car, I put her in the back and sit beside her, and then turn to Spencer who's standing outside of the door.

"Spencer, take my car and take Aubry home, please."

He nods and walks away from us before Bruce turns on the car and drives us away. Blake tries to writhe out of my hold the entire ride home, clawing at me and biting my arm, but I won't let her. She refuses to speak to me but I don't care. I'm not even mad at her anymore, I realize after the fifth time she bites my forearm. I'm just relieved. Relieved she's safe and in my arms, relieved she has to go home with me because all her shit is there, relieved we bought our place together and her name is on the house so she can't just walk away from me. Because walking away isn't that simple anymore, and even if it was, I wouldn't let her.

I rub my forehead and exhale before I kiss her head. "I'm sorry I wasn't here for you today. Again."

She pushes away from me and looks at my face, her eyes red and glazed over from the alcohol and tears. I get the feeling she's going to scoot down as far away from me as she can, and this time I won't stop her. Instead, she surprises me by climbing into my lap and wrapping her arms around me, burying her face in my neck as she begins to sob. My heart crumbles for her, the way it does every time she lets me see her pain. I can't imagine what she went through today, seeing her father for the first time. I squeeze her tight against me and soothe her by running my fingers through her hair, the way I always do, because it's the only thing I know to do when she's like this.

When we get home, I walk out of the car still holding her in my arms and carry her to our apartment. After placing her on the couch, I get her a glass of water and some ibuprofen.

"You feel okay?" I ask quietly as she takes the water and pills.

She hiccups a breath and nods once she puts the glass down.

"Do you want to talk about what happened today?" I ask quietly.

She shakes her head and new tears begin to stream down her face. "I can't."

I get up and walk to the kitchen to see if I can find anything to eat.

"What happened at Mark's office?" I ask after putting some bread in the toaster.

She ducks her head down, but not before I catch the hurt look in her eyes. Her hair creates a curtain around her and all I can make out are her pursed lips.

"Blake, what happened there? Why did you even go? He could've brought whatever you needed over here," I respond with a sigh.

She looks up at me for a long moment with narrowed eyes and tilts her head, as if she's contemplating asking me a question. I raise an eyebrow expectantly.

"Why do you care if I go there or not?" she asks harshly.

I shoot her a confused look. "I just don't understand why you went. You know he would've brought whatever you needed. You didn't have to go there!"

"Are you worried because you didn't want me to run into your dirty little secret?" she seethes.

I gape at her. "What the hell are you talking about?"

She shakes her head slowly, giving me a disgusted look. "You and Barbie. Or Skipper. Or whoever the heck she is! The blond from Mark's office!"

"What?" I ask in a quiet voice as I try to figure out what she's talking about, until it all comes back to me. Oh. Fuck. "No! Blake-"

"Don't." She gets up, clutching the small glass of water in her hand. "Don't you dare. I don't even want to talk about this right now."

She begins to walk the opposite way and I follow, ignoring the chime of the toaster and sprinting around the counter. When I get to our room she's sitting on our bed, her back facing me as she looks out at the view of the city from our floor to ceiling windows.

"Baby, what did she say?" I ask, feeling the adrenaline rushing in waves through my body, my mind running a mile a minute.

Blake turns her head and glares at me. I don't think I have ever seen her so mad...since Sasha, and that scares the shit out of me. While she works her jaw and glares at me, I try to figure out ways to get that lying whore fired from Mark's office tomorrow.

She shakes her head slowly before standing up. "Get out," she demands.

"I'm not going anywhere! Whatever she said, she lied to you, Blake!" I grit, trying to control my own anger. She will not have the last word. Not today. Not with this.

"Get the hell out, Cole. I swear to God-" she starts.

"Shut up!" I interrupt and just as I open my mouth to say something else, she extends her arm and throws the glass she's holding at me. I move out of the way quickly, my eyes following the flying cup as it hits the wall behind me and shatters, pieces of glass flying everywhere around me, just like everything else in my fucking life.

"What the fuck?" I say dumbfounded, unable to grasp what just happened.

"GET THE FUCK OUT!" she bellows so loudly, I'm sure the neighbors can hear us.

I walk over to her, fuming, until we're chest to chest.

"I didn't do anything with that lying slut!" I yell and watch her recoil and back up a step.

"Then why would she say you did?" she counters, placing her fisted hands on her hips.

"Because she's a whore! She tried to do something with me, but I refused and she's pissed. I. DON'T. KNOW. *BLAKE!*" I shout, throwing my hands up in frustration.

She blinks, tears clumping her long lashes together. "Why were you even in that situation?" she asks in a broken voice and my stomach drops.

"Baby," I start, extending my arm to hold her to me, but she backs away further.

"NO. Do *not* baby me, COLE! I was living in somebody's fucking basement with people doing illegal things right outside the door. I lost my baby. OUR baby!" she says, breaking into heaving sob before wiping her face and continuing, "I was emotionally and physically abused...and you...you were out partying?" she whispers hoarsely, crinkling her eyebrows in disbelief as more tears trickle down her face. The pain in her beautiful eyes is so palpable that it makes me want to go back in time and right all of my wrongs. Right all of the things I did when we were broken up. Go back and kick every ex-boyfriend of hers in the head for not being good enough for her. It makes me want to kill Benny and kill Alex and kill anybody who ever hurt her before me. But most of all it makes me want to die for hurting her, for not being there for her, for letting her push me away and thinking that it was okay to walk away.

"No. I wasn't. I swear I wasn't," I say softly, ducking down to look directly into her eyes. "I was a mess without you, Blake. A mess. I couldn't sleep. I couldn't eat. I couldn't think. I went to a little bar down the street with some friends from college for a couple of hours. I had already been drinking, that was all I could do to temporarily numb my pain while you were gone. I got there and drank some more. I got up and went to the bathroom and that girl followed me in. She wanted to do stuff, I didn't...I couldn't. Blake, I couldn't. I wouldn't. I swear on my life, baby. She tried, I told her to fuck off. That's it, I swear."

I take a deep shuttering breath, feeling sobs bubbling deep within my core before I release it. I repeat this a couple times, hoping not to start crying, not now. But thinking something happened to Blake, again. Not being here for her when she needed me most, again. And her wanting to leave me, again. I'm not built for this. I'm not built to deal with abandonment, even if that is what life tried to mold me for, I can't deal with it. Most of all, I can't deal with her abandoning me, and that's what it feels like she wants to do. I don't tear my eyes away from her and when the storm in her eyes begins to dissipate, I allow the current in my body to draw me closer to her.

I clasp the nape of her neck and pull her to my chest before lowering my face to the top of her head. I close my eyes and breathe her in, feeling her tremble beneath me as she cries silently. I hold her tighter and feel my own eyes pool with tears. My breath finally comes back to me when she wraps her arms around my waist. For what seems like the millionth time in my life, I marvel about how vulnerable she makes me feel and how many times I've opened myself up to her, only to end up in heartbreak. I cup her face with both my hands to search her face and make sure we're okay. She gives me a small smile, that smile that never fails to bring me to my knees, and I can't help but smile back.

"You know that I belong to you, right?" I ask as I stroke her wet face with my thumbs.

A single tear runs down her face, which I kiss away.

"I'm sorry," she whispers. "I shouldn't have believed her. I should've known better."

I squeeze her cheeks in my hands and dip my head so that we're at eye level. "I need you to listen to me, Blake. I need to make sure you understand this. When you were gone, you were all I thought about. The only thing that kept me going was knowing you were coming back to me. I was physically sick with worry, and on the two occasions that I tried to associate with others, I failed miserably. My soul belongs to you, Blake. I go where you go. I can't live without you—I don't want to live without you. If you die tomorrow, I die with you. I don't know how many times or how many ways I'm going to have to say that to you for it to stick, but if I have to say it every single day for the rest of my life, I will."

Her eyes glisten and more tears fall freely, but the grip on my heart loosens, knowing that these aren't tears of sadness. I lower my head and kiss her eyes before trailing down her face, consuming her salty tears and leaving loving kisses in their wake. When I reach her soft pouty lips, I lick the bottom one slowly before sucking it into my mouth and letting out a low moan at the feel and taste of it. My hands trail down over the swells of her breasts and continue to the hem of her shirt before I slowly inch it up and place my hands on her tiny waist. She leans into my touch, giving me permission to continue, and I inch my fingers slowly to her breasts, tucking them under her bra and kneading at them gently. She sighs against my mouth and our tongues dance against one another before I pull her shirt over her head and bury my face in her neck, sucking it gently as I unsnap her bra.

When I draw my head back from her, she clutches my dress shirt and pulls me toward her, giving me a sensual kiss as she begins to slowly undress me. She lets my dress shirt fall below us and pulls my undershirt over my head, tossing it to the side before turning her attention to my belt. The tips of her hand tuck into my boxers and she pulls everything down to my feet, assisting me in stepping out of them. While I shake off one of my pant legs, she unexpectedly squeezes me, making me hiss out a breath and my heart speed up. My dick twitches in her hold when she lowers herself to her knees, looking up at me through hooded eyes. When I feel her tongue circle the tip of it, I put my hands on her head and throw my head back with a moan. I begin to draw slow circles on her scalp as she takes me in deeper. Her whimper resonates through my body and causes me to clutch on to her hair.

"Blake," I breathe. "You need to...oh...fuuuuck. You. Shit." I can't form words to let her know that I'm going to come in her mouth if she doesn't stop soon. Instead, I channel every ounce of power in my body to push her shoulders back slightly. She pouts when my dick falls away from her mouth and looks up at me, licking those luscious lips of hers. The way she licks and bites her bottom lip always drives me to the edge. I pick her up quickly, making her squeal and laugh in surprise before I toss her on our bed. I undo her jeans and throw them to the floor along with her panties, leaving her completely naked, just like I like her to be. I trace her leg upward with the back of my hand, as she watches with lustful eyes, her breath coming in pants. I love the way my touch affects her. Hell, I love how the way I look at her affects her. I duck my head and begin to trace wet kisses up her toned legs in the same place I just touched her, until I reach her sweet spot. I take my time here, the way I always do with her. I nip and suck the inside of her thighs, right beside her throbbing middle as she writhes her hips in an unspoken plead.

"Cole," she pants. "Please, do it."

"Do what, baby?" I murmur right before I swipe my tongue once up her slick folds making her gasp loudly. I smile against her and go back to sucking the insides of her thighs, knowing it'll drive her crazy.

"Cole!" she reprimands breathily.

"Hmmm?"

"Please!" she screeches as she moves her hips side to side, trying to get me to cave, but instead I rub my nose against her. Finally she grips the short hair on my head and unsuccessfully tries to keep my face in one spot.

"Tell me what you want me to do and I'll do it," I say huskily against her before sucking her clit into my mouth once and making her bow off the bed groaning. I let go and place a soft kiss on her inner thigh.

"Kiss me, please, please, just do it!" she whimpers.

"I am kissing you, baby," I reply softly as I slide my hands up from her hips and begin to tease her nipples with my thumb and forefinger.

"Oh my God, Cole," she pants as she raises her hips again. "Please lick me," she begs. Damn, that shit turns me on.

My heart pounds against my chest, and I growl against her before devouring her and making her fall apart against my tongue. As she comes down from her orgasm, I hover above her, watching her in awe. She's always beautiful, but never more beautiful than when she lets go, all of her normally worried features relaxing and her gray eyes bright and sated. I would give my left nut to keep that carefree look on her face all day. Before she can completely come down from it, I delve deep into her, making her scream out another one.

I hold my body still for a beat and grind my hips slowly into her. She lifts her hips to urge my thrusts, but I don't pick up the pace, I'm taking my time. I bring my right hand in between us and pinch her clit. "Whose is this, Blake?" I ask through gritted teeth, making her gasp when I pull out completely and slam into her again.

"Yours. Oh GOD. YOURS!" she screams.

"Fuck yes," I hiss as I lower myself to kiss her and plunge my tongue into her mouth while quickening my thrusts. She lets out a strangled moan against my mouth before tilting her head back on the bed, giving me access to her throat, which I fully take advantage of.

"Oh fuck. Cole. Right there. Yes," she cries and I shut my eyes, throwing my head back as I slam into her while I pick her up and sit on the bed so that she's straddling me.

She wiggles against me, but I don't let her take control. I hold her hips and slam her onto me, deeper. Faster. Harder. And then I slow our tempo again, reveling in her cries of pleasure. I lean forward and suck her nipples, smiling against them when she begs me not to stop. I bite lightly on one of them and loosen my grip on her so that she can take over, which she does quickly. As she moves her body up and down and side to side trying to get me as deep inside her as she can, I begin to circle my thumb on her clit and feel her clench around me. We're both covered in our sweat and on the brink of ecstasy when I pull out making her yell obscenities at me. I flip her back over on the mattress and push myself between her legs slowly. We both moan loudly at the feel of her wrapping around me again. She squeezes my body to hers with her legs around me and I know I'm not going to last any longer.

"Look at me, baby," I say hoarsely, and the second she does, we fall together. Crying out each other's names.

dawn

/dôn/


Noun.

The first appearance of light before sunrise.


Synonyms

morning, daylight

# Chapter Twenty

## ~Blake~

Moments later, my eyes pop open when I feel Cole's hands drawing slight circles down my back. I move my face against his hard naked chest, inhaling his intoxicating scent before placing a soft kiss on his pec. He takes a deep breath, causing my head to rise and fall with him.

"I'm sorry I called him," I say, nuzzling against him. His body tenses, as he holds on to me tighter.

"Why would you do that? I don't understand how you, of all people, would want to stay in touch with him, let alone see him," he asks quietly.

"I needed answers, Cole," I respond in a whisper.

He pushes back and cups my chin, tilting it up to look in his hard, serious eyes. "Did you get them?"

The callousness in his voice makes me gulp down nervously, the aftertaste of whiskey, tequila, and Cole swirls down my throat heavily.

He raises an eyebrow, waiting for an answer that I'm not ready to give him. I tear my eyes away from his probing gaze as I try to collect my thoughts.

"I got some, yes," I reply vaguely when I look at him again.

I watch as his jaw twitches and mentally curse myself for not giving him the straightforward answer he expects from me. How do I tell him though? It hurt me enough to hear the words come out of Dean's mouth, but for me to repeat them, to say them to Cole, that would kill me. Without another word he moves from under me and walks to the bathroom, leaving me staring blankly behind him.

Water pools my eyes as they roam his scratched naked back. The sight of that usually makes me smile because I know how much he likes it. Instead, a painful feeling consumes my chest because I feel like that's exactly what I'm doing—clawing at his vulnerability. My chest starts to ache when thoughts of my actions, my words—everything begins to hit me. As I replay my day and remember the worried look Cole had on his face when he found me at the bar, I begin to sob uncontrollably. Oh my God. I place one hand over my heart and the other covering my mouth to try to keep quiet.

I wipe my face quickly and take deep shaky breaths to calm down when I hear the bathroom door open. As he walks over to me, Cole looks at me and shakes his head, defeated, before sitting beside me on the bed.

"Come here," he rasps. When I gain enough courage to look at his face, we stare at each other for a moment, channeling the weight of our sadness onto each other. I scoot over until my thighs hit his and look down at my folded hands. He grabs a fistful of my hair and pulls my head onto his chest, and that's when I can't hold it in anymore and begin to cry.

"I'm so sorry. I'm a horrible friend and a horrible girlfriend," I say in between gasping sobs.

"Shhh, you're not," he responds.

"I am," I cry before wiping my face clean again. "I am," I repeat in a whisper.

He pulls me onto his lap before grabbing both sides of my face. "You are not. Stop saying that. You are an amazing person, you are an incredible girlfriend, and you're my best friend. I just can't handle you shutting me out like that. My entire life I've watched you shut people out, especially boyfriends, and I can't accept that you would do that to me. You never shut me out."

I blink back new tears before he wipes my cheeks with the pads of his thumbs.

"I can't tell you," I say brokenly. "You shouldn't have to bear the weight of everything involving my fucked up past."

He gives me an incredulous look. "You can't be serious," he mutters, shaking his head. "Blake, your past is my past, your present is my present, and your future is my future. I bear the weight of everything that happens in your life. How can you not see that?"

"I do, Cole. I do see it, which is why I know you shouldn't have to deal with more," I whisper, tearing my gaze from his.

He gives me a soft kiss on the lips before carrying me to the bathroom and setting me down on top of the counter. He turns around and sets up the tub, which we've only used once since we moved here. I'm not really into soaking, but I am too exhausted to argue. Once it's filled, he puts his hand in to test the water, lifts me up and sets me in before undressing himself and sliding in behind me.

He begins to massage my shoulders, his soothing touch melting away my anxiety. When he stops, I close my eyes and lean my back onto his chest, letting him wrap his arms around me.

"Baby, you have to wake up," Cole whispers in my ear. I let out a surprised gasp as my eyes flutter open. "Hey, it's fine, I just don't want you to turn into a prune."

I smile and turn my body to look at him, making water swish out of the tub. "Thank you. I needed this." He smiles back and winks at me before climbing out and fetching our towels.

Once we're both dressed for bed, he takes hold of my hand and walks me back to our bed. I look at our intertwined fingers and squeeze them. Ever since I've been back, Cole has a newfound thing for holding my hand. It's cute and makes me smile every time he does it. He knows how to make me feel loved and protected.

"Sleep. We'll finish our talk tomorrow," he murmurs before placing a kiss on my lips.

"I love you," I whisper against his lips.

"I love you more. To the moon and back," he replies before kissing me once more.

I fall into a dreamless slumber and wake up the next morning to the smell of greasy bacon. I put my hand over my mouth and run to the bathroom before leaning over and emptying out everything in my system. I flush and wipe my mouth with the back of my hand when I'm done and get up slowly. When I turn around I find Cole watching me intently, leaning against the doorframe with his arms crossed over his chest. He shakes his head at me before walking back out of the bathroom.

"You're not going to give me a kiss good morning?" I ask with a smile as I watch him walk back to the kitchen.

"Why don't you get dressed and meet me in the kitchen when you're done," he says without turning around. My eyebrows shoot up at his clipped tone and his attitude. I should probably let it go and do as I'm told, but it's clear that he's pissed off and I don't understand why. I stomp to where he is and pull his arm back so he can stop walking and look at me, but he snatches his arm from me and pins me with narrowed eyes.

"Go get dressed!" he says loudly.

I gape at him for a second. "What is wrong with you?" I ask, shuffling behind him when he continues walking.

I decide to wait for his answer on this side of the counter to leave some space between us when he goes into the kitchen.

He huffs out a breath as he places our breakfast on the plates in front of him. "Go get dressed, Blake. I'll have the food and coffee on the table by the time you come back out."

"Are you going to tell me why you're mad at me?" I ask a little quieter.

The only thing audible in the room as he glares at me is the clattering of the utensils when he tosses them on top of the ceramic plates. My eyes roam down his shapely arms and fixate on the movement in his forearms that flex and un-flex as he grips the countertop.

"What's wrong?" I ask again.

"You've got to be kidding me," he mumbles under his breath before turning and slapping the cabinet behind him, making me jump. "Go get dressed so we can talk," he says for the millionth time, through clenched teeth.

I sigh, slumping my shoulders but remaining unmoved. I refuse to leave until I get an answer.

He turns back around and tilts his head. "Let's see, Blake, you went out, got drunk and wouldn't answer my phone calls. You didn't let Aubry answer his phone calls, you didn't let anybody else know where you went. You called a guy who participated in your kidnapping, NOT for the first time, I might add. You didn't want to come home with me, you attacked me because you thought...fine, I'll let that one slide. You wouldn't tell me what you had to talk to that asshole about." He puts his arm up when I open my mouth to say something. "Let me finish. Mainly I'm stuck on the fact that you communicate with this guy regularly and don't even tell me about it."

I try to swallow past the lump in my throat, but end up gasping for air instead. I know I messed up, but hearing him say all of those things and seeing how angry and hurt he is because of me leaves me at a loss for words. I can only stare at him as he looks at me expectantly. I bite down on my trembling lip, and suddenly, it's all too much. I turn back into our room, grabbing some clothes and heading straight into the shower. I leave the door unlocked, expecting him to barge in at any minute, but he never does. When I finish dressing, I go back to the kitchen and find that he's no longer there. When I notice his keys are missing, my heart starts pounding rapidly and I sprint to the spare bedroom, the balcony, the guest bathroom, and it hits me that he just left. He left my breakfast and coffee on top of the table like he said he would, but he's gone. He didn't even leave me a note.

I scramble out of the apartment, bumping into Spencer right outside the door.

"Where is Cole?" I ask hurriedly.

"He said he was going out," Spencer replies.

"Did he say when he would be back? Is Bruce with him?" I ask, jumbling my words together.

"Bruce followed him out, but Cole left in a rush. He looked..." Spencer trails off and looks at his feet, which doesn't help slow down my heart at all. Spencer and Bruce are very professional yet no bullshit guys and they never look away from anybody, so it's obvious he doesn't want to get dragged into this.

"He looked pissed," I say, finishing his sentence. Spencer's brown eyes shoot back up to mine and he nods slowly. My mouth drops open when I turn around and notice a hole in the wall right outside of our door. I take a sharp intake of breath and look at Spencer for confirmation, which he gives me by nodding gravely.

I half-heartedly eat my chocolate chip pancakes and bacon, tossing most of it aside because of my complete lack of appetite. I pace around for an hour before I call Cole's cell phone and get no answer. I call Aubry and get no answer from him either, which makes me even antsier. Next I call Aimee, but she says she hasn't heard from Cole and last spoke to Aubry earlier in the morning before she left the house. After hanging up with her, I growl in frustration and decide to sit on the balcony and wait for him to come back. Another couple of hours passes, and I've called Aubry, Cole and Bruce a total of thirty times. I'm jittery and chewing on my fingers at this point, and decide to call Greg.

"'Sup, Cowboy?" he says as he answers the phone.

"Have you talked to Cole or Aubry today?" I ask desperately.

"No, why? Did something happen?" he asks in an edgy voice.

"No. I don't know," I reply before I begin to hyperventilate.

"Holy shit. What happened? Are you okay? What the fuck happened?"

"I'm not okay," I whisper. "I messed up, Greg. I messed up bad."

I tell Greg what happened last night and this morning, grateful that unlike Becky, he listens without interrupting my story. When I'm done, I sniffle and wipe my nose with the sleeve of my shirt.

"Damn, Cowboy...you really fucked up," Greg says with a whistle.

"I don't know what to do. I was going to talk to him today and tell him everything, but I didn't even get a chance and then he left and now he's not answering and...oh my God. I think I lost him. I really lost him this time, Gregory. He's not coming back," I whimper before I start wailing and gasping for air again.

"No, Shorty, you haven't lost him. You'll never lose him. Never. You just need to talk to him. Imagine how he must feel, put yourself in his shoes. Yes, you fucked up, but you're not going to lose him. Trust me on that. He's too whipped to see anybody but you, Baby Girl," he says softly.

"Thank you, G. I love you. Tell Becks I'll call her tomorrow."

"Love you too."

# Chapter Twenty-One
## ~ COLE ~

I turn into the garage of our apartment and park the car, sighing and leaning my head back on the headrest as I savor the quiet moment. I look at my rearview and see Bruce pull up behind me, and I take another minute, closing my eyes and breathing heavily. The best thing I did today was go to a Cubs game with Aubry. Not that I got my mind off any of this shit, but at least I had a couple of beers and chilled out for a while. I know Blake must've been beside herself because she called us a hundred times, and part of me did feel bad for not answering for her. It wasn't until Greg called to tell me that he spoke to her that I realized how worried she was, but by then the game was tied in the eighth inning, and I wasn't going to leave to console her. I did enough of that last night. Hell, I've done enough of that my entire life, and I'll do it for the rest of it, but sometimes it seems like nothing I do is enough.

To add fuel to the fire, I woke up and started making breakfast for her when her phone started chirping. I checked it, expecting it to be Aubry checking in, and was unpleasantly surprised to see Dean's name staring back at me. Not once, not twice, but ten fucking times. Text messages and calls back and forth between the two of them. I can take a lot from Blake, but that shit is too much. And then I try to get her to talk to me and she refuses? Fuck that.

She didn't even reply when I told her how I felt. She just turned around and left me reeling. I thought we were done putting each other through hell, but apparently Blake has other plans. I shake my head in disbelief before getting out

184

of my car and heading to our place. She's probably asleep by now. After the game, Aubry and I went to a sports bar and had dinner and talked more shit, anything to keep me from coming home early. The more I think about it, the more disgusted I am with myself, because in hindsight, I did want her to worry.

I step in, quietly closing the door behind me. I see her standing in the doorway to our room. Her hair is wild, her face blotched red and her gray eyes have that dead look in them that makes my heart stop beating. She's just staring at me as she chews nervously down on her lip. This. This right here is the kind of shit that makes me hate myself. This right here is what makes me crumble and fall at her feet every single time.

"Hey," I say quietly.

"Hey," she barely whispers in return, casting her eyes down.

I take and let out a harsh breath. "I'm sorry."

She nods slowly and shifts on her feet, her hair curtaining over her face so that I can no longer see her expression.

"I had to get out. I needed a break from all this shit. I'm sorry I made you worry," I explain, even though I don't have to. But this is what she does to me, she makes me fucking crazy when she shuts me out and I desperately need her to let me in. Some of my friends that haven't been around us have given me shit over this because they don't understand our relationship. They say it's not normal, not healthy, and I get it, but we can't change our past. We're just two broken people in love trying to heal each other, and despite everything, we don't want to be with anybody else. We've tried countless times and it's never worked, so I don't care what I look like to anybody else. When it comes to Blake, nobody else matters.

Her eyes are sad when she lifts them to meet mine again, which is still better than emotionless. "It's okay. I pushed you away like I always do. I don't blame you for leaving, and I don't blame you if you don't want to stay with me. I'm sorry. I'm sorry I didn't just talk to you when you asked me to. I'm sorry that I've been so weak lately. I'm sorry that you're the one that has to deal with my paranoia and my attitude and my tears and my secrets and...just everything. I'm sorry about everything. I don't want you to hurt with me, *because of me,* and I know that's impossible if you stay, so I get it," she says with a slight shrug.

My heart is stuck my throat, and I can't even form a coherent reply to that. Instead I walk up to her, watching her as she takes a shaky step back. When I reach her, I place a kiss on her forehead and run the back of my hand slowly down her face before tilting her chin up to look at me.

"I'm not going anywhere," I whisper. "Ever. But you need to stop pushing me away. Your pain is mine, let me carry it with you, for you—I don't care as long as you're with me. I thought we covered this last night and a hundred times before? I want to be with you forever. Forever, Blake. You are everything to me. Now, can I give you that kiss I should've given you this morning?"

Her eyes twinkle as she blinks rapidly. "You're not leaving me?" she asks in a hoarse whisper.

I duck my head and give her a quick kiss. "Never," I murmur before lightly sucking on her bottom lip.

She wraps her arms around my neck and clings on to me. "Please don't leave me like that again. I'm sorry I pushed you away, but please don't leave like that. I thought I lost you for good."

I squeeze her as I stand up straight and carry her to the couch, folding her in my lap as I take a seat.

She kisses me softly before pulling back and cupping my face in her small, cold hands. "I need to tell you something."

I nod and tighten my hold on her. "Tell me everything."

She takes a deep breath. "I'm sorry," she says regretfully and I instantly tense, expecting the worst. "Dean told me that your dad...your dad knew where we were all along," she continues in a shaky voice. "He said he heard Benny talking to someone about me." She shudders at the mention of Benny and I clench my fists.

"Dean says my dad knew where I was when I was kidnapped and he didn't say anything, didn't report it, didn't go get me? And you believe him?" I ask incredulously. She nods slowly with wide eyes. "When I met him, he was just as shocked as everybody else about the entire thing. He didn't even know you were alive."

She tilts her head and searches my eyes for a couple of seconds. "Who put the money into your bank account?"

I blink at her in surprise. "Mark."

"Did you ask Mark?" she asks with a raised eyebrow. "Did you ask him about the farm? Who gave you the farm?"

My heart constricts. "Blake, that's enough!" I say, placing her on the seat beside me so I can stand up. I pace around the room with my hands behind my head as if I've just run a marathon, which is exactly how I feel.

"It's not true. It just can't be true," I state quietly.

"I'm sorry," she says softly. "That's why I didn't wanna tell you."

I take a couple of deep breaths and think about the account I had set up when I was a teenager, the farm that was signed over to me. Now I wish I had paid more attention to details, but I thought hiring a private investigator meant I didn't have to do that shit. Blake comes up from behind me and wraps her arms around me as I stare into the beautiful Chicago skyline. I sigh and lean my body forward, placing my forehead against the cold glass door, and close my eyes. What am I supposed to do with this information? Is it true? Were my birth parents faking their shock to see me alive when I showed up at their house? Did Mark know that they were in on it? Did he know that my parents were going to charity events and climbing up the social ladder, while fake mourning the son they knew was alive and forced to live with a complete stranger at the age of four? Who does that to a four-year-old? What kind of parents do that? A shudder runs through me and Blake tightens her hold on me.

"I'm here, it's okay," Blake coos as she kisses my back. She lets go and steps in front of me, looking at me with pain and sadness in her eyes as she begins to wipe the tears I hadn't realized were falling from my eyes. Funny how the tables turn, and the thought that her pain is this deep, this bad, and most likely worse than I can ever imagine, makes my heart shatter for her. I stand upright and pull her body against mine, breathing her in as we cling to each other like we're the only thing that matters in this world...and to each other, we are.

"What else did Dean say?" I ask, his name losing some of its poisonous taste in my mouth.

She shakes her head under me. "That was all he told me. You got there before he was able to say anything else. He just...he said Benny's been pretty absent lately and he's worried about me."

My heart stops beating at the mention of that heartless bastard. "What about Alex?" I whisper.

"He's...I don't know. I don't know. Dean says I shouldn't worry about him. Something about him talking to Liam...my...uh...my dad."

I pull away from her and cup her face in my hands. "How was that? Seeing him?"

She takes a staggered breath before pursing her lips. "Weird. I recognized him, I guess from the pictures. I felt oddly...comfortable with him. His smell, his-" her voice breaks before she clears her throat, "his voice. I don't know, it was just too much for me, not expecting to see him and then he's there. I couldn't."

We move back to the couch and continue holding each other in silence, mulling over the million questions we have no answers to. Blake unfolds herself from my lap and gets up, pulling her hair into a ponytail.

"You know what? We're getting to the bottom of this. Tonight we're getting to the bottom of this!" she says, determined, looking at the kitchen before turning her gaze toward me. "Get up. We're going to see Mark."

I raise an eyebrow as I look at my watch. "Blake, maybe this time you should call him? You don't know if he's home, it's nine o'clock on a Saturday night."

She narrows her eyes before walking away and picking up her phone on the way to our room. My phone buzzes in my pocket and I take it out to see a text from Connor.

**Connor: Dude, ur girl is fucking crazy. She wants 2 go 2 my grandfather's house. Just called me. WTF?**

My eyes widen as I read his message. "BLAKE! YOU CALLED CONNOR TO TAKE YOU TO BRIAN'S HOUSE?"

"YES! I CAN'T DEAL WITH THIS ANYMORE, COLE! I'M SICK OF SECRETS, I'M SICK OF QUESTIONS, I'M SICK OF NOT KNOWING WHAT THE HELL IS GOING ON!" she shouts from our bedroom.

I take a deep breath as I type my reply to Connor.

**Me: Can you take us?**

**Connor: Hell yeah. B there in 20**

I chuckle at that. Connor reminds me of Aubry sometimes, they're both nosey motherfuckers. Shit. I have to call Aubry.

# Chapter Twenty-Two
## ~Blake~

I fall into a reverie as Connor drives Cole and me toward Brian's house. I stare dumbly at the highway signs, which are my only indication as to where we're headed. I close my eyes to shut everything out and sag against the back seat of the four-door sedan, letting myself get lost in Common's lyrics coming through the speakers. A large hand stilling my bouncing leg snaps me out of my contemplation and I peel my eyes open to find Cole watching me intently.

"You okay?" he asks quietly.

Connor's eyes snap to mine in the rearview mirror and I nod at him before looking at Cole again, still nodding. He squeezes my knee before turning around again. I stare at the back of his head and idly fiddle with my necklace before clasping both hands together on my lap. I look at the clock in the middle of the car that reads 10:15 and just as I'm wondering how much longer we'll be on the road, Connor turns into a driveway. He lowers the window when we get to an iron gate and enters the code that opens it. As we drive up, my leg begins to bounce again on its own accord as I wring my hands together. Cole turns around and covers my hands with his, squeezing gently to affirm that I'm okay. I nod slowly in response.

I take a deep breath and gulp down my apprehension as Connor switches the engine off. Closing my eyes, I silently repeat *I can do this* before getting out of the car and taking Cole's hand as we follow Connor up the steps to the house. He knocks twice before an older lady in a French maid outfit opens it. I frown and tug Cole's arm, looking up at him in question as we walk past her. His replying smirk tells me he's seen her before and thought the same thing—*odd*. I've always loved that Cole and I can have a conversation with just our eyes. I'm not sure if that stems from knowing each other for so long or just the way we know each other.

Connor rubs his hands together and strides to the other side of the house as I look around at everything from the polished off-white marble floors that I can see practically see my reflection in, to the dual staircases on either side of the foyer. We trail behind him slowly, across a long corridor filled with family photos on either side of it. My eyes go from face to face in all of the photos until one catches my attention, making my heartbeat quicken. I let go of Cole's hand and walk toward the picture, willing my breathing to stabilize as I look at it in shock.

"Hey, what's wrong?" Cole whispers.

I look at him with my mouth hanging open before looking back at the photo of a woman that looks like she could be my twin. Standing beside her is an older lady with brown hair and sky blue eyes—Aunt Shelley. I clasp my hands over my face to contain any emotion from seeping through while taking a deep breath. Cole wraps his arms around me and pulls me toward him, and I let him hold me.

"That...that's Sh-Shelley," I whisper hoarsely and watch his eyebrows raise in surprise.

"Your aunt?" he asks with wide eyes.

I nod slowly in response, my mind still reeling over seeing my mother and my aunt, the aunt who took care of me for nine years. The one whose intentions I never had a reason to question before now. She was as alone as I was, sad even, hurt. I shake my head, slowly refusing to believe this is real. I shake it harder for good measure in hopes to wake up, until Cole holds both sides of my face and angles my head to look at him.

"I'm getting you the fuck out of here. Now," he growls with narrowed eyes. "CONNOR!"

"No, Cole!" I say loudly. "NO! I NEED TO KNOW, DAMMIT!"

"Blake, listen to me. LISTEN TO ME!" he says, shaking me by the shoulders when I try to walk past him. My eyes snap to his cold glare and I run through things I can tell him so he'll back off. Before I can say anything, he presses his lips roughly against mine, making the air rush out of my body. My chest is heaving when he backs away and before I have a chance to react, he scoops me into his arms and begins to stalk toward the exit.

I cling to his shoulders and look at Connor, who is now jogging toward us with a confused look on his face. I demand Cole to put me down—still looking at Connor—when I see three men dressed nicely trailing behind him.

"COLE!" The one with salt and pepper hair yells before they break off into a sprint toward us.

Cole turns around, fully facing them as he holds me tighter to his chest. "Fuck all of you!" He shifts so that he's holding my body with one hand. I contemplate getting on my feet but decide not to until he's done with his rant. When they reach us, Cole points at them with his other hand. First at the oldest man, Brian, my grandfather. Then at the man standing on one side of him that I don't know. "You lied to me! You fucking lied to me! You said you didn't know where she was all those years!"

I gasp, realizing that the other man is probably Cole's father, Camden. I squint my eyes and realize that it does look like him, although he looks different when he's on television. Still, he's definitely Cole and Aimee's father, and he does have a mixture of both of his kids in him.

"Brian, what the fuck is he talking about?" my father, Liam, shouts.

"Let the kid talk, Liam," Brian demands as he gestures for Cole to continue and raises an eyebrow. His gray eyes are thunderous as he looks at us impatiently.

Cole puts me down and rolls up the sleeves of his dress shirt before tucking me into his side and holding me there. I look at the three men, Brian, Liam, and the one I assume is Camden, Cole's father. The only one that doesn't look like he's visibly holding his breath is Brian.

"Blake saw a picture of her aunt inside! Her aunt and her mom posing together. What the fuck?" Cole exclaims loudly, throwing an arm up.

"Let's go inside and we can talk about it," Brian says, waving his right hand toward the house.

Connor looks at the three men and back at Cole and me before walking up to us and standing next to me. I feel his fingers brush my shaky hand before he places it in his, and I let him, thankful to have a cousin that takes my feelings into consideration.

"Explain it here. Explain it now, Grandpa. This fucking girl has been through enough! COLE has been through enough! They were kids! JUST KIDS! If somebody took Eli from me like that, I'd fucking kill them without thinking twice. I'd hunt them the fuck down. I wouldn't stop until I found my kid! EXPLAIN IT HERE BECAUSE I WANNA HEAR THIS SHIT TOO!" Connor yells loudly, his hand squeezing mine as he does.

Both Brian and Camden rub their foreheads as Liam stands with his arms crossed, waiting for the men to speak, I guess. I turn my head into Cole's body and breathe him in, reminding myself of what's important and who's important. Reminding myself that at the end of the day, these people are strangers to me and they don't matter. They never did. I sniffle back tears, making both Cole and Connor shift their bodies toward me and look down to make sure I'm okay. I wipe my face on Cole's shirt and let go of Connor's hand as I wiggle myself out of Cole's hold.

"I'm fine," I whisper to them, looking them both in the eye for assurance, before taking a step toward the men. Both Cole and Connor move with me, and it occurs to me that the two men standing behind me can take the men before me in a fight if it came to that. I close my eyes and pray it doesn't come to that, though. Liam's and Camden's eyes have been locked on me the entire time, both in amazement and apprehension, and I imagine it has to do with the fact that I look so much like my late mother.

"Speak," I say, crossing my arms in front of me and tilting my head at Brian in expectation. He chuckles and shakes his head in disbelief, looking from me to Liam and Camden. They all seem to agree on something as their mouths turn up for a second before they look back at me.

"I really didn't know where you were. I swear on that. I found out when Benny called trying to cut a deal with me," Brian says, shaking his head. "I would have looked for you."

"Why was I with Aunt Shelley and why is her picture in your house?" I demand.

Brian exhales before his mouth settles in a grim line. "She was my ex-wife, your grandmother. I had no idea she had you. I didn't know you were alive! She disappeared on me—I only knew she was alive because the kids would come over wearing things that I knew she had made for them; but she didn't want anything to do with me. I respected that and stayed away. I'd burned her enough times to make her suffer anymore," he responds quietly before taking out a pack of Benson & Hedges cigarettes from his pocket and lighting one up.

"Did you know she was sick? For YEARS she was sick! For YEARS she cried every night! For YEARS she talked about love and how you don't give up on real love. For years..." My broken voice trails off when my throat begins to tighten.

Cole places his hand on my shoulder and kisses my head, pleading with me to calm down. And in that moment I am so disgusted to be associated with these people, even if it's just by name, even if it's just by blood, that I'd do anything to erase the memories from that part of my life out of my head forever.

"Why are you two so fucking quiet?" Cole snaps.

I look up to see both Liam and Camden staring at us before ducking their heads. Brian steps forward, flicking his cigarette as he points an accusing finger at Liam.

"You fucking knew, you little bastard!" Brian says gruffly. "YOU MOTHERFUCKER!" he screams at Liam. "YOU KNEW WHERE SHELLEY WAS ALL ALONG!"

"Brian-" Liam starts before Brian's fist connects with his jaw, rendering him speechless.

I gasp just as Cole pushes me behind him, holding my arm with his left hand so I don't move. I sneak a look around him to watch Connor step forward and grab his grandfather. Brian looks at Connor in confusion.

"Grandpa, let me handle this," Connor says, pacifying his grandfather with a hand on his shoulder.

Brian shakes his head somberly and looks at Liam again. "You fucking knew where she was? YOU KNEW WHERE SHELLEY WAS THE ENTIRE TIME? WHERE YOUR OWN DAUGHTER WAS?"

"SHE WAS SAFE THERE, BRIAN!" Liam shouts back.

"SAFE MY ASS! WHO ELSE KNEW?" Brian demands.

Liam closes his eyes and takes a breath before opening them again. "I only knew when Blake was at Shelley's. I lost track of her when she was taken away from there because Mark wouldn't give me any information. Cam knew where Cole was, but never touched base with Maggie, so we didn't find out when Blake got there."

"Maggie? Our friend Maggie?" Brian growls. "And how could Mark tell you and not me?"

Liam shrugs. "Marky got one of guys not to kill the kids somehow but knew they'd go back for them if they were somewhere obvious. I knew they hadn't gotten killed, so I started asking him, following him. But like I said, Marky's smart, wouldn't leave trails. Cam wanted to set up a bank account for Cole, and Marky drafted everything for it. Maggie's information was there."

"You knew where I was all those years and you didn't even think of getting me? Of visiting me?" Cole asks, his voice barely a whisper.

"They would've killed you!" Camden grits. "If I had gone there, they would've killed you! As it is, Benny trailed everything back there looking for Blake, and look at what happened to Maggie then!" he continues.

"DON'T BLAME THIS ON BLAKE!" Cole screams, his breathing becoming ragged.

"I'm not blaming it on anyone but ourselves, Cole! It's nobody's fault but ours! I'm just letting you know what would've happened if they would've tracked you down!" Camden shouts back.

"Your wife was shot dead. My fucking baby girl was shot dead. Oh my fucking...did you kill Cory?" Brian spits at Liam. He shouts the question again, leaving the name rattling in my head for a second too long. I bite down on Cole's forearm to keep from making a sound. He snaps his arm from me and turns around quickly, searching my face.

I shake my head slowly. "Cory is my mom," I explain, my voice barely a whisper.

His jaw works as he narrows his eyes at me in contemplation, a look I know too well. Before I can react, he steps away from me, shooting me a quick warning glare before stomping past Brian and Connor and grabbing Liam by the throat.

"COLE!" Camden screams beside him as he grabs him by the shoulders. "This doesn't concern you!"

Cole lets go of Liam, pushing him back, making him tumble and splay onto the grass before he turns to glare at Camden. "DON'T FUCKING TELL ME WHAT DOESN'T CONCERN ME! ANYTHING THAT CONCERNS BLAKE CONCERNS ME!"

I shuffle my feet over quickly to where Cole is standing and pull on his with both my hands, begging him to step away from them, but he shrugs me off. "Back off, Blake! I'm gonna MAKE THEM understand that you are my ONLY concern! Stand over there!"

I clutch his arm again and look at him with wide eyes, then at Camden and Liam, who's dusting the grass off his pants. Brian and Connor are watching Cole in approval. My breathing begins coming in short bursts and my vision tunnels. When my hands weaken, I drop them from his arms and concentrate on breathing.

"Cole!" I hear Connor shout at a distance and suddenly feel arms holding me up.

"Babe, are you okay?" Cole calls out as I blink heavily, trying to concentrate on his eyes, his beautiful green eyes. I take one last deep breath, feeling my senses returning to me all at once as I sag against him.

"I'm fine," I whisper. "Did you kill her?" I ask, looking directly at Liam, who's standing beside us.

"NO! I would never do that! Benny was trying to shoot me in the arm when I went for my gun, and she stepped in," Liam explains. "I loved your mother."

"There were three shots. Three," I repeat, loud enough to hear my words over the thumping heart in my ears.

Liam casts his eyes down before he looks back at me. "The first shot hit your mother. The rest of the shots were aimed at me."

"But none hit you," I say, searching his body, even though I wouldn't be able to see a wound through his clothing.

"One did," he says, lifting his shirt and showing me the hole on his arm. "I'm sorry, Blake. But I had to keep you safe. Benny's been looking for you ever since you disappeared. If you had been with me, he would've found you and who knows what his revenge would've been to get back at me! I really did lose track when you left Shelley's. Mark wouldn't tell me where you were sent. I did trust him to keep you someplace safe. With everything that had happened between me and Benny, and me and Alex...there just wasn't a safe way of me getting to you without them finding out."

"You went on and got remarried and moved on with your life, though. And they *did* find me, " I supply bitterly, remembering how I felt when Dean filled me in on that piece of information.

Liam exhales. "I'm sorry that they did. And I did get married, but that doesn't mean I forgot about you."

"Do you have more kids?" I ask quietly.

"No, I don't," he responds in a whisper.

"Can we go inside?" Connor leads us toward the terrace, where Cole and I take a seat on the outdoor love sofa, while the others sit around us.

"Don't bleed on the fucking carpet," Brian says to Liam when he comes back with a pack of ice for his hand.

"You didn't get me ice?" Liam asks Brian.

"I don't know if I'm gonna clock you again, boy! Start yappin' about important shit and stop whining like a little bitch!" Brian responds before walking to the bar. "Drinks?" he asks, looking at Cole and me.

I nod feverishly, hoping for anything that can help calm my nerves. Brian comes over with two cups of gold liquid on the rocks. We thank him, as he hands it to us. I take a big gulp of it, feeling the burn in the back of my throat before I go into a coughing fit. Cole slaps my back and mumbles something about me always doing that, which is a total lie, but that's the least of my worries.

"Careful," Brian says with a smirk.

Liam sits down in front of us again after he serves himself a drink and I watch him anxiously, waiting for him to tell his story. When he looks at me and exhales, I shift to pay him closer attention.

"Benny had a plan and it backfired on him. He came into the house thinking he was gonna take me. Your mom got defensive and started screaming at him. She and Benny were close at one point, if you can believe that. Heartless bastard," he mutters under his breath before continuing, "I tried to keep her out of it, but your mom always did what she wanted when she wanted. Shit got out of control, shots were fired, Benny was drunk as fuck and one hit her." Liam's eyes grow sad as he recalls the night.

"Did you forget I met Benny?" I ask angrily. "He's a monster! He...he would've killed me without thinking twice. Shit, he TRIED to kill me!"

"If he wanted to kill you, he would've killed you, Blake," Liam says.

Cole gets up from his seat beside me and crouches down in front of Liam, looking directly at him. "You don't know what she's been through, so you don't get to talk to her like that. You don't get to sit here and defend the man that murdered her mother and almost killed her. You don't get to do anything. As the matter of fact, consider this a gift from me to you, because you don't get to speak to her ever again. She may have come from you, but she's nothing to you."

Liam's eyes widen as Cole's words seep in. "You can't keep me away from my own daughter!"

"WHY DIDN'T YOU FUCKING LOOK FOR HER? WHY DIDN'T YOU LOOK FOR HER WHEN SHE WENT OFF TO

COLLEGE, IF NOT AT MAGGIE'S? YOU'RE A FUCKING DEAD PRICK YOU'RE DEAD TO HER!" Cole screams, the veins in his neck more prominent the louder he gets.

I can only sit here staring blankly at the spectacle in front of me, refusing to side with my birth father in anything because at the end of the day, Cole is right. Liam didn't want me then, so it doesn't really matter now.

"And you," Cole says, turning around and pointing at Camden. "You're dead to me. My only family is Blake. PERIOD. Let's go."

I will myself to move, but can't. I'm still in shock, just staring.

"Baby, please get up," Cole whispers.

I blink at the men a couple of times before looking up at Cole, who is looking at them as well as he grinds his jaw. He tears his eyes off of them and looks down at me, noticing that I haven't moved. He tilts his head, his green eyes laced with pain, anger, and concern. "Do you need me to carry you, baby? Are you okay?"

"I think I'm okay," I whisper back, standing on shaky feet as I wave my goodbye to Liam.

"You're just gonna let him boss you around like that?" Liam asks, bewildered.

"He's right. Everything he said is right," I reply quietly with a shrug.

Liam raises an eyebrow. "I guess the similarities are only skin deep. Your mother would've never let me speak for her," he muses.

I grab Cole's forearm to keep him from moving forward and take a long, deep breath. "Thanks for that bit of information. Maybe if you had been there for me twelve years ago, I would've made a note of it. You weren't, though. I know nothing about you, nothing about my mother, and you know nothing about me, so you shouldn't make assumptions. If I had to make my assumptions about you, I would pretty much say what Cole already said about you. You're a coward for being too scared to go get his own daughter, a deadbeat for going on with your life with your new family not giving her a second thought, and a loser for even pretending that you missed me to begin with. So yeah, I can speak for myself, but I don't have anything nice to say to you. And since the people that DID raise me taught me how to be a lady, I was going to let you off the hook. Now that you got me started though, you wanna get to know me? Fuck you, because the only man I need in my life is the one standing beside me, like he always has been."

I grab Cole's hand before Liam or anybody can say another word and pull him toward the door where we came from, glaring at Camden as I pass him. I stop in front of Brian and examine his face, his glossy eyes, and take a breath.

"Maybe we can get to know each other someday," I offer.

He smiles warmly. "You're always welcome here, baby girl," he says before pulling me into a hug. "Don't let him fool you, your pops did miss you. I'll get to the bottom of that, but I'm glad you put him in his place. Don't believe everything you hear, love. Not even from him. Not even from Shelley. I did try, I did look for her—I sent her flowers with those kids every time I knew they were going over there. She just refused them. Love always tries, and I never stopped."

Tears form in my eyes as I nod at him, thinking of Shelley's sadness over her lost love. I take a breath, blinking, and signal at Connor to get us out of there. When we walk through the corridor again, I pause to look at all of the photos, paying close attention to all of them in detail. I run a trembling hand over the one of my mother with Aunt Shelley, or Grandma Shelley. Cole hugs me from behind and coos sweetly in my ear about how beautiful they were, making me turn around and sob into his shirt as he embraces me.

"This is too much for one person," I muffle against his chest.

"I know, baby. I know," he says quietly as he finger combs my hair.

# Chapter Twenty-Three
## ~Blake~

"So, what do you wanna do for you birthday?" Becky asks in the middle of our conversation about baby bedding.

I purse my lips and switch the phone to my other ear so I can hold it with my shoulder. "I don't know. Nothing. Take a vacation. Tan. I really don't know," I reply with a shrug, making me drop the phone.

"...not know?" Becky asks when I put the phone back up to my ear.

"I don't know, Becks, really. It's not a huge deal, just another birthday, you know I've never really celebrated them anyway."

"Yeah, but you're over that. Maybe you can actually act like a grown up and have a party this year," she suggests perkily, making me laugh.

"Seriously?" I ask with an eye roll, even though she can't see me.

"Yes, seriously! You have never had a party!" she pouts.

I groan. "Becky! We had parties all the time!"

"No, we didn't! We cut a freaking cake between the six of us! That's not a party! I'm talking balloons, invitations, ACTUAL GUESTS!"

I laugh, despite myself. "I'll consider it. I'll look at invitations online or something."

"You can't plan your own party!" she squeals.

"Then why the hell are you telling me any of this?" I ask, annoyed, as she laughs on the other end of the line.

We go back and forth about the party for about an hour, until I finally get her to hang up. She and Greg are staying here for the weekend, and my birthday just so happens to land on Saturday, so that should be fun...or not. I finish doing the dishes before getting my laptop out to search for information on the Bar exam. I'm considering taking it in a couple of weeks since I was already signed up for it, even though I know I'll probably fail since I haven't studied. I just don't care anymore; my heart's not in it like it was before.

Cole has tried to be home a lot more lately and has done some of his interviews through Skype, which is pretty cool. He interviews somebody in our office room, while I watch on in our living room. As I'm dusting the desk where he sits, I spot a little post-it with my name on it. Picking it up curiously, I laugh as I read it.

*B, thanks for picking up my desk! I love you, your future husband.*

Ever since I left the hospital, he's been telling everybody that I'm his wife, and I keep correcting him. So he's decided to call himself my future husband instead. The look on people's faces when he says that term is pretty funny, but the look on his when they ask to look at my engagement ring is priceless. It always leaves him in a jam, which he gets out of fairly quickly. Usually by making up some crazy story about how we had to take it to the jeweler to resize or how I lost it while I was doing dishes.

The ringing of my phone in the other room snaps me out of my distraction and I jog to pick it up. I consider not answering when I see that Dean is calling, but figure I might as well.

"Hello?"

"Hey, chick. Long time no hear," Dean says and I hear him inhale a drag of his cigarette.

"Yeah. What's up?"

"Hmm. Don't wanna talk?" Dean asks, reading my thoughts.

"Not really," I reply bluntly.

He exhales. "Nothing's up. Just wanted to check up on you. Heard you saw your dad and shit."

"Yep, that happened. Fun times," I deadpan.

He laughs. "You mad at me?"

"Nope, nothing to be mad about. I just...I don't really want to make Cole mad...again," I explain. "I know you don't get it and I know he doesn't understand our friendship, but you realize if I had to choose between you-"

"You'd pick him, I know," he offers. "Nothing wrong with that, chick. I'm just looking out for you."

I sigh. "I know."

"I heard your birthday's coming up," he says, changing the subject.

"You hear a lot of things," I reply.

"I do."

"All right, Dean, I gotta go, but maybe we can talk soon?" I ask hopefully. I just have to make sure I don't keep Cole in the dark about our conversations and I know he'll be fine with them. Baby steps, though.

"Hey," he whispers loudly before I can hang up. "I've been following Benny around, listening to his conversations, that sorta shit. You need to be careful, pay attention to your surroundings, pay attention to the people around you. Have those cops come back to talk to you?"

"Yeah, but they left me alone when I told them I really didn't remember anything," I whisper back.

"That's not why," he whispers harshly. "I can't talk right now, but be careful with those cops! And pay attention to your surroundings! I'm following him everywhere, but still. Shit, I gotta go."

"WHAT? DEAN!" I shout at the dead line.

My mouth hangs open as I stare at the blank screen. Noise coming from the other side of the door makes my eyes snap up. I make out moving shadows in the space under the door and gulp down my apprehension as I take a step closer to it. My heavy breathing accelerates when the doorknob turns a couple of times and a man mumbles a low curse. Finally reaching the peephole, I tiptoe up and lean against the door, squinting to make out the tall figure on the other side. He crouches down and sorts through a brief case before standing back up. I let out a shaky breath when our eyes meet and sag against the door before unlocking and opening it.

"What's wrong?" Cole asks with a confused look.

I shake my head. "What happened to your keys?"

"I don't know what the hell I did with them! I just had them in my hands and now I can't find them anywhere!" he replies, flustered.

I lead him inside and take in his nice business attire, navy blue pants, a white long sleeve shirt, gold tie, and a navy blue jacket hanging over his forearm. My eyes wander over his face, his defined jaw, his plump lips, his ever so slightly crooked nose, his beautiful, yet tired, green eyes, his slicked back growing hair. I trail back down his face, licking my lips at the sight of his slightly parted lips.

"Are you going to let me fuck you or are you just going to do it all on your own, standing from there?" he asks, making me smile.

"Nah, you can do it," I reply with a laugh as I wrap my arms around him before kissing him deeply.

"I missed you," he whispers against my hair as he holds me tight.

"You saw me this morning," I say with a smile.

"So?"

I shake my head and let go of him, still smiling, and walk over to the kitchen to serve our food as Cole gives me the details on his day. As I listen to him talk excitedly about the convention he's been attending in a local hotel this week, I find myself replaying my own day. All of my days are the same—I wake up, eat, read, help Aimee study most days, and wait for Cole. That's it. My life has fallen into this unexciting routine that I never imagined for myself. Everybody keeps telling me to give it time, that I can still do what I wanted to do before all of this, but I don't know if I want to. I'm not sure if I can. But what do you do when everything you've always pictured yourself doing suddenly seems stupid?

"What's wrong, babe?" Cole asks, bringing me out of my daydream.

"Nothing, why?"

He puts his fork down and wipes his mouth before holding his hands out in front of him and signaling me to give him mine, which I do.

"What's going on?" he asks, concerned as he draws circles on the backs on my hands.

My shoulders slump and I let out a breath, looking down before replying. "I just don't know who I am anymore. I don't know who I want to be or what I want to do. The whole becoming a lawyer thing seems dumb to me now. I know I can't help the people I wanted to help originally, because the people that have been wronged will always be wronged, and the system won't change that."

My eyes flutter to his, fully expecting him to be giving me an incredulous look. He surprises me by smiling at me instead. "You have time. You have the rest of your life to figure out what you want to do. I'll help you, we all will. You can still take the Bar, though. You worked hard to get to law school and you worked hard to get through it, baby. You shouldn't give up just because some bastards decided to fuck with your plans. What about social work? You can figure out how you can help kids that have been through similar things that we went through. There are a bunch of kids that get taken from their homes every day. Maybe not kidnapped, but taken away from terrible parents."

I smile as I listen to all of his suggestions, thankful that he's willing to help me find what's right for me. I don't know what I did to deserve this man in my life, but I'm glad I have him. We spend the rest of our night on the computer, researching social workers and attorneys that work with them until I decide that I am going to take the Bar exam, and I'm going to pass it.

The next morning as Cole and I shower together, he tells me about some sports gala we have to go to next week. He suggests I call Becky and talk to her about wardrobe since she's gone in the past and will be there as well. Once he leaves for the day, I start splitting up the box of memories that I have. I leave the things I actually want to remember and look at in one, and toss the things I don't care about in the other. I sort through the photos I got from Aunt Shelley and examine all of the faces carefully. I empty out one of the manila envelopes on the floor, seeing her family photos in a different light now that I know they're my family too. One by one I put them in the box of things I don't want, pausing when I hear three loud knocks on the door.

As I unfold myself from the floor, I idly wonder if it's Spencer telling me he's going to lunch. Instead I see a man wearing a fitted black T-shirt with brown scruffy hair. His hazel eyes look serious when they finally look from the floor to the peephole, and I wonder what the hell he's doing here. Opening the door slowly, I stick my head out to look around and see Spencer at the end of the hall.

"What are you doing here?" I ask with wide eyes.

"Can I come in?" he asks, tucking his hands in his pockets.

My eyes trace the black outline of the tattoo on his left arm, squinting as I try to figure out what it is. Seemingly reading my mind, he takes his hand out of his pocket and turns his arm over, giving me full view of a crest with three lions in the middle. I nod in appreciation, making him chuckle.

"I don't think Cole would like it if you and I were alone in our home," I respond.

"Don't blame him," Dean says with a shrug. "I'll be quick. I feel bad about leaving you hanging like that."

"Just talk."

"Alex freaked the fuck out after you left and when he found out what happened...what Benny did to you, Alex kicked him out," Dean starts, nodding in confirmation as my mouth drops open. "Yeah. He said he doesn't want him around, period. So I've been trailing Benny and...I dunno, Blake, I just have a really bad feeling about this shit."

"Dean, why do you work with these people? Why? You said they were family, but why?" I ask quietly.

"My mom married Jamie O'Brien when I was little, chick. I don't know anything else," he says with a shrug. "This is my life. Alex and Benny were long gone by the time I got to their house, but still...they're family."

I raise an eyebrow. "What about your sister?"

"Sandra's safe," he replies quietly. "My other sister..." his voice trails off.

"She's the girl? The one you couldn't help?" I whisper.

He nods, his eyes looking grave, as if I opened up a wound he thought he'd covered.

"I'm sorry," I whisper.

"It was a long time ago," he responds.

"What does it have to do with me though? Why does Benny still want to get to me?"

When he exhales I catch a whiff of the cigarette he smoked before getting here. "Word is, Liam screwed Benny over and took the money. Benny wanted revenge and you were it...*are* it, really."

"Liam doesn't want me. He doesn't care about me," I say with an eye roll.

The side of Dean's mouth turns up. "Trust me, chick, he wants you. He raised you for four years—you don't have memory of that? That man loves you, B. I'm not a father, so I don't have firsthand experience, but even as an uncle, I know that once you have a kid under your wing, you're not gonna do wrong by them."

"Not everybody feels that way."

Dean shrugs. "True."

"Whatever," I mumble. "Are we done?"

Dean searches my face before tucking my hair behind my ear. "Yeah, we're done." My breath hitches when he leans in close to my ear. "Don't trust those cops, Blake. And be careful with your guard dogs."

I look from Dean's serious eyes toward Spencer at the end of the hall and shake my head, exhaling a shaky breath before saying goodbye to Dean. I head back inside my place and lock the door behind me. A cloud of doubt consumes me for the rest of the day as I think about everybody in my life and how little I can trust the ones I thought I was safe with. I decide to bury my thoughts in my law books yet again and forget about the world around me.

# Chapter Twenty-Four

## ~ COLE ~

I pace around the bedroom taking a series of deep breaths before deciding to wake her up. I don't know why I'm so nervous. Actually, I know exactly why I'm so nervous. My plan could backfire on me completely, and if it does, I'll never forgive myself for it. Blake thinks I've been gone on business a lot lately, and I have been but not all of it has been business. Nobody told me remodeling a house was going to be so damn difficult. Well, nobody other than Aubry and what the hell does he know about remodeling homes? Apparently more than I do. He should've been a damn architect instead of going into advertising.

I close my eyes and relish the silence, the calm before the storm, if you will, before striding over to Blake and kneeling down beside her.

"Baby," I whisper, brushing her long unruly hair away from her face, "you need to wake up."

Her replying grumble brings a smile to my face, and I repeat the gesture a couple of times before placing a kiss on her nose.

"What?" she asks, clearly annoyed to be losing sleep, and I can't really blame her. I kept her up way past her bedtime last night.

"Wake up, babe. It's your birthday," I say quietly.

Her long lashes flutter open, and she pins me with that sultry gaze that does inexplicable things to my insides. As much as I'd love to continue my exploration of last night and find out how many times I can make her come in a row, I decide to stand and give her enough room to get on her feet.

I consider going into her closet and picking out an outfit for her, but walk to the kitchen instead because I don't want to start a fight this early in the morning and definitely not on her birthday. Once the coffee is made, I take out a bowl and start making her favorite pancakes. As I'm flipping them, I hear the door of our room open and I turn around to watch her stumble out, still looking half asleep but cute as hell with her wet hair and short summer dress.

"Morning, birthday girl," I greet her with a smile that turns into a laugh when she glares at me.

"Thanks for breakfast," she says quietly, still pretending not to be impressed by my birthday wish, even though her eyes are smiling. I feel her eyes on me as I scribble down a little note for her. When I'm finished with it, I read it over twice for good measure:

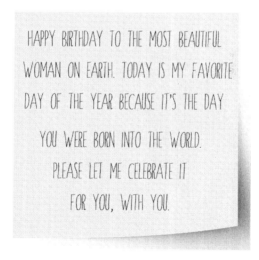

HAPPY BIRTHDAY TO THE MOST BEAUTIFUL WOMAN ON EARTH. TODAY IS MY FAVORITE DAY OF THE YEAR BECAUSE IT'S THE DAY YOU WERE BORN INTO THE WORLD. PLEASE LET ME CELEBRATE IT FOR YOU, WITH YOU.

I place the note on top of the counter and pull her close to me, looking her in the eye before I kiss her thoroughly.

"Eat, I'm going to get a few things for us."

Once I'm in my closet, I grab a bag and pack the clothes I'd set aside for the weekend before quickly sorting through the drawer where I keep my watches and grabbing one. I go into Blake's closet and grab a handful of her underwear, not caring which ones I choose since she won't be wearing or keeping any intact anyway. I get two of her dresses from the hangers and pack those as well, along with a pair of shorts, T-shirt, and bathing suit, just in case. I don't get any of her bathroom things, I figure mine will do, and worse case, we can always take a trip to Target.

When I turn around, I find Blake leaning against the door with her arms crossed and a huge smile on her face. My eyes trail her body slowly, from her cute toes in the open toe wedge sandals she's wearing. I continue up her calves and pause where the hem of her dress meets the top of her knees, visualizing myself slowly sucking and planting wet kisses past that. My heart beats faster in my chest and my breathing quickens as I stride toward her. I caress her cheek with one hand and bring it lower, brushing and parting her bottom lip with my thumb as I stare longingly into her clouded eyes. Her tongue darts out and she takes my thumb into her mouth, making my breath hitch.

I throw the duffel bag on the floor and run my hands along both sides of her body, reaching behind her and grabbing a handful of her ass while I lift her to me. She wraps her legs around me, throwing her arms around my neck before pulling my hair at the nape of my neck. I groan, closing my eyes as she bites down on my bottom lip before sliding her tongue into my mouth. She squirms in my hold as my grip tightens and I take a step forward, crushing her back onto the wall behind her. Our mouths break apart long enough for us to look at each other and relay the weight of our love, our need, our lust, before our tongues meet again in a wild dance.

Placing the majority of her weight on the wall behind, I place my hands on her toned, silky thighs before sliding them under her hitched dress where I massage over her thin cotton underwear. I nuzzle against her neck and relish in the quickness in her breath, placing soft kisses along her jaw while drawing circles over her core. She squirms, arching her back and pushing into my hard on, cutting all coherent thoughts from my head.

"Want me to take you here or on the bed?" I manage to groan out through an intake of breath.

"I don't care," she whimpers. "I want you."

Using my left arm as a bench under her ass, I back away and deftly unbuckle my belt with the other hand, quickly lowering my zipper.

"Take off my pants," I murmur against her lips, lowering the V of her dress and sucking a nipple into my mouth, making her gasp loudly. "Take them off," I demand as I nip her softly, making her groan.

"Can't," she pants. "Can't do it."

I let go of her breast with a pop and place my face in front of hers—her eyes look as wild as I feel. And even though I had her last night and the night before that, and many nights before that; in this moment, I can't think of anybody I've wanted more than this woman. I know there never will be anyone else because she's it for me, always has been. I place both hands below her and walk to the bed, throwing her back on the mattress, kicking off my shoes and lowering my pants quickly before springing free from my boxers. She sits up on her knees licking her lips, looking at me through hooded eyes as she crooks her finger for me to step toward her. My heart pounds loudly against my chest as I walk up to the bed. The side of my mouth turns up when she places her head against my chest, right under my chin where she reaches as she kneels up completely. I dip my head to kiss her lips, but she stops me by placing a finger on my lips and shaking her head and mischievously bites down on her pouty bottom lip. Her fingers slide over my shoulders and down my body. The way she admires my body makes me glad I hit the gym so damn hard, even though I know Blake doesn't care about any of that shit. When her small hand grips my dick and squeezes, I feel the air leave my body and rush back.

She leans forward on the bed, placing her weight on her on her elbows and leaving her ass exposed as she looks at me through her fluttering lashes, still holding my cock. I throw my head back when she draws circles around it with her tongue before taking some of me into her mouth. She continues to rock her body to and fro, my dick hitting the back of her throat every time she leans toward me. I fist a handful of her hair, trying to control myself from holding her face onto my dick, which is hard to do when I feel her hot mouth on me one second and going away the next. I take hold of her, sliding slowly out of her lips and back her up, pulling the hem of her dress and throwing it to the other side of the room to leave her completely exposed, only wearing a tiny pair of blue panties. I slide my fingers into them from the top, scrunching them in hand and ripping them off.

"COLE!" she yelps, looking at me in disbelief.

I return with a wolfish smile before pressing my lips roughly against hers. "Turn around," I say gruffly. "You taunted me for a little too long with the view of your perfect round ass and I want to enjoy the full thing."

"Wha..." she begins, but I cut her statement short by grabbing her by the hips and pulling her close before flipping her body so that she's facing our wooden headboard.

As she positions herself on all fours, I take advantage and bring my hand around her, sticking my pointer and middle finger into my mouth before lowering it to her clit. She lets out a low moan as I rub against her before sticking them inside her and bringing them back out, repeating the process a couple of times until she arches her back and moans loudly, letting me know that she's close. I take my hand away from her, placing one on her shoulder and the other on my dick to lead it inside of her before I slide into her slowly.

"Cole," she gaps.

"Yeah," I rasp before picking up the pace.

She yells out my name again as she clenches around me, her desire coating me more than I already was.

"Shit, baby," I growl, letting go of her shoulder to rope her hair and pull it back toward me so that I can lean forward and suck on her earlobe.

"Oh my GOD!" she shrieks as I pound into her quickly, feeling my balls tighten with every thrust.

"I'm gonna come, Blake. I'm gonna come," I groan. "Are you ready?"

"YES! YES!" she screams, making me grip her hair tighter.

"Tell me you're mine, Blake," I murmur, feeling her shiver at my breath against her ear.

"I'm yours," she pants.

"Fuck yes," I growl, dropping my hand from her waist and bring it around her to pluck her nipples, taking her over the edge.

"Only mine," I groan as I unload inside her while she screams profanities.

She sags against the bed when I let go of her hair. I push inside her one last time, before leaning down and kissing her neck and down her back.

"Did I hurt you, baby?" I whisper against her spine.

"No," she says, muffled against the sheets. "I think I'll survive."

I smile against her and slide out, picking her up and walking her to the bathroom.

"Shit, we're so late!" I mutter when I look at the time on the nightstand.

"So worth it," she replies against my chest. "Thank you for helping me start off my birthday with a bang."

I give her a confused look because of her choice of words, but then smile widely, realizing that maybe my girl is finally letting go of her tainted past.

"I love you," I say in response as I kiss her head.

"And I love you," she says. "Only you," she continues, sighing against me.

# Chapter Twenty-Five
## ~Blake~

After the tenth huff and eye roll, I let Cole cover my eyes with a blindfold.

"Thank fuck!" he says in an annoyed tone once the bandana is secured on my face.

"Shut up," I reply before sagging into the seat of his Escalade.

"Just relax, baby. We'll be there before you know it," he says, turning on the ignition and pulling out of our parking spot, after voicing that he had to wait for Spencer to trail behind us.

He turns up the radio and laughs when I groan at his choice of station, which is ESPN radio, as usual.

"Can you let work go for one day and listen to music like a regular person?" I complain.

"I was getting to that!" he says with a laugh before changing to some dance-y Nas song that I immediately start to bob my head to, picturing him doing the same thing.

When Ludacris comes on the track, Cole starts rapping along and for the remainder of the song, I forget that I have my eyes covered and stop trying to figure out where we're going. I have my suspicions, though. The last time Cole blindfolded me like this was years ago. We went to a Bed and Breakfast, and with all the little hints that Becky and Aimee have been dropping lately I think he may be proposing to me soon. I smile as I think about the romantic gesture and how lovely it would be for him to take me back there and propose in a place that means so much to me. That was the first time we spent the night together in every way, and warmth fills me at the thought.

"Are we far?" I venture to ask after the fifth rap song plays.

"Not too far, no," he replies taking my hand in his and placing a kiss over the top of it before lacing his fingers through mine and placing it on his lap.

I take a breath and tuck my feet under me, tapping my feet together before I sigh in boredom again. When the song switches to an R&B song I've never heard I stop tapping my feet and smile at the soothing voice coming from the speakers. My smile broadens when Cole kisses my hand again and starts to serenade the beautiful words to me, happy tears filling my eyes. He raises his voice even louder, making me giggle as I picture how he must look. We reach a red light as the song comes to an end and I find myself pouting, which he laughs at before leaning in for a kiss.

"What song was that?" I ask, smiling against his lips.

He backs away with a chuckle, eyes twinkling before he winks at me. "Adorn. Apparently I can give Miguel a run for his money."

I laugh along, but make no reply. As much as I loved that he sang it, Cole cannot give a professional singer a run for his money...period.

"You definitely get an A for effort," I reply, biting down on my lip before falling into a fit of uncontrollable laughter when he starts poking and tickling my side.

We banter for a while, before Cole turns on an unpaved road and announces that we've reached our destination. He lets go of my hand and unties my bandana, letting it fall to my lap. I blink rapidly to clear the tiny dots from my vision, knitting my eyebrows together as I look at the deserted roads around us, trying to figure out where we are. My eyes stay trained on the profile of his face as he pulls onto a dirt road, admiring his golden skin and the way his turned up mouth showcases the dimple on his cheek. When I see him furrow his eyebrow at whatever is in front of us, I turn my attention and body forward, gasping loudly as my hands fly to cover my mouth.

"Oh my God," I mutter under my breath as water pools my eyes before I look at him. "Where are we?" I whisper.

He gives me a small smile, placing the car in park. "You know where we are," he says, tilting his head.

"But how?" I ask, still at a loss for words.

"With a lot of work and a whole lotta love," he replies as he unbuckles his seatbelt and jumps out of the truck.

I place my hands over my rapidly beating heart, trying to bury the conflicted feelings that threaten to overpower my happiness. I turn my gaze slowly back to the red barn house before me, surrounded by the meadow that we used to play in as children, and smile as tears trickle down my cheeks. I wipe them away quickly and take a breath when Cole opens my door and gestures me to step out. Before my feet hit the ground, he scoops me up and swings me in his arms, making me squeal and giggle against his chest.

"Let's go inside," he says excitedly, walking toward the house.

He sets me down in front of the four white wooden steps and holds my hand, walking me toward it before letting go and taking a familiar looking mint blue box with a white ribbon out of his pocket and handing it to me. My eyes widen and my heart flutters as I untie the ribbon and open it to find a house key on it. After tracing the key with my finger, I look up to find him watching me with naked amusement.

"Thank you," I say, shaking my head and smiling before leaning up on my tiptoes and pressing my lips against his.

"Anything for you," he replies cordially as he takes the key from me and opens the door.

Stepping in, I close my eyes and inhale the rich scent of wood that fills my nose, before opening them back up and looking around at the cozy living room.

"It has three bedrooms, so it's not huge but we can always add to it," he offers as I look around with a smile plastered on my face.

I take in the mostly bare white walls that surround us, with the exception of a fire place on the right side. I walk over to it and take in the smiling faces in the frames that adorn the mantel. Pictures of us as teenagers with our friends, with Maggie, in the house, at the lake, in the Taco Bell parking lot, on the high school football field, in our high school graduation. I continue exploring, walking toward the hallway to the right side and stepping into the first room, which is completely empty.

"I figured you should have a say in what we do with this one," he says behind me.

I nod and walk to the room across from it, poking my head in and opening the door to find two desks, one white and one dark wood.

"We can work from here when we wanna escape the world," he offers and again, I nod before I step out and walk past a guest bathroom and toward the last door.

My breath hitches when I open the door to the master bedroom, and I find a beautiful, yet simple king size bed low to the ground, with a beautiful white upholstered headboard behind it. To my right is an antique vanity with a round mirror and a small stool, and beyond that is a closet. I walk over to the closet first, finding a T-shirt hanging and a pair of worn shoes on the floor. I look over my shoulder and raise an eyebrow at Cole, who is leaning against the doorframe with his arms crossed over his chest watching me closely. I walk to the bathroom next and smile at the sight of my favorite shampoo and body wash. The same color toothbrushes we have at our place are on an iron-looking holder, and white fluffy towels are placed on a rack by the shower. I can't help but love the simplicity of it, all of it.

"Who built this?" I ask curiously when I turn and walk back toward him.

His mouth twists into a wry smile. "Not me, if that's what you're asking." He chuckles. "I hired a company. I told them what I wanted, though. I figured you would appreciate that it's not huge. Seems more homey, I think. Do you like it?"

"Do I like it?" I ask, bewildered. "Cole, I freaking LOVE it! This is...it's everything." My voice is barely a whisper as I finish the last part. I never thought I would feel such peace coming back here, not after everything, especially not after everything that's happened recently.

"We've been working on it for a while. I wanted it to be done for my birthday, actually..." he starts, trailing off before finishing. I lean into him, wrapping my arms around him and placing my head on his chest contentedly.

"Thank you," I whisper. "So much."

He wraps his arms around me and kisses the top of my head before pulling back and brushing my cheek with his thumb.

"Anything, baby," he says, smiling as he taps the tip of my nose and leads me back out to the living room. "You haven't seen the kitchen yet."

Movement catches my eye as I step over the threshold between the living room and the kitchen area, and I squeeze Cole's hand in apprehension.

A loud gasp escapes me when "SURPRISE!" is yelled, followed by pink confetti tossed at me from all different directions. My jaw unhinges and my eyes dart to the people I love that are standing in front of me. And I forget about the history of secrets that plague this house because it is once again a place of happiness for me. When I tear my gaze from their faces, I notice the pink "Happy Birthday, Princess" banner that hangs over the white kitchen cabinets and the sprinkled cupcakes on the table in the center, and I'm transported back twenty-three years.

Back to the day when ringing gunshots woke me up. My breathing shallows as I stare blankly at the cupcakes, envisioning the pink Hello Kitty alarm clock clearly on my nightstand. Running down the stairs and passing the very same banner that greets my blurry eyes now, the blood on the cupcakes, on the floor, on my clothes. My mother's lifeless gray eyes burning a hole through mine as large, loud men yell back and forth. My father being carried away over someone's shoulder and Mark's kind eyes and arms taking me away from it all. Taking me from one dark place to another. I blink the memory away and look back into the green orbs that have been my one constant in times of both despair and happiness, and I'm reminded of the reason I'm here. Aunt Shelley's words of wisdom ring true in my head, and I'm thankful that unlike me, Cole has never second-guessed us. He's never questioned whether or not we were better off apart because even during the years that I tried to keep my distance, he was there. Those truthful eyes that I've held on to during the most difficult times in my life have never left me. He's never left me, and I know he never will.

My daydream is interrupted by various arms wrapping around me and kisses on my cheek.

"Happy Birthday, Blakey!" Becky says quietly as she presses her cheek against mine. Greg and Aubry give us a group hug as Aimee takes my hands in front of me, and Cole stands off to the side smiling and letting them shower me with attention.

"Thank you...so much. You guys..." I say, failing to create a coherent sentence through my emotion.

"All right, all right, give her space!" Cole says, his voice dripping in amusement as he walks toward us and pulls me out of their circle.

He turns me by the shoulders so I can see my friends and take in the decor again, before leaning into me. "Do you like your kitchen?" he murmurs against the spot right below my ear.

"Yes," I reply with a shiver.

"And the decorations are okay?" Cole asks quietly, concerned.

I nod rapidly. "Yes, they're perfect," I whisper.

He turns me around again, signaling our audience with his head before looking down at me and brushing my bottom lip with the pad of his thumb, his long stare rocking every inch of my body. Aubry walks up to us and gives me a hard wet kiss on the cheek. He walks off while laughing at my disgusted grunt.

"Why do you always have to be the funny guy?" Cole asks Aubry, who's still laughing, making the rest of us laugh along.

He takes a deep breath as he takes both my hands. His eyes grow more serious with each second that passes. "Blake, if you don't like any of this let me know."

"I love it! Please stop saying that already! It's getting annoying," I reply, cracking a smile.

His lips twitch and he begins to lower his body, making my eyes bug out of my face and my breath halter when he settles on one knee. New tears pool my eyes and my hands swing to my mouth, covering it before a throaty sob escapes me when I see him reach for a little black velvet box on the table.

He takes a breath, his green eyes twinkling as he looks at me. "Blake, I feel like I've spent an eternity declaring my love for you and maybe I have. Hell, I'm sure I've been doing that for centuries. And as difficult as you can be, as stubborn as you are, and as big of a pain in my ass as you are, I wouldn't want to spend any of my time in any lifetime chasing after anybody else. You're it for me. You always have been and always will be. I can't picture myself loving anybody but you, there's nobody else for me. You are the most fierce, selfless, caring, compassionate, and loving human being I know. And I wanted to do this—build this house, throw this party—for you. So that we can replace the not-so-great memories you have with new ones, better ones, happier ones. I want to spend the rest of my life making happy memories with you. You're the love of my life, my best friend, my soul mate, my partner in crime. Blake Brennan, will you do me the incredible honor of adding wife to that list?" he asks in a hopeful voice.

Sobs rake through my body once he finishes, and my eyes drop from his to the ring he's holding in his hand, which I can't even make out through my tears. I look back into his eyes, nodding furiously, but begin to wail when I try to voice my response. I hear, but don't fully register the wild cheers coming from our friends, our family. I continue to sob, looking from his face to the twinkling diamond ring and back to his face.

"No pressure," Cole says with a chuckle, looking toward our friends and back to me.

I finally gather my wits and shout, "YES! OH MY GOD! YES!" Extending my shaky left hand to him, he carefully places the ring on my finger. I wipe my eyes swiftly and admire the three stones on the platinum band, more tears trickling down my face, even though I'm smiling as I remember our discussion about the three stones and what they stand for.

Cole places a kiss on the ring and stands smiling down at me, letting go of my hands and grabbing both sides of my face. "I love you. To the moon and back, baby," he says before crashing his lips against mine.

"I love you too. So much," I whisper, still crying against his lips, giving him one last kiss.

"Let me see the ring!" Becky squeals as we break apart.

"Oh great, here we go," Cole mumbles under his breath.

"Shut up!" she says, slapping his arm and pulling my hand toward her.

"Holy shit!" she exclaims, wide eyed. "You did good, Cole!"

Cole chuckles and nods his head in appreciation as Greg and Aubry step forward to look at the ring.

"The boy did good!" Greg says in agreement.

"Shit, it only cost him-" Aubry starts but is cut short by Cole's glare.

"It's beautiful, Blake," Aimee chimes in before hugging me from the side. "I'm so happy we're going to be sisters—officially."

I smile at her and give her a kiss on the cheek before going around and doing the same to every single one of them.

"You deserve it, Cowboy," Greg says as he pulls me into a bear hug and keeping me there.

"You do," Becky agrees with a smile as she steps toward us, her bulging belly stopping in front of me. I smile down at it and place a hand on either side, feeling at peace and genuinely happy for the first time since I saw her pregnant. I gasp, jumping slightly when I feel movement on my right hand.

"That was the baby?" I whisper in amazement.

Becky nods quickly and smiles. "She keeps doing that."

"She?" I ask surprised.

"He," Greg corrects beside me.

I look back and forth between them, confused. "So you don't know yet?"

"Nah, we're going to find out when she delivers," Greg says. "But it's definitely a boy!"

Becky rolls her big blue eyes. "Gregory, we're not going to talk about this again!"

I laugh and shake my head at my crazy friends before rubbing Becky's belly a couple of times and walking back to my fiancé.

I sigh contently on his chest, leaning into his hold when he places his chin on my head. "Was that epic enough for you?" he asks quietly.

I back away from him and look up, holding his face in my hands. "That, Mr. Murphy, is what I call beyond epic."

He beams at me before dipping his face to mine and sucking my bottom lip into his mouth. "Hm. I can't wait 'til these people leave. I haven't had sex with a fiancée before."

A laughed gasp escapes me and I slap his chest playfully. "Cole!"

"What? It's true—I gotta take advantage of that! I hear once you have a wife, the sex cuts down...by a lot," he says with a shrug, chuckling when I narrow my eyes at him.

# Chapter Twenty-Six
~Blake~

As it turns out, even a small three-bedroom home cannot keep our clan away, and they end up deciding to stay over. While we're thrilled to spend time with them, especially with Greg and Becky since we don't get to see them often, trips to Wal-Mart for air mattresses is not how we envisioned spending the night. Not sleeping in our bedroom is also not how we imagined we would spend our engagement night, but since Becky is pregnant, we didn't think it would be right for her to sleep on a sucky air mattress on the floor.

I sigh loudly, looking around at the mess we have to clean up and wondering if Cole and I are spending the night again or heading back to Chicago with everyone else.

"You're not cleaning this up," Cole raps beside me, making me jump.

"I didn't know you were awake," I reply, turning my body toward him and caressing his arm.

He gives me a lopsided smile. "I just woke up. How can you be so pretty in the morning?" he muses as his eyes scan my face.

"I'm not," I groan, throwing my head back on the mattress. "This bed sucks."

He chuckles. "You are," he replies as he covers my body with his, opening my thighs with his and settling his weight between my legs. "You're the most beautiful creature ever made...and you're right, this bed sucks ass."

"You're just saying that because you want to have sex," I say with a laugh as I look at him, thinking the same about him.

He tilts his head as he regards me. "Nah, we're going to have sex anyway, I don't have to sweet talk you into doing that."

My laughter is cut short when he grinds against me, the hardness in his boxers making me gasp and tilt my pelvis toward it.

"Are you guys up?" Aubry asks with a knock on the door.

"Motherfucker," Cole mumbles under his breath, closing his eyes and exhaling as he clenches his hands on the pillow under my head. "AUBRY, WILL YOU EVER STOP COCK BLOCKING?" he shouts loudly, making me laugh. "He's an asshole. We'll have to take a rain check," he says before kissing me and backing away from me.

I pout as I watch him pull a white shirt over his head and adjust his hard-on in his boxers before he gets up and steps into a pair of blue basketball shorts. When he opens the door, I catch a glimpse of Aubry and Greg laughing when they see Cole step out and shake my head when I hear Aubry complain about Cole slapping him in the back of the head. Some things never change. I lie back down with a smile on my face and extend my arm to admire my ring for the millionth time. I look around the empty room, thinking of things we can do with it before getting up and heading to the shower. Once I'm dressed, I get the things we bought for the bathroom yesterday on our eventful trip to Wal-Mart and start putting everything in its place.

"I still think we should've gotten the tin trashcan, not that bamboo looking one," Cole says from behind me, making me drop the trashcan.

"Dammit! You scared me!" I say, turning around to face him.

"Sorry," he apologizes with a shrug. "Everything else looks good, though," he says with a smile as he looks at the shower curtain and toilet paper holder.

"Yeah, because you picked those out," I say with an eye roll.

He laughs and pulls me into a tight hug before letting me go and slapping my butt on his way to the sink.

"Your pancakes are done," he says, muffled as he brushes his teeth.

"Thank you," I reply over my shoulder before walking to the kitchen.

As we eat breakfast, Becky flips through a bridal magazine she bought yesterday, and even though I've always loved the idea of places like Wal-Mart having everything you need under one roof, I wish they didn't sell so many unnecessary things like bridal magazines. After I tell Becky that I don't care what colors my wedding are and assure Aimee that I haven't even thought about picking a date yet, I begin to scroll through my phone and check my missed calls and texts. I have one from Connor apologizing for not being able to make it last night and congratulating us. I reply and hover over a text message from my ex-boyfriend, Russell. I open it and smile as I reply.

**Russell: Hey, just wanted to check up on you. I haven't spoken to you since you got out of the hospital. Hope everything is okay. Lunch soon?**

**Me: I'm good, thank you! Sure, let me know when you're free.**

The couch sinks beside me and I look up to see Cole pursing his lips, clearly trying to hide a smile.

"What?" I ask, confused.

"Nothing. You better be wearing that ring if you go to lunch with him," Cole replies.

"Why are you looking at my phone?" I ask in shock.

"I'm not. He is," Cole says with a smirk, pointing his head in Aubry's direction.

I turn around and narrow my eyes at Aubry. "Nosey bastard."

Aubry laughs and messes up my hair, the way he does when he wants to get a rise out of me, but I decide not to give him the pleasure. Instead I finger comb my hair with a huff and shut my phone off before stuffing it in my purse. I get up from the couch to get a cupcake and pivot around when I'm reaching the table.

"And for the record, I will never take it off," I say in response to Cole's previous statement. Failing to keep my cold glare, I end up smiling at the way his eyes light up.

After we clean up, Greg and Becky leave to visit their moms before they head back to Chicago. When Aubry announces that he's going to visit Maggie's grave with Aimee before he leaves, I suggest that Cole and I go with them. Aubry and Cole have gone back there since the burial, and it's something that I've wanted to do but have never brave enough to do it. I look at all of the tombstones as we walk through the cemetery and wonder if my mother was buried here, or anywhere. A sign catches my eye that reads: Ask about our two for one deal. Because that's not morbid, I think to myself with an eye roll.

My breathing increases the closer we get to the spot that I remember her casket lowering in. The day replays in my head like it happened yesterday. I keep seeing myself scrubbing her blood off the ground, seeing the blood in my hands, tasting the iron in my mouth. When we reach her tombstone, I take a shaky breath before I kneel down in front of it, feeling the weight of her loss on my shoulders.

Whoever said loss gets easier with time, clearly hasn't loved and lost. I blink back forming tears and scoot over, placing my hand on Aubry's, who is kneeling beside me staring blankly at his mother's name on the stone. His blue eyes are dim, empty when he looks at me, and I can no longer hold my tears in. I sniffle back a whimper and cast my eyes away from his, shuddering when he holds my hand and squeezes.

"Stop," Aubry whispers. I nod in response, not daring to meet his eyes again, unable to bear the emptiness in them. "You need to stop blaming yourself for something you had no control over."

I gulp back my heartache, drowning my self-hatred along with it and exhale a shaky breath before meeting his eyes again. "I know," I whisper in agreement. "I know," I state a little louder, trying to convince myself as much as him.

I let go of his hand and scoot right up to the gray stone, placing my hand over it and tracing her name slowly with my finger before moving on to the bottom. A custom stone lays on the ground that reads, "Loving mother, aunt, and friend. An angel who earned her wings long before she made it to heaven." I trace it, blinking back tears and smiling at the truth in those words.

As I'm silently apologizing to Maggie one last time, a surge of wind brushes through me, making my hair wave wildly away from my face. I close my eyes and take a deep breath while lifting my face to the gust, filling my lungs with fresh air. When I release it, I let go of the guilt I've been harboring over words I should've said and things I could've done differently. I let go of the stored up sadness I have over knowing I won't feel her hand on mine or have her advice to rely on. I know that Maggie would hate to see me this sad; I know she would never want me to feel anything but happy, fulfilled. And last, I let go of my handicapping fear, because as I sit here and think back on my life and the things I've been faced with, it hits me just how short and fragile it is, and how little room there is for fear of the unknown. I exhale into the wind, allowing myself to bask in the clarity I've been craving for years. When it settles, I peel my eyes open and feel a sense of peace.

"Are you okay?" Cole asks as he squeezes my shoulder gently.

I wipe the tears away from my face and offer him a smile. "I think so."

He returns my smile and helps me off the ground before walking up to Aubry, who is hugging Aimee. Cole and Aubry look at each other for a moment, speaking with no words. They nod and pat each other on the arm before we all walk back to the car feeling lighter than we did when we got here.

# Chapter Twenty-Seven

## ~ COLE ~

My eyes are trained on her ring finger as I secure my tie, and she sleeps soundlessly. Thinking back on my life, I don't think I've ever felt this content. I look at the time on my watch, wishing I had five extra minutes to crawl back in bed with my girl, but as tempting as she looks snuggled up in our plush covers, I would definitely run late. I sigh heavily, tearing my eyes from her slightly parted lips and messy dirty blond hair and walk quietly toward the door, careful not to wake her. In the kitchen I turn on my cellphone and switch on the television, sitting in front of it as I wait for my coffee to brew.

When my phone vibrates on my lap, I look down to find two missed calls from Colleen, my birth mother, and a text message from Erin. I scroll to the text message first.

**Erin: OMG! Did you propose?!? Tom told me he saw Greg the other day! If it's true, CONGRATS!!!!!**

I smile at the text message, thinking that Erin Andrews is definitely one of those girls that you hold on to. I know I would've if it hadn't been for Blake. Fortunately for Tom Buck, Erin's boyfriend, Blake came back to me. And even more fortunately for me, I didn't stop fighting when Blake wanted me to give up on her, on us.

I shake my head when I hear the coffee pot brewing and press down to check my voice messages while getting up and flicking off the television. Holding my phone to my ear with my shoulder, I serve myself a to-go cup and close it. The sound of Colleen's sad voice pours through and I instantly think of Aimee and what she's told me about her mother hurting over Camden's betrayal. I know I shouldn't punish Colleen for something her husband kept from her, but it's hard not to. The first message is yet another apology, which I huff at because I'm so damn sick of them from everybody. The second is a congratulations and invite to a charity party she's hosting in a couple of weeks. I consider deleting the messages and forgetting I ever heard them until I hear what the charity is for—foster homes.

I walk back to our room, opening it slightly to find Blake still sleeping. I take a breath and stride over to her, leaning over and breathing in her fresh scent before placing a kiss on the side of her head. I back away slowly and flinch when she stirs.

"Cole," she whispers in a grumble that makes me smile.

"Yeah, baby?" I whisper back, knowing she's still asleep.

"I love you. Be careful," she mumbles as she flips over to her stomach.

Why those three little words make my heart skip a beat every time she says them is beyond me. But they get me every single time. I love it.

"I love you too. Sleep tight."

My eyes widen when the time on the dresser catches my attention, and I see that it's already seven-thirty. I walk out quickly and close the door behind me, locking it from the inside before picking up my coffee and bolting out of the apartment.

I signal Bruce, who's standing at the end of the hall, over with my finger and walk to the elevator quickly, while taking out my phone and making sure the crew is already setting up for today's interview. Luckily, the network has been accommodating in letting me work anywhere and hasn't locked me into working in the studio. I've spoken to Blake about it a couple of times and she says she would move anywhere I need to, but I don't think leaving Aubry behind and moving to Connecticut is really something she would be interested in. It works out better when I travel to the athletes' locations anyway, even if it is a pain in my ass to get on an airplane for a one-day trip, sometimes multiple times a week. I can't really complain though, I'm doing something I never thought I would be and getting paid good money.

I text message Erin back my thank you and confirm that I did indeed get engaged over the weekend. Instead of calling Colleen back, I call Aimee to see what she thinks of the whole thing. Out of everything that's happened, I'm thankful that I was at least able to connect with my sister again. That alone has been worth the fucking heartache I've been through with these damn people.

"Hello?" she answers with audible exhaustion.

"Hey, did I wake you up?" I ask concerned.

"Nah, I had Aubry wake me up before he left so I could start studying for this fucking exam. I swear, I'm never going to law school again," she says with a groan.

I laugh. "Obviously, you already went once. Why would you go back?"

"Shut up, you know what I mean," she snaps, which makes me laugh again.

"Have you not had coffee yet?"

"No. Aubry went to the store yesterday WITH a list and forgot to buy coffee. But don't worry, he bought beer!" she says in annoyance.

"Yeah, he's a genius," I reply with a laugh, as I shake my head at his stupidity. "Your mom called and left a message about some charity event she's hosting. What do you know about that?"

"Hmm, other than I've been dragged to it every year of my life? Nothing. It's boring. People dance, there's food, a lot of important people usually go—athletes, politicians, you name it. You like the cause, I'm sure, so you'd enjoy it...Blake would, too. Aub and I will be there," she replies. "My dad won't be, if that's what you're really asking."

I rub my forehead before resting my elbow on the car door. "All right. And you know for a fact he's not going? What about Mark, does he go? And Brian?"

She exhales a breath. "There's really no telling, Cole. Sometimes they do, sometimes they just send money. I'm not the right person to ask about the guest list. I can find out and call you back if you want, but I know Mom really...she feels horrible. She's physically sick over this shit. She's...she's leaving my dad," she says, her broken whisper snagging at my heart.

I close my eyes wishing I had something nice to offer her: a condolence, words of encouragement, anything. "Are you okay?" I ask quietly.

"I mean, it's just weird, I guess. It's not like we were this big happy family or anything, but still."

I nod my head in understanding because I think I get it, a dysfunctional family is better than no family at all. And that's when I decide that I'll go to the charity event Colleen is hosting.

# Chapter Twenty-Eight
~Blake~

I stifle a laugh when I hear Spencer grunt in the seat beside me as I take a sharp turn onto Michigan Avenue.

"Sorry," I lie with a smile.

Cole's been using the Escalade lately, even leaving it at the airport when he goes out of town for work, so I get to use the black Audi A5 that we leased when he got his own show. Normally I don't drive any of the cars since I only use them when I'm going someplace in a hurry, and Spencer ends up driving me. I still prefer taking the L to get around, but I have way too many things to get done. It's hot out, so I'd rather sit in air conditioning, even if it means paying an obscene amount of money for parking.

Once I find a space in a parking garage, I toss the keys over to Spencer before walking across the street as he trails behind me. I scramble through the herd of business suits, looking over my shoulder periodically to make sure I haven't lost him before reaching the large glass doors of the mall. A masculine hand wraps his hand on the metal handle at the same time I do, and the scent of cinnamony-cigarettes wrapping around me startles me to a halt, as the door swings open.

"Missed you, chick," he murmurs low against my ear, so that only I can hear him.

My heart runs a mile a minute. I turn to him, wide-eyed, with my mouth hanging open and find him watching me in amusement. He places his forefinger under my chin, as if to playfully close my gaping mouth, and snaps me out of my shock.

"What the hell are you doing here?" I whisper harshly, snapping my head bewilderedly in all directions, even though I don't know exactly what I'm looking for.

"It's a public mall, I'm pretty sure I'm allowed to be here," he replies, making me look back toward him.

I cross my arms, raising an eyebrow. "What store are you going to?"

His smiling hazel eyes scan my face before trailing slowly down my body and back up. I watch his smile waver and his eyebrows pull together as he steps forward and jerks my hand quickly.

"You got engaged?" he asks in a low voice, looking from my hand to my eyes and back to my hands a couple of times.

I nod as he drops my hand from his. "Yeah, last week," I reply quietly with a small smile.

He scratches the back of his neck as he looks around the crowded mall before turning his attention back to me. "Congratulations," he offers with a small smile. "Are you happy?"

"I am. Very," I reply, smiling as my mind drifts to the moment Cole proposed, the house, my friends.

"Good. I'm glad, chick. I really am," Dean says, bobbing his head before tilting it to look at me.

"Thanks," I reply with a shrug. "Do you...do you want to go shopping with me?" I ask awkwardly.

The side of his mouth twitches. "Why not?"

"I have to get a dress though. Fair warning," I respond, raising an eyebrow.

My hand brushes his when we begin to walk beside each other, and I tense when he holds it in his. I turn toward him with probing eyes as I wiggle my hand out of his.

"Spending time with a friend is always fun," he says, squeezing my hand before I take it back completely.

"Friend," I confirm seriously.

Dean shakes his head with a laugh. "Yes, friend. Get over yourself!"

I roll my eyes at his statement and smile as we continue our walk around the stores. I spot a pair of shoes that I instantly fall in love with, but after searching for a dress to no avail, we take a break and go to the food court. Spencer appears beside us while I'm taking a bite of pizza and unexpectedly hands me his cell phone.

"Mr. Murphy wants to speak to you," Spencer announces in a serious tone.

My insides twist at the sound of his name, and my eyes shoot from Dean to Spencer before they land on the phone he's handing me.

"Hello?" I answer, my voice barely audible.

"Please tell me you're eating lunch with Russell," Cole says through clenched teeth.

I shut my eyes closed tightly. "I'm not," I whisper, not hearing my own voice over the sound of my pounding heart.

"You've got to be fucking kidding me, Blake!" he yells before huffing a breath. "I thought we went over this? I don't want you near him, ever. You need to cut ties with that part of your life. Enough is enough!"

I rub my forehead and open my eyes to look at Dean who's sitting across from me, watching me intently. His twitching jaw and hands fisted on the table tell me that he hears every word Cole is saying to me. "Can we talk about this later?" I ask Cole in a low voice.

He exhales into the line. "Are you going home now?"

"I still need to get a dress."

"We can go look for one tomorrow...together," he replies, his tone serious.

"I'm already here, Cole," I mutter with an eye roll that makes Dean snicker.

"I don't like him, Blake. I don't fucking like him," he says with a sigh.

"I know, but it's not what you think," I respond, defeated.

"I'll be home in an hour. If you're not there when I get there, I'm coming to the mall to get you," he says before hanging up, not giving me a chance to say anything.

I narrow my eyes at Spencer as I hand the phone back to him and push my slice of pizza aside, no longer hungry. Dean and I look at each other for a couple of seconds or minutes in complete silence; the only noise is that of the chatter around the food court.

"He really loves you, you know?" Dean says after a while.

"I know," I agree with a sigh. "But he can be a bit overprotective sometimes."

Dean's lip twitches. "I've noticed. That's not a bad thing, though. Sometimes you need that in your life...you definitely need that in yours!"

I purse my lips and nod in agreement, my mind drifting to Cole and the many times he's unnecessarily been overprotective of me.

"Whatever, he's pretty awesome even if he's a little annoying sometimes," I reply with a laugh and watch Dean's eyes sparkle in amusement.

I stand up, taking the balled up paper of my Jimmy John's sub and cup of pop to throw out. When I come back to the table, Dean is still sitting there, leaning back on his chair with his arm over the seat beside him and his legs splayed open, not a care in the world. I laugh, rolling my eyes at him as I approach.

"What did you have to buy?"

"Socks," he replies, shrugging the arm he has placed on his lap.

"Socks?" I ask, sputtering in laughter.

"Yeah, you can never have too many socks. Don't your socks magically get lost when you wash them?"

I purse my lips at his question. "I guess? Cole does the laundry." I shrug.

A slow smile spreads over his face. "Huh. I woulda never thought that. Lucky girl," he replies in his amused tone.

We say our goodbyes in the food court and I go home to wait for my petulant fiancé. I toss the bag in my room and kick off my shoes before heading to the kitchen to open up a bottle of wine and prepare our dinner. I head to the balcony to water my plants and as I'm walking back inside, I hear the front door swing open and close. I tread back to the kitchen quietly and bite down on my lip when I see Cole striding toward me, carrying his suit jacket over his forearm. My breath hitches at the sight of him in his charcoal gray suit and unbuttoned dress shirt with loosened tie. I can tell he's been running his hands through his rumpled dark hair, and I give him a sad smile when he stops walking just steps away from me. His exhausted green eyes meet mine. He stares at me for a long moment before closing his eyes and taking a breath. When he opens them again, he tosses his jacket over the couch and continues to walk to me, his eyes blazing into mine. My heart rate spikes up when he stands flush against me. So close that the tip of my nose is touching his blue and gray tie and all I can smell is Cole as my chest heaves against his white dress shirt.

"What am I going to do with you?" he asks, cupping my chin and turning my face toward his. His deep voice makes my body hum and shiver slightly. "Do you know how worried I am every time I leave for work? Do you realize that every time I know you're out I think of a hundred different things that can happen to you and relive that day all over again? Every. Single. Goddamn time. So when I find out that you're WITH one of the guys responsible..."

I take a step back so that I don't have to tilt my head as much to look at him. "I didn't ask him to meet me there. I haven't spoken to him since...in a while," I reply, reaching up to caress both sides of his face, the stubble along his jaw tickling my palms. "He happened to be there and we had lunch. I know you don't like him and I get why you don't, but you weren't there, Cole. If it weren't for him..." I shrug, dropping my hands from his face, unwilling to finish my sentence.

He pulls me into his chest and cloaks me in his arms, resting his head above mine. "I don't understand it, baby. I really don't. And I don't want you to see him. I get that he protected you and got you out of there, but I hate the way he looks at you. And knowing that he was with you that whole time...when you were...I just can't deal with it. I can't even stand the thought of someone else being there for you when it should've been me."

I snuggle into him, closing my eyes to savor his touch. "I'm yours, Cole. Only yours."

He lets go of me and holds me at arms' length, grazing over my face with the tips of his fingers as he looks at me adoringly. I close my eyes and part my lips slightly when he brushes over them, continuing down my bare shoulder and gently down my arm, stopping over the ring that adorns my index finger. He turns it on my finger a couple of times before adjusting it back in place. My eyes flutter open when the smell of his minty breath hits my face and we lock gazes again.

"You are," he replies quietly. "Mine."

I yank his tie, bringing his face close to mine until we're nose to nose. "Forever," I say, looking into the deep green eyes that make my head spin.

"Forever," he growls against my lips before crashing his mouth against mine.

# Chapter Twenty-Nine

## ~Blake~

I run my fingers under my eyes in an effort to perfect my eyeliner and take a breath as I wipe the foggy bathroom mirror with my hand towel. I dab on some light lip gloss with the tip of my finger and smack my lips together a couple of times before deciding that I look as good as I can make myself look. Running my hands through my loose waves, I take a deep shaky breath and plaster on a smile.

My heels clink on the hardwood floor as I walk to the living room to wait for Cole who's in what is now known as his home office, doing an interview. I sag down on the couch and switch on the television and find that it's already tuned in to Cole's segment. My mouth dries when the camera goes from the guy he's interviewing back to Cole, already dressed in his tuxedo for tonight's event and looking damn good. After a couple of seconds listening to them ramble on about the Miami Dolphins' new team, I switch it off and walk to the mirror to look at myself again. I thought I looked fine, but seeing how great he looks makes me want to fix up my hair a little more. I grab my soft curls with one hand and bring them up to the back of my head, trying to figure out how to clip them there and drop them, letting them cascade over my shoulders, when Cole's reflection appears in the mirror.

His eyes blaze as they rake slowly over my body, and he runs his tongue between his teeth before moving it over his lips. I pivot around and look down, suddenly feeling shy under his gaze. The sound of his dress shoes patter against the hardwood floor as he walks toward me. I bring my face up slowly, breathing in a whiff of his scent when he's close enough for me to revel in it. I tilt my head, my lips parting slightly, and my body heating up from the desire in his eyes as he lets his eyes roam over me once more.

"You look...amazing," he finally says hoarsely. "That dress-"

"You really like it?" I ask hopefully. "I loved it when I saw it. I figured I would go with black since it's an evening thing, but I've never really been to anything like this-"

"Stop. You look beautiful. Beyond beautiful. You look fucking edible in that dress."

A small smile touches my lips and my heart swells in appreciation for this man, who could make me feel sexy in just about anything. Still not at eye level with him despite my five-inch heels, I lean up to kiss him, but he holds my arms and takes a step back, shaking his head slowly.

"Let me see the back of that dress again," he says in a low voice.

I turn around quickly, feeling my hair swing with me and hit his body before I collect it up in my hands again so that he can see the low cut on the back of it. He caresses my back with the back of his finger close to the edges of dress, making me shiver as he pays close attention to the dip that's dangerously close to my butt. He draws the U of it a couple of times before sliding his finger inside of the fabric.

"This is really low," he murmurs, closing the gap between us so that his mouth is over my ear and his chest is practically flush against my back. Even with his hand between us, I can feel him hard against me and see the heat in his eyes in the mirror in front of us. I let go of my hair and throw my head back against his chest. My eyes flutter closed when he moves his hand to hold my pelvis and pivots against me. He brings both hands in front of me and moves them over the thin fabric of my dress, placing them over my sensitive breasts, teasing them.

"You're not wearing a bra?" he asks with a strained voice, still at the shell of my ear.

My breath hitches in response, and he pinches my nipples, making me whimper and open my eyes quickly.

"No," I reply breathlessly.

"You're trying to kill me," he says, narrowing his eyes at me in the mirror. "You're trying to fucking kill me tonight."

I bite down on my lip and push my hips back with a low moan, feeling his breathing increase in my ear.

"Baby, don't start something you can't finish," he warns hoarsely.

"You started it," I pant, slipping my hand behind me and cupping him over his pants. He groans deeply.

Loud knocks on the door make us both pause and let out deep breaths. Cole drops his hands from my breasts and clears his throat, not taking his blazing eyes off mine in the mirror.

"Be right there!" he yells at the door before lowering his head and biting my earlobe. "We'll finish this later...you need earrings."

"Damn it. I knew I was missing something," I say under my breath.

"You haven't been in your closet, have you?" he asks, shaking his head and letting out a chuckle as he adjusts himself in his pants.

"No," I reply, confused.

"Well, you may want to go now," he says, walking toward the front door.

I walk back to our room and to my closet. I've had the dress hanging on the bathroom door for a couple of days, and rarely go into my closet since I keep my underwear and lounging clothes in the drawers in the bathroom, but I'm pretty sure I got my shoes out of there. As I'm trying to sort out my confusion, I open the door to my walk-in closet and switch the light on, gasping when I find a vase full of huge sunflowers beside a wrapped present on the small table in the middle. I beam as I walk toward it, wondering what in the world he could have gotten me now. I touch the yellow petals lightly and smile at his gesture, always the romantic. He got me the same flowers when we went on our first date together. I pick up a small envelope with my name on it and tear it open, finding a note from him:

> TONIGHT IS OUR FIRST DATE AS AN
>
> ENGAGED COUPLE—
>
> LET'S MAKE IT AN UNFORGETTABLE ONE.
>
> I LOVE YOU X ∞

I smile and place the note beside the vase and begin to unwrap the present, careful not to tear the wrapping paper that has the word *love* written all over it in different colors. My eyebrows knit together when I find the Jimmy Choo shoebox that the shoes I'm wearing came in. I open it, finding a smaller box in it wrapped in the same paper. I groan when I realize the game he wants to play, which he knows I absolutely hate. His laughter erupts behind me, and I roll my eyes as I face him.

"I love you and I love the flowers and the note and the gesture, but why do you always do this to me?" I ask exasperated.

He's smiling as he strides toward me and taps the tip of my nose with his finger. "Because I love how cute you look when you're frustrated. It's fun!"

"So not fun," I mumble under my breath, making him chuckle.

"Hurry up and open it! We're already running late."

I sigh and tear the wrapping paper of this box a little faster than the last and find another small box inside of that one. I grit my teeth to keep from cursing or saying anything mean and take another deep breath as I tear through the next box with wrapping paper, finally finding two Tiffany blue boxes. I bite down on my smile and pick one up.

"That one first," he interrupts, making me look at him with narrowed eyes.

I put down the smaller box and pick up the other one, opening it to find a pair of breathtaking diamond chandelier earrings. My mouth drops open as I take in how shiny they are. They drip perfection and expensiveness, and my mind battles between wondering how much they cost to whether or not I can pull off wearing them.

"They're beautiful," I whisper in awe, looking from the earrings to Cole and back to the earrings. I place them over the back of my hand and swallow as my eyes drift from the earrings to my equally as shiny engagement ring and back to the earrings. "They probably cost a fortune, Cole," I murmur, looking back into his eyes.

He furrows his eyebrows and looks at me like I'm crazy before placing a kiss on my lips and taking the earrings from me. "Blake, if the world was for sale, I'd buy it for you. Don't worry about how much they cost. Put them on and open the other box so we can go."

I nod, picking up the other box and opening it to find the skeleton key he replaced for the one I lost when I was taken. I smile when I see he picked the one with nothing at the top of it, just a beautiful skeleton key. He brings his hand out in front of me and turns it over so I see a small engraved message on the back of it. I bring it closer to my face and read: **You own me.** Placing the box on the counter, I shift my body and pull his face down to mine and kiss him deeply. My heart thumps against my chest when I feel him run his hands down the sides of my body and back up until he reaches my face and separates our mouths.

"We need to go," he whispers against my mouth, biting my bottom lip and pulling it into his mouth. "That dress makes me wanna do really...really dirty things to you."

I close my eyes and take a steadying breath, letting my hands drop from his face and backing away with my new earrings in my hand. Once I put them on, we fix our clothes and step out of my closet, flipping the lights off and leaving the messy wrapping paper to be picked up later. Cole grabs his jacket and shrugs it on. I watch as he fixes his bow tie while we walk to the elevators, making me stumble a step and curse when he reaches to steady me.

"You really suck at walking in heels," he mutters with a low laugh.

"Shut it. You're distracting to walk around," I snap back, turning my face to hide an embarrassed smile.

He places his hand on the nape of my neck as we reach the elevator and escorts me in before turning around and instructing Spencer and Bruce to take the next one. The men exchange confused glances but don't argue with Cole as the elevator door closes. Before I can look up to question him, he backs me into the elevator wall and moves his hand from my neck to pull on the bottom of my hair and crane my neck. I swallow loudly, seeing his eyes boring into mine before he dips his head and places kisses along my jaw and down my neck as he lifts the skirt of my dress and tucks his free hand under it. My shallow breath increases when his mouth reaches my chest and his fingers flick over my underwear. I close my eyes and not for the first time tonight I wonder if we should cancel on this event and go back to our room.

"I really shouldn't have told Colleen we would be there," he murmurs against my nipple before biting it through the material.

I moan softly, trying to concentrate on what he's saying and keep my eyes from rolling to the back of my head at the feel of his touch. He drops his hands and takes a step back when the elevator chimes, letting us know we reached the lobby. I let out a frustrated groan, leaning my head against the wall behind me. He chuckles and reaches for my hand to guide me out of the elevator, leading me to the front of the building.

"Where are we going?" I ask in confusion.

"Limo," he replies, tipping his head at Pat, the doorman that's holding the door open for us.

"Oh. Why a limo? Are a lot of people going with us?"

He drops my hand and stops walking, turning his body around to look at me. "Nope, just you and me," he replies with a grin and twinkling eyes that make my insides do somersaults.

"Oh," I whisper.

"Oh," he mocks with a raised eyebrow.

I duck my head and step into the limo, lifting my dress so that I don't step on it and slide over to the other side to give Cole room to enter behind me. I look outside and see him talking to Spencer and Bruce before he stops in front of the driver. I watch the driver's confused face as Cole gives him directions, telling him what streets to take. I can't help but laugh at the sight; he must think Cole's crazy.

Cole slides in beside me and smiles at my questioning look before facing forward and taking his cell phone out.

"You have more phone calls to make?" I ask quietly, trying to hide my annoyance.

He ignores me, only taking his eyes off his phone to look at the glass that separates us from the driver roll up before going back to his phone. I let out a breath and reach for the clutch purse to take out my own phone, but Cole stops me and tosses the purse further away from me along with his own phone. I shift in my seat to face him, my heart threatening to sputter out of my chest from watching his eyes heat up as they trail over my body.

"Sit in that seat," he says gruffly, pointing at the seat across from us.

"Why?" I ask in confusion.

"Just do it."

As I stand, hunching over awkwardly to sit across from him, I feel the back of my dress hike up and gasp when he places both hands over my butt and squeezes.

"Put your knees on the seat," he orders hoarsely.

So I do, gasping loudly and lurching over to grab onto the seats when I feel his hot breath over my exposed backside. He trails his tongue along my ass cheeks, sucking and biting until he reaches the backs of my knees and makes his way back up. When he repeats the motion on the other side, he takes my underwear down with him, making me wiggle out of them.

"You should've never worn this dress," he rasps before burying his face into me and sliding his tongue over my folds, making me bite down on my lip to keep from moaning loudly. "Or these shoes," he says, tapping on each heel. "Don't move," he orders before stepping away from me.

I look over my shoulder and watch him clicking the buttons of the radio and stopping when J. Cole's music blares through the car. His eyes trail down my back, fixed on where I'm naked before he looks at my face again. His eyes never leave mine as he shrugs off his jacket and tosses it, undoing his cufflinks and tie and tossing those along with it. The limo phone rings beside him and he answers, replying yes and no before hanging up. My hands grip down on the seat when the car begins to move and I look out the window in front of me suddenly feeling exposed, even though I know they can't see me through the tints. Cole shifts behind me and places a wet kiss on my shoulder. I turn my face to his, offering him my lips, which he takes before raining kisses down my bare back until he reaches my butt again.

I turn my head and arch my back, watching as his face disappears below me. I throw my head back and close my eyes in abandonment when I feel his tongue *there* again, shaking my core. With each flick of his tongue I feel my body quiver a little more, and just when I feel like I'm on the brink, he backs away.

"Turn around," he orders, his voice laced with need.

I open my eyes and turn so that I'm facing him. He unzips the side of my dress and pulls it over my body, laying it over his jacket before undoing his belt and lowering his pants so that they pool to his knees. I place my legs on the seats beside me, opening myself for him and watching from under my lashes as he springs free from his briefs.

My breath falters at the carnal need in his eyes as he looks at me and begins to stroke himself. My lips part and my heart hammers in anticipation. I lift my hand from the seat to touch myself with it, but he stops me, dipping his head and growling as he buries his face between my legs again, sending a tremor through my body. His fingers reach and twist my nipples at the same time that his tongue grazes me again, making my back arch and a loud moan escape me as I'm pushed over the edge.

He kisses his way up my body to my breasts, pulling each one into his mouth, and before I come down from my orgasm, he pushes into me, making me cry out louder as another one ripples through me.

"That's right," he rasps against my ear as he grinds into me.

I bite down on Cole's shoulder when the car hits a bump and he pushes deeper into me, switching positions so that he's sitting on the seat and I'm straddling him. He drives me into me, pulling my hips and lifting himself at the same time and all I can do is toss my head back and get lost in the moment.

"So good. You feel so good," he says roughly. "I'm so close. Look at me."

I open my eyes and bring my face to his, pushing myself up with my knees on either side of him and watching as his lips part and beads of sweat form on his temple. His eyes are hard on mine as he bites down on his lower lip. I feel his muscles tense, letting me know he's on the brink. He lets go of one side of my body and brings his hand between us to massage my clit, making me pulsate around him again as we both reach our climax. Our cries of pleasure get drowned out in the music.

"I love you," he whispers against my shoulder, our bodies heaving in exhaustion.

"I love you too," I respond, closing my eyes against him.

Cole helps me clean up and dress before dressing himself and handing me a handful of Kleenex to dab my face with. I open up the mirror in my clutch and fix my eyeliner and lip gloss before touching up my hair as best I can...and pray that nobody knows what we did on our way to the event.

"I told you I was going to fuck you in that dress," he says, taking a seat beside me and holding my hand in his.

"You did," I reply before taking a deep shaky breath. "I didn't realize you meant *before* the event though."

"Neither did I...until I remembered we had a limo," he says with a chuckle. "I'll be sure to thank Colleen for that later."

My eyes widen and my mouth pops open when I turn my face to his. "Oh my God! It just hit me that I'm going to meet your mother tonight!" I shriek in disbelief. "I can't believe we just did that!"

Cole laughs, his shoulder shaking me along with him. "You lived with my mother, Blake. Colleen-"

"Is your birth mother, Cole. And she's trying. Aimee says so all the time. Don't rule her out," I reply quietly before placing a peck on his cheek.

# Chapter Thirty

## ~ COLE ~

I spot a lot of familiar faces as we walk around the gala and look down at Blake to find her smiling as she looks around the room. The walls have photos of smiling children playing sports, reading books, watching movies, running around and doing what kids do. Noticing her smile broaden, my eyes follow her line of sight and see Aubry walking toward us holding Aimee's hand.

"You took for-fucking-ever to get here, dude," Aubry greets us as he gives me a quick hug and pat on the back before moving to say hi to Blake. He and Aimee switch places for me to kiss her on the cheek.

"My mom's been asking for you, she thought you weren't coming," Aimee adds with a smile.

I look at my watch. "We're only thirty minutes late," I reply.

"Yeah, but you're never late!" Aubry retorts.

Blake laughs and tugs my hand. "He's not very happy that I made him late," she says, looking up at me, her huge gray eyes sparkling in amusement.

I smile at her and dip my head to kiss her. "Oh yes he is," I reply against her lips.

"You two are sickening," Aubry says in faux disgust before taking Aimee's hand and placing a kiss on it.

I roll my eyes and let them lead the way to where Colleen is standing with a group of people. We wait until she's finished talking and she turns her attention to us, smiling brightly when she sees me, which I return. Now that I'm here in front of her again, my heart feels lighter, and I want to kick myself for not wanting to see her again. Her eyes move from mine to Blake and her smile disappears. She stares at Blake with an open mouth, and as she steps forward, she extends her hand and brushes Blake's face with it, her eyes swelling with unshed tears. She takes her hand back and covers her mouth, blinking a couple of times, unable to stop tears from trickling down her face which she wipes away quickly.

"It's so nice to meet you," Colleen whispers. "I'm sorry. It's just...you look exactly like your mother. I knew you would, but seeing you..."

Blake lets go of my hand and takes Colleen's hand in hers and placing a kiss on her cheek. "It's okay. It's nice to meet you, Colleen. Did you know her well?" she asks quietly.

Colleen nods her head. "Very," she whispers back. "We were great friends for a long time."

They smile sadly at each other before Blake drops her hands and steps back to my side. Colleen turns her attention to me.

"Thank you for coming, Na...Cole. It means so much to me," Colleen says quietly as she leans up to greet me with a kiss, which I return.

"Thank you for inviting me. It's a good cause," I reply.

"It is," she says with a bright smile before looking at Blake again. "I hope we can all catch up and get to know each other."

"We'd love that," Blake responds cheerfully.

I look at her and she looks at me with pleading eyes that I can't argue with, so I let out a breath and nod in agreement. Then we follow Colleen around so she can awkwardly introduce me as her son and tell Blake's story.

After talking to what seems like two hundred people in the room, Blake and I find our seats next to Aubry and Aimee's and see Connor's name on the table with us. Aimee waves her hand and explains that a lot of people come to these events, and Connor usually doesn't make it even when he says he will.

"Don't count me out just yet," Connor booms behind us, making me laugh.

I turn around and look at him in surprise when I see he's wearing a tuxedo and has a pretty brunette on his arm that's smiling in apprehension.

"This is Sandra," Connor announces before introducing us all to her. When he gets to Blake he pauses and gives her a pointed look that leaves me confused. Blake's smile widens and she stands.

"It's so great to meet you, Sandra. I'm Connor's cousin," Blake says, which confuses me even more.

"Good to meet you, Blake," Sandra says, smiling happily.

"Your son is absolutely adorable, I've seen a million pictures of him. He looks like trouble," Blake continues.

"Oh, you have no idea! Like father, like son," Sandra says with a laugh.

"I am not trouble!" Connor says as he looks at Sandra in adoration, and I realize who she is.

Once we settle down in our seats again, Mark shows up with his date, who Blake also happens to know and talks to for a couple of minutes.

"How do you know all these people?" I whisper as the food is being served.

She smiles. "Sandra is Connor's ex but not really ex—it's complicated. He's always talking about her. I'm surprised you don't know who she is. And Mark's date I know from his office," she says in a low whisper.

"Got it," I reply before taking a sip of champagne and leaning back into my seat.

All of us fall into easy conversation for the duration of our meal before Blake excuses herself to go to the bathroom.

Aimee also gets up and accompanies her, tossing her napkin aside before walking rapidly after her.

I crinkle my eyebrows when the waiter brings over the dessert and I realize that I've been so enrapt in conversation that I hadn't noticed Blake taking a little too long in the bathroom. I look around, pivoting my body in my seat to look for her but don't see any sign of her or Aimee.

"Aub, is it me or have they been gone a long time?" I ask curiously. Women always take long in the bathroom—I've learned that over the years. But something doesn't feel right.

"You're right," he responds as his eyebrows knit together.

A loud shriek rings through the ballroom and the feeling of dread that was threatening to consume the pit of my stomach, does. My eyes shoot to Connor's as I get up and take off into a sprint in the direction of the screams. I hear stomps behind me and assume Connor and Aubry are following, maybe Mark, but don't care enough to look. My vision tunnels and my ears clog as I look around anxiously for the bathrooms, bumping a couple of people out of my way in the process. My shoulder crashes into a blur of brown hair when I round the corner and I grab on to the feminine figure to steady her. My heart rate spikes even higher when I look past Aimee and realize she's by herself.

"Where is she?" I shout, shaking Aimee by the shoulders.

"There! There!" Aimee shrieks, pointing at the door as she runs toward it again.

"Aimee!" Aubry screams behind us and grabs her as she tries to shake out of his hold, shouting that she has to get to Blake.

I turn the knob of the door she pointed at and find that it's locked. I slam my shoulder into it as hard as I can once, twice, three times before I decide to start kicking it.

"GET THE FUCK OVER HERE, CONNOR!" I yell loudly.

He runs quickly to me and pulls out the pistol from his back, making people around us scream in alarm and start to scramble in every direction.

"Get out of the way!" he shouts, pushing me aside.

"Give it to me!" I demand, earning a 'you've got to be kidding me' look that I don't have time for.

"Are you fucking crazy? You're not using my gun!" he shouts back, pushing me away and aiming it at the doorknob.

Screaming coming from the kitchen doors makes our heads snap in that direction before we take off running that way.

# Chapter Thirty-One
## ~Blake~

"WHAT DO YOU WANT FROM ME?" I yell loudly as Benny walks me through the commercial kitchen of the hotel. The chefs and everybody else dressed in white drop everything to either scream or put their hands up. "HELP ME!" I scream, looking at them with wild eyes, not understanding how they could just be standing out of the way watching this happen.

"Yeah, yeah, stay out of it unless you want your head capped!" He spits, pushing the barrel of the gun into the back of my skull, making me close my eyes and shiver at the bite of it. "Well, Blake," he starts, my name rolling off his tongue in disgust. "Your father gave me some interesting information yesterday. Your father," he chides with a throaty laugh before pulling my hair back roughly and making me yelp at the pain. He walks me to the back door, pushing my chest into it with an elbow in the middle of my back. He turns my face so that the tip of my nose brushes the scar on his left cheek before he shifts and we're nose to nose. "Turns out...that I'm your uncle. Or that's what Liam wants me to think. Dumb fuck. We're gonna find out the truth, but I call bullshit. Liam wants to save his ass, wants to keep you safe, wants to screw me over as usual. We're gonna see how true that is when I call him now and make him listen to me splitting your face open like he did me. Let's see how much he likes to feel helpless."

I gasp and screw my eyes shut as my chest heaves against the metal door. I open my eyes and turn my head slightly at the absence of the gun on my head and catch a sharp blade through my peripheral vision that makes me yelp and frantically turn the doorknob beside me. I push it open, letting it hit the rail beside it and scramble outside. I pray that my heels don't slow me down as I take the four concrete steps as quickly as my dress allows and begin to run with him on my tail. He yanks me back by the hair and presses the tip of the blade to my naked lower back.

"Don't fucking move," he demands gruffly.

"Please, Benny! Don't do it! Please!" I beg in a broken, dry sob as he walks me to the wall on the other side of the stairs. He pushes me onto it and holds the blade in place as I arch my back away from it. He places his ringing phone on the landing between the back door and the top of my head.

When a man answers on the fourth ring, Benny tightens his hold on my hair, making me screech.

"Liam! I'm here with your girl, Blake. I was just filling her in on the news. Figured I'd test out how true it is by decorating her face a lil' with this blade here. You remember when you did that to me, Liam?" Benny asks in amusement.

I bring my hand out from under me to dry my tears and look at him in disgust as he talks on the phone, holding the knife close to my face with one hand and my hair with the other.

"DON'T YOU FUCKING DARE!" Liam screams through the line.

"Oh, but I dare, Liam. I do dare. You gonna take back what you said or wait until she's nothing but shreds?" Benny asks sharply.

"SHE'S ALEX'S KID, BENNY!" Liam yells loudly. His admission makes my mouth drop open, and for a moment I wonder if the loud ringing in my ears is altering my hearing or if he really just said that. "CORY WAS PREGNANT WHEN I MARRIED HER!"

"He was in jail, you piece of shit!" Benny yells back, the emphasis of his words spitting on my face. "Stop trying to get out of this one, Liam!"

Benny positions the knife to the corner of my eye where my tears are running and he wipes them with the flat side of the knife, making me flinch.

"Stop crying, girl!" he growls, narrowing his stark eyes at me as loud sobs rake through my shuddering body.

"Benny! She got pregnant before Alex went to jail! He's gonna fucking kill you for this if I don't get you first!" Liam shouts over my sobs.

I kick my leg up, trying to hit him and hoping to nail him between the legs, but he shifts and barks out a laugh. He looks at me with crazed eyes and pushes me down again as I struggle against him, trying to push off his heavy body. I kick again, making contact with his leg. He laughs as he pins me harder against the concrete.

"You wanna do this the hard way, huh?" he asks through gritted teeth, turning my body to face him. From the corner of my eye, I can see his tight grip around the blade that he brings toward my face. I screw my eyes shut as I continue to struggle against him but await my impending punishment. A whimper, followed by loud sobs escape me when I feel the sharp blade meet my hairline.

"Please don't!" I shout, my guttural voice a stranger to my own ears. "Please," I plead once more, feeling woozy when I smell the blood streaming down my face. I hear a shout from afar and feel the blade leave my face.

My eyes pop open at the sound of ringing shots, immediately followed by the wind getting knocked out of me as Benny's body pushes fiercely into mine. I try to gasp for air before another shot rings off. Benny pushes into me again, driving me deeper into the wall. He languidly pushes his body away from me and turns around, bringing his gun out in front of him, as if in slow motion. He pulls the trigger twice, shelling out two bullets. My horrified eyes follow the direction his arm is pointing, and I let out a loud scream when I see his target. I feel my senses come back to me all at once, and I scream again before lurching forward and pulling Benny's shooting arm down with all my strength, making his body crash down to his knees. I wrap both hands around the gun in his hand and yank it out, tossing it aside before I start running across the alley.

"NO!" I shriek when I see him fall on his knees before I reach him. I take off my shoes and throw them behind me and continue running as fast as I can, not caring what I may step on.

When I reach him I crash down on my knees and put my hands over his face, over his hair, before my eyes trail to his stomach where his white shirt is drenched in blood. He shifts his body sideways and falls to the ground, landing on his side in a thump.

"DEAN!" I shout desperately.

"I'm fine," he rasps before going into a coughing fit. "You okay, chick?"

"YOU'RE HURT!" I shriek, unable to hide the sheer panic flowing through my veins. My eyes brim with tears as I press down on the wound on his stomach.

"Are you *okay*, chick?" he repeats, his voice dimming and his eyes blinking heavily.

I touch my head and yelp at the sting my fingers cause on the cut in my hair line, but I'm not gushing out blood, and it doesn't hurt too much. I look down at myself, blinking tears onto my face, and find that my dress is drenched in blood. I pat myself with one hand, feeling no holes in my dress and decide that I'm fine. Rattled and cut, but fine.

"Yes! Keep your eyes open!" I demand, looking into his exhausted hazel eyes. Before he can reply, I begin to sob loudly, my entire body shaking as I press into his wound with both hands. "What were you doing here?" I ask between sobs.

"Followed him," he replies in a hoarse whisper. "Heard him talking to Liam. Heard."

"Okay, no talking. No talking. HEEELP!" I yell at the top of my lungs despite the pounding headache I'm feeling. "I need an ambulance! HELP! PLEASE HELP!"

"Shhh...'skay, chick. I'll be fine," he says, bending a leg to try to sit up.

"No! Don't move!" I demand. "Oh my God, please don't die. Please don't die," I beg as my chest heaves in sobs, and I look down at the blood covering my hands and forearms.

The doors bang open behind me, and I look over my shoulder to see Connor holding a gun in his hand, with Cole on his heels. They spot Benny on the ground and Connor aims at him and shoots him in the back of the head. I scream loudly, hurling over at the sight of blood and chunks of things splattering everywhere.

"BLAKE!" Cole yells as he rushes toward Dean and me.

I sob harder when he reaches us and wraps his arms around me. He looks down and sees my hands holding Dean and takes out his phone to call the police, not letting go of me with his other arm. After telling them where we are, he looks at Dean and explains his condition. As Cole is on the phone, I press down a little harder, making Dean flinch and grunt under me.

"Sorry," I whisper. "You said you didn't kill for anybody."

"I don't," he whispers back, the side of his lip turning up.

I raise an eyebrow in question, my clattering teeth and shivering body not letting me argue. He coughs out a laugh before gasping for air a couple of times. I scramble to sit up on my knees and place a hand under his neck.

"Okay, new rule, no talking," I say as tears roll down my face. He closes his eyes when I massage the back of his neck before pinching it to make him open them again. "Eyes open. Please let me see your eyes."

They flutter open and he smiles sadly. "I don't kill for anyone, chick. You're not just anyone, though," he says, answering my question.

I grit my teeth to keep my loud sobs inside. "Thank you for saving me again," I say, my voice barely a whisper as I gulp back the ball in my throat.

He shakes his head slowly, the hair on the back of his neck brushing against my open palm. "Thank you for helping me right a wrong," he responds solemnly.

My heart constricts in my chest as we stare at each other for what seems like an eternity, until I finally tear mine away from him and bury my face into the jacket of Cole's sleeve, letting his scent wash a sense of tranquility over me. He kisses the top of my head and hangs up the phone before placing his hands over mine on Dean's abdomen helping me hold him together.

"Thank you for saving my girl again," Cole says, breaking the silence.

"No big deal," Dean replies with a small smile. "She's been a good friend to me...my only friend, really. Other than Con," he adds looking at Connor, who's walking back to us with Sandra. Sandra picks up the speed when she sees her brother laying on the street beneath Cole and me.

"What happened?" Sandra shrieks, falling to her knees beside his face.

Sirens approach and lights hit our faces, making us squint our eyes and turn our heads unanimously toward them. The paramedics get a stretcher and run, pushing us out of the way and questioning what happened as they load Dean onto the stretcher. We pick ourselves up from the floor, Cole scooping me up into his arms as he stands and walks toward the ambulance.

"I need a minute," I tell Cole when we reach the paramedics that are loading Dean into the ambulance.

Cole puts me on my feet and I climb into the ambulance, waving off their warnings.

"I can still be your friend," I say when I reach Dean's face.

"Good. I think I'll need one after all this," he replies before the paramedics ask me to get on or get off. I get off and let Sandra hop in to accompany her brother, promising that I'll visit him.

I rush back into Cole's arms, burying myself in them and suddenly feeling lightheaded. Aubry and Aimee rush toward us from the other side of the police tape the cops are putting around us. My vision tunnels as I look around, the lights dimming around me, noises fading and my body weakening. I feel my knees and body sag before falling into a hard cradle that smells like Cole. Like home.

sun·light

/ˈsənˌlīt/


Noun.

Light from the sun.


Synonyms

sunshine, sun, daylight

# Chapter Thirty-Two
## ~Blake~

It's been two days since Benny's attack. Two days of me waking up in cold sweat nightmares because the look of his face is haunting me in my sleep. Two days and I'm still scrubbing myself and taking four showers a day. Two days since my freedom was promised to me, yet his words have done nothing but clink around in my head. Dean is still in the hospital and today is the day that I'm going to visit him. Two days after he saved my life. Again. I toss around before sitting up and swinging my feet over the edge of the bed and standing.

"You okay?" Cole asks groggily.

"Yeah, going to get water. I'm fine."

I walk to the door and unlock it, opening it slowly before striding to the kitchen and opening the fridge. I'm not sure I'll ever be able to sleep with my bedroom door unlocked. I'm not sure if I'll ever learn to let go of minor details that have kept me locked up inside myself for so long.

Footsteps startle me as I lean in to get a bottle of water and I gasp, pulling my hand out quickly and dropping one on my foot.

"Babe, you need to see someone," Cole says, flicking the light on, making me blink rapidly while he rubs his eyes.

"I'm fine," I mutter under my breath and lean over to pick up the water bottle, but he stops me midway.

He picks it up for me and unscrews the top as he hands it to me. His tired eyes are serious as he looks at me. "If I'm not fine," he says, air quoting, "there's no possible way that you can be. We can go together."

My shoulders slump and I cast my eyes from his, leaning into his bare chest when he steps forward and holds me. "I just keep seeing him, hearing him," I whisper against him.

"I know," he whispers as he finger combs my hair softly.

I close my eyes and nod slowly. "He said Alex is my father," I whisper, voicing it out loud for the first time since I heard it.

His hand stills in my hair and he holds me tighter, his chest pushing into my cheek as he breathes in deeply. "It doesn't matter," he murmurs against my head. "It doesn't matter who our parents are, Blake. We are our family. I am your family. You are my family. That's it. That's all that matters."

I move my head up and down, robotically in agreement, but when I close my eyes I picture Benny's face, his words, and Alex crying over me in that basement. Apologizing to me for what he did. Apologizing to Cory. His one brown eye looking at me in agony as he saw me, and for a moment, it all makes sense—he saw her in me.

"Blake, breathe," Cole says as he lowers my body to the floor and holds my shoulders down. "Breathe in. Breathe out." He repeats the steps until I begin to follow his directions. When I take the last deep breath, I know I beat the impending panic attack. I close my eyes and fall into his body, hoping he'll catch me again.

The next time I blink my eyes open, I'm wrapped up in Cole's warm arms and he's tracing the stitches on my hairline-courtesy of Benny's knife.

"You didn't go back to sleep?" I ask quietly, pulling away a little, not wanting him to touch things that taint me.

He tilts his head and gives me a small smile. "You're beautiful, you know that?" he whispers, going back to tracing my stitches.

Water pools my eyes and I shake my head softly. "I'm going to have a scar...forever," I whisper back.

"So am I," he responds gravely. He leans into me and sprinkles soft kisses around my stitches before pulling back and looking at me, his eyes so full of intensity and love that it makes my heartbeat quicken. "Scars are a part of the healing process," he says quietly while tracing it again with his fingers. "We're going to be okay."

I nod slowly and close my eyes as I lean into his touch. We lay together for a while, holding each other.

"I made an appointment to see a therapist today," he says after a while.

My body goes rigid. "Can we go another day?" I ask in a whisper.

He tightens his hold on me, burying his face into my neck and taking a breath. "Normally, I would be okay with that, Blake, but no. We're not going to start pushing this back. The appointment is at two o'clock and that's when we're going. Today."

I feel myself stop breathing. I don't know if I can do this. I don't know if I can speak to somebody about my nightmares, about my past, about what's happened to me in the past year. I don't know if I want to. It's not like I haven't been to a therapist before, I have. But I usually leave out things I don't want to delve into and with Cole there with me I know that won't happen. And ultimately, I'm scared.

He pulls back from me and tilts my chin to look at him. "We're scars, baby, we need to start our healing process...together. You don't have to be scared. I'll be there with you. We'll hold each other's hands through it, like we always do," he says softly.

I blink back my tears. "Can we visit Dean in the hospital after?" I whisper.

"Yes, baby. We'll go there when we're done," he replies as he kisses the tip of my nose. "And when we're done there,

Aimee is going to come pick you up and you're going dress shopping with her while I go pick out suits with Aubry."

Once I manage to close my mouth and swallow, I furrow my eyebrows. "We don't have a wedding date yet. Or a location. We haven't even talked about it!" I reply with a short laugh.

"Next week. Courthouse," he says, getting up from the bed and adjusting the elastic of his black boxer briefs.

I blink a couple of times to make sure that this isn't some weird dream I'm having, and sure enough looking around, I realize that it's real. I lie back in an exhale and watch his back retreat to the bathroom as I try to figure out what I wanted for a wedding and come up short. I never really wanted anything because I never thought I would actually get married. I mean, of course it was fun to pretend that Cole and I would get married someday, but we were teenagers when we used to talk about it. I guess the courthouse is fine. My eyes drift closed again with that thought in mind.

Vibrating sounds wake me up, making me swing my hand to my nightstand as I blindly feel around for my phone. I pick it up and swipe the screen with my eyes still closed.

"Hello?" I mumble groggily at the still vibrating phone. I suck my teeth and finally pull my eyes open to look at it and swipe over Aubry's sapphire blue eyes. "What?" I bark out.

"Somebody's moody. Why are you still sleeping? It's like twelve," he says.

"What do you want?" I groan.

"Just checking to see how you're doing."

"Fine. I'll talk to you later," I respond, really hoping to go back to sleep.

"Wait! Cowboy, I have a question for you," he says, making me rub my eyes and sit up with a sigh.

"What's up?" I ask, trying to stifle a yawn.

"Cole called me about looking for suits later for your wedding. He says you're just gonna go to the courthouse. You okay with that?"

"I guess," I respond with a shrug. "I hadn't really thought of a wedding or anything. Why? What do you think?"

"I think you guys deserve a real wedding. You have the money. I know Momma wouldn't want you guys just going to a courthouse and getting married. I still own her house, you know. Haven't been able to sell it," he says, letting his sentence float around in my mind for a bit.

"I thought you were renting it?" I ask, confused.

"Yeah well, they didn't pay me for the past three months so they got booted."

"I don't know, Aub. I mean, as nice as that would be, I'm not sure Cole would be okay with it."

"Just wanted to put it out there, Cowboy. I think you guys should think this through a little. I know you just wanna be married and it doesn't matter where you do it, but it should be memorable, don't you think?"

I nod my head in agreement before realizing he can't see me. "Thanks, Aub. I'll think about it."

I stretch my body before getting up to get ready. Once I'm out of the shower, I wrap a towel around myself and step into my closet, stopping at the dying sunflowers on my little table. I smile at the memory as I step into my jeans and put on my blouse before taking out the skeleton key to put around my neck. Aubry's words swim around in my head as I put my hair up in a high bun and I wonder how I should bring it up to Cole.

"Hey, beautiful," Cole says, making me jump and turn around.

"Hey," I reply with a smile.

"You're in a better mood, I hope," he says with a grin as he pushes off of the doorframe and strides over to me.

I wrap my arms around his neck and stand on my tiptoes, leaning into him when he scoops me up and sits me on the table behind me. I place feather kisses on every inch of his face before reaching his lips and placing one there. Not letting me back away, he grabs both sides of my face and groans deeply as he delves his tongue into my mouth.

"I love you," he murmurs against my lips. "Even when you're being a pain in my ass."

I laugh, rolling my eyes and slap his shoulder lightly. "I love you too."

"I love how that looks on you," he says, picking the key up from my chest before letting it fall back in place.

"Me too," I respond before clearing my throat. "I have a question," I start, training my eyes on the back of his shirt collar as I pluck it with my fingers.

He cups my chin to make me look at him. "What is it?"

"Do you really want to get married at the courthouse?" I ask in a small voice.

His eyebrows knit together as confused eyes scan mine. "You want a wedding," he says finally, his lips spreading into a victorious smile. "You want a wedding!"

I feel my own smile broaden as confusion clouds my thoughts. "Why are you so excited about that?"

"Because you, Blake Brennan," he says flicking my nose with his and placing a peck on my lips, "want to celebrate the fact that you're going to be mine." He places another kiss on my lips. "You, Blake Brennan, want to throw a party," he continues in between kisses. "You, Blake Brennan, want to celebrate something with guests. Do you not see what a big deal that is?"

I laugh against his lips and wonder if he's lost his mind completely this time, but before I can say anything else, we're interrupted by my rumbling stomach.

"I guess I finally have something worth celebrating," I respond with a nonchalant shrug.

His smile falters as he looks into my eyes, caressing my face with the back of his hand. "You're worth celebrating, baby," he says quietly before clearing his throat. "Does this mean we can't get married next week?"

"Let me call Becky and find out," I reply with an eye roll.

"Cool. I'll go make you breakfast," he says, setting me down on my feet before walking away.

I pick up the phone and text message Aubry letting him know that a wedding is definitely on but not to worry about Maggie's house just yet. I think I have the perfect location for our nuptials, and I want to figure out how to keep it a surprise from Cole for once. I dial Becky's number, biting down on my lip to keep from bursting out the news as soon as she picks up.

On our way to the therapist, Cole and I go over wedding colors, flowers, and honeymoon locations.

"You wanna get married on the farm?" he asks, slowing down for a red light.

"Maybe."

"Maybe, huh?" he asks, trying to stifle a smile as he leans in to tickle me.

"Stop!" I plead in between giggles. "Just let me get the invitations and then you'll find out where, but the farm is a maybe."

"Shouldn't I be part of this?" he asks, pressing the accelerator. "Last time I checked, two people are getting married next week and I happen to be one of them."

"It's going to be small, Cole. Just let me handle it. Please? I've never planned a party in my life," I pout, trying to make him feel guilty.

He leans in and pokes my rib cage again, making me shift in my seat and laugh. "Don't play that card on me. That's your own fault."

When he parks outside of the building and turns off the car he looks over at me. "It's your wedding, Blake. As long as I'm the groom, you tell me where to go and I'm there—no matter where you want to get married."

"Thank you," I whisper before leaning over the center console of the car and kissing him.

"I pick the music though," he says when I back away from him.

Our visit with the therapist goes over by thirty minutes, and we agree to meet with her once a month unless we feel the need to go back before then. Once we started talking about our past, we can't seem to stop. Both of our issues seem to stem from the night we were kidnapped and thrown in other homes. Dr. Laura seems to think that even though we grew up in great homes, we always held on to the feeling of abandonment from that night. My pain runs a little deeper since I experienced the abandonment twice and then recently went through the kidnapping and loss of the baby. Even though I feel like I'm in a good place about the loss, it hurts that somebody could be so cruel and wanted to take my life so badly.

We're both silent on our way to the hospital, our minds both jogging with everything we talked about. I know I should let things go, but I can't bring myself to just close a chapter of my life that I don't understand. I just don't understand that night and why it happened and I don't think I'll ever fully be okay with it until I do.

"What are you thinking?" Cole asks, interrupting my thoughts as he pulls into the parking garage of the hospital.

"I just don't get it. They did all of that for money. Everything was about money. We were taken over some deal gone wrong. And why did Alex take me again if all he did was apologize to me when I was in that basement?" I ask, burying my face into my hands in frustration.

Cole places his hand on my shoulder. "You just have to let some things go, babe. Does it really matter why it happened? It happened. We survived. Hell, we had each other all those years and we didn't even know it was us. We got through it together, just let it go."

# Chapter Thirty-Three
## ~Blake~

Hospitals make me queasy. Everything about them makes my stomach convulse—from the monotone colors to the smell of latex and syringes. I take a deep breath and check in with security before following her directions to Dean's room. Cole holds my hand as we walk the eerie hallways and I make an effort not to look into the open rooms. With each room we pass, I wonder the same things: how many people have died in there, how many lives were saved, how much blood was lost, who put them there?

Cole stops walking, making me stumble over my feet and look up startled. I follow his eyes to the man walking toward us dressed in jeans, a black shirt and black jacket layering his broad shoulders. The grim look on his face turns into shock when he spots us, before settling on grief. He stops a couple of feet away from us, close enough so that we can hear him, far enough so that Cole can't hurt him. The patch that covers his missing eye makes him look more human, less horrid than the glass eye did.

Cole's hand painfully tightens around mine as Alex's eye burns into me, making me shift from foot to foot before I take a deep breath and stare back.

Alex rubs his hand over his forehead. "I'm sorry for everything, Blake. I was in too deep with Benny. He was wrong, but he was my brother and if I hadn't done what I did, I don't think you'd be here right now. But I'm sorry for taking you away from your life, your loved ones. I'm sorry for...Cory...I'll never forgive myself for letting Benny go into the house before I did..." he says, his gruff voice breaking.

"Is it true? What Benny said?" I ask quietly as tears sting my eyes.

"What'd he say?" Alex asks, his shoulders slumping.

I tilt my head. "That you're...that Liam isn't my father...you are."

Alex's eye widens and he places his hands on his chest, taking a step back as if I've punched him before he regains his cool and clears his throat. "That's impossible. Cory married Liam when I..." he gasps, looking at me as he shakes his head roughly. "I...that's impossible. I'm sorry," he says, his voice barely audible before he rushes off, leaving me standing feeling shell-shocked at his reaction.

Cole pulls my hand, turning my body to face his, and cups my cheeks with one open hand. "You don't need them," he says through gritted teeth. "He's nobody."

I blink rapidly before tears can consume my vision and nod. We walk to Dean's room and knock on the door, pushing it open slightly at the sound of voices.

"Come in!" A female voice shouts from inside, and when we step in, I see Dean laying on the bed with Sandra on one side and the most adorable blond toddler sitting at Dean's side.

"Hey," I greet with a smile looking straight at the little boy.

"Hey," Dean and Sandra say unanimously.

"Hope it's okay that we came by," Cole adds behind me.

"Of course," Dean replies. "Come in, take a seat. Elijah, this is Blake and her boyfriend Cole. Blake is your daddy's cousin."

"Fiancé," Cole corrects.

Dean chuckles, flinching and holding his stomach. "He doesn't know what that is."

The little boy scrunches up his adorable nose and scratches his head. "Does that mean you're my cousin too?" he asks, looking at me and ignoring Cole's comment.

"Yeah, I think so," I reply with a laugh.

"What's your name again?" he asks, tapping his chin with his little finger in contemplation.

"Blake," I respond with a smile.

"That's a boy's name!" Elijah chides. "My friend's name is Blake and he's a boy like me."

"Well, my friend Greg thinks my name is a boy name too and you know what he calls me?" I ask, placing my hands on my hips.

"What?" Elijah asks, his blue eyes opening wide.

"Cowboy!" I exclaim before erupting in laughter at the sight of his face.

"That's for a boy!" Elijah says, giggling loudly.

"Yeah, my friend is silly," I reply, ruffling his blond curly hair.

I look at Dean, who's watching me interact with his nephew with a small smile on his face. "How are you feeling?"

"I've been better," he replies with a shrug. "I got drugs and the cops off my back for now, so I guess I can't complain too much."

"They're still questioning you?" I ask in disbelief. "I told them everything that happened that night!"

"You know how it is. Don't worry about it, chick. I don't regret what I did, so whatever happens happens," he replies nonchalantly.

My mouth drops open and I stare at him, not believing what I'm hearing.

"Careful, flies can get in there," Elijah says, sticking a finger in my gaping mouth.

I back away and close it before narrowing my eyes at Dean. "You can't throw your life away because of me!"

"Chick, just stop talking for once," Dean says with a groan. "Did I ever tell you I went to law school?" he asks, changing the subject.

My eyes and my mouth drops open again before I snap it closed rapidly, not wanting a fly or Elijah's dirty hand to get in there. "No. You said you never went to school!"

"Well, I lied. I went to school, I just didn't finish, so it doesn't really count now, does it?"

"Umm...I'm pretty sure that constitutes as counting, Dean," I mutter with an eye roll.

"How far did you get?" Cole asks, sounding interested.

"Eh...I did a year before I stopped," Dean replies as he looks at his sister for confirmation.

"Yeah, I think you did a year and a half," Sandra confirms.

"Whatever. Point is, I threw my life away once already and back then it was really for nothing. This time, if anything does happen at least I'll be okay knowing that I saved a life or two," Dean finishes.

"Thank you," I respond quietly. "But I won't let you throw your life away. You need to go back and finish law school."

"Why? Are we going to open up a firm together?" Dean asks with a sly smile.

"I don't think so," Cole mutters quickly, making us all laugh.

"I'm serious, I want to help you if you're in trouble," I say firmly.

"Well, take your Bar and ace it, then we'll talk," Dean says with a wink.

"Oh! We're getting married next week!" I announce excitedly and look back to see Cole's face light up at that. "You guys are invited if you want to come."

Dean lets out a laugh. "I've never seen you this excited."

"I'm not sure I ever have been," I answer honestly.

"If Connor is invited I'll probably tag along," Sandra says with a shrug when I look at her.

"He is and you are too. Oh! Can we use your kid?" I ask, biting down on my lip.

Sandra and Dean laugh as Elijah looks on curiously. "You want him to be a ring bearer or somethin'?" Dean asks, cringing between laughs.

"Uh...yeah?" I ask with a cringe.

"Well, you may want to make sure you give him fake rings. The last wedding he was in ended up costing us a fortune," Sandra says, laughing as she wipes tears from the sides of her eyes.

"Oh Lord," Cole mutters behind me. "Why do we need a ring bearer?"

We all start laughing together, Elijah joining in even though he has no clue what the joke is. As Cole and I are walking out and Dean is thanking us for going to visit, Connor walks in, earning a loud shriek from Elijah. He jumps up on the bed, making Dean groan in pain, before he climbs off and runs to his dad. Watching Connor pick him up and swing him before kissing both of his full cheeks is a beautiful sight, only trumped by the following, which is Connor carrying Elijah while he gives a huge kiss to Sandra.

That is what family looks like, I think with tears in my eyes as I wave my goodbye to Dean and walk away holding Cole's hand.

We step into the empty elevator and press the parking garage button before Cole backs me into the elevator wall behind me. He ducks his head and leans into my ear, running his soft bottom lip up and down the outer shell.

"One day, baby," he whispers before sucking on my earlobe. "You're going to have so many little Coles running around, that you're not gonna know what to do with them." My breath hitches when he gyrates his hip into my pelvis. "We're going to have our own little baseball team," he continues to whisper seductively. "And you're going to be the hottest mom to ever walk the planet."

He runs his lips down my jaw and to my mouth, kissing it deeply when he reaches it and backing away when the elevator chimes.

"I'm probably going to be fat," I reply breathily.

"I won't care," he responds with a shrug and a smile.

My eyes trail down his ridiculously fit figure and I wonder how true his statement is right before I make a mental note to sign up for a spinning class or four.

Later that night after dinner, Cole heads to the gym and I curl up in front of the TV with a cup of ice cream in my hand. As I flip through channels I find Father of The Bride playing and leave it on. The dynamic of families has always been intriguing to me, I guess since I never had what you would call a normal family. The only thing I know about normal families is what I've learned from the Cosby's, the Tanners, and all the movies I watched growing up. In retrospect, I think the reason I got stuck on Home Alone was because the kid had a big family and they left him. Completely forgot about him and went on vacation while he battled with those two bad guys throughout the movie.

I sniffle back my tears as I watch Steve Martin walk his daughter down the aisle and put my ice cream down before I lose it completely. I wipe my face when I hear the door open and the keys tossed on the kitchen counter, but Cole takes one look and rushes to me, kneeling down in front of me to ask me what's wrong.

"I...I don't have anybody!" I wail. "I don't have a father to walk me down the aisle!"

"Oh, baby," Cole coos sadly. "I'm sorry," he says, pulling me down to the floor and sitting me on his lap. "I didn't even think about that. Is that why you're so hung up on the dad issue?"

My lip quivers as I exhale a shuddering breath. "No! It's not like I'm going to ask him to walk me!" I sob. "I don't know what's wrong with me!"

"Shh...it'll be okay. Would you want Mark to walk you?" he asks quietly, drying my tears with his thumbs.

I shake my head slowly as new tears roll down my face. "I should've never started watching that stupid movie," I mumble under my breath, turning to switch the TV off.

"You have the right to feel sad, Blake. It sucks to not have a normal family, it does. But you need to stop classifying what a family is by the movies and shows you watch. We may not have had a mom and a dad growing up but we always had love and we always had each other. We learned everything that people learn from their families from each other. You have two brothers, you have a sister, now you're gaining another sister. You have me. Your life is full of love, babe. Full of love."

I swallow back my tears and nod with a smile as I let his words sink in. My life is full of love.

I jog into the bathroom as Cole showers and open the door, coughing when the steam hits me in the face. "I'm going out, I'll be right back."

"What? Where are you going? What time is it?" he asks anxiously, turning around to meet my eyes.

"It's nine, I'll be back soon, I swear," I say quickly.

"Take your phone! Remember we don't have security anymore!" he shouts when I close the door and shuffle my feet back to the living room.

"We don't need them anymore!" I shout back loudly before scribbling a note telling him where I went.

I pull out my phone on the way to the elevator and make a quick phone call. In the elevator I make small talk with a cute little old lady who tells me all about the hot young men that live in our building. I laugh at her description of a tall handsome man that wanted to help her with her groceries and wonder if she's talking about Cole. When we get to the lobby, I wait for her to step out before rushing to the parking garage as I wave at Pat, the doorman, on the other side.

Taking the short drive, I park in his building and wonder how long it's been since I visited because everything looks updated. I take the elevator up to the twenty-second floor and knock on his door, waiting for him to answer.

"'Sup, Cowboy?" Aubry says, opening the door wide.

I shoot him a confused look when I see he's shirtless and wearing swim trunks.

"I was gonna go to the pool when you called," he explains with a shrug.

"Sorry. I had to talk to you about something," I start, tossing my purse on the kitchen counter and sitting on a stool before pivoting it toward him. I take a breath and look at him, his blue eyes questioning me. "Will you walk me down the aisle and give me away to Cole?"

Tears fill my eyes as I await his response and take in the shocked expression on his face. He puts his hands over his heart. "Me?" he asks quietly.

I nod. "You're my best friend, you've been my rock for as long as I can remember, you held me up more times than I can count. You kept me from freaking out when I was thirteen and got my period in the middle of school. You watch movies with me when I'm depressed and kept me from dating guys that weren't boyfriend material. You were with me when my heart went from broken to shattered and held my hand through it all. I don't know what a father is supposed to do for his daughter but knowing what I know, which isn't much, I think you pretty much qualify for the role. So, will you walk me down the aisle when I get married next week?" I ask hopefully as I wipe tears from my face.

Aubry takes a step forward and cups my chin. "I would be honored to, Cowboy. Thank you for asking me," he whispers before crashing my face into his chest and holding me there.

We pull apart when we hear somebody sniffling behind us. Turning around, we find Aimee wiping tears away from her face. "I'm sorry, I was studying but I heard and I just...that was so nice," she says with a cry before walking over and giving me a hug.

"Would you like to be a bridesmaid, Aimee?" I ask quietly against her shoulder.

She gasps loudly and backs away from me. "Hell yes!" she exclaims, making us laugh.

"Does this mean Greg's gonna be the best man?" Aubry asks.

My eyebrows shoot up. "Good question. I don't know, I didn't even tell Cole I was asking you to walk me," I reply with a shrug at the same time the doorbell rings.

"Well, I guess he'll find out now," Aubry murmurs as he walks off.

When he swings the front door open, Cole is standing on the other side with his arms folded at his chest. His lips form a grim line as he works his jaw and narrows his eyes at me. I smile and offer a small wave as I shift from foot to foot before he stomps over to me.

"Why the hell did you leave while I was in the shower? I thought you were going to run to the grocery store or something and then I find a little note that says you're coming to Aubry's! Were you gonna have a fucking sleepover without me too?" Cole fumes, his eyes boring into mine.

Sputtered laughter escapes my lips before I can hold it back. I bring my hands over my mouth to cover it, but it's futile since Aubry and Aimee join in, making me laugh even harder. "A sleepover, Cole? Really?" I ask in between laughs. "When have I ever had a sleepover that didn't involve you?"

His lips curl up, forming a slow smile and he raises an eyebrow as he strides to me. He tilts my chin to look at him and dips his head, placing soft kisses along my jaw until he reaches my ear. "That's a good question," he murmurs, making my eyes close and my body hum. "I like to think that your sleepovers only ever involved me," he rasps, nipping my earlobe and sucking it into his mouth, making a shiver run through me. "Did they?" he asks huskily, brushing his nose up and down my earlobe. "Was I the only man you ever let share a bed with you?" he continues, his voice making my heart go into overdrive, so much so that I have to remind myself to breath and that there are other people in the room with us.

"Cole," I breathe. "Please stop."

"What am I stopping?" he asks, making my breath hitch when he licks the shell of my ear.

I bite down on my lip to keep from making any embarrassing sounds in front of Aubry and Aimee, who I'm sure are enjoying the show.

"Please," I whisper.

Cole backs away and looks down at me, his green eyes twinkling as he flashes his smile and that darn dimple that makes me want to bite him and slap him at the same time. "Why'd you come over here without me?" he asks as he places a kiss on my parted lips. I begin to laugh when he continues. "Is it about where the wedding is gonna be? Aubry, by any chance do you know where this wedding is taking place?" Cole asks, tilting his head at Aubry.

My laughter instantly dies and I take off into a sprint toward Aubry, jumping on him to cover his mouth with both hands. "Don't you dare say anything, big mouth!" Aubry's body shakes in laughter under mine, and he bites the inside of my hand, making me yelp and let go. "Ouch! Bastard!" I yelp, punching him on the arm.

"My lips are sealed!" Aubry says, still laughing as he pulls me into his side and ruffles my hair.

"Let her go, dick," Cole warns playfully as he pulls me by the arm.

"His lips are sealed because I haven't told him the location," Aimee says, shaking her head. "I gotta go back to studying. Blake, I fucking hate you for not having to study this much."

She walks off, closing the door behind her and the three of us take a seat in the living room, Cole pulling me into his lap as soon as his ass hits the sofa and Aubry siting across from us.

"I came to ask him to walk me down the aisle," I say quietly, shifting my body to look at Cole.

He looks from me to Aubry and back to me before a smile appears on his face. "That's such a great idea, baby," he says, tucking my head under his chin.

I fall asleep in his arms in the middle of the Cubs game they have on and wake up when he stands with me in his arms.

"I can walk," I mumble sleepily. "I'm not a baby."

He cradles me closer to his chest and I drift off again until my butt hits the seat of his passenger seat and I'm startled awake.

"We'll pick up your car tomorrow," he says before closing the door and walking to the driver's side.

# Chapter Thirty-Four
## ~Blake~

I take a deep breath and pace around the bathroom as I wait. Ninety-seconds is a long time when you're waiting for such a vital answer. My heart picks up speed when I walk over to it and see that there's something written on the screen. I screw my eyes shut and bite down on my lip as I lift it up, not knowing what I want the answer to be in the first place. I take one last deep breath in through my nose and out through my mouth and look down.

**Pregnant :)**

My hands begin to shake as I stare at the little screen in disbelief. The smiley face throws me off for a second. What if I didn't want to be pregnant? I think before a smile spreads over my face and a mixture of exuberant laughter and tears erupt from within me. I hop up excitedly, covering my mouth to keep my excited shrieks low. I open my sock drawer and hide the stick in the back before gathering up the opened box and throwing it in the bag to get rid of evidence. Cole isn't home, but I don't want to risk him finding out yet.

I walk to the kitchen with an extra bounce in my step and get the trash bag to take out while grabbing my phone to call Becky. I dial her number and shriek my news as soon as she greets me, jumping up and down enthusiastically at her answering scream.

"What made you take it?" she asks once we've calmed down.

I shrug. "I don't know. I was sleeping the majority of the day, my tits are extra sore, I feel gross all day even though I haven't thrown up, I haven't gotten my period in well over a month now!"

"I'm so excited!" she shrieks again. "What'd Cole say?"

"I haven't told him yet," I reply, biting down on my lip.

"Oh?"

"I think I'll tell him on our wedding night," I respond, wiping my free hand on my jeans.

"True and what a great wedding present! He's going to be so exciiiteeddd," she sings.

"I know," I reply with a laugh. "You want me to pick you up on Thursday?"

"Sure! We get in at noon so we should have plenty of time to shop before we leave for the hotel. Does he know where the reception is yet?"

"Nope," I reply with a smile. "Unless Big Mouth found out and told him."

Becky laughs. "Yeah, I wouldn't put it past him. You better not tell him you're pregnant unless you want Cole to find out in five minutes!"

I'm able to get some studying done before Cole gets home, but it doesn't occur to me that we have no dinner until I hear him walk in the door. I scramble to put my things away rapidly and greet him at the door, the smell of pizza stopping me dead in my tracks. Suddenly I feel like I haven't eaten in days and I quicken my steps, reaching him and taking the box out of his hands. Before I even have time to process what I'm doing, I place it on the kitchen counter, open it, and take a big bite of a slice, my chewing only slowing down when I feel his eyes on me.

"When was the last time you ate?" he asks in his pissed off voice, making me look up to find him with his head tilted sideways as he squints at me with his arms crossed.

"Lunch," I reply before taking another bite. My eyes widen and I drop the pizza before quickly wiping my hands on a napkin. "Ohmygod, I'm sorry! I didn't even say hi!" I scoot between the stools and go around the counter to wrap my arms around him, nuzzling into his chest. "Hi baby, thank you for the pizza and for always smelling so good. I missed you and I love you."

His answering chuckle vibrates through my body, coiling my insides and instantly making me want him. I run my hands flat on his hard chest up to his tie and untie it while looking up at him and licking my lips. I see the way his throat bobs when he swallows and his eyes darken as he watches me slowly undo the buttons on his dress shirt.

"Remind me to bring you pizza every night," he says hoarsely, roaming his hands all over my back and down the sides of my body before reaching back up and cupping my sensitive breasts. I throw my head back with a moan, placing my hands on the waistband of his pants as he continues to massage my breasts over the thin material of my cotton shirt. "No bra. I approve," he murmurs, dipping his head and flicking my hard nipple with his tongue.

Pleasure shoots through me and he wraps his arms around my back, bringing me flush against him as he places feather kisses over my neck working up to my jaw and finally landing on my mouth with a searing kiss. He backs away a few inches and rubs his nose against mine before sighing a breath and gazing into my eyes.

"I missed you too," he whispers against my lips. "Let's eat so we can finish what we started."

My stomach rumbles at the mention of food, making Cole shake his head and set me on my feet. I take out a notepad as we eat to go over the guest list again, just to make sure we didn't miss anybody, not that we're having the wedding of the century or anything. We've decided to keep it small and intimate, only inviting people that we truly want to share that day with.

"Have you thought more about inviting Colleen?" I ask after taking a sip of water.

Cole wipes his mouth and exhales a breath. "I've thought about it, but I really don't know. On one hand I think why not, and on the other, I don't know if I want her there. What if she tries to bring him?" he asks in reference to Camden, making my heart sink for him.

"She won't, but if you want her there, I think she should be there," I respond quietly. "As sick as it is, Camden didn't think he was doing anything wrong, Cole. I mean...he made sure that you were okay and had money. I know it doesn't make what he did right and I hate him for it, but I think he thought it was the only way."

"Yeah, that's what makes it worse," Cole scoffs. "Whatever. I don't need him. Just invite Colleen, I guess."

I place my hand on his, offering him a small smile. "Okay. Let me get your invitation," I whisper, hopping off the stool and placing a kiss on his cheek before walking to our room and into my closet. I kneel down and get my all-things-wedding box out from the corner, opening the lid and sorting through things I've collected in the past week. I smile brightly when I find the box with invitations and open it, taking out the one I custom-made especially for him and putting the rest away, before deciding I should show him how the rest of them look as well.

When I go back to the kitchen, I find him typing furiously into his phone and the table is cleared of everything except the notepad. Standing on the balls of my feet, I place a kiss on the back of his neck that makes him shiver and put his phone down. He pivots the stool to face me and bites down on his lip, looking at me with mischievous eyes as he grabs my hips and pulls me between his legs.

"Nope. None of that right now," I warn, putting his invitation between our faces.

"Finally!" he groans. "I've never heard of a groom getting invited to his own damn wedding!"

I laugh and swat his hands when he tries to reach for me again as I back away and wait for him to open the envelope. He opens it carefully, and I watch as his mouth pops open when he takes out the folded ivory card stock with a half-moon on it. He looks at me and smiles before continuing to open it by pulling the moon up and unfolding it flat. My eyes are on his as they scan it and his smile broadens when he gets to the bottom. He shakes his head, placing it beside him and looking at me in awe.

"Come here," he says gruffly.

I walk over to him, letting him pull me into his arms and hold me in silence as he places occasional kisses on my forehead as his chest rises and lowers against me.

"I've been waiting my entire life to make you my wife," he whispers against me. "I wouldn't miss it for the world...besides, you haven't given me many options," he adds with a laugh, making me laugh along.

"Do you like where we're getting married?" I ask equally as quiet.

He backs away to look at me with a huge grin on his face, his eyes glowing. "I couldn't have picked a more perfect place."

I smile and run my hands over his invitation, flattening it to look at it again.

I, Blake Brennan, would like to invite you, Cole Murphy, to marry me in the place where I let you think you made me yours for the first time. The truth is, I was yours from the day you hid my Baby Alive doll and traded it for a G.I. Joe. I was yours the day you kissed my knee when I fell out of the tree you made me climb with you. I was yours when you warmed me with your body in the back of that van. And when you opened your eyes and looked into my soul the day I got to Maggie's house. I was yours when you slept beside me on the floor the day I got attacked. I was yours when you erased any memory I had of a first kiss by covering my lips with yours that night on Halloween, and when you took me to the Bed & Breakfast I want you to give me your name in. After Saturday, I will be yours for an eternity. And if you ever decide to go to the moon to show me just how far you'd go to prove your love for me, take me with you because I never want to live without you.

Love,

Blake (your fiancée–for now).

RSVP: yes _ yes _ yes _

"I figured I should reply to all of those notes you've written me," I say with a smile as I look at it.

"I think I'll live with you not writing back. I don't think you can top this one anyway," he replies as he stands and scoops me into his arms and begins to walk to our room.

"I haven't shown you the real invitations yet!" I squeal.

"You can show me later, we have unfinished business to take care of." He dips me, biting my neck and making me yelp.

# Chapter Thirty-Five
## ~Blake~

Walking hand in hand with Cole, enjoying a gorgeous Chicago day as we head to a high-end jewelry store on Michigan Avenue, I feel like my life can't get any better. I think we're both slowly getting to a good place in our lives as individuals and growing stronger as a couple. I lean into his arm and swing my free hand into somebody, straightening my body to apologize. My heart drops when I see Liam looking back at me, apologizing at the same time. We both freeze in place, getting pushed by all sides because of our sudden stops. I'm thankful that Cole's arms hold me from being flung with the traffic of bustle of people around us.

"Hey." He looks at me with serious chocolate eyes.

"Hey," I respond quietly.

"Let's go, babe," Cole urges, pulling my hand.

"I've tried calling you," Liam says, ignoring him. "I would really love to talk to you. I know you don't want anything to do with me, with any of us, but just one chance to explain—that's all I want."

I swallow the knot in my throat as I look into his solemn eyes. "Is it true? About Alex being my dad?"

Liam exhales sharply and Cole pulls on my hand again. "Yes, but to me, you were mine, Blake. I was the one who was there for your mom through her pregnancy, in the hospital. I was the one changing your diapers, cleaning your cuts and kissing your bruises."

"You were also the one who willingly gave her up!" Cole bites, standing in front of me to block me from Liam's view.

"For her safety! She was living with her grandmother! An amazing woman, I might add! I fucked up not being able to find her after that, I know I did! I've been paying for that for twenty-five years, dammit!" Liam shouts.

"So have I," I whisper, mostly to myself.

"So has she!" Cole yells back at the same time. "We both have. But you were an adult! You and Camden were adults! We were FOUR!"

I move off to the side closer to the building, yanking on Cole's arm so he can move with me, and Liam follows.

"I can't speak for Camden, his decisions are his. But I'm sorry, I really am. Like you said, you were four. And you were being taken care of by lovely people. I was an adult, I had to...have to live with my decisions every day knowing that I could've done things differently. Knowing I was dealing with a...look what's done is done. I know I can't change that. I know you may never forgive me, but know that I am truly sorry. Truly," he says, looking directly into my eyes so I can feel the weight of his apology.

"Okay," I reply, cutting Cole off before he starts again. "I think I'm finally at a place in my life that I can take your apology and maybe even Alex's and move on."

"Maybe one day we can get together," Liam suggests, making Cole mutter curses under his breath.

I look at him one last time—his smooth skin, brown eyes, dark hair, the lines around his mouth—and steady myself when a gust of wind flows through us, allowing me to smell him...rain. I look down at myself, my still flat but promising stomach and smile sadly. "Maybe one day," I whisper before pulling Cole out of there and continuing our walk into the stores.

"I'm proud of you," Cole says, placing a kiss on my palm.

I respond with a smile and let him lead me into the jewelry store.

I wipe my hands on the ivory gown I'm wearing for the fourth time this morning and take a couple of shaky breaths. Never in a million years would I have thought I would be nervous today. I keep reminding myself that it's just us, and I'm marrying the only man I was meant to be with, but it's not enough. My stomach is still turning, and all I can do is take deep breaths to keep me from wanting to run to the bathroom and vomit. Becky comes up behind me in her navy bridesmaid dress with an ivory sash and smiles brightly. Her red hair is picked up into a sophisticated up-do. She stands closely behind me, pushing her enormous belly into my back, while she massages my scalp. My eyes close and and my lips part at the feel.

"Sit," she orders, pushing my head down so that I sit on the chair in front of the mirror. "You look stunning. Calm down. Deep breaths. This is your day!" she says with a smile as she fixes my loose curls to cascade down my back.

"I know! I don't know why I'm so nervous!" I reply, exhaling.

"Well...have you given him his present?" she asks with a raised eyebrow.

I shake my head and sigh, feeling my stomach somersault at the thought. I'd planned on giving it to him before the reception, then after the reception, then I thought I'd just send the box over with Greg and let him record Cole's reaction but I don't want to miss it, so I settled on after. Now I'm wondering if I should just send it over after all. I groan at my own indecisiveness, making Becky giggle.

"Stop worrying! And don't move, I'm going to put this clip on your head now," she says sternly, putting a bobby pin in her mouth to open it with her teeth before putting it in my hair. She repeats the process a couple of times until the front part of my hair is held away from my face. She tightens it, making me flinch and takes out a silver comb I haven't seen before. I turn around, crinkling my eyebrows at it, and give her a questioning look.

"It's your something borrowed," she explains with a shrug.

"Who did you borrow it from?" I ask cautiously. I know it's not hers because she and Greg eloped in Vegas when we were in college and she didn't wear a veil.

"It was in your family box, silly!" she says with an eye roll. "You never sorted through the entire thing, did you?"

I gasp, my eyes widening. "The stuff Aunt Shelley left me?"

"Yeah," she says slowly, looking at me with an uneasy expression. "I thought maybe you'd want to wear something of hers."

I take the comb from her hand and examine it. It's small and silver with diamonds and just the thought that Shelley wore this at her own wedding, to the man she loved until the day she died, regardless of how sad their story was, makes tears sting my eyes.

"You don't have to," Becky whispers, seeing my sad expression.

"No, I want to. Thank you," I whisper.

"She left a note with it," she whispers, handing me a stained, folded paper.

I take it with shaky hands and unfold it. Seeing her handwriting takes my breath away, and I sniffle back tears to read it.

*I hope you use this someday*
*No matter how difficult a marriage*
*can be, love is forever. I hope both your*
*love and marriage last a lifetime.*
*I know you've chosen wisely.*
*I love you always,*
*Shelley*

I fold it back up and hold it close to my heart as Becky leans down to hug my shoulders.

"I wish she could've been here. I wish Maggie could've been here," I whisper hoarsely.

"Me too, babe. Me too," Becky whispers back, placing a kiss on my head. "Let's get you ready. No more crying on your wedding day!"

I laugh and fan my eyes, taking a couple of breaths to keep my emotions at bay. Aimee comes in wearing her bridesmaid dress as Becky adjusts my veil with the silver comb.

"You look breathtaking," Aimee breathes. "The most beautiful bride ever. My brother is going to die when he sees you."

"Thank you," I smile. "You guys don't look so shabby either!"

"Oh please, I look so fat in this. I can't believe you chose this material knowing how pregnant I am!" Becky exclaims, making us laugh. "Yeah, keep laughing! I'm going to make sure to renew my vows when you're eight months pregnant!"

"You still haven't given it to him, right?" Aimee asks in surprise.

"Nope, not yet," I reply.

"Good. Can you do it in front of us? I'm dying to see his face!" she squeals.

"I know, right?" Becky adds in excitement.

"We'll see," I say with a laugh.

A knock on the door makes us simmer down and check ourselves in the mirror one last time before opening it and letting Aubry come in to get me.

His blue eyes look at me from my feet to my head, and he smiles his huge, show all perfect teeth goofy grin before he walks over to me and embraces me. "You look stunning, Cowboy. Stunning. I got something for you," he says, letting go of me and reaching into his pocket to take out a small box.

I smile up at him. "You're definitely one of the most handsome men here," I reply, opening the little box to find a silver necklace with a cowboy hat on it. I laugh as I run my hands on it and look back up at him. "I love it! Thank you so much!"

"You're welcome. It's from Greg too, he helped pick it out," Aubry responds, shrugging one shoulder. "Are you ready to make Cole the happiest motherfucker alive?"

I nod, exhaling a breath and tuck my arm into his, winking at my girls over my shoulder.

"Okay, I gotta go. I promised Sandra I'd help Elijah practice walking WITH the rings on the pillow. God help us, I hope that kid doesn't lose them," Aimee says with a sigh.

As we walk down the hall I curse at myself and tell Aubry to wait for me while I go back to the room quickly. He helps Becky go down the stairs and I wave off his promise to be back up in time to help me carry the train of my dress. I go back into the room and shuffle through our things in search of my phone, finally finding it beneath my discarded jeans. I click on the screen and find a voice message, which I ignore to type Cole a quick text and smile when I press send. Curiosity gets the best of me and I dial to check the message, my heart dropping to my stomach when I hear the gruff voice on the other end.

"Blake, it's Alex," he starts before clearing his throat. "I heard you were getting married today. Had a long talk with Liam yesterday and just wanted to say sorry again. I want you to know that your mother was the love of my life. I would've done anything for her. Maybe someday you'll forgive me and we can talk. I...I'm so sorry. I can't believe I kidnapped my own daughter. I can't believe I treated you that way after all these years." His gruff voice is full of emotion and trails off before he coughs into the phone and speaks up again. "Maybe you'll never forgive me, but I want you to know that I'm sorry. I'm sorry for everything. Have a good wedding day. I wish...I wish things could have been different. Maybe someday you can give me a chance to make them better." He exhales. "You're beautiful, just like your mom. I know she's smiling down on you today. If you ever need me...I'm around..."

I take deep shaky breaths, blinking back tears that threaten to heave through my body.

"Hey, what happened?" Aubry asks, making me drop my phone and snap my head up to look at him.

"Nothing," I respond. "I'm ready."

As promised, Aubry helps me with my dress as we walk down the stairs, and in that moment I realize that I have conquered more this past year than I have my entire life. Walking slowly down the flight of stairs, I reminisce on how far I've come and smile at the overwhelming happiness I feel. When we reach the last step, Aubry steps down in front of me and reaches for my hand, pausing to pose for the camera beside us. Aimee and Becky walk toward us and help fix the back of my dress before giving me kisses on the cheek and walking out into the courtyard where the ceremony is about to start.

Aubry holds my hand in his as we stand in front of the closed doors. He shifts his body so we're standing looking at each other, his blue eyes searching mine.

"You sure you're okay?" he probes.

I sigh. "I am. Alex left me a voice message apologizing for things."

"And?" Aubry presses.

"And I don't know. Is it weird that I don't care as much anymore?"

"No, it's not. Maybe you finally realized that the family you have is the one that's important," he replies with a shrug.

"I think so," I whisper with a smile.

He bends down and places a kiss on my cheek before straightening his jacket. "Now let's go get you married."

When Christina Perri's "Arms" begins to play, our cue to begin our walk down the aisle, the gentleman standing beside the doors pushes them open and we step out to the courtyard where our guests are looking on. I take a moment to look around at the faces of our guests: Dean, Connor, Sandra, Mark, and Colleen. I smile at them before turning my eyes to the man waiting for me at the end of the aisle. Waiting for me like he always has been, and when the doors close behind us, I let Aubry lead me to him. All thoughts of who may or may not be my family vanish when I look into his green eyes, because he's my family. My home.

# Chapter Thirty-Six

## ~ COLE ~

I told myself I wasn't going to cry, that crying was for wimps. But seeing Blake holding my brother's arm as she walks toward me in that beautiful lace form-fitting dress she's wearing makes my heart skip a couple of beats. And when her gray eyes look into mine, I feel the air swoosh out of my body. Aubry drops her hand when they reach me and I lean in to give him a tight hug.

"Congratulations, bro," he whispers against my shoulder.

I want to reply but I'm afraid of what my voice will sound like if the ball closing my throat lets me get the words out. I hold out my hand and Blake places hers in it. I bring it up and kiss the top of it while looking into her eyes. "You look beautiful," I say, my voice sounding hoarse in my own ears.

"You do too," she replies in a whisper, making me laugh.

We turn around and face the priest for him to start the ceremony and follow his instructions, but his words are lost on me after we do the sign of the cross. All I can do is stare at this gorgeous woman beside me. She looks more radiant than ever before, if that's even possible, and I can't help but smile at her. I'm snapped out of my reverie when she nods her head toward the priest and goes to stand up, Aimee and Becky rushing to her side to help her. I shoot them a glare, but they both roll their eyes at me as if to dare me to say anything, but what the hell, I think I can help my girl get up without their help!

We stand facing each other, holding each other's hands as the priest reads another sermon. He asks us if we have our own vows or would like to recite his and I put my hand up to stop him.

"I have my own," I reply, earning an arched eyebrow and amused smile from Blake.

"I do too," she says, completely flooring me because I wasn't expecting that from her at all. The customized invitation she made me the other day surprised me enough.

The priest signals her to go first, and she crinkles her cute little nose at him before clearing her throat. She takes a step toward the priest to whisper something in his ear that makes his white eyebrows raise high in his forehead before he nods and whispers something back that makes her laugh.

"Okay," Blake starts before licking her lips. "I didn't write this down so bear with me," she says, taking my hands in hers and squeezing. "I can't tell you what love is, I really don't know that there's a concrete definition for it. But I can tell you what love is to me. When I was younger it was the way I got butterflies in the pit of my stomach every time your name was mentioned, it was the way my mind only wanted to think of you; daydream of you. The way I yearned for you and laughed louder when I was with you. You made me feel safe, cherished and happy despite my unhappiness. And even now, all these years later, now that the butterflies aren't as lively as they once were...don't worry they're still there..." she adds with a chuckle before she sniffles "You make me feel all of those things. Once upon a time I was willing to give up those laughs, those butterflies, and the smiles you gave me because I wanted to put your safety first—like I always will—but I realize now that I'd rather keep you safe by my side, because I don't feel safe when I'm not by yours. Love is the feeling of safety you give me, the peace that washes over me when you're around. Love is knowing that one day when I'm old and my body aches, my heart won't, because I'll be with you. Thank you, Cole for teaching me what love feels like. And most of all thank you for never giving up on me even when I was ready to give up on myself."

I take a shaky breath and bite the inside of my cheek, not allowing myself to cry in front of all these people, regardless of the bursting feeling in my heart. I lift her hands to mine and kiss them before wiping the tears from her cheeks with my thumbs.

"I have something for you," she whispers before turning around and getting a dark wooden box with a clasp and handing it to me. I furrow my eyebrows as I look down at the box that reads *All You Need is Love* and pop the clasp open. I am thoroughly confused when I see the tissue paper and wonder if I should have read the little programs she made for the ceremony after all. I flap the white tissue out of the way and gasp loudly when I see the positive pregnancy stick that stares back at me. I pick it up, looking from the stick to her and back to the stick and hand the box over to Greg behind me. I hold the stick up in victory, a smile taking over my face as the stupid tears that were threatening earlier now roll down my face and I don't give a shit.

"WE'RE HAVING A BABY!" I bellow, announcing it to our guests and wedding party, making them erupt in loud cheers.

"I can't believe you didn't tell me, Cowboy!" Aubry shouts from the first seat.

Blake laughs and shrugs her slim shoulders, and I look down at her body before lifting her into a hug and kissing her face and mouth, earning loud warnings from everybody. The priest laughs as he tells me that the kiss is at the end of the ceremony.

"We're having a baby," I repeat quietly as I look into Blake's tear-filled eyes. "I can't believe I didn't know it," I whisper, touching her slightly round lower stomach. "I just thought you were eating a lot because of the Bar."

Blake laughs. "Gee, thanks!"

"Can we continue the ceremony now?" the priest asks. "You should definitely get married before celebrating the baby. Well, you should've gotten married before that but we'll look past it."

I chuckle and wipe my face with the backs of my hands before wiping Blake's again.

"Okay, my turn!" I announce after clearing my throat. "'Though I doubt I can beat that! Blake, I promise that I'll be with you when life gets bad, when it's down, when it's up. I'll be with you when you doubt and when you want to run away I'll be there to hold you close to me. I promise to let you rent those sucky early nineties movies you're obsessed with. I'll even recite lame lines with you. I'll water your plants when you don't feel like doing it because I know how much it kills you when they die on you. I'll be there when you need to talk and hold your hand when you don't want to. I'll be your shoulder when you need one to soak and laugh at your jokes even when they're not as funny as you think they are. I've loved you for half a lifetime, and I'll love you for many more beyond this one. Thank you for making me the happiest man in the world today. Really. The. Happiest. Man. In. The. World. Thank you for accepting to be mine forever, and for accepting me to be yours. I love you and will be with you, fighting for you until the end of the world. I love you for loving me, and I love you for allowing me to love you. I love you to the moon and back. Forever."

She squeezes my hands and wipes her face with the free hand before Becky hands her a tissue to dab her tears with. The priest finishes saying the words he wants to say and asks the crowd if anybody intervenes in our marriage, to which nobody replies before asking for the rings. We both thank Elijah for taking good care of them and place the rings on each other's fingers. The priest pronounces us husband and wife. When he gives me permission to kiss my bride, I bend my knees and scoop her up giving her a searing kiss, pouring all the love I feel for her, all the happiness I'm flooded with, everything into it. I set her back on her feet as our guests and the other guests of the Bed and Breakfast cheer and clap loudly.

I look down at her and smile proudly. "My wife, my beautiful, pregnant wife. Congratulations, Mrs. Murphy," I whisper before dipping my face to kiss her again.

"Congratulations, Mr. Murphy. My husband. My family," she replies against my lips.

# Epilogue

*Five years later*

*~Blake~*

A lovely peal of laughter follows me as I make my way down the stairs, past the Ninja Turtle Happy Birthday banner and into my kitchen. I pull on the little hand behind me and bring her little body beside me, careful not to step on the scattered puzzle pieces on the ground. I come to a screeching halt when I reach the threshold of my kitchen and see the booths that surround the island are turned over and the floor is smeared with green icing from the cupcakes that toppled over the counter. My heart rate spikes up, my eyes widening when I see the door is wide open.

"Mommy?" Carley, my two year old says skeptically as she tugs on my shaky arm.

I don't reply, don't think. I just pick her up and place her on my hip, holding her tightly while cradling her head to my chest.

"Cole?" I call out, my voice barely audible through the pounding in my ears.

"Mommy, what happened?" Carley asks in a quiet concerned voice against my neck.

"Shh. Hold on, baby," I coo pressing her head into me again while covering her ear. "COLE!"

I turn at the sound of loud footsteps behind me, Carley's little legs swinging in movement with my body. I sigh loudly in relief when a flustered Cole appears before me. His khaki shorts, legs and sneakers filled with mud and leaving a trail behind him in the house. His blue Chicago

Cubs T-shirt drenched and sticking to his hard chest, the defined ripples of his abs and arms seeping through. His eyebrows are set in a frown, his jaw clenched and his green eyes are wild until he sees me holding his little girl and suddenly he takes a breath and a slow smile appears on his face.

"Hey," Cole says walking toward us. "That fu..." He flinches before he finishes. "Freak..." I raise an eyebrow and he takes an annoyed breath looking between Carley and I. "THAT DOG! Miles is a psycho!"

Carley and I fall into a fit of laughter and I set her down carefully when she tries to shimmy out of my hold. Her blonde curls bouncing as she skips to her dad in her green tutu and black tights.

Cole crouches down to her level. "Little, I'm dirty. I can't pick you up," he pouts, pushing his bottom lip out for effect. I bite down on my own to fight the urge to jump on him and bite it myself.

"I don't care, Daddy!" Carley says holding her arms up, always willing to get dirty, which is funny considering her older brother hates being dirty.

"I do though, honey. You look too beautiful to get dirty. I like your shirt. Did mommy get it for you?" Cole asks with a smile as he looks at her adoringly.

"Nope," she replies with a pop. "Aunt Becky!"

"Where's Miles?" I ask, interrupting their conversation. "You do realize people are coming over in an hour, right? The cupcakes are ruined, the floor is a mess. Aubry called ten minutes ago saying that Logan and Riley keep talking about the bounce house..."

My voice trails off and my breath hitches when Cole stands up and peels his shirt over his head, the sides of his body flexing calling my attention as he pulls it off. When he straightens and tosses the shirt over his shoulder, he shakes his head and I get lost staring dreamily at this man that I married five years ago and I've known forever, yet still catches me off guard when he does things that make him look like he belongs in a damn TV commercial.

"Daddy! You're wetting!" Carley shrieks with a giggle.

"Carley, clean up. Go put your dolls away," Cole says, taking her little hand and spinning her toward the living room, his eyes never leaving mine. The way he looks at me makes the desire in my body ignite and my mind forget about the messy house I need to clean up.

He begins to move toward me, his sneakers squeaking on the hardwood with each step he takes. He licks his lips slowly as his eyes travel over my body seductively, making my heart skip a couple of beats and my chest rise and fall heavily in anticipation. His footsteps stop in front of me and I crane my neck to look at him. My eyes dragging along his defined jaw, the smiling lines around his mouth that have become a little more visible over the years, and lastly, stopping on his eyes. His blazing, hooded, sexy, mischievous, tantalizing eyes. I try to control my breathing, which is increasing and embarrassingly loud at this point.

"You," Cole starts, his voice low and raspy as he caresses the side of my arm with the tips of his cold fingers, making me shiver. "Look too beautiful to clean this up." I nod slowly, agreeing to anything he says, anybody would at this point. "So perfect," he whispers dipping his head and placing a soft nibbled kiss between my neck and my shoulder. My head tilts on its own accord to give him easy access. "The hottest mom on the planet," he continues in a husky voice, trailing the tip of his nose along my neck and jaw. Suddenly his head snaps up and he looks into my eyes; his eyes wild and full of need. "I want to take you back to our bed so bad right now," he says hoarsely, taking my hand in his and placing it over the front of his shorts. "So. Bad."

He holds my hand there and ducks back in to place his lips on my jaw, raining soft kisses along it up to my ear. His heavy breathing prominent over it, before his tongue flicks over my earlobe. "I want to taste you so bad right now," he whispers in my ear as he nibbles on the lobe. My eyes flutter closed and I bite down on my lip with a groan. "You should go shower," I say breathily.

"You should shower me," he retorts as his mouth continues to work on my ear, my neck, and over my throat.

"You should go right now," I respond, my voice full of longing.

"You should take me," he rasps.

"I should," I breathe.

"You should," he confirms as he hikes up my sundress and runs his hand along the inside of my thigh.

"Daddy!" Carley calls out behind us, making us both groan loudly.

"Yes, sweetheart?" Cole asks into my neck, his voice muffled.

"Miles took dolly outside!" Carley whines.

"Oh fuck, Miles. I completely forgot about that dog," Cole mutters.

He lifts his head and fixes my dress, looking at me intently. "I still need a bath," he says, his lip forming a slight smile. "A good one. A really detailed wash," he continues, sealing my impending response with a kiss. He turns around and jogs outside, shutting the kitchen door behind him as I watch.

I'm still watching the door, my mouth hanging open when it opens back up and Cole reappears. "And don't clean up! Go to the store with Carley and buy more cupcakes. I'll pick up the mess the dog from hell caused."

I laugh at his accurate description of our rescue Boxer, Miles. He's really the most adorable dog, but he is absolutely insane. The kids love him to death, though. Especially Logan. The thought of Logan jars me out of my thoughts and I begin to scramble around the house, picking up the scattered puzzle pieces and tossing them in the nearest toy bin.

"Carley, did you pick up your dolls?" I ask when I find her playing with some in the living room.

"Yes," she mopes. "Miles has dolly."

I look at her, cupping her thin little chin and tilting it up to me. Her big gray eyes are sad when they look into mine and I offer her a reassuring smile. "It's okay, daddy will get her back. You wanna go with mommy to the store?"

She instantly perks up and bobs her head. "Yes!"

Once I load Carley into her car seat, I take out my phone and dial Aubry's number to check on their status. My nerves begin to kick in at the thought of them bringing Logan over too soon and him seeing the mess of the house.

"Hello?" Riley answers, his breathing loud and audible.

Shortly after Cole and I got married, Aubry and Aimee followed suite and took the plunge. They decided to wait on having children for a while, until one night when they saw a news report about a poorly kept orphanage, and they decided to adopt. They first met Riley when he was just shy of a year old, but didn't get custody of him until he was two. We were all for it and supported them throughout the long process. Since adoption is what I concentrate on the most these days, they asked me to take charge of all of their legal work. Aimee works alongside Mark in his law firm as a criminal attorney, and works long hours so she couldn't concentrate on the case as much as she would have liked. Between the law suit that the orphanage was facing, and everything surrounding the adoptions taking place, it took them over a year to take Riley home. But once he got there, it was as if he'd always been part of the family. He and Logan are in the same classroom, the same little league teams, and like the same things so they're basically attached at the hip.

"Hey, Ry, what are you guys up to?" I ask as I settle into the drivers seat and switch the air on. It's a hot day in May, which is a change from the cold front we had last week.

"Hey Aunt Blake, we're playing basketball with dad. Can we go to the party already? Is the bounce house there?" Riley asks excitedly.

"No, Ry. Let me talk to your dad, please," I reply.

"Mommy! Goldfish!" Carley whines from the back seat, pointing at the small carton of Goldfish I have sitting in the cup holder.

I sigh and place my cellphone on speaker, opening the carton and handing it to her.

"Thank you, Mommy," she says sweetly once she has it on her lap.

"You're welcome, sweetie. Be careful!" I say, internally pleading that she doesn't make a mess in my just cleaned car.

"Hey," Aubry says suddenly, his voice filling the car.

"Uncle Auby!" Carley shouts from the backseat.

"Hey, sugar!" he coos. "How's my favorite Ninja Turtle doing?"

"Good," she giggles.

"Are you going to jump in the bounce house with me?" he asks sweetly.

"Hmmhmm!" she replies through a mouth full of Goldfish.

"Cool! See you later!" he says. "What's up, Cowboy?"

I take a deep breath before letting it out slowly as I look at the front of my two story, white colonial home. I close my eyes and throw my head back onto the headrest. "Miles messed up the house. I'm on my way to get new cupcakes while Cole picks up. Everything is a mess, Aubry. A mess."

He lets out a laugh. "I told you Boxers were crazy dogs! But noooobody listens to Aubry!"

I roll my eyes. "You've never had a dog, why would anybody listen to you?"

"Because I know people with dogs, obviously."

"Whatever," I mutter. "Give us another thirty minutes."

"You want Aimee to go to the store for you? You sound stressed."

"I'm fine," I reply. "Thank you though."

"You're tired, Cowboy. You need to rest. I don't know why you didn't just let us take Lo to the park or the arcade or something, you know he didn't need a party," Aubry says sternly.

"I'm fine!" I respond. "I really am. And he wanted a party."

Logan has been asking me for a party since the school year started. He didn't really care to invite his entire classroom, but he did request a bounce house and for it to be Ninja Turtle themed. Who am I to turn down a four year old's simple request?

"All right, well call me when you want us to head out," Aubry responds before hanging up.

I pull the car out of the driveway and maneuver my way around our neighborhood. All of the trees are blooming and leaves are green. A beautiful sight after the cold winter we had. By the time I pull up at the store and park, I notice that Carley is fast asleep. Of course she is. I squeeze my eyes shut and bang the back of my head with my headrest, cursing myself for not taking up Aubry's request to have Aimee do this for me. My phone begins to vibrate in the console and I force myself to peel my eyes open and look at it. When I see Alex's name lighting up, my heart spikes up a little.

"Hello?" I respond as calmly as I can.

"Hey, do you need any help with anything?" he asks, his voice gruff and unsure.

I gulp down a breath. "I...are you busy right now?" I ask quietly, cringing slightly while doing so even though I know I'm ready for this.

"No, do you need something? Is everything okay?" he stammers.

"Everything's fine," I sigh as I draw circles over the hem of my white sundress. "But I've been parked in front of Dominick's for the past ten minutes and Carley fell asleep and I really don't want to wake her up and Cole's home picking up for the party and Aubry has Logan and-"

"I'll be right there," Alex says cutting me off.

"Are you sure?" I ask holding my breath.

"Of course, Blake! You need help and I told you I would always be here if you needed me. I wasn't kidding," he replies, his gruff voice as soothing as it can be.

I let out a long breath. "Thank you. I'm in the truck."

"See you there."

I hang up the phone with a shaky hand and glance at my sleeping beauty in the rearview mirror. Her lips are parted and her head is lolled to one side letting her curls hang freely. I unbuckle my seat belt and lean over the center console as best I can to adjust her head while I wait for Alex. It took a while for me to let my guard down when it comes to Alex, and still, my walls aren't completely down. Maybe they never will be, but I'm trying. He's trying. He's been trying for a while now. He sent Cole and I weddings gifts, sent us gifts for Logan throughout my pregnancy, called often. I close my eyes as my memory drifts to the day Logan was born and a small smile touches my lips.

*I got home from a long day of reading through a case I was dealing with when I was still working in litigation, before I decided that I wanted to become an adoption lawyer and help good people become parents. I called out to Cole as I stepped inside and took my coat off, brushing off* scattered leaves that had clung onto my dress. My pregnant belly bulging and my pelvic bone hurting more than usual. I looked at the stairs with slumped shoulders before making my way up. When Cole found our two story home, it took him months to convince me that we were going to be okay getting stairs. I was hesitant to buy it until I took the tour of the house and fell in love with the antique feel of it. Now I couldn't imagine living anywhere else, even if it did take me a while to warm up to the idea of a staircase.

"Cole?" I said out loud once more, stopping on the fifth step to take off my flats because even those were uncomfortable on my feet.

"In here, babe!" he called out from Logan's room.

I rounded the corner and passed our room making my way over to our soon-to-be son's room. I stopped and smiled at Cole's confused face as he eyed the socks, the onesies, and laughed when he stared at the breast pump with an intrigued look.

"What are you doing?" I asked, still laughing.

His face shot up to mine, a smile spreading over it. A smile I knew all too well and made me back up a step. "I think we should probably test this thing out before you really have to use it, don't you think?" he teased.

I shook my head, horrified. "No! I am not looking forward to that thing. Haven't you heard Becky's horror stories?!"

Cole laughed. "Babe, Becky has horror stories about everything!"

I sighed, slumping against the doorframe. "Yeah, but still..." My voice trails off as I look around the sports themed room. The walls are navy with autographed baseballs, basketballs, and footballs that sit on dark wooden shelves. The crib is dark brown, matching the shelves and the blankets are sports themed. I roll my eyes when I notice that Cole took out the football shaped toy box and placed it in the corner of the room-again, even though I keep storing it in the closet. I run my bare foot over the glossy floor that Cole had custom made to look like a basketball court and survey my eyes over the basketball hoop in front of the crib.

A small laugh escaped me. "You do realize that newborns don't do a single thing right?"

Cole's hands stopped stuffing the baby bag and he looked at me again, furrowing his eyebrows. "Robinson does a lot," he argues.

"Robinson is almost a year old," I explained with a smile, thinking of Becky and Greg's adorable baby boy.

Cole shrugged. "Whatever. Logan's gonna have the coolest room ever."

I laughed. "Yeah, hopefully we don't have to change it in two years when he starts liking Toy Story or something."

His mouth hung open. "We are NEVER changing this room! He's going to love sports. Watch!"

I bit down on my lip to keep from laughing again and walked over to my adorable husband. He turned his body toward mine when I reached him and caressed my face as he lovingly looked into my eyes. He ran his hands down my face, over the sides of my breasts, landing on my enormous belly and leaned down to kiss my lips before placing them over my belly.

"Logan, you're going to love sports! We're never changing this room and if you ever decide that you'd rather see Buzz Lightyear over the awesome room your dad worked so hard on...we're switching rooms," he murmured against me, kissing it once more.

I laughed, shaking my head and grabbed both sides of his face to pull him in for a kiss and just as our lips were about to touch, I felt uncontrollable goo rushing down my legs.

I gasped loudly. "Ohmygod! My water!"

Cole's eyes widened and his mouth popped open. "It broke!?"

"Yes!" I squealed pulling away from him to look down, horrified at the puddle at my bare feet. "This is so gross!"

"Holy shit! What the fuck should I do?! Don't move!" Cole said frantically, jogging out of the room and reappearing with two towels in his hands.

He threw one on the floor and one around my waist before scooping me up in his arms and walking me to our bedroom. He placed me down when we got to the bathroom and held my shoulders. I looked up at him, tears forming in my eyes at the thought that this would probably be our last time alone in this bathroom.

"Are you okay?" he asked quietly, lifting my face with a hand on either side of it to look at me with concerned eyes as his chest rose and fell quickly.

"I feel fine. I don't even have contractions," I replied, crinkling my eyebrows at the thought.

He nodded and I could see he was trying not to freak out over this. "Do you want me to help you shower before we go?" he asked, his eyes darting to the shower, me, the empty bag on top of the counter.

I smiled and brought my hand up to his face, smoothing his worried eyebrows with the back of it. "I'm fine, Cole," I repeated calmly. "I'll shower while you finish packing up."

He let out a breath and nodded a couple of times, his worried eyes not straying from mine. "You'll tell me if you get a bad contraction?"

"I'll tell you," I replied, getting on the tips of my toes to reach his lips.

The sound of Adele's One and Only blaring from my phone brings me back to the present. I slide it to unlock, wishing Cole wouldn't have set that as my ring tone when he bought me the phone because it's so loud.

"Hey," I answer quietly, eyeing an undisturbed Carley. She sleeps as heavily as her father.

"Hey, what's your status? Did you get the cupcakes?" he asks breathlessly.

"Carley decided to take a nap so I've been sitting in the parking lot. I'm waiting for Alex to get here so he can help me," I explain.

Silence.

"Hello?" I say, taking the phone away from my ear to make sure we didn't get disconnected.

"Yeah. How did that happen?" Cole asks.

I sigh. "He called. I was tired. Carley's sleeping. You're busy, Aubry's busy. I don't know," I reply quietly.

"I think it's good," he responds. "He's coming over for the first time today and he's been good to us. He cares about the kids, about you. I think it's good that you're letting him help you. You know I can drop what I'm doing and go over there, right?"

"I know," I reply with a smile. "But I'm fine. I'm ready."

Silence.

I laugh. "Cole?"

"Yeah. I'm here," he says. "I just never thought I would hear you say that. Especially after you kicked him out of the hospital when he went to go visit you and see Logan."

My shoulders slump. "I know," I whisper, tears filling my eyes. "I just wasn't ready. I feel so bad about that now. He's a good man...right?" I ask even though I know he is. He's shown me how good he is over and over and never stopped proving himself, even when I turned him down and didn't let him see his grandchild.

"He is, Blake. I wouldn't let him near you or our kids if I didn't think he was," Cole responds with a sigh.

I look up and see Alex' black mercedes pull into the parking space in front of me. "He's here, I gotta go."

I hang up the phone and put it in my purse as Alex walks toward my door. His blond hair is slick back with gel and reaches the nape of his neck and he's wearing a black patch and a black T-shirt, which makes his blue eye stand out more than usual. He smiles warmly as my window lowers, and I greet him with a smile of my own.

"Hey," he greets, his eye searching my face the way he always does when he sees me, before he looks into my backseat and sees Carley, which makes his smile widen even bigger. "She's a good sleeper."

I look over my shoulder. "She is," I reply smiling.

When I look back at Alex, he's still watching Carley. "You make beautiful kids, Blake."

Water fills my eyes and I bite down on my cheek to keep them at bay. "Thank you."

He looks at me then, his eye glistening and full of emotion. "So do I," he whispers hoarsely.

A couple of tears escape my eyes when I blink rapidly. I sniffle and wipe them away quickly.

"Sorry," he says. "I just...I'm in awe of you. You're such a good mother, such a good wife...and you're my daughter. I just..." His voice breaks and he clears his throat. "I wish Cory was here."

I smile sadly, placing my hand over the one he has resting on my door and squeeze. "Me too," I whisper. "But I'm glad you are."

He gapes at me and his body shifts back as the shock of my words hit him.

"Mommy," Carley calls out groggily behind me, snapping us out of the moment.

"Hey Little, you're finally awake!" I say with a smile.

Alex steps away allowing me to put the window up and turn off the car. He offers me his hand, which I thank him for and take as I climb out of the truck. He follows me as I walk behind the truck to get Carley out of her seat.

"Should you be lifting her?" he asks in a concerned voice.

"I kind of have no choice," I reply with a laugh, placing Carley on my hip.

"I can...I can carry her?" he offers.

I stop wrestling with my purse for a second and look at him, unsure.

"I don't have to," he says quickly.

"Carley, will you go with Alex?" I ask, holding my breath.

Carley smiles, showcasing her little teeth and the dimple on her right cheek. "Yes!"

Alex and I both let out an audible breath as I hand her to him. Once we get a cart, he sits her down carefully and pushes it as we walk through the store. We make small talk about my job, and he fills me in on Dean's whereabouts.

"Have you spoken to Liam?" he asks as he loads the things we bought onto the check out belt.

I downcast my eyes from his. "I haven't."

Liam and I kept in touch for a while, we still do but not as much as we used to. When I do see him, it's around Brian's house and that started to become awkward when he found out that Alex and I were actually getting along. The fact that Liam is good friends with Cole's dad doesn't help much since Cole absolutely despises him. He refuses to forgive him or speak to him. Thankfully that isn't the case with his mom. Colleen is the sweetest grandmother and helps us out in any way she can. After she finalized her divorce from Camden, which became a huge scandal, she ended up moving twenty minutes away from us and comes over almost daily to see the kids.

Alex grumbles something under his breath and shrugs.

"I can't believe you still talk to him," I say with a shake of my head and lean down to fix Carley's dangling shoe. "He married the woman you were in love with while she was pregnant with your kid...I don't know. It's just...crazy."

When I bring my face back up, I find Alex watching me intently. He nods his head. "True. But he took care of her when I couldn't. He took care of you...when I couldn't. I hated him for years, you know? Hated him."

I look at him expectantly, waiting for him to expand on that. When he realizes I'm not going to budge, he finally exhales a breath and offers me a small smile. "But I hated myself more."

I nod and take out my wallet to pay but Alex beats me to it, handing the cashier money for everything.

"It's my grandson's fourth birthday," he explains to the cashier when she looks between us. She shrugs and takes his money.

Alex loads everything in my trunk and puts Carley in her seat, promising to see us at the party later.

When we get home, Cole meets us outside and takes the bags down before getting Carley and taking her inside, and I'm relieved to see the house back to normal when I walk in. The dog is in the yard, the kitchen is picked up and clean, no mud tracks on the floor. It's perfect. For the next couple of hours we work on the rest of the stuff as the party company sets up the bounce house and Carley watches a movie. The doorbell rings while I'm placing the last cupcake topper and Cole is evening out the table cloth. We both straighten up, our eyes meeting as he walks around the table and stands in front of me.

"You need to take it easy today, okay?" he says.

I nod my head slowly, my eyes not wavering from his as he looks at me intently. When he licks his lips slowly my eyes dart to his mouth for a second.

"I love it when you look at my mouth like that," he says in a low voice that makes me bite down on my own lip as he leans into me, his breath hitting my eyelids before landing over my ear. "And I love the way you smell," he rasps while running his nose along the brim of my ear. "And the way you take care of our kids," he continues, placing a kiss near my earlobe. "And the way you love me," he adds with another kiss. "And the way you let me love you," he says sucking on my neck, making me moan. He continues to trail kisses over the swells of my breasts and down the center of my stomach until he reaches my belly button. "And the way you look when you're carrying my kids in here," he says kissing my pregnant belly before he gets up and looks at me again. "I love you, Blake Murphy."

I gulp down loudly, trying to control my tears and fast breathing. "I love you, Cole Murphy."

He runs the pad of his thumb over my bottom lip slowly, his green eyes heavy as he looks at me. The doorbell rings two more times and Carley obviously informs us that someone is there. Cole dips his head and kisses me, leaving no trace of my mouth un-sated before slowly untangling his tongue from mine and backing away from me.

"So much," he says and pivots his body, breaking into a sprint to get to the door.

"Hey! Happy Birthday, kiddo!" Cole says enthusiastically, picking up Logan and swinging him around a couple of times.

"Thank you, Daddy," Logan responds before turning to give his sister a hug.

I place one hand over my heart and the other over my stomach, smiling, grateful for the amazing family I've been given. Logan runs to me and I crouch down a bit, opening my arms to hug him.

"Happy Birthday, baby," I greet, picking him up and kissing his ruffled brown hair. His gray eyes shining bright.

"Thank you, Momma," he says with a smile. "I wanna go to bounce house!"

I shake my head and laugh. "Do you like all of the Ninja Turtle stuff? Say thank you to daddy for putting up all the decorations," I say with a raised eyebrow.

"Thank you, Daddy," Logan says turning around to face Cole.

Aubry, Aimee, and Riley continue to walk in, greeting us as they look around. Connor and Sandra arrive next with Elijah, who's too smart for his own good at eight years old. Colleen shows up next followed by Mark, Brian and lastly, Alex. Greg and Becky call us through FaceTime so that Logan can see his cousin Robinson, whom he adores.

"Dude! You should've seen it!" Aubry shouts as I make my way outside with drinks. "Logan has some serious vert!"

I groan, rolling my eyes as I hand him his beer. "Can you please stop talking about the way my kid jumps?"

"Cowboy! You gotta put him in basketball! No joke, Cole, he fucking jumps higher than I do!" Aubry exclaims

"That's because you can't jump for shit," Cole replies with a laugh.

"Yeah dude, you suck at basketball," Connor says. "Remember the time you sprained your ankle...WALKING TO GET WATER?!" he adds as he goes into a full out belly laugh, the rest of us joining him.

I laugh at the memory, wiping the tears from my eyes as I walk back inside to get more drinks. Aimee and Sandra join me in the kitchen to help me put out snacks and we sit down for a while and talk about the usual: husbands, kids, work, and lack of time to shop or do anything for ourselves.

When the sun takes the day and the party is over, all of our guests leave with the exception of Colleen and Alex. They help us clean up, both of them echoing Cole's pleads for me to sit down and put my feet up. I take an exhausted Logan and Carley to the living room and cradle them close to my side and watch an episode of Max and Ruby, which I am absolutely dying for them to stop liking so much, as we wait for them to finish.

"Mommy, when is baby coming?" Logan asks, sleepily laying his head over my stomach.

"Soon, baby. Next month you and Carley will have a little brother to share your toys with," I reply kissing the top of his head as I run my fingers through Carley's tangled hair.

Logan raises his head and looks at my stomach. "He's gonna play with my Ninja Turtle?" he asks scrunching his little nose.

I laugh lightly. "Yes he will."

Logan nods once and looks back to the television.

"I'm heading out," Alex says, making the three of us turn our heads.

I make my way to get up but he puts his hand up to stop me. "You guys look too comfortable there. I just wanted to thank you again," he says quietly, his eye bouncing between each of our faces, cherishing the moment.

"You're welcome to come back," I offer with a smile.

His chest rises and falls once. "Thank you," he replies with a smile.

He walks over to us and places a kiss on each of our heads before turning around and leaving.

"Our grandpa is awesome," Logan says, causing my eyes to widen and my heart to skip a beat.

"Yeah?" I ask, unsure.

"Yeah! He bought me numchucks!" Logan replies excitedly.

"Nun-chucks," I correct with a smile.

Logan smiles and nods quickly.

"Yeah, he is pretty cool..." I say, my voice trailing off.

Colleen comes into the living room and says goodbye to us, turning to Cole and giving him a big kiss on the cheek and slapping his face lightly. "You're working tomorrow?" she asks.

Cole sighs, running his hand through his hair as his eyes land on mine. "I am."

"Don't worry, I'll come over and take care of her for you since you think she's going to break," Colleen teases while I laugh.

Cole purses his lips. "I don't think she's going to break...I just prefer to know she's okay and not overdoing things while she's pregnant."

"Sure," she says laughing as she walks out.

Cole closes the door behind her and comes back to the living room, plopping down beside Logan and putting his arm around us as he leans his head against mine.

"We did good," he whispers.

I look into his eyes. "We did good," I confirm with a smile.

After bath time, I lay Carley down while Cole gives Logan his bath. I decide to jump in the shower while they do their usual routine and when I come out, I find the house is dark except for the light coming from Logan's bedroom. I tiptoe to his door and lean against the doorframe to watch them quietly. Logan is tucked into his bed and Cole is sitting on the oversized football beanbag beside him with a book open. I cross my arms over myself and shiver at the air that hits my bare arms and watch as Cole reads to our son.

When he looks up and finds me standing there, he stops reading and smiles at me. His eyes filled with a love that reaches deep within me and makes my own heart stir. I place my head on the wall and continue to look at him as he reads. Not for the first or last time, thanking the universe for giving me this man. This perfectly imperfect man that loves me so much it's almost unimaginable. I'm thankful for the family we have together, the one we've made and the one we've gained over the years. My life feels as complete as it can possibly feel. I run my fingers through my hair and over the scar on my hairline, the part of my life that is gone but will never be forgotten. And I'm thankful that we made it out of that together, and that we're no longer the broken people we once were. Cole clears his throat and I blink my eyes, realizing that I have tears streaming down my face. I wipe them away as he looks at me, his bright green eyes the only thing visible in the dim light...the only thing visible to me in any light.

He smiles then, that big smile with the dimple that I had no chance of ever not falling in love with, and he reads from memory. His eyes never swaying from my own...

*"Big Nutbrown Here settled Little Nutbrown Here into his bed of leaves. He leaned over and kissed him good night. And he laid down close by and whispered with a smile: I love you, right up to the moon...and back..."*

To you, reader:

To everybody who read There is No Light in Darkness when it came out and (im)patiently waited for this one.

The ones who reviewed it.

The ones that took the time to email me to tell me how reading it made them feel.

The ones who took the chance and one-clicked without knowing what they were getting into.

This one's for you.

Thank you from the bottom of my heart for lending me your time, your mind, your heart, your eyes. It truly means the world to me!

I love you all. To the moon and back,
Claire

Ps. Yes, I will be posting an epilogue online for those who want to read one ;).

Catch me (if you can) on:

FB: facebook.com/ccontrerasbooks
Twitter: @ClariCon
Gmail: CContrerasbooks@gmail.com

# Acknowledgements

Cole & Blake, thank you for giving me such an interesting story to write. I hope I did it justice!

Christian: Thank you for telling me what tie goes good with what shirt and suit combination, for answering strange questions like, "is it drive through or drive-thru"? "Do you really have to use those huge cans to make heroin like in Breaking Bad?" Basically, thank you for being my own personal Google. And for accepting me. And loving me. I love you.

Abraham and Moses: Thank you for believing in me so blindly. You don't even know what I do, yet when you see my book somewhere you point, you smile and yell, "THAT'S YOUR BOOK!" That alone pushes me to keep doing this. Because I love it, and I want you both to have something you feel this way about someday.

My fam (mom, Jay, Barbara, Rudy, Dan, Noah): Your undying support means the world to me. Thank you so much. I love you.

My "critical critics": Jessica, Ashley & Sandra (Turtle): Every time you had chunks of this story in your hand, I felt like I couldn't breathe. That, I think, is the sign of a great reader. Thank you for being such amazing readers, critics, not holding back, and helping me throughout this journey.

Barbie Bohrman (my McCartney): Thank you for letting me bounce ideas off you even when I blurted out spoilers (oops! LOL). You're going places and I can't wait to see you shine! Write on.

SL Jennings: For all of your help, listening to my rants, calming me down when I wanted to trash it for a third time. Thank you <3.

MJ Abraham & Angie McKeon: I look forward to our chats every day. Thank you for believing in me, pushing me, and talking non-sense with me. Totally off topic, but...lol

Lisa Chamberlain: Thank you for pausing your life to write my blurb, read my story, and give me amazing feedback! I'm waiting...

Lori Sabin aka rockstar editor. I am in awe of you and so thankful to have been able to work with you in this incredible journey. Your words mean the world to me. Thank you for everything!

My Fight Club Crew...rule #1...;) LOVE YOU GIRLS!

MY ANGTFT girls: AL Zaun, Karina Halle, Madeline Sheehan, EL Montes, Gail McHugh, LB Simmons, Melissa Brown, Calia Reed, Laura Howard, Katja Millay, Michelle Valentine, Trevlyn Tuitt, Nikki D, Nikki N, Elaine Breson, Cindy Brown, Stacy Bentley, Rose Hunter, Lisa Paul, Antoinette Candela, Kendall Grey, Evan Taylor, Janine Olsson, Kahlen Aymes, ...thank you for making this process so much fun. For the laughs, the vents, for just being you. Thank you.

AL Zaun: Thank you for always looking out for me and helping me when you have your own writing and things going on! And for being Cole's biggest fan!

Taryn: My favorite jerk. Thank you for being my cheerleader, making me laugh and cry, for your texts, memos, and snail mail (even if you do send me glitter and things I want to kill you for).

My betas/readers: Trisha (thank you, thank you, thank you for your encouraging words), Michelle Finkle, Christine, Natalie, Mari, Justine, Nikki, Sam, Brigitte.

Angela McLaurin (Fictional Formats): For doing this on such short notice and making it look more beautiful than I ever anticipated it looking.

Sarah Hansen: For making this cover even more amazing than the first one, which is a difficult task since the first one is stunning.

Stepha, Blanca, Anabelle, Diana, Lidia, Karlla- THANK YOU for your support. I love you!

Reviewers & straight up **amazing** supporters: Rachel Zilkoski-Keenan, Jodie Stipetich, Christine Estevez, Bridget Peoples, Jennifer Mirabelli, Juliana Cabrera, Fred Lebaron, Trisha Rai, Orquita Rahman, America Matthews, Daisy Esquenazi, Kimberly Shackleford, Stephanie Horning, Tessa Teevan, Dianna Almanzar, Jen Dale, Andrenella Dielingen, Melissa Mascolo, ALL of my KBs, Crysti Perry, Jen Dale, Tessa Teevan, Abigail Ketner, Shey Houston, Robin Prete, Lizzy Henriquez, Sarah Lowe, Becky Lowe, Yvette Huerta, Ciara Martinez, Megan Hand, Megan Simpson, Jennifer Roberts-Hall, Anne Brewer, and Jennifer Hagen.

Other authors that ROCK hard and have helped me in this process: KA Linde and J.Sterling, thank you <3.

The bloggers, you guys really amaze me. Your love for reading, your beautiful reviews, the way you push our books. AMAZE ME. Thank you. Thank you for reaching out and letting me know you loved TiNLiD, thank you for sharing it with your readers. My Secret Romance Book Reviews, Angie's Dreamy Reads, The Autumn Review, Mommy's Reads and Treats, Sweets by Steph, Fiction & Fashion, Shh Mom's Reading, Devoured Words, Aestas Book Blog, Guilty Pleasures Book Reviews, Three Chicks and Their Books, Indie Bookshelf, Jessica's Book Review, Romantic Book Affairs, Reality Bites Let's Get Lost, Wine and My Kindle, The Book Blog, Bridger Bitches, Up All Night, Sugar and Spice, Sweet Reads, Book Bitches, and so many others that I may have missed but appreciate dearly.

# Return to Me
## by Adrianna Luca

a contemporary romance novel coming late 2013

# Chapter One

## eight years earlier

Luke took one last deep pull on his cigarette and flicked it into the grass. Blowing out the dry smoke, he removed the low country boil from the grill. He had been preparing the pot soon after he arrived at the lake while the guys set up the table and the women spoke with one another. The lake was a part of their youth where memories were laid down and never forgotten. It only made sense for them to get together here after the past few years of being apart. He squatted down and poured the steaming pot into a colander with a basket underneath to receive the draining water. Now that it was finished and needed to cool, Luke wanted his girl in his arms.

Luke spotted Olivia standing barefoot with her back to him staring across the lake. She was in her blue and white striped bikini, which showed way too much damn skin in his opinion. Her sexy lean legs were tan and firmly in place while she stood with something clearly on her mind. Her dark wavy locks were swept up in a messy tie where a few strands managed to escape landing around her slender neck. Surrounding the lake, the massive trees were tall and thick with a wide variety of green foliage. The trees were at a height where they arched slightly over the winding lake creating a shadow over the water. And when the wind blew, he could hear the trees sway with the most incredibly cool breeze brushing against his hot summer skin. Livy looked so small and lost standing there by herself.

In a lazy saunter, Luke made his way over to Livy. When he was standing behind her, he placed his hands smoothly onto her sun kissed shoulders. He leaned down and quietly sang behind her ear, "Why you makin' me fall in love with you, no complications, just easy and smooth love like the summer breeze that drifts through the leaves, baby lean into my kiss, every man needs his own whiskey girl like this..."

A small giggle escaped Olivia.

"Penny for your thoughts?" Luke asked as he wrapped his arms around Olivia's slender waist, squeezing her tight to him. There wasn't any breathable space between them now. Leaning down, he placed his chin onto the curve of her shoulder. "What are you thinking about in that pretty head of yours?"

Sighing she paused before she answered. "Nothing...just thinking what a great day it's been." Olivia placed her hands on top of Luke's, threading her small fingers through his big ones. She caressed the back of his warm hands with her thumbs, circling them slowly against his skin.

Turning his head slightly alongside hers, his stubble lightly grazed the side of her smooth face. He asked, "You sure, baby? You look like you have a lot on your mind." Luke gently pressed a kiss to the side of her neck. She smelled like a blend of the sweet tea she loved to drink and coconut. He inhaled and kissed her once more, rubbing his nose softly against her neck.

Olivia trembled from the small contact. "Just here looking at the beautiful lake, watching your brother's rough house, thinking how today was so wonderful. One of the best days of my life. Wondering about where everyone will go now that we've all graduated college. What kind of jobs everyone will get."

Luke paused briefly before he replied. "I think I'm going to need more than one penny."

Luke and Livy chuckled together as she relaxed into him, laying her head back against his chest as they slowly rocked side to side. The sun was stronger this time of year and he could feel the heat beating down on his bare shoulders. It didn't bother him though. He was born and raised in the South, so the exceptionally high temperature was nothing new to him. It was actually a welcoming feeling against his skin, one that he loved to feel. In fact, he detested cold weather and couldn't imagine why anyone would want to deal with it.

Olivia continued to fix her eyes straight ahead, unwavering. He sensed something was swirling around in that mind of hers. Not wanting to push, he dropped it and figured she'd speak when ready.

"Yo, Luke! The food done yet? I'm starvin'!" Colt hollered.

Shaking his head, he reared back and yelled, "Y'all can get your own damn food!" He'd be dammed if he was going to let his girl out of his arms. Luke brushed the strands of hair out of the way and then leaned back down, kissing Livy's neck tenderly, grasping her a little tighter. Absolutely nothing would take this away from him. He felt pure bliss. Luke had his girl in his arms and that's all that mattered. In a moment as simple as this, he fell in love with Livy a little more each day.

Leaning against a giant Oak Tree in his now dry swim trunks, Luke's arms were crossed firmly in front of his bare chest. He was unmistakably irritated that a tick started in his jaw. They'd just spent an incredible day by the lake with their closest friends swimming and grilling like old times. Luke even sang songs and played his guitar, some along with the radio and others off the top of his head. The singing was mainly for Olivia's pleasure. He loved to watch her face display a dozen different emotions while he sang. Her beautiful brown eyes would light up before concealing them as if she didn't like it. But he knew her all too well. Her eyes would focus in on the guitar while his fingers strummed the chords. When he added, 'whiskey girl' to a song, he'd lay it on thick causing his southern drawl to come out in a raspy and husky sound, grabbing her attention. Livy's heated eyes would drift up to meet his and they'd lock in place. Whiskey girl had become a nickname he used for her and her alone.

All of their friends had left the lake now, and they were having a heated discussion- more like an argument- with Livy about the future. Luke was trying in vain to keep his emotions at bay. Olivia took him completely by surprise with her thoughts and truth be told, it wasn't sitting well with him. He couldn't say he was completely blindsided by it, he felt earlier that she was holding back, but still, he wasn't expecting this.

Tension mounted between them as Luke said, "What do you mean you want to leave Georgia? So you're telling me you're better off somewhere else? This right here baby," he said, hitching up his thumb and pointing to the woods behind him, "is the real deal. This is where your heart is, where your friends and family are. It's your home. You're not going to get much better than this." Luke rubbed his chest as tightness gripped him inside just thinking about it, an unfamiliar feeling creeping in.

He paused, placing his right hand over his heart and said, "It's also where...I am. Take it or leave it. What's it going to be?"

Sitting under the tree on an old wool gray blanket gave her very little reprieve from the sweltering sun. Olivia bit the inside of her lip as she glanced up at Luke with her big, round chocolate eyes. She could swear she heard his voice crack at the last statement he made. It was as if he was saying take me or leave me. Goodness, did it hurt to hear that since she had no intention of leaving him to begin with.

"Take it or leave it... what is that supposed to mean, Luke?" Olivia spat out with bite. Shaking her head, she pulled up her knees to her chest, wrapped her arms around and looked away. Olivia felt sick as she replayed the words in her mind.

Luke didn't respond, instead he just stood there silently, stubbornly. She looked back up into his green eyes and saw that they held a mixture of confusion and a hint of pain yet his body radiated confidence as he spoke. Subtly, she shook her head and sighed, so frustrated by how difficult he was to read.

Luke looked so good standing there with his deep olive tan and messy sandy blonde hair that had dried unevenly from swimming in the lake earlier. His hair was longer than most men's and full of different shades of dirty blonde that women would pay top dollar for. The strands curled just at the tips framing the sides of his handsome face. He kept pushing it away but it would just fall back. His black board shorts hung low on his waist, showing off the slight v that dipped into his suit. It wasn't pronounced, but the thin strip of dark hair driving up from beneath caught her attention. Luke wasn't overly defined or full of ridiculous bulging muscles, but he was toned to the right amount of perfection for her.

Olivia loved Luke deeply and probably always would. He was her first real boyfriend- not counting all the losers she dated in high school. Luke was pretty much her first real everything. They began dating before college and as luck would have it, they ended up at the same university. But she wasn't destined to live in a small town forever. Olivia aspired beyond the life she was dealt, she worked hard for it. Why couldn't he comprehend her need to at least give it a shot outside of Georgia? She wasn't breaking up with him, she just wanted to see what else was out there. Surely he would understand... Or perhaps even go with her should she ultimately decide to leave?

A current of air silently glided off the lake and through their little spot. The trees swayed causing the sun to filter through the green leaves and land onto her bronzed skin. Olivia bit the inside of her lip, a habit she had when she was nervous. She worried that the decision she was about to make could change so much between them. She knew what she wanted; city lights, a little snow, the hustle and bustle of busy streets, and most of all, a secure life where she wouldn't have to rely on anyone again. But she couldn't figure out why, deep down, she had a notion that what she was about to say could tear them apart.

Olivia was picking at her nails as she tried to think of an answer that would be the "right one." Answering his question with trepidation, she said in a soft voice, "I...I want more. I want to see what other places have to offer. Maybe you want to leave with me? We could go together? I would like to experience life outside of this small town, Luke. And... you should want that too, for both of us. Isn't there anything you want?"

"I know what I want. I'm lookin' at her," Luke said to her in a barely audible voice, his eyes piercing hers. Luke was wound tight. Pushing off the tree with his back, the grass was hot, crumpled underneath his feet as he increased the space between him and Livy. Pissed wasn't even the word to describe what he was feeling at this very moment. Maybe agitated? Maybe fuming? He wasn't sure. It didn't matter. Luke reached into his pocket and pulled out a cigarette. He titled his head to the side, cupped the tip of the cigarette with his palm as he flicked his lighter and lit it. Taking a deep drag and exhaling, he was trying to interpret exactly what she was saying. Did Olivia just say, in so many words, that she wanted to leave? That she wanted to see if there was more out there for her? What else did she need? Did he hear her correctly? Blinking rapidly, he just shook his head and kept walking away. What the hell was he then? Nothing to her? Did the past four years mean absolutely zilch?

Of course Luke wanted Olivia to do what made her happy, he'd do anything to satisfy her, but without him? He'd just assumed that they'd stay in Georgia together. The thoughts began to eat him up inside. Was he being selfish wanting Olivia to stay here with him? Probably. Did he give a shit that he was about to be a prick? Nope. Not a damn.

Luke turned back toward Olivia with newly found determination. Pinching the cigarette between his thumb and forefinger, he gritted his teeth as he said, "Fine. Leave. If that's what you want, then go. I hope you find what you're looking for. But know this, I won't be waiting for you when you come back, 'cause baby, you'll be back. This place is in your bones. Mark my words."

Standing up, Olivia had fire in her eyes as she stomped over to Luke, her hair blowing frantically in her face. She was just a few feet away now and seething in exasperation, her hands forming fists at her sides. Irritation rolled down her clammy skin in rippling waves that heated her to the core. Leave? Luke just told her to leave?

"Luke! You're being stupid! We're young, fresh out of college and have our whole lives ahead of us. How do you know you're supposed to stay here? How do you know there isn't more waiting for you somewhere else?" Olivia yelled, throwing her arms around as she spoke. "Is this enough for you? To be confined to this little town where everyone knows everything? Is that what you want?"

Luke stood stock still, his eyes narrowing in on her. This woman was making his blood boil, and not the way she usually did either. He had a feeling he knew where this conversation was going but didn't want to accept it just yet.

With sheer purpose in his eyes, Luke took one last pull inhaling, flicked it and crossed the short distance to where Olivia was standing. He blew the smoke out and eyed her as if he'd just spotted his prey, ready to devour her.

Reaching behind and grabbing the back of her head, he fisted her hair in his hand close to her scalp firmly. He used his left arm to circle her waist and pulled her flush against his body. Her back ached and her stomached pressed into him. He heard her breath catch as he held her tight. God, how he loved her. Loved her for some time now. Damn. Maybe even longer than the four years they've been dating, but now it felt as if she was leaving. He could feel it and was prepared to do anything to get her to change her mind. Call him selfish, he didn't want to see her go.

Leaning down close enough to almost touch his face with hers, he searched her eyes as he said in a whisper, "You're enough for me, woman. You. I want what you want and I thought it was to be here. But now I'm seeing that we might not want the same thing." Shaking his head, he said, "What changed, Liv?"

Luke could feel Livy's body soften up against him. He loved that he had this effect on her. Dense hot air circulated them and flowed between them, making it hard to breathe. He'd like to believe that it was the humidity in the air right now, but they'd always had such chemistry together. He'd be fooling himself thinking otherwise.

Luke stared down into Olivia's dark brown eyes. He brushed his lips gently across hers and never losing eye contact he said against them in a breathless whisper, "Did you hear me, baby? You. I said you're enough for me. Am I not enough for you?" Then he pressed his mouth down onto Olivia's soft, lush lips. He wanted, no needed, to show her how much she meant to him.

Slowly, he slid his tongue across the seam of her mouth, causing her to part her warm lips just slightly. He tenderly pulled her bottom lip into his mouth and nibbled on it. She tasted like the damn sweet tea that she was always drinking which fueled him more. She felt so good against his mouth as he gently started to suck on her lush bottom lip, caressing it with his tongue.

In charge of the moment, Luke slid his tongue into Olivia's mouth. The split second it touched her tongue, he put everything into that kiss, crushing her to him. Pulling her tighter so she couldn't move, he kissed her. He kissed her for all the days he'd known her. He kissed her to show her what she meant to him. He kissed her as if his life depended on it. And he kissed her like it was the last chance he was ever going to get. He devoured her lips with vigor. It was as if he was overpowered with this need to convince her to change her mind. With a kiss. And he would damn well do anything to get her to stay. Olivia was his girl, always.

Olivia couldn't even think straight at this point. Luke's kisses always made her dizzy with need, turning her body soft and pliable. She could feel his body hardening against her and she loved it. His kisses were the most erotic thing she'd ever experienced. They turned her on more than anything else he did. Well, almost. He seriously had skill when it came to using his mouth. It may have been a hot summer day, but the only heat she felt was coming from Luke.

Luke's tongue danced along with hers in perfect harmony. He pushed in and pulled out gradually and then slid back and forth from side to side. Olivia glided her hands up Luke's arms, over his broad shoulders and into his sandy thick hair pulling him into her. It wasn't as if there was much room left for him to be closer, but she wanted more of him. Moaning into his mouth, she kissed him back with the same intensity.

Needing to come up for air, Olivia pulled her head back slightly to breathe and opened her eyes. They were both gasping heavily into each other's mouth when she saw the raw passion and need in the depths of his eyes. In this moment, Luke's eyes said more than what words could ever say.

Of course you're enough for me, always have been... she thought to herself while she traced her hand down the side of his face. How could she ever leave him?

South Fork was a small town, but she sure did love it. No matter where she went, it was always going to be home. On one hand she wanted to stay here after being away at college for the past four years, but on the other hand she had to see what the world held for her. She didn't have the support Luke had with his parents. It was the complete opposite for her; Luke didn't know how fortunate he was.

Olivia stood on the tips of her toes and pressed her lips to Luke's warm cheek, hugging him close to her and taking in his scent. The sun was shining pretty hard today, but she couldn't tell if the heat was coming from the sun or how agitated he was at the moment. Pulling back, she noticed his scrunched forehead was making creases between his beautiful emerald eyes. His eyes held so much feeling in them and would change shades to the emotion he was going through. She didn't want to ruin the wonderful day they had with their longtime friends. Not wanting to upset him any further, in that instant she made the decision to tell him what he wanted to hear.

"You know... Let's not talk about it anymore. It was just a thought. I want to enjoy the rest of the day with you. We haven't seen our friends in so long and I'm looking forward to spending time with everyone before reality sets in and we have to look for jobs. You know I'm a planner and always looking ahead. It was merely a thought and wanted to discuss it with you. Nothing more. Honestly. "

What she failed to tell Luke was that she had already agreed to an interview. If the interview went well, there was a strong possibility she would accept the position. Dropping that kind of news wouldn't be easy after Luke's reaction today. Olivia prayed nothing would be regretted down the line, though she was sensing that some things just couldn't be avoided.

## Find out more about Adriana Luca:

https://www.facebook.com/AdriannaLucabooks

http://www.goodreads.com/book/show/17937579-return-to-me

24597720R00194

Made in the USA
Lexington, KY
24 July 2013